CRIMSON INK

Lucius Qayin

Crimson Ink

Lucius Qayin

ISBNs:

978-1-951434-61-8 (Hardcover)

978-1-951-434-60-1 (Trade Paper)

Copyright © 2024 by Lucius Qayin

All rights reserved.

All rights reserved. No part of this publication may be reproduced, distributed, or transmitted in any form or by any means, including photocopying, recording, or other electronic or mechanical methods, without the prior written permission of the publisher, except in the care of brief quotations embodied in critical reviews and certain other noncommercial uses permitted by copyright law. For permission requests, write to the publisher via email at the address below.

inquiries@luxoccultapress.com

The story, all names, characters, and incidents portrayed in this production are fictitious. No identification with actual persons (living or deceased), places, buildings, and products is intended or should be inferred.

All interior pages artwork : Rasa

All Artwork © 2024 by Rasa. Used with permission.

First edition 2024

Published by:

Lux Occulta Press (an imprint of Bune Holdings)

Contents

Introduction	1
1. Inked Beginnings	15
2. Shadows of Crimson Ink	31
3. Whispers of Power	49
4. Unwilling Destiny	67
5. Doubts and Dilemmas	87
6. Guidance in Shadows	107
7. A Leap into Darkness	125
8. Hidden Realms Revealed	145
9. Allies in the Night	165
10. The Cost of Power	183
11. Temptations of the Mark	201
12. Betrayal's Sting	219
13. Gathering Shadows	239
14. The Path to Power	257
15. Ordeal of the Mark	277
16. A Twist of Fate	295

17.	Hunted	313
18.	Return to the Fray	331
19.	Eclipse of Conflict	351
20.	New Dawn Rising	369
21.	Ink of a New Era	387

Introduction

The city woke up with a yawn of buses and the clinking of coffee cups. I followed suit, rubbing the sleep from my eyes, feeling the pull of the day ahead. I left my small apartment, tucked away above an all-night diner that always smelled faintly of grease and burnt toast. The sun hadn't quite mustered the courage to climb above the skyline, and the streets were painted in hues of gray and dawning gold.

Crimson Ink sat nestled between a pawn shop with barred windows and a florist teeming with urban greenery. I pushed open the door, its chime announcing my arrival to the empty parlor. The place was a sanctuary where art met flesh, and if you listened closely enough, you could hear the hum of countless stories etched in ink.

My morning ritual was sacred—wipe down the leather chairs, mix fresh ink, lay out sterilized needles like a surgeon preparing for operation. Each motion was deliberate, meditative even. The click of bottles and snap of latex gloves provided a familiar soundtrack as I prepped for the day's appointments.

The first client arrived just as I flicked on the neon 'Open' sign—a regular named Marco who had sleeves of mythical creatures that seemed to dance upon his skin. He grinned wide, revealing a gold tooth that caught the light.

"Alex, my man! Ready to add another beast to the zoo?" His voice echoed in the still-quiet shop.

"Always," I replied with a nod. "What's it gonna be this time?"

"A phoenix," he said with a twinkle in his eye. "Rising from ashes right here on my chest."

I smiled at his choice—rebirth, transformation—it suited him. Marco had stories that would make your skin crawl or your heart ache, depending on how much whiskey he'd had.

As I sketched out the design, my hand moved with an ease that felt like second nature. Lines flowed like water from my fingertips, creating shapes and shadows that promised life beyond their two-dimensional prison. When I glanced up at Marco, his eyes were fixed on the drawing, alight with anticipation.

"That's wicked," he murmured as if witnessing magic—a response I never tired of.

While setting up my station, I caught sight of myself in the mirror—black hair a tad too long falling into my eyes, which today looked more sea-storm than sky. Tattoos snaked up my own arms—each one a testament to moments of personal triumph or folly.

Marco settled into the chair as I pulled on my gloves. The machine buzzed to life in my hand like an eager insect waiting to taste nectar. As I worked on transferring the phoenix onto his chest, each puncture of skin was a note in an intimate symphony only we could hear.

There was something else in that symphony though—a faint whisper that wasn't from me or Marco or even from this realm. It happened sometimes when I tattooed—visions flickered at the edge of my sight like shadows flitting through sunlight. It was part of what made me good at this; not just technique but something older humming through my veins.

I could sense more than just Marco's excitement—I felt his hope for change and it fueled each stroke of ink like wind to fire.

Hours passed as we talked about everything and nothing—music pulsing softly in the background while outside life in the city marched on. The phoenix took shape beneath my hands; its wings spread wide across Marco's chest as if ready to take flight right there in Crimson Ink.

By late afternoon, Marco stood admiring our collaborative creation in the mirror. Satisfaction swelled within me—there was power in marking skin; an exchange between artist and canvas that left both changed forever.

He clapped me on the back hard enough to make me stumble slightly. "You're something else, Alex," he said earnestly before heading out into the waning light.

The door closed behind him with a soft jingle and for a moment there was silence—a sacred pause between chapters.

Then came Violet—her hair living up to her name—a college student with nerves that jangled like loose change but eyes full of determination.

"I want something... different," she stammered slightly as she showed me her sketchbook filled with doodles and dreams rendered in graphite smudges.

I leafed through her ideas—a kaleidoscope of abstract patterns and celestial bodies—until one caught my eye: an intricate design that seemed both ancient and otherworldly; familiar yet foreign stirring something deep within me.

"This one," I pointed to it with a certainty that surprised us both. "It's perfect."

Violet beamed as if she'd been seen truly for the first time. "Really? You think?"

"I know," I assured her with a confidence that wasn't entirely my own—the design resonated within me; an echo from a past life or perhaps something woven into my very DNA.

As I prepared Violet for her first tattoo experience—explaining each step with patience—I couldn't shake off that sense of recognition; that design belonged somewhere on her skin as if it had always been meant for her.

My hands hovered over her waiting arm—the buzz of anticipation hung heavy between us like charged air before lightning strikes. With every drop of ink that seeped into her skin under my steady hand, I felt an awakening—a silent acknowledgement from whatever magic pulsed within me recognizing itself mirrored in those lines and curves now becoming part of Violet forever.

* * *

The needle hummed a low, steady rhythm as I guided it across Violet's skin. The ink bloomed under the surface, shaping itself into a pattern that felt as old as time. She lay still, her breath measured, her trust in my hands implicit.

The design we chose—a twisting vine with delicate flowers—seemed to grow organically from her shoulder blade, curling towards her heart. I infused each stroke with care, knowing that this mark would be a part of her story forever.

"Does it hurt much?" I asked, breaking the silence that had settled between us like a comforting blanket.

She exhaled softly, "It's bearable. Feels like... more than just a needle, though. Like you're drawing out something from inside me."

Her words caught me off guard. She wasn't wrong; the tattoos I crafted often did more than just sit on the skin—they interacted with the person, sometimes in ways even I didn't fully understand.

"You're very perceptive," I said, my focus unwavering from the task at hand.

Violet smiled faintly and closed her eyes again. As the needle danced across her skin, the air in Crimson Ink thickened subtly, charged with an energy that often accompanied my work.

A chime from the front door pulled me back to reality. I glanced at the clock—late for a walk-in but not unheard of in our line of work. With a few final touches on Violet's tattoo, I cleaned my hands and stepped out to greet the newcomer.

He stood near the entrance, his eyes scanning the dark interiors of Crimson Ink with a mixture of curiosity and reverence. The man was cloaked in a long coat despite the mild weather outside, his attire speaking of someone who cherished anonymity.

"Welcome to Crimson Ink," I greeted him. "I'm just finishing up with another client. Can I help you?"

He turned towards me slowly, his gaze piercing yet not unkind. "I was told this is where one comes for tattoos of... a certain caliber."

I raised an eyebrow at his vague hint of something more—something otherworldly perhaps? "That's right," I replied cautiously. "We pride ourselves on our custom designs."

He nodded, his lips curling into a knowing smile. "I'm looking for something unique—a piece that holds power."

The word 'power' lingered in the air between us like smoke from an extinguished candle. My heritage tingled at the base of my skull—a sensation that often accompanied conversations veering towards the arcane.

"I might be able to help you," I said slowly. "But power can mean different things to different people."

His eyes held mine for a moment longer before he reached into his coat and produced an aged piece of parchment that looked like it belonged in one of the antique books lining our shelves rather than in someone's pocket.

"I seek the Mark of Power," he said simply as he unfolded it before me.

The drawing on the parchment was intricate—a web of symbols and shapes that spoke of ancient rituals and hidden knowledge. It was familiar yet elusive; part of me recognized it from somewhere deep within my heritage but couldn't quite place it.

My pulse quickened as I traced my finger over the lines on paper, feeling them thrum with an energy that called to my own bloodline.

"Where did you get this?" My voice was steady but inside, questions raced through my mind.

"A gift from an old friend," he said cryptically.

I hesitated before responding; part of me wary of entangling myself further in what was clearly more than just a tattoo request but another part—the part tied to my supernatural lineage—thrilled at the challenge.

"We should talk about what this mark means to you before we proceed," I suggested.

He agreed with a nod and took a seat on one of the plush armchairs we kept for consultations like these—conversations that went beyond simple design choices and delved into realms most people never knew existed.

As we talked, Violet emerged from the back room—her new tattoo covered with a protective film. She thanked me with genuine warmth in her eyes and promised to recommend Crimson Ink to all her friends before slipping out into the night.

Turning back to my enigmatic client, whose name I still didn't know, I realized how deeply I'd been drawn into this already. The Mark of Power wasn't just any tattoo; it carried weight beyond its visual form—it had purpose and consequence tied to it.

"I'll need time to study this," I told him after we'd discussed his request at length. "Designs like these aren't taken lightly."

He nodded understandingly and rose to leave as mysteriously as he had arrived. "I'll return tomorrow night then," he said before stepping back into the cityscape outside our doors—the normal world blissfully unaware of what transpired within these walls.

Alone now, surrounded by ancient artifacts and dim lighting that seemed all too fitting for such revelations, I spread out the parchment on my worktable and let out a breath I didn't realize I'd been holding.

Intrigue twisted within me like vines on Violet's tattoo—a mix of excitement and trepidation as I pondered what accepting this commission would mean not only for myself but potentially for those around me as well.

As silence enveloped Crimson Ink once more, punctuated only by the distant sounds of city life beyond its walls, I leaned over the parchment—the first step taken into depths unknown yet irresistibly compelling.

* * *

The mysterious man had left, his presence lingering in the parlor like the hum of a charged wire. The Mark of Power he'd asked for twined in my thoughts, an insistent vine wrapping around my consciousness.

I stood there for a moment, lost in the pulsing echo of the supernatural connection I'd felt with the Mark, before shaking it off and turning to tidy up my station. That's when the chime above the door jangled, heralding another customer.

"Hey Alex," came a voice that wrapped around me like a well-worn jacket—comfortable, familiar.

"Hey Frankie," I greeted without turning around, knowing by his tone it was my regular, a man with more ink on his skin than blank canvas. He liked to joke that he was my personal gallery.

Frankie sauntered over, his eyes flicking to the design still displayed on my computer screen. "That's some heavy mojo you're playing with," he said with a nudge of his eyebrow.

I quickly minimized the image, a small flush creeping up my neck. "Just a client's request."

He chuckled, easing himself onto one of the plush waiting chairs. "You always were good at understating things. It's in your blood."

His words hung there between us—a subtle reminder that Frankie knew more about me than most. I busied myself with rearranging my inks, avoiding his knowing gaze.

"Speaking of blood," Frankie continued as if reading my thoughts, "your dad stopped by the other day while you were out. Left something for you." He nodded toward the counter where a small, ornately carved box rested—something I hadn't noticed before.

My pulse quickened as I approached it. Dad rarely left things for me; our relationship was complicated by what I was—or rather, what I wasn't entirely sure I wanted to be.

The box felt warm to the touch as if it held its own heartbeat. Lifting the lid revealed an old photograph nestled within—a picture of my parents on their wedding day. Mom looked radiant, her smile reaching her eyes which sparkled with human joy; Dad beside her appeared noble but there was something otherworldly about him even then.

Underneath the photo lay a feather—an iridescent plume that seemed to shift colors as I turned it in the light. It was from one of dad's kind—his people—a benign supernatural entity whose name felt like a secret perched on the tip of my tongue.

I replaced both items and snapped the box shut with more force than necessary. "Thanks for letting me know."

Frankie watched me with an unreadable expression. "He seemed... proud," he said slowly, choosing his words with care.

A small laugh escaped me before I could stop it; it was hollow and more bitter than I intended. "Yeah? First time for everything."

He didn't press further, sensing my reluctance to delve into family history—a history that left me caught between two worlds.

A few hours slipped by as Frankie and I talked shop—ink and skin, lines and shading—the dance of distraction perfect in its rhythm. He left just as dusk settled over the city like a blanket tucking in for the night.

I locked up behind him and made my way through back streets that hummed with unseen life. The city had its own magic after dark—a kind that seeped into your bones if you weren't careful.

The apartment above Crimson Ink welcomed me home, its walls filled with echoes of memories too dense to parse at this hour. The box sat heavy in my bag as I tossed it onto the kitchen table.

I showered off the day's grime, letting water cleanse away traces of ink and sweat—the residue of touching others' lives so intimately. Afterward, wrapped in an old robe that had seen better days, I stood before the window watching night creatures flit between streetlights below.

My reflection caught my eye—pale against dark glass—and for a moment, I saw him behind me; not really there but always present—my father with his enigmatic smile and eyes that held galaxies within them.

"Who am I?" The question whispered out into silence—an echo bouncing back without answer.

It wasn't long before restlessness drove me from my apartment back down to Crimson Ink—the parlor somehow more welcoming than empty rooms above.

The keepsake box called to me again; this time I allowed myself to take out the feather, running fingers over its smoothness—an anchor to a heritage I couldn't fully grasp or reject outright.

I studied the photograph once more—my parents looking back at me from their frozen moment of joy—and wondered how much of their legacy lived within me. My mother's warmth? My father's mystery? The convergence that made up Alex?

I returned both items to their wooden crypt and placed it on a shelf high enough that it demanded effort to reach—a metaphor if there ever was one for how I dealt with that part of myself.

Midnight crept upon me as I began sketching new designs—each line an attempt at understanding or maybe just escape. That's when she walked in—a figure cloaked in shadow and purpose—her arrival punctuating night's stillness like a question mark demanding attention.

She paused at the threshold before stepping inside fully—into light that painted her features in sharp relief and shadows that whispered secrets best left unspoken.

"I need your help," she said simply, but her eyes held complexities—a maze where truth waited patiently for those brave enough to seek it out.

I motioned toward one of the chairs near my work station—an invitation to share space and maybe more if fate deemed us aligned on this peculiar night.

* * *

The woman's entrance into Crimson Ink sliced through the usual hum of conversation like a blade. Cloaked in purpose, she had an air that made my skin prickle. I glanced around; the buzz of the tattoo guns fell silent one by one, as if the very atmosphere of the parlor bowed to her presence.

"Alex," she began, her voice a silken threat, "I need your expertise."

Her eyes, a sharp contrast to the shadows that seemed to cling to her, fixed on mine. I recognized that look—the kind that heralded trouble.

"Sure," I replied, gesturing toward my station. "What are you looking to get?"

"Not here," she said, her gaze darting around the parlor. "Somewhere private."

The back room wasn't just for storage; it was where sensitive conversations happened away from prying ears. I led her there, acutely aware of the weight of her stare on my back.

Once inside, she leaned close, her breath cool against my ear. "The Mark of Power. You know it?"

I nodded, remembering the mysterious man from earlier. "It's come up."

Her eyes narrowed. "The Gang's interested in it. Damien's got everyone looking."

Damien—the name sent a shiver down my spine. Leader of the vampire gang that operated out of Crimson Ink under the guise of night and ink.

"I'm not involved with—"

"You are now," she interrupted. "You're going to help us find it before they do."

A mix of fear and defiance surged within me. "And if I refuse?"

She smiled then, and it was all teeth—predatory. "Don't."

The door creaked open, sparing me from having to answer. Victor strode in, his imposing figure filling the doorway.

"The boss wants an update," he grumbled, his eyes locking onto our visitor.

She didn't flinch at his entrance; if anything, she seemed amused by it.

"Tell Damien I'm making progress," she said smoothly.

Victor's gaze shifted to me then—a silent warning that had my heart racing.

"You too," he added before turning on his heel and leaving as abruptly as he'd arrived.

I let out a breath I hadn't realized I was holding and faced the woman again.

"Who are you?" I asked, though I wasn't sure I wanted to know.

"Evelyn," she said simply. "And you're going to help me beat Damien at his own game."

The encounter left me shaken as I returned to the main floor of Crimson Ink. The shop was a hub for those seeking more than just ink on skin; it was where magic intertwined with flesh. But beneath that facade lay something darker—the vampire gang's stronghold in the city's underworld.

As the day waned into evening, snatches of conversation from patrons brushed past my ears like whispers from the shadows themselves.

"...heard Damien's got half the city turned over looking for some ancient symbol..."

"...Evelyn doesn't think it's here, but you know how she gets—like a dog with a bone..."

"...they say whoever gets that Mark first will have power like we've never seen..."

Each word twisted in my gut—a coiling serpent preparing to strike.

Later that night, after locking up, I took a detour through alleys shrouded in secrets and smoke from distant fires—a shortcut home that doubled as a path through whispered rumors and clandestine dealings.

A hushed voice stopped me in my tracks; two figures loomed ahead in the dim light—a deal unfolding under cover of darkness.

"...the Mark's no joke," one said nervously. "They say it holds real power—ancient stuff."

His companion scoffed. "You believe those fairy tales? It's just a tattoo."

I edged closer, hidden by shadow, curiosity overpowering caution.

"It ain't just ink when it comes from Crimson Ink," came the reply laced with fear and awe. "That place... there's something about it—something old and hungry."

Old and hungry indeed—Crimson Ink held secrets within its walls that would turn even the bravest soul pale.

Slipping away unnoticed, I pondered their words as I continued home through streets that felt more alive at night than during daylight hours—a city breathing secrets with every gust through narrow alleys.

I unlocked my apartment door and stepped inside—the false safety of four walls did little to ease my mind. Damien's influence stretched far and wide; no one in this city was untouched by his reach or blind to his power.

And now Evelyn wanted my help—to go against Damien? To seek out this Mark before he could claim its power? The thought sent adrenaline coursing through me like an electric current—dangerous but invigorating.

As I sat down at my drafting table littered with designs and sketches, one image beckoned—a circle entwined with intricate symbols and glyphs: The Mark of Power.

My hand hovered above it as if drawn by an unseen force; this wasn't just another tattoo—it was a beacon calling out into depths unknown, promising power or perhaps peril.

And there I sat—a pawn caught between two formidable forces: Evelyn with her calculating gaze and Damien with his unseen yet palpable command over all he surveyed.

But amid their games of shadows and supremacy lay an unsettling truth—I wasn't just a pawn. There was something within me they both needed; something about my lineage that made me more than human or benign entity alone—something they couldn't replicate or understand fully.

The realization brought both clarity and dread; for in this game where bloodlines were as important as bloodshed, what did it mean for someone like me?

As midnight crept closer, blanketing the city in its somber embrace, sleep eluded me while thoughts raced—a storm brewing within as dangerous as any that raged outside these walls.

Chapter 1

Inked Beginnings

T he sun hadn't even breached the horizon, but I was already tracing the contours of my latest design, the graphite whispering across the textured paper. My small apartment, cluttered with canvases and ink bottles, thrummed with a silent energy that matched my racing heart. There was something about the predawn stillness that sharpened my focus, allowed my thoughts to roam free in the realm of possibilities.

A pot of coffee bubbled in the background, its rich aroma wrestling with the faint scent of antiseptic and pigment that lingered in the air. The steam kissed the windowpane, painting it with transient fog as I sketched. A well-worn leather-bound book lay open beside me; its pages yellowed with age and heavy with secrets. It was a compendium of tattoo lore passed down through generations, a testament to a lineage part human, part something... more.

The tome spoke of symbols that could bind or release, protect or curse, all hinging on the intent and skill of the artist. It whispered of my ancestors' pact with benign entities from realms unseen, a pact that coursed through my veins as much as ink through my pen.

My phone chirped—a reminder that time, regardless of one's heritage, waits for no one. With a sigh, I set aside my sketch and moved through my routine. My apartment was nothing if not a mirror to my inner life—organized chaos. Canvases lined against one wall boasted splashes of color and half-formed dreams. On shelves sat figurines from every mythology known to man—and some known only to those who believed in more than what met the eye.

I pulled on black jeans and a faded band tee, attire that doubled as both work uniform and personal statement. My hair was an untamable mass; I ran fingers through it in a futile attempt at order before giving up and letting it fall where it wished.

A glance in the mirror caught the shimmering lines at the edge of my jaw—a subtle tattoo nearly invisible unless you knew where to look. A protective glyph inherited from my non-human side; it pulsed gently against my skin like a heartbeat. It reminded me every day that I straddled two worlds—one foot in each and belonging fully to neither.

With coffee cup in hand, I turned back to the book for a moment longer, running a finger over an illustration of an ancient sigil said to grant immense power to those who wielded it responsibly—or ruin to any who dared misuse it.

The shop wouldn't open for another couple hours, but there was always prep work to be done—needles to be sterilized, stations cleaned, designs finalized. Crimson Ink was more than just a business; it was an extension of me—of who I was and who I aspired to become.

Stepping out into the brisk morning air cleared my head further as I locked up behind me. The city was stirring awake; its pulse quickened with each passing minute as early risers shuffled along sidewalks and cafes began grinding their first batch of beans.

I passed murals splashed across brick walls—some legal, others not so much—but all breathing life into otherwise dreary alleyways. Art was everywhere if you took the time to look; it colored every inch of this urban canvas we called home.

As I made my way toward Crimson Ink, nestled between a twenty-four-hour diner and an antique bookstore whose owner claimed they were witch-adjacent (whatever that meant), I felt anticipation building within me like ink in a well-shaken bottle.

Today would be different; I could feel it in my bones—the way you feel an incoming storm by the prickle on your skin or the charge in the air.

But for now, I'd savor this quiet interlude before flinging open the doors to whatever awaited me within those walls lined with designs born from both imagination and ancient heritage—a heritage I both revered and wrestled with each time my needle touched skin.

* * *

The city's heartbeat throbbed in my ears as I locked my apartment door behind me. Sunlight streamed through the high-rises, casting geometric shadows that crawled over the pavement like silent, spectral creatures. I descended the steps, feeling the pulse of the city sync with my own.

Morning commuters flowed around me, a river of purpose and haste. Coffee aromas wafted from open doorways, mingling with the exhaust from idling buses. I sidestepped a child chasing an errant soccer ball, their laughter ringing clear above the din.

My path took me past the glass facades of corporate behemoths, reflections warping and stretching my figure into a specter of the mundane world I straddled. Here, magic was confined to fiction and sleight of hand—a stark contrast to the ink that flowed beneath my skin, humming with latent energy.

Turning down an alleyway, I exchanged nods with the fruit vendor whose stall marked the transition from daylight's domain to the shadow's embrace. His eyes flickered to my forearms, covered in intricate sleeves of my own design. His gaze held a question he'd never voice; he knew better than to ask.

As the alley opened up onto a narrow backstreet, I found solace in the quiet. The thrum of traffic faded to a whisper. Here, between crumbling brick and forgotten stories, lay the bones of an older city—one that remembered ancient magic and whispered its secrets through cracked windows and rusted fire escapes.

A cat slinked across my path, its eyes glowing like embers in the dim light. It paused to regard me with a knowing look before disappearing into a gap between buildings. I couldn't help but smile; even the city's felines carried themselves with an air of mystery here.

Crimson Ink emerged at the street's end, its facade an echo of times past—gothic arches framing stained glass that never saw full daylight. The door creaked on aged hinges as I pushed it open, welcoming me into its sanctuary.

The interior exuded an otherworldly charm. Velvet drapes hung heavy on iron rods, and chandeliers cast warm light over displays of ancient artifacts. My fingers brushed over a set of weathered leather-bound grimoires as I passed—their spines crackling like dry leaves underfoot.

I heard them before I saw them: soft murmurs from private rooms where art met flesh met magic. The familiar buzz of tattoo machines was a lullaby for those who sought to wear their power on their skin.

I shrugged off my jacket and draped it over the counter before making my way to the back where preparations awaited me—a ritual unto itself. Bottles of ink lined up like soldiers ready for battle; each hue held potential for enchantment.

I rolled up my sleeves and set to work mixing colors with practiced precision. The scent of antiseptic mingled with lavender and sage—my personal touch to cleanse and calm the space.

Today's appointment book lay open on the counter—names etched alongside time slots in a neat script that belied the chaos each session could unleash. Today would be different though; today marked an intersection between fate and choice—a day when paths would converge at the tip of my needle.

A knock on the front door snapped me back to reality—a client early for their reckoning or perhaps just seeking shelter from a world that didn't understand them. That was fine; here at Crimson Ink, we understood more than most.

I smoothed down my black tee, emblazoned with our shop's logo—a serpent entwined around a quill—and made my way to greet whoever sought entrance into our realm.

The bell above the door chimed as it swung open...

* * *

The bell above the door chimed its eerie, melodious tune as the first client of the day stepped into Crimson Ink. Sunlight struggled through the shop's tinted windows, casting a lazy glow over the polished black floors and the walls adorned with designs that seemed to pulse with life.

"Morning, Alex," greeted Mariah, a regular whose sleeve I'd been crafting for months. Her eyes sparkled with anticipation.

"Morning," I replied, pulling on my gloves with a snap. "Ready to add the finishing touches to your phoenix?"

She nodded, rolling up her sleeve. "I've been looking forward to this all week."

I guided her to my chair, the leather creaking softly under her weight. My workstation gleamed with meticulously arranged inks and needles. As I prepped my tools, Mariah watched with an eagerness that never failed to stoke my own excitement for the craft.

I dipped my needle into the fiery red ink and began. The buzz of the machine melded with Mariah's steady breathing. The lines flowed from my hand like an extension of my own energy—precise and sure.

With each stroke, Mariah's eyes drifted closed, a serene expression taking over her face. "It's strange," she murmured after a while. "Every time you tattoo me, it's like I can feel it... coming alive."

A smile tugged at the corner of my mouth as I continued to work, weaving not just ink but a wisp of magic into her skin—a warmth that would resonate with her spirit.

"It's all part of the experience here at Crimson Ink," I said, keeping my tone light while masking the depth of truth in those words.

Hours passed, and soon Mariah's phoenix was complete—a creature of myth seeming to rise from the ashes right on her arm. She examined it in the mirror, awe etched on her face.

"I swear it's more than just art," she said, tracing the lines as if they held secrets only she could understand.

After Mariah left, a new customer entered—a man with a sharp suit and sharper eyes. He introduced himself as Victor and explained his desire for a tattoo that embodied power and ambition.

As he settled into my chair, I flipped through my sketchbook filled with designs that were more than mere drawings; they were potential gateways to abilities untold.

Victor pointed at an intricate lion design—the symbol of a leader, fierce and unyielding. "That one," he said decisively.

"An excellent choice," I acknowledged as I prepared my station once again.

I sketched the outline onto his upper arm before starting in on the shading. Victor remained silent throughout the process but kept glancing down at his emerging tattoo with a mixture of fascination and something else—recognition?

"This feels different than any other tattoo I've had," he said finally, his voice laced with intrigue.

I kept my focus on the tattoo but replied casually, "Every artist has their signature touch."

By evening Victor left with more than just ink under his skin—he carried an air of confidence that seemed magnified somehow.

The day wore on with more clients coming and going—each one leaving with a piece of magic that they could feel but not fully grasp. They spoke of sensations like whispers in their ears or adrenaline coursing through their veins when they looked upon their new tattoos—whispers of enchantment laced within every drop of ink I laid down.

As dusk settled outside Crimson Ink's windows, casting long shadows across its interior, I cleaned my station for what felt like the hundredth time that day. The soft clink of bottles and clatter of equipment filled the room as I worked through my routine methodically.

The door opened again—this time admitting a woman whose presence seemed to dim the lights even further. Her gaze held centuries within them; she was no ordinary client.

She approached me slowly, her footsteps barely making a sound on the wooden floorboards. "Alex," she began in a voice that resonated deep within me. "I seek something unique—a tattoo that embodies not just strength but protection."

I studied her for a moment before nodding silently. This was not going to be just another appointment; it was an unspoken challenge—one that called to every fiber of my being both human and otherwise.

I motioned toward my chair silently inviting her to sit down while my mind raced through designs ancient and powerful enough to meet her request.

As she settled into place, draping her coat over the armrest, moonlight peeked through a break in the curtains and played across her skin—an empty canvas waiting for me to work my dual heritage into something tangible.

We didn't speak as I prepared; words were unnecessary when such understanding hung thickly in the air between us.

My needle hummed to life once more as night embraced Crimson Ink completely—the only illumination now came from my lamp casting dramatic highlights over us both.

With each line etched into her skin I felt something profound—a connection between artist and canvas deeper than any before; it was as if our very spirits conversed silently while ink merged indelibly with flesh.

Her eyes met mine occasionally in silent acknowledgment—of what transpired between us; an exchange beyond mundane comprehension but familiar all too well in this hidden world we inhabited.

Time became irrelevant as we continued—each moment stretched taut like thread ready to weave destiny itself into existence upon this woman's skin—a testament to protection imbued by lineage both human and supernatural entwined within me—Alex of Crimson Ink.

* * *

The needle hummed, a steady drone that blended with the pulse of the city outside. The woman beneath my hands, Evelyn, was getting a phoenix etched into her back. She wanted rebirth, to start anew after a life marred by too many endings.

Evelyn winced as I shaded a feather on her shoulder blade. "How do you do this day in and day out?" she asked, her voice taut with the sting of the needle.

I paused, dabbing away excess ink with a practiced hand. "You get used to it," I said. "But then again, I grew up around needles and ink. It's in my blood."

"Really?" She tried to crane her neck to look at me. "Your parents were tattoo artists?"

I smiled, pressing gently on her shoulder to keep her still. "Not exactly. Let's just say that artistry runs through my lineage in... unconventional ways."

Evelyn's interest piqued; I could see it in the tilt of her head, the furrow of her brow softening. "Unconventional how?"

I glanced around Crimson Ink, ensuring we were alone; these tales were not for all ears. The walls whispered their silent consent, the ambient magic that seeped through the brickwork humming in quiet agreement.

"When I was about eight," I began, guiding the needle once more over Evelyn's skin, "I discovered that my family was different. My grandmother on my father's side lived in this old, vine-covered house out in the countryside—more of a cottage really."

Evelyn's muscles relaxed under my touch as she listened.

"She had this garden," I continued, "a wild thing, overflowing with plants you couldn't find in any botanical guidebook. I used to help her tend to it during summers."

A shiver ran down Evelyn's spine—not from pain but from anticipation. I could feel her curiosity as palpable as the buzz of the tattoo machine.

"One evening," I said, "we were out there just after dusk had settled like a cloak over the sky, and she was teaching me how to prune the whispering willows." I chuckled softly at the memory. "Those trees... they'd murmur secrets if you listened close enough."

Evelyn laughed lightly. "Whispering willows? Are you pulling my leg?"

"Not at all," I assured her with a smile that held more than a hint of nostalgia. "They were real enough for us."

My hands worked steadily as images from that night flickered through my mind like old film reels.

"Anyway," I said, "there was this pond near the edge of her property—always looked like liquid obsidian under the moonlight." The needle dipped into skin again as I spoke. "We never went near it because Gran said it was home to spirits."

"Spirits?" Evelyn asked, skepticism lacing her voice even as fascination held her rapt.

"Yes," I replied softly. "That night though, Gran wasn't paying attention and dropped her pruning shears into the water." My hand never wavered as I recalled how those shears had sunk silently into darkness. "She cursed under her breath and told me to stay put while she went to fetch a net from the shed."

"But you didn't stay put," Evelyn guessed.

I shook my head slightly, though she couldn't see it. "Nope. Curiosity got the better of me." The phoenix under my needle seemed to flare with life for a moment—a trick of light and shadow—and then settled back into stillness on Evelyn's skin.

"I crept up to that pond," I murmured, my voice almost blending with the hum of the tattoo machine now. "The surface was so still it looked solid—like you could walk right over it."

"And did you?" There was an edge of eagerness in Evelyn's question.

I hesitated for a heartbeat before answering. "Yes... but not on purpose." The memory was clear as glass—the sensation of slipping forward when the earth gave way beneath my sneaker.

"The next thing I knew," I said with a wry grin at the recollection, "I was up to my waist in water colder than winter's heart."

Evelyn gasped softly; perhaps she felt that cold too for an instant.

"I panicked," I admitted. "Started thrashing around trying to get out when suddenly everything calmed down—the water, me... everything." My hands paused over her skin; even now it felt like something sacred had touched me that night.

"A pair of hands pushed me up and out of that pond." My voice was barely above a whisper now; some secrets demanded reverence when spoken aloud.

Evelyn turned slightly despite herself; eyes wide and bright with wonder met mine in a moment shared across time and space.

"Hands?" Her voice mirrored mine—a hushed awe threading through each syllable.

"Yes." A breath escaped me—a ghost of laughter or perhaps something else entirely—as I resumed working on her tattoo. "Gran found me dripping by the pondside, staring at where those hands had been."

"And what did your grandmother say?" Evelyn asked after a beat filled only by ink sinking into skin and two hearts beating in tandem—one from excitement, one from remembrance.

"She just smiled," I said softly as though sharing an ancient secret between bloodlines—"a knowing smile that told me there was more to our world than what lay before our eyes."

We fell into silence then—a comfortable hush punctuated only by my needle and Evelyn's steady breathing—as if both of us needed time to absorb what lay between words unsaid and secrets half-revealed.

As if on cue with our shared contemplation, a chime echoed through Crimson Ink—the door announcing another seeker of magic etched into flesh—but neither Evelyn nor I turned toward it immediately; we remained locked in an unspoken understanding that some moments are too precious to break away from too quickly.

* * *

The bell above the door chimed, slicing through the hum of the tattoo machines like a sharp knife. My hands, steady moments before, now faltered ever so slightly on the skin of the client under my needle. I glanced up through the web of dark iron chandeliers dangling from the ceiling. A shadow pooled at the entrance of Crimson Ink, a figure detaching itself from the darkness outside.

She was tall, clad in a tailored coat that seemed to drink in the dim light of the parlor. Her hair was an obsidian waterfall cascading over her shoulders, framing a face that was both severe and mesmerizing. She scanned the room with eyes like shards of midnight until they found mine and held.

My pulse quickened; I couldn't help but feel like prey under her gaze. I wrapped up with my current client, a regular who wanted nothing more than roses twining around her wrist—ordinary ink for ordinary skin. "Take care of that now," I murmured as she admired my handiwork, "and come back if you need any touch-ups."

The mysterious woman waited, a statue by the door. My client left with a pleased smile and a wave, leaving me alone with this enigmatic presence.

"Alex?" The woman's voice was rich velvet laced with steel. She stepped forward, heels clicking against the aged wooden floor like a metronome counting down.

"That's me," I replied, standing to meet her full height, which rivaled my own. "And you are?"

"Call me Valeria." She offered no hand to shake, no smile to warm the chilled air between us. Her eyes seemed to bore into me, searching for something I wasn't sure I wanted her to find.

"I take it you're here for some ink?" I tried to keep my voice level despite the unease coiling in my gut.

"Not just any ink," she said as she moved closer, inspecting the framed designs on the walls as if they were pieces in a gallery. "I'm here for your talents specifically—your unique gifts."

My brows knitted together at that. How much did she know about what ran through my veins—about what set me apart from every other artist wielding a needle?

"What kind of tattoo are you looking for?" I steered us towards one of the private rooms reserved for special clients—those seeking more than mere decoration.

Valeria followed, her presence filling the space behind me like smoke. "One that holds power," she answered simply as we entered the dimly lit room adorned with ancient symbols and relics from times when magic was more than just myth.

I gestured towards the chair at the center of the room. "Take a seat and we can discuss your design."

She perched on the edge of the leather seat, coat whispering around her like wings folding in. "I don't want a design from your walls or books," Valeria said crisply. "I need something... personal. Something only you can create."

My hands rested on my tattoo station, fingertips grazing polished metal and sterile packages. Her words were an echo of others who'd come before—those who knew or guessed at my lineage—but there was an intensity in her demand that set her apart.

"And why is that?" I probed while arranging my tools with practiced ease.

"Because," Valeria leaned forward, shadows playing across her angular face, "you're not just any artist, Alex. Your bloodline is rare—even among those who dabble in magic."

A shiver ran down my spine at her acknowledgment of my heritage—the half-human part easy enough to see; it was what lay beneath that most never saw.

"What do you know about my bloodline?" The question came out sharper than intended.

Valeria's lips curved into a semblance of a smile that didn't quite reach her eyes. "I know enough to seek you out above all others."

Her words hung heavy in the air as I took in every detail about her—the controlled posture, an aura that spoke of old power barely contained beneath her skin, and eyes that held centuries within their depths.

"So," she continued, "will you craft something for me? Something... binding?"

The request sent alarms ringing through my mind—a binding tattoo was not something to be taken lightly. It held implications far beyond skin-deep beauty; it could be shackling or liberating depending on its purpose and its creator's intent.

"What's it for?" I kept my voice steady despite my racing thoughts.

Valeria's gaze locked onto mine once more—a challenge or perhaps an invitation to understand something deeper about this woman before me.

"It's for protection," she said at last but paused as though weighing each word before it left her lips. "Protection and power—a safeguard against those who would see harm come to me."

The gravity in her tone suggested enemies lurking in shadows far darker than those within Crimson Ink.

"And what do you offer in return?" My question wasn't about money; currency held little weight when bartering with spells woven into flesh.

"A favor," she answered smoothly. "One within your capabilities when you deem it necessary to call upon it."

A favor from someone like Valeria could be invaluable—or it could be damning. Yet intrigue gnawed at me with sharp teeth; this woman knew things—things perhaps about myself that I had yet to uncover.

"I'll need complete honesty," I stated firmly while reaching for parchment and charcoal to begin sketching out possibilities swirling in my mind—the intertwining of protection and power made manifest through ink and magic.

Valeria nodded once, solemnly conceding to my terms. Her story unraveled slowly as I drew—the tale of old vendettas and new threats—a life spent navigating treacherous waters where trust was scarce and allies even scarcer.

With each detail shared, each line etched onto paper then transferred onto skin, I realized this tattoo would be unlike any other I'd created before—a piece intertwining our fates more intricately than either of us could've imagined when she first stepped through Crimson Ink's door.

* * *

Valeria's request hung in the air between us, heavy like the scent of incense that lingered in the corners of Crimson Ink. She knew of my lineage, a fact that sent a ripple of unease through me. Most folks wandered in seeking art, a piece of magic to wear on their skin. But Valeria? She wanted more than ink; she sought a piece of me.

"Protection and power," she had said, her voice a melody that resonated with something ancient within me. "I offer you a favor in return."

A favor. The currency of the supernatural world was never as simple as it sounded. I mulled over her words, the gravity of the transaction not lost on me.

"What kind of favor?" I probed, keeping my voice steady.

Her lips curled into a knowing smile. "One that matches the weight of your gift."

I let out a breath I didn't realize I was holding and motioned for her to follow me to my workstation. The chair creaked as she settled into it, and I pulled on my gloves with practiced ease. My tools were ready, my mind less so.

As I sketched the design onto transfer paper, the hum of the tattoo machine filled the silence between us. The drawing flowed from me – an intricate weave of symbols and sigils, each one a testament to protection, each stroke an invocation of power.

When I pressed the stencil onto her skin, Valeria's eyes met mine. In them, I saw oceans and storms, an unspoken promise or perhaps a threat. It was hard to tell with her kind.

"You're sure about this?" My voice betrayed none of my inner turmoil.

"As sure as night follows day," she replied with an unwavering gaze.

The needle dipped into crimson ink – my signature blend – and as it touched her skin, Valeria's favor became a bond that neither time nor tide could break. The design came alive under my hand, each line infused with energy that pulsed against my fingertips.

It wasn't just ink; it was alchemy.

Hours passed in what felt like moments. The tattoo took shape – an armor etched in flesh – and with each addition, Valeria's aura grew stronger until it filled the room with an electric charge.

As I wiped away the last traces of blood and ink from her newly marked skin, she sat up and examined my work in the mirror. Satisfaction flickered across her features like shadows at dusk.

"Thank you," she said simply, but her eyes held centuries of secrets.

The bell above the door chimed as she left, her departure as enigmatic as her arrival. I was alone again with nothing but the lingering magic in the air to keep me company.

I cleaned up silently, lost in thought. What had I just woven into being? What would Valeria's favor entail? Questions swirled around me like leaves caught in an autumn wind.

A chime from my phone snapped me back to reality – a message from an unknown number:

"I'll call upon you soon."

It had to be Valeria; who else?

The night beckoned me to close up shop. As I flipped off lights and locked doors behind me, the city's heartbeat seemed louder than usual. Streetlights cast long shadows that danced around my feet as I made my way home through the maze of alleys and side streets that crisscrossed the neighborhood.

That's when it happened – a flicker at the edge of my vision. A shape too deliberate to be dismissed as a trick of light or an errant plastic bag caught in the breeze.

I turned sharply, but nothing was there except for empty space and the distant murmur of city life. Still... something prickled at the back of my neck, a sense that eyes watched me from just beyond where light met dark.

Shaking off the feeling, I continued on but couldn't shake the cold finger tracing down my spine. It was as if some part of me recognized what lay hidden – a fragment inherited from whatever supernatural ancestor lurked in my bloodline whispered warnings.

A breeze swept through the alleyway, carrying with it whispers not meant for human ears. They caressed my senses before vanishing into silence once more. A shiver ran through me; this wasn't just another evening walk home.

My pace quickened until I stood before my apartment door fumbling for keys that seemed all too eager to evade my grasp. Once inside, safety wrapped around me like a blanket – but only for a moment.

I drew all curtains closed and made myself some tea trying to push away unwelcome thoughts about visitors both seen and unseen. Yet comfort remained elusive; every creak of settling wood or sigh from aging pipes sent adrenaline coursing through me again.

There were worlds hidden within our own – this much I knew all too well – yet tonight they felt closer than ever before. An intuition whispered that things were shifting beneath the surface like tectonic plates destined to collide.

Restlessness settled over me like dew upon morning grass; sleep would not find me this night. Instead, I poured over ancient texts and scrolls passed down through generations searching for anything that might explain this unease or predict what loomed on horizon's edge.

It was during these hours when night waned toward dawn that something new caught my attention: A passage speaking of bonds forged in ink and favors owed by moonlight's grace... And there it was again – another flicker outside my window; fleeting but undeniably real.

Chapter 2

Shadows of Crimson Ink

T he next night.

The first rays of dawn hadn't yet kissed the city's skyline as I made my way through the quiet streets. The pre-morning hush felt like a cloak, enveloping me in its brief illusion of peace before the day's chaos unfurled. My steps echoed against the cold concrete, a steady rhythm that matched my heartbeat. I was heading to Crimson Ink, the place that had become both my sanctuary and my battlefield.

I unlocked the front door, the familiar jingle of bells above it cutting through the silence. The parlor greeted me with its rich scent of ink and antiseptic, mingling with a faint trace of something ancient and indefinable. I flicked on the lights, their glow chasing away shadows that clung to corners like cobwebs. It was in these early hours, before the world woke up, that I felt most attuned to the energy pulsing through this place.

My morning routine unfolded with practiced ease: setting up my station, sterilizing equipment, and laying out designs for today's appointments. As I organized my inks—each color a weapon or a blessing in my hands—I sensed a shift in the air, a subtle prickling at the back of my neck. It was an unspoken signal; they were here.

The door swung open without warning, admitting a draft that carried whispers of power struggles and dark intentions. They strode in like shadows given form—The Vampire Gang.

Damien entered first, his presence commanding immediate attention. He moved with an air of authority that made space seem to bend around him. His eyes were dark pools of enigmatic knowledge, betraying nothing of his thoughts. He glanced around Crimson Ink with a proprietary gaze before settling on me.

"Alex," he greeted, his voice smooth as velvet yet edged with steel. "The day begins anew."

I nodded, keeping my expression neutral as I replied, "It does indeed, Damien."

Behind him trailed Evelyn—her elegance sharp as a blade's edge. She held herself with poise that spoke volumes of her rank within this hierarchy. Her gaze flickered over me like a caress laced with danger; she always seemed to be calculating angles and advantages.

"Morning," she said with a smile that never quite reached her eyes.

Victor lumbered in next, his stature towering and his movements deliberate—a stark contrast to Damien's refined grace and Evelyn's lethal charm. He offered me a curt nod, acknowledging my existence but nothing more.

I watched them disperse throughout Crimson Ink as if it were their kingdom—and in many ways, it was. The gang members took their places around the shop: some lounging on the leather couches reading newspapers as if they weren't soaked in darkness; others whispering among themselves, casting furtive glances around as though plotting their next move.

Damien settled into his usual spot near the back where he could oversee everything from his secluded throne. A few acolytes hovered near him like moths drawn to flame, eager for any morsel of attention he might deign to bestow upon them.

Evelyn paced gracefully around the parlor, inspecting every corner with meticulous attention to detail. Her fingers trailed over surfaces lightly dusted by time itself—a silent testament to her dedication and perhaps her aspirations beyond what she currently held.

Victor stood apart from the others, his role clear as he scanned for threats or disruptions. His imposing figure served as both shield and warning; none would dare challenge Damien's rule while Victor stood sentinel.

As I continued prepping for my first client of the day—a simple piece infused with strength—I couldn't help but eavesdrop on their exchanges.

"Have you secured it?" Damien asked one of his acolytes in a low tone that nonetheless carried across the room.

"Yes," came the hushed response. "It's safe."

Damien nodded once before turning his attention back to a thick tome laid open before him—a book so old it seemed whispered about in legends rather than read by mortal eyes.

Evelyn circled back toward me then stopped abruptly beside my station. She leaned down slightly under the pretense of admiring my designs but whispered so only I could hear her words over the hum of machines warming up for use.

"Keep your wits about you today," she cautioned softly before straightening up and offering me another smile—this one tinged with genuine concern hidden beneath layers of duplicity.

My fingers paused over a needle cartridge; Evelyn rarely offered unsolicited advice without reason or personal gain behind it. What did she know that I didn't? Or was this another test?

As I resumed my preparations without acknowledging her warning aloud—the safest course—I pondered what unseen currents were at play within these walls today.

The council members arrived shortly after—veterans draped in shadows and secrets who advised Damien from just out of sight but never out of influence. They settled into quiet discussions near him while occasionally casting sharp glances toward Evelyn or Victor or even myself—assessing allies and potential threats alike.

A younger vampire approached Damien with deference bordering on reverence; he whispered something into Damien's ear that drew a rare flash of interest across his face before he dismissed him with an imperceptible nod.

Alliances shifted within moments; acolytes exchanged wary looks while council members murmured amongst themselves—a silent storm brewing beneath calm surfaces.

As I lined up ink pots meticulously by shade—blackest black to blood red—I couldn't help but feel like another piece on their chessboard; moved according to plans I was only partially privy to but wholly affected by nonetheless.

The morning light began filtering through frosted windows casting dancing patterns across dark wood floors when suddenly all activity ceased; every member turned toward me expectantly.

Damien rose from his seat—an unspoken command that silenced any remaining whispers—and approached me with purposeful strides that ate up distance between us effortlessly until we stood face-to-face once more.

* * *

The buzz of my tattoo machine blended with the low hum of conversation, a soothing backdrop to the steady hand I kept as I etched an intricate design into my client's skin. The woman beneath my needle lay still, her breaths measured, trusting in my ability to give form to the magic she sought. Yet even as I focused on my craft, snippets of conversation from The Vampire Gang pierced the room's tranquility.

Damien's voice, smooth as aged whiskey, drifted from his corner booth where he sat ensconced in shadows. "Ensure the shipment arrives undetected. We can't afford another mishap," he instructed, his tone suggesting the weight of consequences should failure occur.

Victor's reply rumbled like distant thunder, "No one will suspect a thing. The docks are under our control."

The assurance in his words did little to ease the tension coiling within me. My city, a sprawling canvas of light and shadow, now seemed more ominous with each whispered secret I overheard.

Evelyn's heels clicked against the floor like a metronome dictating the rhythm of our fates. "The East End coven grows restless," she remarked, her voice carrying the chill of a winter breeze. "They question our authority."

A murmur of dissent rippled through the council members gathered around her, like leaves rustling before a storm. Their concerns, veiled in quiet tones, spoke of territories disputed and loyalties tested.

I pressed on with my work, my client oblivious to the power plays unfolding around us. The scent of blood and ink filled my nostrils – a potent mix that anchored me to the present moment.

As I dipped my machine into a pot of deep crimson ink, Victor's booming laugh broke through once more. "We've got those amateur necromancers right where we want them."

I couldn't help but shudder at the thought of what that entailed – manipulation and coercion were their tools just as much as fangs and fear.

My heart raced; not just from eavesdropping on their sinister dealings but from knowing I existed within their orbit—a reluctant satellite caught in their gravitational pull.

Evelyn leaned closer to Damien, her voice dropping to a purr only I seemed able to catch. "And what of the Mark of Power? Any progress on locating it?"

Damien's reply came soft but firm, "Patience, Evelyn. Such things cannot be rushed."

A bead of sweat trickled down my spine. The Mark of Power was no mere myth; it was real and within this city's confines. It held secrets that could unravel the delicate balance between our worlds.

"Once we have it," Damien continued, his tone dark as pitch, "our dominion over the city will be uncontested."

Their words weighed heavy on me like chains threatening to drag me into an abyss I wanted no part of. But there was no escape – not when your very bloodline entwined you with forces beyond your control.

A new voice entered the fray – one of The Acolytes – young and eager to prove his worth. "There's talk among the shapeshifters; they're organizing."

Damien's laughter sliced through the air, cold and dismissive. "Let them scheme," he said. "They pose no real threat."

As hours slipped by and night fell heavy outside Crimson Ink's stained-glass windows, I remained vigilant amidst the ink and skin—my artistry a shield against their darkness.

A Council member spoke up next, her voice like silk over steel. "The witches seek an audience with you regarding recent... disturbances."

Disturbances? My hand paused for a mere second before resuming its dance across flesh. What sort of disturbances warranted such caution in her tone?

Damien's response was clipped and authoritative. "Arrange it for midnight tomorrow. It's time they remembered who truly rules this city."

With every revelation spoken within these walls, unease grew within me like ivy creeping up an ancient ruin.

"Remember," Evelyn intoned sharply to an Acolyte whose eagerness had likely outpaced his discretion earlier. "Discretion is our greatest ally."

I couldn't agree more as I fought to keep my expression neutral while marking another person with power they barely understood.

My needle moved with precision over curves and edges as if tracing constellations meant to ward off evil or perhaps call forth something divine. And all while around me circled predators discussing territories and pawns in hushed tones laden with implications.

"Have we considered potential... traitors among us?" The Council member's words slithered across the room like smoke seeking out cracks in armor.

"Always," Damien replied without missing a beat. His confidence was unshakable – a fortress built upon centuries of cunning and survival.

The air grew thick with unspoken suspicions as alliances shifted like sand beneath tides in their world—a world where power ebbed and flowed at the whim of creatures ancient and ruthless.

And there I stood amidst it all – Alex – tattoo artist by day and something far more complex by nightfall. My hands worked magic upon skin while my mind raced with strategies on how to navigate this labyrinthine underworld without becoming another casualty in their endless games.

Each revelation from The Vampire Gang wove a tapestry rich with intrigue but fraught with peril—a tapestry I was now inexorably part of whether I willed it or not.

And so I continued my work under watchful eyes—both seen and unseen—as pieces moved silently across a chessboard that spanned an entire cityscape shrouded in mystery and magic.

* * *

The bell above the door chimed, a sound that usually brought a surge of anticipation. But today, it heralded a shiver down my spine, as if it tolled for something ominous lurking just beyond the threshold of Crimson Ink. The man who entered was a walking contradiction to the warm afternoon light that spilled onto the dark wooden floors. His eyes darted around the parlor like a cornered animal, and I could almost smell the fear rolling off him in waves.

"Welcome to Crimson Ink," I said, keeping my voice steady. "How can I help you today?"

He approached me, each step measured, his gaze lingering on the ancient artifacts lining the walls before finally meeting mine. "I need a tattoo," he muttered, his voice barely above a whisper.

I motioned toward one of the private rooms. "Sure thing. Let's discuss your design in here." As we walked, I couldn't help but notice how his hands trembled slightly at his sides.

Once we were settled into the room with its walls draped in velvet and the gentle hum of the sterilized equipment waiting to be used, I asked, "What kind of tattoo are you thinking about?"

He glanced at the door as if expecting it to burst open at any moment. "Something... to keep me safe."

I leaned back in my chair, eyeing him with a mix of concern and curiosity. "Safe from what exactly?"

He hesitated, and I watched his Adam's apple bob as he swallowed hard. "From them," he said under his breath. "The Vampire Gang."

My heart skipped a beat. There was no mistaking the tremor in his voice or the haunted look in his eyes – this man had danced with darkness and still felt its icy fingers trailing down his back.

I reached for my sketchpad and began drawing as I spoke. "I can create something that symbolizes protection." My fingers moved with practiced ease even as my mind raced with questions.

He watched me for a moment before nodding slowly. "Yeah, protection... That's what I need."

The room filled with silence save for the scratch of pencil on paper as I sketched an intricate amulet design known for its warding properties. The stillness was deceptive; it felt like we were both holding our breaths, waiting for something dreadful to leap out from behind the shadows.

As I worked on refining the design, I could feel his eyes on me – wide, desperate eyes that had seen too much. It wasn't just any client sitting across from me; it was someone who had witnessed firsthand what happens when you get entangled with creatures like The Vampire Gang.

"Will this really work?" His voice broke through my concentration.

"It's more than ink and needles," I replied, locking eyes with him to convey my sincerity. "There's power in these symbols – ancient power."

He nodded again but said nothing more. We settled into an uneasy silence while I finished up the drawing.

"I'm ready," he finally said, and there was a new determination in his tone that hadn't been there before.

As I prepped my equipment and went through the familiar motions of putting on gloves and pouring ink into tiny cups, my thoughts drifted to Damien and Evelyn – to their elegant menace and how effortlessly they wove their web of influence through every corner of this city. They had their hands in so many lives; it was only a matter of time before someone got caught in their snare.

I glanced up at my client's reflection in the mirror as I began transferring the design onto his skin. His jaw was set firm now; whatever fear he'd walked in with had transformed into resolve under the weight of necessity.

The buzz of the tattoo machine cut through the room like a siren's call as I began etching protection into his skin – line by line, shade by shade.

"You don't have to talk about it," I said after a while, sensing that there was a story behind his fear that might never find its way into words.

He exhaled slowly, watching as dark ink formed patterns on his flesh. "I made deals with them... deals I thought were simple at first." He paused as if each word was being pulled from deep within him. "But nothing is simple when it comes to vampires."

I nodded but kept my focus on the tattoo – this wasn't just art; it was an anchor for him now—a lifeline cast into turbulent waters.

As minutes stretched into hours and layers of ink built upon each other to form an emblem of safety, I couldn't shake off the feeling that this parlor had become something more than just a place where skin met ink. It was a sanctuary for those caught up in supernatural currents too strong to swim against alone.

The machine finally fell silent; only our breathing filled the space between us as I wiped away excess ink to reveal the completed tattoo – bold and intricate against his pale skin.

"It's done," I said softly.

He stood slowly and moved toward the mirror, examining my handiwork with wide-eyed wonder before turning back to me with an earnestness that cut right through me.

"Thank you," he said. "I can never repay you for this."

A wry smile tugged at my lips as I cleaned up my station. Repayment wasn't necessary; helping him felt like pushing back against forces that thrived on fear and domination – forces like The Vampire Gang lurking outside these walls.

As he left Crimson Ink with cautious steps that carried more weight than when he entered, there was no doubt left in my mind: every soul that sought refuge here added another layer to Crimson Ink's legend—a place where magic thrived amidst danger, where tattoos were more than just body art—they were talismans against an ever-encroaching darkness.

* * *

The hum of the tattoo machine ceased, and with it, the tension in my shoulders relaxed. Mariah, my latest client, rose from the chair, her eyes wide with the fresh thrill of ink embedded in her skin. The serpent coiled around her arm seemed to pulse with an energy that mirrored her satisfaction. I wrapped her tattoo with a practiced hand, my mind slipping from the precision of my work to the murkier thoughts that lurked beneath.

"Thank you, Alex," Mariah said, her voice soft yet vibrant. "It's exactly what I needed."

"Take care of it," I reminded her as I often did, though my advice was more than just aftercare—it was a cautionary tale spun from ink and magic.

She nodded and left, the chime of the shop door closing behind her like the final note of a song. The quiet settled over Crimson Ink like a shroud. Alone now, with only the faint city sounds permeating through the walls, I allowed myself to sink into the worn leather of my drafting chair.

My mind wandered to the whispers and shuffles of The Vampire Gang earlier in the day. Damien's presence loomed even in his absence—a shadow cast over every corner of my shop. His underlings had exchanged furtive glances and spoken in hushed tones about necromancers and witches as if these were common topics of discussion over morning coffee.

I had no illusions about my place here. My heritage and abilities made me valuable, but they also made me vulnerable—a pawn on a chessboard where I couldn't see all the pieces. It was one thing to give someone a protective amulet etched into their skin; it was another to be embroiled in a world where such protection was necessary for survival.

I rose and paced around my shop, fingertips grazing over surfaces imbued with spells for safety and secrecy. The weight of unspoken promises lingered heavy in the air—promises like the one I'd made with Valeria. The binding tattoo had sealed an agreement between us; its lines were like chains linking us together through unknown futures.

The vampires' conversation replayed in my head—the Mark of Power they sought was not just a trinket or symbol. It held significance beyond what I understood, and its importance had them circling each other with wariness reserved for enemies rather than allies.

I paused before a mirror that hung crooked on the wall, catching my reflection in its silvered surface. My eyes searched for signs of what I'd become since delving deeper into this hidden world—did I appear different? Did I wear my fear as openly as Mariah wore her serpent?

The door chime jangled again, slicing through my introspection. In walked a figure shrouded in a hooded cloak that seemed out of place amidst the city's concrete landscape—a stark reminder that no moment of peace lasted long in this life.

"I need your help," came a voice muffled by fabric.

I nodded slowly, wordlessly inviting them to sit. As they did so, removing their hood, their face remained obscured by shadows—not just any shadows but ones tinged with magic.

"What brings you to Crimson Ink?" My voice remained steady despite the unease that settled like frost on my skin.

They hesitated before speaking again. "I have heard you can grant protection through your art—protection from those who lurk in darkness."

My heart quickened; another soul seeking refuge from predators I knew all too well. The pattern was becoming too familiar, each thread weaving tighter around me until I felt enmeshed within their dark tapestry.

I cleaned my hands methodically at the sink before responding. "Protection can be given, but it's not just about what's on your skin—it's about what you carry within."

Their gaze met mine for a fleeting moment before dipping away—enough for me to see the resignation buried deep within their eyes.

"I carry enough within me to know when I am outmatched," they confessed. "And so I come seeking armor against forces beyond my control."

Armor—I mulled over the word as if it were foreign on my tongue. Wasn't that what we all sought? A way to shield ourselves from things we feared yet could not flee?

As I prepared my tools for another session of magic-infused artistry, doubt crept along the edges of my mind like creeping vines. With each tattoo I etched onto seeking flesh, was I drawing unwanted attention? Was each drop of ink another beacon for forces far greater than myself?

The air grew heavy with anticipation as I poised myself above their outstretched arm. My hand hovered as if guided by some unseen force dictating where to place each line—each barrier against darkness.

But darkness had many forms; it wasn't always lurking in alleys or hiding behind fangs and claws. Sometimes it whispered sweetly about power and protection while ensnaring you with invisible threads until you found yourself bound by promises you didn't remember making.

The needle buzzed to life once more as skin yielded beneath its dance—the dance of protection or perhaps entrapment? Only time would tell which melody we were truly moving to.

I worked silently, letting muscle memory guide me while my thoughts continued their restless journey through shadowy possibilities and half-heard conversations.

And there it remained—an uneasy truth hanging over me like Damocles' sword: by intertwining myself with these beings and their clandestine affairs, had I already sealed my fate? Or was there still time to unravel these threads before they pulled too tight?

The design took shape under steady hands—interlocking patterns meant to ward off evil—but even as I created this shield for another soul, doubt lingered like an unwelcome guest whispering tales of entanglement from which there might be no escape.

* * *

The bell above the door chimed, slicing through the low hum of whispered conversations and the soft buzz of tattoo machines. The familiar sound usually signaled a new client or the return of a regular eager to add to their canvas of skin. But today, it heralded something else—something that made the air feel charged, thick with expectation.

I looked up from my sketchpad, charcoal dust smudging my fingertips. He stood there, Damien, his presence commanding immediate attention. The Vampire Gang had been fixtures in Crimson Ink for weeks now, but he had always remained an enigma, a shadow overseeing his minions from a distance.

His eyes found mine, locking on with an intensity that seemed to see past the ink-stained walls of my shop and into the tangled threads of my dual heritage. He strode toward me, his movements fluid and predatory, the other vampires parting before him like mist.

"Alex," he greeted me, his voice a smooth baritone that resonated through the cramped space. "Your reputation precedes you."

I wiped my hands on a nearby cloth, standing to meet him halfway. "Damien," I acknowledged, feeling his name roll off my tongue with a mix of caution and curiosity. "To what do I owe the pleasure?"

He leaned against one of the workstations, his gaze never wavering from mine. The other patrons seemed to vanish into the background; even the hum of activity dimmed under his watchful eyes.

"I've been watching you," he said casually, but there was weight behind those words—a gravity that pulled at me with an uncomfortable force.

"You and half the city's underworld," I quipped, trying to keep my tone light. Yet, underneath the banter, unease coiled in my gut like a restless serpent.

His laugh was low and genuine, as if he found my discomfort amusing. "True," he conceded. "But few possess your... unique talents."

I folded my arms across my chest, feeling suddenly vulnerable under his gaze. My tattoos itched on my skin—a reminder of power I wielded but seldom understood.

"And what would you know about my talents?" I asked.

Damien pushed away from the workstation and closed the distance between us in two measured steps. His proximity sent a shiver down my spine—fear or anticipation; I couldn't tell.

"I know enough," he whispered. The menace was subtle but unmistakable. "Enough to recognize that you're wasted on these mundane transactions."

I bristled at his words. Crimson Ink might have been many things—a haven for supernatural beings seeking solace in art or power—but it was never mundane.

"This is more than just business for me," I replied firmly.

He tilted his head slightly, regarding me with newfound interest. "Is it now? Then perhaps you'll be open to a proposition."

My pulse quickened at the suggestion—dangerous possibilities skittered through my mind like shadows at twilight.

"What kind of proposition?" I ventured.

Damien's smile held secrets I wasn't sure I wanted to uncover. "One that could elevate your craft... expand your influence beyond these four walls."

The idea tugged at me—appealing to both sides of my nature—but something in Damien's demeanor warned me that whatever he offered came with strings attached.

"And what would you want in return?" I asked, steeling myself against whatever temptation he might dangle before me.

He stepped back and ran a finger along one of the tattoo machines as if admiring its potential for artistry—or destruction.

"Let's just say... a collaboration," he replied cryptically. "I have resources that could be beneficial to someone like you."

The way he said 'someone like you' made it sound like an invitation into a world I had long resisted—a world where blood ran deeper than ink and power came at a price paid in shadows and silence.

I considered him carefully, aware that this conversation was as much about gauging each other's strength as it was about forging alliances.

"And if I refuse?" I challenged quietly.

Damien's eyes glinted with dark amusement. "You have free will—for now." His voice dropped to a murmur only I could hear. "But remember this: In our world, it's better to be feared than loved—if one cannot be both."

His words hung in the air between us like an unspoken threat or perhaps a promise—a riddle wrapped in allure and warning.

As he turned to leave, blending back into the throng of vampires and mortals alike, I was left with a sense of disquiet churning inside me. My hands felt cold despite the warmth of the shop around me; even my own artwork seemed foreign under Damien's shadowy influence.

His encounter left questions clawing at my mind: What game was Damien playing? And more importantly—what role did he expect me to take within it?

My fingers absently traced over a half-finished design on parchment—a symbol of protection infused with power from both realms of my existence—and I wondered if soon I would need such protection myself.

* * *

I flicked on the crimson neon sign of Crimson Ink, the hum of electricity syncing with the pulse in my veins. Today, the air inside felt thick, charged with an anticipation I couldn't quite place. As I prepped my station, the glass jars of ink reflected back at me like a collection of dark, liquid eyes, each holding secrets I had yet to coax from their depths.

The door creaked open and a gust of wind toyed with the chimes, casting an eerie melody through the parlor. My next client, shrouded in shadows that seemed too dense for mere daylight to create, stepped across the threshold. There was something about this one; they moved with a purpose that seemed to stir the air into whispers.

"Welcome to Crimson Ink," I said, masking my curiosity with practiced ease. "What can I create for you today?"

The figure pulled back their hood, revealing eyes that held millennia within their depths. "Something... binding," they replied, their voice a low murmur that seemed to resonate with the very walls of the shop.

As we settled into the rhythm of ink and skin, I couldn't shake the feeling that today's work would etch more than just flesh. The design flowed from me as if it had been waiting for this moment—a series of intricate knots and weaves that promised strength and secrecy.

Hours bled away as I worked, and as the final line connected, sealing the pattern into their skin, a pulse of energy shot through me. The air crackled, and every shadow in Crimson Ink deepened. For a moment, it felt like we were not alone.

"Your craft is remarkable," they praised, their gaze lingering on their fresh tattoo before sliding back to me with unnerving focus.

I nodded my thanks but remained silent. Compliments were currency in this underworld of ours; too often they bought silence or feigned allegiance.

The door swung open again and Damien entered, flanked by Evelyn and Victor. Their presence sent ripples through the charged atmosphere.

"Alex," Damien greeted me with a nod that felt more like a king acknowledging a subject than an equal greeting another. "Your talents continue to impress."

I watched them move through my shop like they owned it—and perhaps in some ways they did—examining my work on today's clients with an appraising eye.

"Thank you," I replied cautiously. "But my work here is personal."

Damien chuckled—a sound devoid of humor. "Everything is personal when power is involved."

My skin prickled at his words; they held weight and portended change. Change that could unravel or reweave the fabric of this city's supernatural tapestry.

A subtle gesture from Damien had his entourage spreading out through Crimson Ink as if on cue. Victor lingered near an ancient bookshelf housing texts some would kill to possess. Evelyn moved like a wraith between shadow and light, her eyes never resting in one place for long.

Their orchestrated movements weren't lost on me; this was more than a casual visit.

"Is there something specific you're looking for?" I asked Damien directly.

He flashed me a smile that never reached his eyes. "Just ensuring our interests are protected."

The coded message was clear: They considered Crimson Ink part of their territory now—my talents included.

The evening wore on with an edge of tension sharp enough to slice through steel. The final client left with fresh ink drying on their skin and a newfound confidence in their stride—a parting gift from my craft and whatever magic it carried.

Alone now, save for The Vampire Gang's continued presence, I began my closing ritual: wiping down surfaces, securing ink pots, covering designs sketched for future appointments.

That's when it happened—a disturbance so subtle at first that I almost missed it amid the quiet hum of ending another day at Crimson Ink.

In one of the private rooms reserved for special clients—where magic was both sealed within skin and summoned from beyond—I caught sight of something unusual. A flicker in the air like heat above pavement on a sweltering day disturbed my peripheral vision.

Curiosity drew me toward the room before caution could catch up.

Inside, Damien stood alone amidst a swirl of shadows that seemed to writhe at his command. He murmured words too low for me to catch but carried an ancient resonance that vibrated through the floorboards up into my very bones.

With each syllable he spoke, those shadows coalesced into forms both wondrous and terrifying—beasts wrought from darkness and nightmares that bowed before him in deference.

Evelyn appeared at my side without sound or warning. Her breath was cool against my ear as she whispered urgently: "Don't interfere."

Her words were needless; fascination rooted me in place as much as fear did.

Damien's display was not meant for mortal eyes—or mine which straddled realms neither fully human nor wholly otherworldly—but here I stood witness to power raw and untamed.

I could feel it now—a shift within Crimson Ink itself—as if its very walls recognized Damien's dominion over these forces or perhaps feared them as well.

The shadow-beasts dissipated as quickly as they formed, leaving behind only echoes of their existence—and Damien standing triumphant among fading wisps of darkness.

His gaze met mine across the room; there was no surprise there—only an acknowledgment that secrets had been shared without consent given or sought.

This was The Vampire Gang: mysterious in motive and dangerous in nature—a reminder etched into my memory as indelibly as any tattoo I'd ever inked onto willing flesh.

Chapter 3

Whispers of Power

I leaned against the cool, rough brick wall just outside the private room, the murmur of conversations filtering through the parlor. Words floated up, laced with a mix of reverence and fear. They were talking about the Mark of Power—a design so ancient and potent that even uttering its name seemed to charge the air with electricity.

Victor, with his broad shoulders hunched over a tome as thick as my thigh, was saying something to a new apprentice, his voice a low rumble. "They say it's not just ink on skin—it's like grafting a piece of the universe onto your body, tapping into raw power."

The apprentice, a wiry kid with more piercings than years under his belt, nodded, eyes wide as saucers. "But who could wield such a thing without getting consumed by it?"

Their words clawed at my chest, and I straightened up. In my pocket, my fingers brushed against a folded piece of paper—a sketch of that very design I'd drawn last night during my restless hours of research. I shivered despite myself.

Evelyn swept through the room with her usual grace, her hair cascading down her back like a river of night. Her voice was softer but carried no less weight as she spoke to Mariah, who was flipping through one of my design books. "It's more than just power—it's a legacy, an heirloom of sorts. Not everyone is destined to bear it."

Mariah looked up at Evelyn, curiosity etched on her face. "But if someone did... if someone was chosen for it?"

Evelyn's lips curled into a knowing smile that didn't quite reach her eyes. "Then they would step into a role that's been vacant for centuries."

I stepped back into the shadows as they passed by my hiding spot. My mind raced—what did Evelyn know about the Mark? And why did it feel like Crimson Ink had become ground zero for all things revolving around this mysterious design?

A pair of regulars lounged in the waiting area—Trent and Lucas—local college kids who fancied themselves as amateur urban explorers and supernatural enthusiasts. They huddled over Lucas' phone, scrolling through what looked like pages from an old grimoire.

"Look at this," Trent whispered, tapping on the screen with an excited grin. "The Mark is said to have been created by a cabal of ancient sorcerers as a key to unlock divine potential."

Lucas shook his head in disbelief. "But no one knows where it is or what it really does, right? It's all just legends and ghost stories."

"Until now," Trent replied with a sly wink.

I exhaled slowly and turned away from their conspiratorial banter. The weight of their words settled in my stomach like stones in water—sinking deep and stirring up silt from long-forgotten places.

The front door chimed, heralding another customer's arrival—an older woman draped in shawls that clung to her like shadows. She moved directly toward me with purpose in her stride.

"You must be Alex," she said in a voice that held traces of an accent I couldn't place.

"That's me." I managed to keep my tone steady despite the way my heart thrummed against my ribs.

"I've heard about your talents." Her eyes were sharp, piercing even in the dim light of Crimson Ink. "And about this Mark everyone is whispering about."

I folded my arms across my chest to hide any telltale tremors. "Rumors are just rumors," I replied carefully.

She smiled then—a cryptic curling of lips that made me feel like she knew more than she let on. "Perhaps," she said before glancing around the parlor filled with artifacts and inked flesh. "But sometimes there's truth hidden within them."

Our conversation hung there for a moment before she walked away toward Damien's office without another word.

The door swung open again; this time two figures stepped inside—a couple that seemed out of place amid the gothic charm of Crimson Ink. They wore business attire and carried themselves with an air of importance that set them apart from the usual clientele.

They approached me directly, their gazes lingering on my work displayed on the walls—images born from ink and magic.

"We're looking for something unique," the woman said without preamble. Her partner nodded along silently.

"And you've come to Crimson Ink." I offered them a polite smile while gauging their intentions; they didn't seem like they were here just for tattoos.

The man finally spoke up; his voice was measured but carried an undercurrent of urgency. "We've heard whispers about a new design... something powerful."

My smile didn't waver even as my insides twisted into knots—the Mark again. It was becoming impossible to ignore how these threads were weaving together into something inevitable.

"I'm not sure where you're getting your information," I began cautiously, but the woman cut me off with a wave of her hand.

"Let's not dance around it," she said crisply. "We represent interested parties who are willing to pay handsomely for information—or better yet—the acquisition of such designs."

The offer hung between us—a tempting fruit dangled from a branch just out of reach. But behind its sweet veneer lay thorns ready to prick at my conscience.

I tilted my head slightly, letting them think I was considering their proposal while inside I wrestled with implications far beyond monetary gain.

"You know how to reach me when you're ready to discuss further." The woman slid her business card across the counter before they both retreated back through the door they had come in.

Left alone once more amid the buzz and hum of Crimson Ink's daily life, I pondered their words and what accepting such an offer would mean—not just for me but for whatever balance we had managed to maintain within these walls where magic met skin and secrets kept us bound together tighter than any ink could ever manage.

* * *

I leaned against the cool leather of the tattoo chair, my fingers tapping a silent rhythm on the armrest. The couple before me, their eyes alight with the promise of power, continued to dangle temptation like a jeweled pendant. They wanted the Mark of Power, and they believed I could ink it onto their skin.

"I understand your... curiosity," I began, my voice measured, betraying none of my own fervent interest. "But such designs are not just drawn. They're born from something deeper, more ancient than you might realize."

The woman's gaze narrowed slightly, a flicker of impatience—or was it desperation?—dancing in her eyes. "We know what we're asking for, Alex. And we're prepared to offer you whatever you want for it."

I let a slow breath escape through my nostrils as I pondered her words. Whatever I wanted? The possibilities surged through my mind like a tide rushing over the shore.

"Let me think on it," I finally replied, keeping my expression neutral. "Such decisions can't be rushed."

As they left, ostensibly satisfied with my noncommittal response, I felt the weight of countless eyes upon me. The Vampire Gang lingered in the shadows of Crimson Ink like wraiths in a crypt, their presence heavy and oppressive.

My mind raced as I wiped down the chair and prepped for the next client—a canvas eager for a splash of magic upon their skin. Subtlety was key now; I couldn't afford to draw unwanted attention or suspicion from Damien and his cohorts.

During lulls between clients, I mingled under the guise of casual conversation. Victor was hunched over his texts again when I sidled up to him.

"Ever wonder what it's like?" I asked casually, nodding towards the ancient book in his hands.

Victor looked up, his brow furrowing in thought. "To hold such power? Sometimes. But then again, who wouldn't?"

"Stories say that Mark can change a person," I mused aloud, hoping to sound merely pensive rather than probing.

"Change or corrupt," Victor muttered, turning back to his reading. "It's a fine line."

I filed away his words like precious coins in a vault and moved on.

Evelyn was perched at the front desk when I approached her next. She had an air about her—a sense that she swam in deeper waters than most.

"Quite the legend that Mark has become," I remarked offhandedly while reorganizing some flyers on the counter.

Evelyn glanced up at me, her eyes cool but not unkind. "Legends often have roots in truth," she said cryptically.

"But what truth?" I pressed lightly.

She smiled faintly, as if amused by a private joke. "That would be telling."

Our exchange was cut short as the bell above the door chimed and new clients entered, eager for their appointments.

I retreated to my workstation but kept an ear out for any snippets of conversation that might float through the air—each word another piece to this ever-growing puzzle.

The day wore on; ink flowed from my needles like rivers of destiny upon skin after skin. Yet beneath each piece of art lay an undercurrent of unease—a tension coiled tight within me.

It was during a brief moment alone in the back room that I heard it—a whisper carried on silence itself.

"...the Mark's power is not just strength," murmured a voice outside my door—one of Damien's council members speaking to another in hushed tones. "It's said to be a gateway—"

A gateway to what? My heart hammered in anticipation, but before more could be revealed, footsteps scattered the conversation like birds at the sound of gunfire.

I couldn't afford to be caught eavesdropping—not when Damien had eyes everywhere and trust was currency best spent wisely.

That night after closing up shop, I found myself pacing across my apartment floor—a lion caged by his own thoughts.

Damien had shown interest in my abilities; he'd seen something within me that sparked his attention. Could he know about my lineage? About the potential magic coursing through my veins?

I stopped mid-stride as realization struck me—a flash of lightning across a stormy sky. If Damien suspected anything about my heritage... he might also suspect that I knew more about the Mark than I let on.

The risk was palpable now; every move needed careful consideration. My search for answers about this elusive Mark had to remain undetected—or else invite peril upon myself and those around me.

Sleep proved elusive that night as plans and counterplans danced through my mind—a chess game played against shadows and whispers where every piece moved with silent intent.

By morning's first light breaking through curtains heavy with dust and time, resolve had settled within me like sediment in still water—I would find out more about this Mark of Power without tipping Damien off to my search.

Crimson Ink opened its doors once again to those seeking transformation through ink and magic—yet beneath its welcoming facade lay secrets both old and new that threatened to unravel at the slightest tug of curiosity's thread.

As clients came and went, bearing fresh marks upon their bodies—each one an echo of some deeper yearning—I continued to weave my web of inquiries delicately among them all: The curious apprentice eager for knowledge yet wary enough not to overstep; The cautious artist guarding against too keen an interest from those who wielded power like daggers cloaked beneath silk.

My questions floated through conversations as light as air—never too pointed or persistent but always listening for that elusive note that might sing of hidden truths regarding this enigmatic Mark whose shadow stretched long across our world's hidden face.

And so days passed—a dance between light and shadow where every step held weight yet appeared weightless; A play where each actor held their cards close while seeking glimpses into others' hands without revealing their own intentions too soon or too clearly amidst this intricate masquerade we all performed beneath Crimson Ink's ancient roof.

* * *

The door to Crimson Ink creaked open, slicing a line of dim light across the shop's polished floor. The figure that slipped inside seemed to merge with the shadows, a whisper of power cloaked in the anonymity of a hooded cloak. I caught the scent of old parchment and a whiff of something like ozone—a storm trapped in fabric.

"Welcome to Crimson Ink," I called out, my voice steady despite the churn of apprehension in my gut. "How can I help you today?"

The figure paused, hood obscuring their face. The silence stretched between us like a taut wire. Then, in a voice smooth as silk and equally enigmatic, they spoke.

"I believe you have knowledge I seek, Alex. Knowledge of the Mark of Power."

Their words struck a chord within me, resonating with the weight of hidden truths and unspoken dangers. My hand instinctively moved to cover my own forearm where ink lay dormant beneath my skin—designs that hinted at my heritage but revealed nothing of my secrets.

"And who might I have the honor of speaking with?" I kept my tone light, masking the quickened pace of my heart.

"A friend," they said, "or perhaps an ally, depending on what you choose to share."

I leaned back against the counter, crossed my arms. "I'm all about sharing—but the price has to be right."

The figure moved closer, their movements fluid as if they glided rather than walked. A sense of power emanated from them, something ancient and formidable.

"The price will be fair," they assured me. "But first, tell me what you know about the Mark."

I pondered their request for a moment before responding. "It's a design shrouded in legend. They say it grants its bearer incredible strength, maybe even immortality. But like any source of power, it comes with its share of risks."

The air around us seemed to hum with anticipation as they digested my words.

"Risks? Such as?" They tilted their head ever so slightly.

"Such as attracting unwanted attention," I replied, gesturing around us at the parlor which now doubled as a chessboard for vampire games and hidden agendas. "Or finding out that power can consume just as easily as it can elevate."

A small nod from under the hood suggested understanding—or at least acknowledgment—of my words.

"You speak wisely for one so young," they remarked. "The Mark has been lost for centuries; its designs scattered to the winds of time. What makes you think you can recreate it?"

My pulse quickened at their implication. Did they know more than they let on? Or were they fishing for confirmation?

"I don't deal in absolutes," I said carefully. "But there's power in ink and skin—a language older than any spoken word."

They drew closer still until I could make out dark eyes beneath the hood—eyes that seemed to hold galaxies within them.

"And if someone were to request such a tattoo?" They reached into their cloak and pulled out an object wrapped in velvet cloth.

I glanced at the parcel before meeting their gaze once more. "That depends on who's asking—and why."

With deliberate slowness, they unwrapped the cloth to reveal an amulet—a twin to the one inked on my last client's skin for protection against these very creatures that now frequented my shop.

"This amulet belonged to one who bore the Mark," they said softly. "It's said to be a key."

A key? My mind raced with possibilities—could this be what Damien and his crew were searching for? Or was this another piece in an ever-growing puzzle that extended beyond even their reach?

"Why show this to me?" I asked.

"Because you are more than you seem, Alex," they replied cryptically. "And because time is running short."

I could feel their urgency now—a current that flowed beneath their calm exterior.

"Time for what?" I demanded.

"For choices to be made," they answered enigmatically before placing the amulet back within its velvet confines and sliding it across the counter toward me.

I didn't reach for it—not yet. The weight of destiny seemed tied up in that small gesture.

"What choices?" My voice was firmer now; demands made under pressure often yielded more truth than polite inquiry.

The figure straightened up, regarding me with those deep cosmic eyes.

"The choice to stand with those who seek balance or those who would tip the scales for their own gain," they stated plainly. "The choice to use your gifts for greater purposes or to hide them away out of fear."

Their words hit home with uncomfortable precision—I had been teetering on that very precipice myself.

"And if I choose balance?" My question hung between us like mist over water.

"Then perhaps we can work together." The figure finally lifted their hood, revealing features both striking and indistinct—as if constantly shifting between possibilities. "My name is Kaelan, and there's much we need to discuss."

* * *

The evening draped Crimson Ink in shadows, and I couldn't shake the feeling that something pivotal was about to unfold. Damien and his inner circle had gathered in the back room, a space usually reserved for private tattoo sessions or the rare, more esoteric magical work. Tonight, though, it was a sanctum for whispered strategies and vampire politics.

From my spot at the front counter, I sketched absentmindedly, the designs flowing from my pen more out of habit than intention. My ears strained for fragments of conversation, snippets that might clue me in on Damien's plans. But they spoke in hushed tones, the words slipping through my grasp like sand through fingers.

A door cracked open, and I glanced up. Victor stepped out, his expression unreadable as he gave me a brief nod before heading to the front door. The gap he left behind became my illicit window into their world.

Damien's voice floated through the crack with a resonance that demanded attention. "The Mark of Power... It's resurfaced," he murmured, a blend of awe and something darker lacing his tone.

I froze, pen hovering above paper. My heart thrummed against my ribcage as if trying to keep pace with the significance of his words.

A woman I didn't recognize—her voice sharp like shattered glass—replied, "It's just a myth, isn't it? A story to keep fledglings in line?"

"Hardly," Damien retorted with a scoff that seemed to rattle the very air. "It's real, and its bearer could shift the balance of power irrevocably."

The room erupted in a low rumble of voices, each member voicing their concern or disbelief. I could almost see them—a coven of night creatures circled around ancient texts and relics—conjuring schemes from the ether itself.

Damien continued, silencing them with his command. "Excitement should be tempered with caution. Whoever wields the Mark will become a beacon—a target for all."

A chill raced down my spine at his words. The Mark of Power was more than just an intricate design, it was a siren call to those who craved dominance over others.

"Then we must find it first," another voice said—a deep baritone that resonated with authority.

Damien hummed in agreement. "Yes, but we must move carefully. The Council is already wary of our influence; we don't need to draw more eyes upon us."

Their voices dipped lower again, details of their plan shrouded in secrecy. I knew then that they were playing a game much larger than any tattoo I'd ever inked onto skin—a game where lives were chips on a bloodstained table.

As the conversation continued beyond my earshot, unease twisted in my gut like a coiled serpent. Damien was right to be concerned; such power wasn't meant for those who sought it out of greed or ambition.

My hand found its way back to paper, moving on its own accord as if trying to purge my thoughts onto parchment. The design that emerged wasn't one I recognized—it was intricate and ominous, woven with symbols that seemed ancient even to my eyes versed in magical iconography.

Suddenly aware of my own focus on the forbidden conversation, I shook off the trance and crumpled up the paper. It wouldn't do well for Damien or anyone else to see what had spilled from my subconscious.

"Alex." Evelyn's voice sliced through my reverie as she approached me from behind. I turned to face her; her expression held an earnestness that tightened something inside me.

"You heard?" she asked quietly.

I nodded once, unwilling to admit just how much I'd overheard—or how deeply it unsettled me.

"Be careful," she whispered before slipping past me toward the gathering in the back room.

Her warning echoed in my mind long after she disappeared from sight—two simple words that felt like an anchor in turbulent waters.

I glanced down at my hands—stained with ink and responsibility—and wondered how long before they would be forced to wield power beyond their means or design a destiny that wasn't mine to dictate.

The door shut with finality then, leaving me alone at the counter once more—the divide between their world and mine as clear as the barrier between night and day. But as much as I wished to deny it, those worlds were colliding—and fast.

* * *

I closed the shop early, the last sliver of daylight melting into the city's silhouette. The click of the lock echoed in my ears, a resounding seal on a day steeped in hidden agendas and cloaked threats. My heart drummed a staccato rhythm as I ascended the narrow stairs to my apartment above Crimson Ink. The place doubled as a sanctuary and research den, walls lined with shelves groaning under the weight of ancient grimoires and modern texts on supernatural phenomena.

The room hummed with the latent energy of countless incantations, spells once spoken in hushed reverence or desperate cries. I settled at my desk, a heavy, scarred thing that had known the weight of many secrets. My fingers danced over the keyboard, coaxing it to life. The glow from the screen painted my face in cold light as I plunged into the depths of hidden knowledge.

Hours bled into each other as I scoured digital archives and scanned encrypted forums known only to those who tread the line between the seen and unseen. My heritage whispered through my veins, an unspoken guide as I sought out fragments of lore about the Mark of Power. Whispers of its existence had always lingered on the fringes of my consciousness, a specter at the edge of understanding.

The Mark was no mere design; it was a legacy etched in flesh and spirit, an ancient covenant between bearer and power itself. Every source spun tales of its might—how it could bend reality to its wearer's will or shatter minds with unbridled force. The symbols within it were not merely for show; they were keys to doors that should have remained shut.

I found an obscure text buried beneath layers of cyphers—a digital copy of a tome so old its original pages would crumble at a touch. The text was written in a language that predated modern tongues, but I understood it as if it were my mother's voice whispering through time. A chill crept up my spine as I translated passages detailing rituals and sacrifices made to infuse the Mark with power drawn from beyond our realm.

"Bearer beware," it warned, "for with great might comes a burden no soul should endure." The text hinted at a price paid not just upon receiving the Mark but continuously, a toll that exacted pieces of one's essence until nothing remained but raw power—and an empty vessel.

Images flickered before me—artifacts unearthed from forgotten ruins; symbols that mirrored those dancing across my sketches; faces twisted in ecstasy and agony as power surged through newly marked skin. The lore was clear: those who sought the Mark did so at their peril, for it was not merely an amplifier but also a conduit for forces untamed by human or vampiric hands.

A diagram caught my eye—a geometric pattern that spiraled into infinity, at its center lay the heart of the Mark. As I traced its lines with my gaze, they seemed to shift subtly, aligning with some unseen axis. It wasn't just a static image; it was an invitation to unlock something within myself or within the fabric of reality.

I couldn't shake the feeling that there was more to uncover, layers beneath layers waiting to be peeled back by hands both willing and wary. The Mark wasn't simply power—it was history made manifest, will crystallized into form.

I leaned back in my chair, muscles tense from hours hunched over forbidden knowledge. My mind raced with possibilities and dangers—of paths that could lead to enlightenment or ruin. A sip of cold coffee did little to clear the fog of weariness clouding my thoughts.

There were connections here I hadn't yet drawn—threads weaving through history that tied the Mark to events long past and yet unfurling still. It spoke of cycles repeating and power changing hands through bloodlines thought extinct.

I sifted through online databases for any mention of bearers throughout history—names rose from obscurity only to vanish again as if erased by time or intention. Each one had altered the course of their era in ways both overt and subtle before meeting ends shrouded in mystery.

My search brought me to forums where whispers turned into debates among those who believed themselves enlightened. Some claimed knowledge of bearers walking among us today; others scoffed at such notions as fantasy—a myth perpetuated by those craving significance in an indifferent universe.

Yet amidst these discussions lay accounts that resonated with truth—tales shared by those whose ancestors had borne witness to feats defying explanation. They spoke not only of power but also consequence—the fracturing of minds too fragile for such gifts, families torn apart by forces they could neither comprehend nor control.

A knock at my door shattered my concentration like glass upon stone. My pulse quickened—visitors at this hour were rare and rarely brought good tidings. I rose from my desk and approached cautiously, every sense heightened by hours spent immersed in lore rife with warnings.

I opened the door to find Evelyn standing before me—her eyes wide with urgency and something akin to fear lurking within their depths.

"Alex," she began, her voice barely above a whisper but carrying weight heavy enough to anchor ships. "We need to talk."

* * *

The shop door chimed, a harbinger of the unknown as a silhouette melded from the twilight into the parlor. Crimson Ink breathed around me, its walls echoing with whispers of past incantations and secrets etched in skin. The newcomer's presence seemed to thicken the air, casting long shadows that clawed at the edges of my vision.

"Alex," the figure's voice was a soft hiss, "we need to talk."

I wiped my hands on a cloth, setting aside my tools of trade. The weight of my heritage pulsed at my temples, a reminder that some conversations bore consequences heavier than ink.

"You know why I'm here," they continued, a hood shrouding their face in mystery.

I nodded, though I knew it was the Mark of Power that lured them like moths to a flame. "Speak then. Time's never been a friend in this place."

They stepped closer, and I caught a glimpse of eyes like coal, smoldering with urgency. "The Mark you seek... it's not just ink and myth. It's alive, in ways you can't fathom."

Chills cascaded down my spine. I had heard tales, sure, but to hear such words uttered aloud lent them an eerie solidity.

"What do you mean 'alive'?" I asked.

"It breathes through those it claims, intertwines with their very essence until they're indistinguishable from its power."

I considered this with care. The thought had crossed my mind in darker moments—the notion that some tattoos were more than art or protection; they were entities unto themselves.

"Who are you?" My voice didn't tremble, but it carried the weight of my dread.

"A friend," they replied cryptically. "Or an enemy. That depends on you."

The parlor felt colder then, as if their words siphoned warmth from the room. A shiver ran through me—not from fear but from recognition. This dance with danger was familiar; it mirrored the duel between my human side and something older within me.

"And what do you want from me?"

Their hood dipped as if acknowledging a checkmate move on a chessboard only they could see. "To warn you. The Mark is coveted by many, but understood by none. You toy with forces that will not be leashed."

My hands clenched involuntarily. Their warning felt like a gale foretelling a storm; something monumental loomed on the horizon.

"Why tell me this?" Suspicion laced my question.

"Because you're at the heart of it all, whether by fate or by choice." They took a step back, blending once more with the shadows that seemed too eager to embrace them.

My mind raced as I processed their words—a riddle wrapped in enigma. "Heart of what?"

But they were gone as swiftly as they'd appeared, leaving behind an echo of menace that clung to the walls like cobwebs.

I stood there for moments—or was it hours?—grappling with their warning and its implications for my future. My search for knowledge about the Mark had always been driven by curiosity and an unspoken need to understand my own power. Now it seemed that quest had placed me squarely in the crosshairs of an unseen conflict.

Evelyn emerged from the back room, her eyes scanning mine with practiced concern. "What happened?"

I exhaled slowly, trying to tether myself to reality once more. "A visitor," I said simply.

Her gaze flickered around the now-empty parlor before settling back on me. "What kind of visitor?"

"The kind that leaves more questions than answers." I walked over to lock the front door—no more clients tonight; I had enough on my plate without adding fresh ink into the mix.

Evelyn leaned against the counter, arms folded as she watched me move about the shop, extinguishing candles and securing cabinets filled with our most potent artifacts.

"You're spooked," she observed quietly.

"I'm... aware," I corrected her without turning around.

Aware that every decision now carried weight beyond mere artistry; aware that whatever path I chose next could ripple through realms seen and unseen; aware that for all my knowledge and skill, I stood at the precipice of an abyss gazing into unfathomable depths.

"Talk to me," Evelyn urged.

I sighed and leaned against the counter opposite her. "Someone came with a warning about the Mark—said it's alive and dangerous."

She arched an eyebrow—a silent prompt for more details which I didn't have.

"They said I'm at the heart of whatever's coming." My laugh was humorless—a defense mechanism against encroaching fear. "They called themselves a friend or enemy based on choices I've yet to make."

"That's... cryptic." Concern etched Evelyn's features even deeper.

"And utterly inconvenient." I ran a hand through my hair—a futile attempt to soothe frazzled nerves.

Evelyn pushed off from the counter and approached me. "Whatever this is about, you're not alone in it."

Her words bolstered me more than she could know—Evelyn was steadfast when everything else felt like shifting sands beneath my feet.

"Thanks," I murmured sincerely before adding with feigned bravado, "Let's just hope your faith in me isn't misplaced."

She offered a smile that didn't quite reach her eyes—she knew too well how treacherous our world could be—but her next words were firm and filled with conviction.

"It's not."

We locked up Crimson Ink together and stepped out into night's embrace—the city's pulse thrumming beneath our feet like a heartbeat urging us forward into whatever lay ahead. As we parted ways under streetlights casting pools of gold on rain-slicked streets, her warning echoed back to me: Be careful.

Chapter 4

Unwilling Destiny

The chime of my phone sliced through the silence like a scalpel, precise and unwelcome. A single message glowed on the screen, its contents brief but its weight colossal. "Come to the back room. Now." Damien's summons, terse as it was, left no room for hesitation.

A knot tightened in my stomach as I set down the tattoo machine, its hum fading into nothingness. The ink I'd been using seemed to congeal with my sudden apprehension. Each step toward the back room felt like wading through molasses, my heart thudding against my ribs.

I rapped lightly on the aged wood of the door before pushing it open. The dim light within couldn't dispel the shadows that clung to every corner, nor could it soften the cold edge in Damien's eyes as he turned to regard me.

"You wanted to see me?" My voice emerged steady, belying the turmoil beneath my calm exterior.

Damien leaned back against an ornate desk littered with ancient texts and arcane artifacts. "Alex," he began, his tone as smooth and dangerous as a blade sliding from its sheath. "Your talents have not gone unnoticed. But there's more to you than mere artistry, isn't there?"

I held his gaze, aware that any sign of weakness could be exploited. "I don't know what you mean."

A half-smile flickered across his lips, and he gestured for me to take a seat opposite him. I complied, settling into the chair with deliberate nonchalance.

"Let's not play games," he said softly. "I've seen how you work—how the tattoos you create resonate with a power that's more than just skin-deep."

My fingers tightened on the armrests. Damien was fishing, but for what? I had to tread carefully; one slip could send me tumbling into waters too deep and treacherous to navigate.

"I give people what they ask for," I replied evenly. "Nothing more."

Damien chuckled, a low sound that sent shivers skittering down my spine. "Oh, but you give them so much more than that." He paused, eyes narrowing slightly as if he were trying to peer into my very soul. "The Mark of Power—what do you know about it?"

The question hit like a punch to the gut. The Mark had been consuming my thoughts since whispers of its existence began to circulate through Crimson Ink.

"It's just a legend," I said with a shrug that felt too casual even to me.

"Legends often have roots in truth," Damien countered smoothly. He stood and paced slowly around the room, hands clasped behind his back like a professor lecturing an attentive student. "This legend holds particular interest for me—and now for you."

My pulse quickened at the implication of his words. Involvement with Damien meant danger; everyone in the supernatural underworld knew that.

"Why me?" I asked quietly.

Damien stopped pacing and leaned in close, his presence overwhelming as he invaded my personal space without actually touching me. "Because you're not just anyone, Alex." His voice dropped to a whisper that held an edge of iron. "You have connections—connections that could prove beneficial."

Connections? Was he referring to my heritage? Did he know about my lineage—my part-human, part-supernatural blood?

"And if I refuse?" The words left my mouth before I could stop them.

His expression darkened like a storm cloud rolling in fast. "Refusal isn't an option."

The air in the room grew thick with unspoken threats. It was clear: Damien had chosen me for whatever game he was playing and expected me to fall in line.

"Fine," I said after a moment's silence, injecting a hint of reluctance into my voice while masking my growing resolve to learn more about his intentions. "What do you need from me?"

A satisfied smile crept across Damien's face as he resumed his seat across from me.

"I need your expertise," he said simply. "You will help us find the Mark of Power."

The directness of his demand struck me harder than any veiled threat could have. Helping Damien and his gang find something so potent was akin to setting a match to dynamite.

"And what's in it for me?" My words were cautious but deliberate; showing interest might afford me some leverage—or at least information.

"Protection," he replied instantly, as if anticipating my negotiation tactic all along. "And power beyond your wildest dreams."

I suppressed a snort at that last promise; power was never given freely in our world—it came at exorbitant costs.

Damien reached into his jacket pocket and pulled out something small and metallic—an amulet I recognized from earlier encounters—and placed it on the table between us.

"This belonged to the last known bearer of the Mark," he said, watching me closely for any reaction.

I feigned indifference even though every fiber of my being screamed for caution; objects like these were never merely trinkets but talismans charged with purpose and history.

"We begin tonight," Damien declared abruptly, standing once again. "Prepare yourself."

With those final words hanging between us like a guillotine's blade poised mid-air, he strode out of the room without another glance back.

I remained seated for several moments longer than necessary before standing on unsteady legs—the conversation replaying over and over in my mind like an eerie echo bouncing off unseen walls.

As I emerged from the back room into Crimson Ink's main parlor area again, faces blurred around me: clients awaiting their turn under my needle, acolytes discussing hushed secrets they thought no one else could hear—the usual symphony of sights and sounds now underscored by an unsettling sense of urgency that had settled deep within my bones.

Tonight would be pivotal—I could feel it in every whispering shadow that clung stubbornly to Crimson Ink's walls.

* * *

Damien's fingers traced the spine of the ancient tome laid out before him, his touch light as if caressing a lover's back. He paused, fixing his gaze on me, eyes piercing through the dim light of the back room. I swallowed hard, feeling the weight of his stare as it bore into me.

"I've watched you," he began, his voice a low hum that filled the space between us with a charge I couldn't ignore. "Your hands... they don't just create art, Alex. They weave power."

I leaned back against the wall, trying to appear nonchalant, but my heart betrayed me with its frantic rhythm. I could see shadows dancing at the edges of the room—servants of Damien's will.

"You flatter me," I replied, forcing a smirk. "But last I checked, every tattoo artist at Crimson Ink weaves a bit of power into their work."

He chuckled—a sound smooth as velvet and just as deceptive. "Come now. We both know you're not 'every tattoo artist.' Your lineage..." He let the words hang, an unspoken acknowledgment of my half-human, half-supernatural heritage.

My grip tightened on the armrests of my chair. "What about it?"

"It makes you valuable. Unique." He stepped closer, and I could smell the age on him—like earth after rain, ancient and relentless. "I want that uniqueness to work for us. Exclusively."

The air seemed to grow thicker with each word he uttered, and I fought to keep my breathing steady. "Exclusively," I echoed, testing the word on my tongue as if tasting a new flavor—one bitter with constraint.

"Yes." Damien pulled a chair from the corner of the room and sat opposite me, leaning forward. "You have a gift that transcends mere talent or skill. It's in your blood." He pointed to his own arm where one of my tattoos resided—a snake that seemed to slither under his skin with every subtle movement he made.

"You want me to tattoo only members of your gang?" The question felt stupid even as it left my lips; Damien was not known for sharing toys.

"Not just tattoo," he corrected with a pointed look. "I want you to research, develop new magics for ink—ones that can benefit us in ways we haven't yet imagined."

The proposition sank its claws into me; it was tempting to delve deeper into the potential of my craft without restrictions. But this was Damien—the price would be steep.

"And if I refuse?"

His smile didn't reach his eyes. "You're smart enough to know that's not really an option."

I stood up abruptly, my chair scraping loudly against the floor. My mind raced with thoughts of escape routes and allies—though in truth, neither seemed particularly promising at that moment.

Damien rose with a grace that belied his strength and crossed to where I stood. He towered over me slightly; not enough to be imposing but sufficient to remind me who held the power in this room.

"You need protection," he said softly, almost kindly if I didn't know better. "There are others who would exploit your talents far more ruthlessly than I ever would."

I scoffed. "And here I thought you were just looking out for your own interests."

A shadow passed over his face before he regained composure. "It can be both."

I weighed my next words carefully; each syllable was a step on a tightrope strung high above an abyss.

"Say I agree—what happens next?"

"We start tonight." His response was immediate—as if he'd anticipated my tentative acquiescence all along. "There's someone who requires your services."

The mention of 'starting tonight' sent a jolt through me; whatever illusion of choice had been presented was just that—an illusion.

"Who?"

"You'll meet them soon enough." He glanced at his watch—an anachronistic piece that seemed more for show than utility—and then back at me with an expectant look.

A cold shiver ran down my spine as realization dawned on me: agreeing to Damien's terms meant surrendering more than just my independence—it meant entwining myself further within this web of darkness that already clung too tightly around me.

"I need some assurance," I said slowly, trying to negotiate from what little ground I stood on.

"Assurance?" His brow arched in mock surprise.

"That this partnership," I emphasized the word with air quotes, "doesn't end up with you owning me."

Damien considered this for a moment before nodding once. "Fair enough." He reached into his pocket and produced an intricately carved wooden box—no larger than a deck of cards—and placed it on the table between us.

"Inside is a token—a promise," he explained as he lifted the lid revealing an amulet similar to but distinct from the one he'd given me earlier—the metal glowed faintly under the low light. "This will bind our agreement; it will protect you from others but also serve as... let's call it collateral for your loyalty."

I eyed the amulet warily—it was beautiful and foreboding in equal measure—a symbol of bondage masquerading as protection.

"Bind our agreement how exactly?" My voice barely concealed my distrust.

He chuckled again and closed the box with care before sliding it across to me.

"In ways only old magic can ensure." Damien stood up straighter then glanced toward the door as if hearing something beyond my senses. "Time is precious—do we have an accord?"

My hand hovered over the box; each decision felt heavier than any tattoo machine I'd ever held.

The door creaked open behind him—Evelyn peered in with an unreadable expression—and suddenly everything came into sharp focus: this wasn't just about tattoos or power or even survival—it was about choices and their irreversible consequences.

And as Damien waited for my response—the shadows still at his beck and call—I knew one thing for certain: whatever choice I made would change everything.

* * *

Damien's silhouette loomed over me, a dark monument against the soft glow of antique lamps. Crimson Ink was a fortress of secrets and shadows by night, its walls heavy with the whispers of ink and blood.

"You've got quite the talent, Alex," he began, his voice smooth like the slide of a knife's edge against skin. "And I'm offering you a chance to expand that talent, to reach heights you've never dreamed of."

I could feel the weight of his gaze, measuring me, calculating. He paced slowly around my work station, fingers trailing along the polished surface where my tools lay neatly arranged.

"But let's not kid ourselves," he continued, his tone shifting ever so slightly, a dark undercurrent beneath his words. "This isn't just about opportunity. It's about survival."

My hands gripped the edges of my chair, knuckles whitening. Damien paused behind me, his presence like a cold draft in a closed room.

"I can protect you, Alex. Protect this quaint little shop of yours," he murmured close to my ear. "There are things out there that would love to take a bite out of someone with your... heritage."

The implicit threat hung in the air between us like smoke. My heart raced. This was no mere business proposition; it was a devil's bargain cloaked in velvet promises.

"And what if I refuse?" My voice came out steady, though inside I felt anything but.

Damien chuckled softly, circling back into view with the grace of a predator.

"Refuse?" He tilted his head slightly as if considering an absurd notion. "I'm afraid that's not an option. You see, you're already part of this world – our world. And there are consequences for those who don't play along."

He stopped directly in front of me, locking eyes with mine. His were fathomless pools reflecting centuries of cunning and cruelty.

"Think about your grandmother," he said casually as he picked up one of my tattoo machines, examining it with feigned interest. "Such a spirited woman."

My breath hitched in my throat at the mention of her – a veiled threat against the one person who mattered most to me.

"You wouldn't dare," I managed to say through gritted teeth.

Damien placed the machine back down with care and leaned forward on his palms.

"I would prefer not to," he admitted smoothly. "But we all have our roles to play."

I felt trapped, caught in the web Damien spun with his words and implications. There was no doubt that his protection came at a price – one that involved servitude and silent complicity.

"So what do you want from me?" I asked, already knowing that whatever it was, it would cost more than I was willing to pay.

"For starters," he said as he straightened up and clasped his hands behind his back, "exclusive tattoos for my gang. Tattoos that are... potent."

His eyes glinted with unspoken knowledge – knowledge of what I could do with ink and magic combined.

"And then?" I pressed on, even as dread coiled in my stomach.

Damien's lips twisted into a semblance of a smile.

"And then we find the Mark of Power," he declared as if announcing an inevitable victory.

I took in a deep breath, trying to steady myself against the tide that threatened to sweep me away.

"You're asking me to dive into unknown waters without so much as a life vest," I pointed out.

"On the contrary," Damien replied smoothly as he reached into his jacket pocket and produced an amulet – its design intricate and menacing all at once. "This will be your life vest."

He extended it toward me and reluctantly; I took it from him. The amulet was cold against my palm, pulsing with an energy that seemed hungry and alive.

"This binds you to me," Damien explained. "It will protect you from other... parties who might wish you harm."

The amulet felt heavy in my hand – not just physically but symbolically too. It was an anchor chaining me to Damien's whims and ambitions.

"But remember," he added with pointed clarity, "it only protects you from others – not from consequences should you decide to cross me."

I understood perfectly what he meant: Damien himself was now my greatest threat as much as my so-called protector.

"So when does this mission start?" I asked him after a long moment filled only by the distant hum of city life beyond the parlor walls.

"Tonight." Damien checked an ornate watch clasped around his wrist – another piece bespeaking old wealth and older secrets. "There is no time like the present for such endeavors."

He turned on his heel then and made for the door without another word or backward glance – confident in his control over me.

Alone now in Crimson Ink's dim interior, I clenched my fist around the amulet until its edges bit into my skin. Choices were made for me tonight under veiled threats and coercive promises; choices that would ripple through my life like stones cast into still waters.

As silence settled around me once more, one thing became clear: despite Damien's talk of protection and opportunity, this game we were embarking on had only one guaranteed winner – and it wasn't going to be me unless I played very carefully indeed.

* * *

The amulet felt heavy in my palm, its surface cool and oddly soothing against my skin. Damien had left, but his presence lingered like a shadow at the edge of my vision. I traced the intricate patterns on the amulet, each line a whisper of promises and threats. My fingers stopped at the center, a hollow that seemed to pulse with an energy that wasn't entirely its own.

I closed my hand around it, feeling the weight of Damien's offer. Protection and power—two things that seemed so appealing, yet I knew they came shackled to an unspoken cost. I'd seen enough in this city to understand that nothing was ever truly free, especially not from someone like Damien.

My mind raced as I considered my options. On one hand, aligning with Damien could provide me with resources I'd never dreamed of having access to; on the other hand, it could drag me deeper into the underbelly of a world I'd tried so hard to navigate from the fringes.

The parlor was silent around me, save for the distant hum of traffic outside—a reminder that life continued relentlessly beyond these walls. Yet here I was, standing at a crossroads that felt like it could alter not just my life but the very fabric of this hidden world.

Evelyn's warning echoed in my mind: "Be careful." She knew the dangers better than most. But what choice did I have? The thought of being bound to Damien sent a shiver down my spine, but refusing him wasn't just turning down an offer—it was potentially painting a target on my back.

I sighed and walked over to my workstation, laying the amulet down next to my sketchbook filled with designs and half-formed ideas. The contrast between the amulet's ancient power and my modern tools wasn't lost on me. They were both instruments of change in their own way.

Leaning back against the counter, I closed my eyes and let out a breath I hadn't realized I was holding. Fear twisted in my gut—a fear not just for myself but for what accepting this offer could mean for those who crossed paths with Crimson Ink.

The shop door chimed, pulling me from my thoughts. My eyes snapped open to see Mariah stepping inside, her presence a gentle reminder of why I loved this place so much.

"Everything okay?" she asked, her voice laced with concern as she took in my troubled expression.

"Yeah," I lied smoothly. "Just one of those days where you question every decision you've ever made."

She chuckled softly and approached me, her steps light and easy—the antithesis of how I felt at that moment. "Well, if it helps any," she said as she reached out and gave my shoulder a reassuring squeeze, "I've never once regretted walking through these doors."

Her words should have comforted me; instead, they added another layer to my turmoil. How many others felt safe here because of what Crimson Ink represented? And how quickly could that sense of safety shatter if I allowed Damien to use this place for his own ends?

I managed a small smile for Mariah's sake but quickly excused myself under the guise of needing to tidy up before closing time. She waved goodbye and promised to return soon for another session—a session that now held an uncertain future.

As she left, silence enveloped me once more. My gaze drifted back to the amulet, its patterns seemingly mocking me with their intricate dance. The room felt smaller somehow—as if the walls were inching closer with each passing second.

This wasn't just about tattoos or even about supernatural politics anymore; it was about identity and choice. Could I live with myself if I became just another tool in Damien's arsenal? Yet could I survive turning him away?

I moved around the shop mechanically—cleaning instruments, wiping down surfaces—my actions devoid of their usual care and attention. Every stroke felt heavy with indecision.

Then it hit me—the real source of this dread wasn't just fear or entrapment; it was about losing myself in this bargain. With every tattoo I crafted, I poured a part of myself into it—a connection between artist and canvas that went beyond ink and skin.

To be forced into creating something against my will would sever that connection—it would make each piece feel hollow... tainted.

A part of me whispered that maybe this was just part of growing up—learning when to compromise and when to stand your ground. But as night began to fall outside, casting shadows across Crimson Ink's interior, compromise felt like surrender.

My hand hovered over the amulet again; its presence taunted me—a physical manifestation of the decision looming over me like an executioner's blade. It offered protection but at what cost? Would wearing it bind me not just to Damien but also seal away parts of who I was?

The clock on the wall ticked away seconds that felt like hours—each one pressing upon me with an urgency that bordered on desperation. Soon Damien would expect an answer—an answer that could alter more than just my life but also tip scales in a game where even kings could fall.

A low growl rumbled from deep within me—a primal sound borne from frustration and anger at being cornered like some frightened animal. But wasn't that what they wanted? To see how far they could push before Alex—the artist who danced with magic—broke?

No—I refused to break.

But refusal alone wouldn't be enough; whatever path lay ahead would require cunning and strength perhaps beyond what I possessed alone. And yet... within those shadows might also lie opportunities—chances for leverage if only I dared look closely enough.

My gaze settled on a design spread across one page of my sketchbook—a phoenix rising from ashes—a symbol not just of rebirth but resilience as well.

Perhaps there lay my answer not in flight or fight but transformation—allowing myself to adapt without losing what made me...me.

As darkness settled around Crimson Ink like a cloak drawn tight against chill winds outside, determination took root deep within—a determination not merely to survive this night but emerge from it more than when it began.

* * *

I stood there, the weight of Damien's gaze pressing down on me like a shroud. The amulet he had placed in my hand felt colder than it should, a tangible reminder of the choice I faced. I turned it over, watching the way the dim light of the back room glinted off its intricate surface, casting patterns on the wall that looked almost like warnings.

"I don't have much of a choice, do I?" My voice came out steadier than I felt. It wasn't really a question; we both knew that. The silence that followed hummed with unspoken truths and unyielding power.

Damien's lips curled into a semblance of a smile, not quite reaching his eyes. "You always have a choice, Alex. It's just that some choices come with... greater consequences."

The amulet pulsed against my palm as if in agreement. There was something about it that felt alive, a whisper of the past or maybe a hint of the future. It was unnerving.

I nodded once, decisively. "Alright, Damien. I'll work for you exclusively." My words echoed in the stillness, marking the end of one life and the beginning of another.

"Create your art for my gang," he said, his voice smooth like velvet but with an edge that could slice through steel. "And help us find the Mark of Power."

I slipped the amulet over my head and tucked it beneath my shirt, close to my skin where its constant chill would be a reminder of this moment – this pact that I had sealed with a being as dangerous as he was alluring.

Damien extended his hand, and I took it without hesitation. His grip was firm and cold, his touch devoid of life yet brimming with an ancient force. As our hands parted, I knew there was no turning back now.

Back at my station, my hands moved on their own accord, sketching designs that seemed to flow from some hidden well within me. Clients came and went, their skin now canvases for enchantments that would bind them to Damien's will just as surely as the amulet bound me.

Hours blurred into days, and days into weeks. Time lost meaning as I worked tirelessly under Damien's watchful eye. He brought me books filled with arcane symbols and forbidden lore that whispered secrets in languages long forgotten by mortal tongues.

The shop transformed around me; once a haven for those seeking magical tattoos imbued with protection or power, Crimson Ink now became something darker – a nexus for clandestine deals and silent pacts signed in blood and ink.

Every drop of color I etched into skin became a testament to my new reality – one where choice was an illusion and freedom a distant memory. Yet amidst this new existence, something within me resisted, an ember of defiance refusing to be snuffed out.

Evelyn watched me with worried eyes whenever she visited. She never spoke openly about her concerns – she didn't need to. Her presence alone was enough to remind me of what was at stake: not just my soul but the delicate balance of power within our hidden world.

"You've changed," she said one evening as she watched me finish up a complex sigil on a client's arm.

I cleaned my tools methodically before answering her. "I had to."

She nodded slowly but said nothing more on the matter. Her silence spoke volumes more than any words could have conveyed.

Night after night, I lay awake in bed with the amulet's chill against my chest and sketches strewn about me – each one bringing me closer to unraveling the mystery of the Mark of Power but pulling me further from who I once was.

I found myself at crossroads in every design I conjured up – could I imbue these tattoos with enough subtlety to serve Damien's purposes without fully succumbing to his control? Was there room to maneuver within these confines he'd set for me?

The questions haunted me even as my reputation grew; whispers of 'the artist who can weave fate with ink' echoed through streets shrouded in shadow and secrets.

One evening as dusk crept over the cityscape like spilled ink across parchment, Damien entered Crimson Ink with an entourage of his closest followers. They surrounded him like planets orbiting their sun – darkly radiant in their adoration and fear.

"Show me what you've learned," he commanded softly but firmly as he approached my station.

I hesitated only for a heartbeat before presenting him with sketches that were more than mere images; they were spells waiting to be spoken aloud by needle and ink on willing skin.

Damien examined each piece carefully before fixing his gaze on mine. "Impressive," he conceded with a nod that felt like benediction from a fallen god. "But we need more if we're to find the Mark."

The word 'more' echoed ominously in my mind long after they had all left for the night. More what? More power? More risk? More sacrifices?

As I cleaned up alone in the quiet aftermath of their visitation, every stroke of my brush felt like another step down an unfathomable path laid out before me by forces beyond comprehension or control.

In this world where darkness whispered promises too enticing to ignore yet too perilous to embrace without caution, I'd become an architect of destinies not entirely my own making – yet still intricately tied to every beat of my conflicted heart.

* * *

Damien's words hung in the air like a thick fog, the weight of his expectations pressing down on my shoulders. The amulet he gave me felt cold against my skin, a constant reminder of the pact I'd unwittingly made. My shop, once a sanctuary of creativity and freedom, now brimmed with the tension of unsaid threats and uncharted territories.

The night wore on, and I worked my needle into skin with an intensity that mirrored the chaos swirling in my mind. Every buzz of the machine was a whisper of the power I wielded and the danger it invited. Damien had left hours ago, his presence still lingering like a shadow cast by the moon's pale light.

Closing time crept up on me, a welcome end to an evening fraught with unease. The last client of the night—a woman whose aura flickered with both strength and sorrow—left with a phoenix rising from ashes on her back, a symbol of rebirth that seemed more poignant now than ever.

I locked the door behind her, flipping the sign to 'Closed.' The silence that followed was both a relief and a haunting companion. I began to clean up, methodically wiping down surfaces and putting equipment away, each movement deliberate and grounding.

A creak from the back room sent a shiver down my spine. My heart hammered against my ribs as I reached for one of the iron rods we kept hidden beneath the counter. It was laughable how such a mundane object became my chosen weapon in a world where fangs and dark magic were real threats.

"Alex," a voice called out from the shadows, smooth as velvet yet edged with an unmistakable warning. It wasn't Damien—no, this voice was different, unfamiliar yet somehow expected.

I turned to face the source, rod held firmly in hand. A figure emerged from the darkness: one of Damien's council members—an ancient vampire whose name never reached my ears but whose reputation painted him as ruthless and sagacious.

"I'm closed," I stated firmly, though my voice betrayed me with its slight tremor.

He stepped closer, his movements fluid like smoke drifting through still air. "You've entangled yourself in a web more intricate than any ink you've laid into skin."

My grip on the rod tightened as I met his gaze—piercing blue eyes that seemed to see through every defense I had. "And what web would that be?" I challenged, even as dread coiled within me.

"The web of power," he replied simply. "Damien may offer you protection, but there are greater forces at play here than you can fathom."

I swallowed hard. "What do you want?"

"To warn you," he said softly. "The Mark of Power is not just an artifact; it's an apex of forces that could shift balances we've maintained for centuries."

His words felt like pieces to a puzzle I wasn't sure I wanted to complete. "Why tell me this? What's your stake in it?"

He chuckled dryly. "Let's just say not all of us are keen on Damien's vision for domination."

I couldn't help but snort at that. "And here I thought vampires were all about hierarchy and control."

"There are those among us who value balance over conquest," he said with a pointed look. "The Mark... it's not something to be wielded lightly."

"I never intended to get involved with any of this," I admitted.

"Intentions matter little in our world," he said as he took another step closer. His proximity sent an electric chill through me—a warning from my very blood about the predator before me.

"Damien is cunning; he will use your talents for his gain until there's nothing left but an empty husk." His voice was almost compassionate now, or as close to it as someone like him could get.

I lowered the rod slightly; his intent didn't seem hostile—just alarmingly candid. "What would you have me do then?"

"Be cautious," he advised. "Watch not only what is asked of you but also what is taken without asking."

I nodded slowly; his warning etched into my thoughts alongside every line I had ever inked onto skin.

"Remember," he continued as he began to fade back into darkness like mist at dawn's first light, "not all allies show their fangs, and not all threats come with snarls."

And then he was gone, leaving me alone with only echoes for company.

The shop felt colder now—emptier—as if his presence had siphoned away any remaining warmth. I stood there for long moments before finally setting down the rod and finishing my closing tasks mechanically.

Once everything was in its place, I stood at the threshold between Crimson Ink and the city beyond—a city unaware of the shadows that danced just out of sight. The cool night air brushed against my face as I stepped outside and locked up behind me.

My mind raced through our conversation again—the council member's warnings playing over in my head like a haunting melody. Damien's intentions were clear: use me for his ascent to greater power within this hidden world we both inhabited.

But it wasn't just Damien now; there were others—others who saw me not as an asset but as a pivot point for something much larger than any single ambition or desire for control.

As I made my way home under streetlights casting their pallid glow upon empty sidewalks, uncertainty trailed every step. With each revelation came new questions: Who else knew about the Mark? What would they do to obtain it? And most importantly, where did that leave me?

A pawn? A player? Or something else entirely?

In that moment of solitude amidst slumbering buildings and whispered secrets carried by nocturnal breezes, one thing became painfully clear: choices loomed ahead—choices that would shape not just my fate but potentially that of many others hidden within this urban labyrinth.

The night gave way to no answers—only deepening shadows that promised more intrigue and peril with each passing hour.

Chapter 5
Doubts and Dilemmas

I sat in the dim light of my apartment, the only glow emanating from a single lamp perched on a corner table piled high with books and sketches. The soft hum of the city's nocturnal life filtered through the half-open window, but it felt distant, like a world I was no longer a part of. In the quiet, my mind spun with thoughts that refused to settle – thoughts of deals made under duress, alliances as fragile as spider silk, and tattoos that held more than just ink.

The weight of the amulet around my neck was a constant reminder of the pact I'd struck with Damien. It felt heavier than it should, like it carried not just its physical mass but also the burden of what it represented. Protection, he had said. But at what cost?

My hand traced over the designs in my sketchbook – a serpent shedding its skin, a phoenix rising from ashes – symbols of transformation. I had to transform too; to adapt to this new reality where Crimson Ink was no longer just mine, but a pawn in Damien's game. But even as I sketched these symbols of rebirth, I couldn't shake off the dread that clung to me like a second skin.

A part of me had been tempted by Damien's offer – who wouldn't be? Power, protection... these were seductive promises in our precarious world. But another part recoiled at the thought of being tied to his dark undertakings. I'd always taken pride in my work, in the way my tattoos could bring strength, comfort, or simply beauty to those who sought them out. But now? Now my art was at risk of becoming something I didn't recognize – something tainted by Damien's sinister intentions.

I closed my eyes and leaned back against the worn couch cushions. The fabric had started to fray at the edges, threads pulling away much like I felt myself fraying under the pressure. In those moments of darkness behind my eyelids, I saw flashes – Mariah's awed expression as her tattoo came to life on her skin; Victor's smirk as he felt the lion roar into existence on his arm; Evelyn's enigmatic smile that hinted at secrets untold.

I opened my eyes again and let out a breath I hadn't realized I was holding. These were more than clients; they were people whose lives intertwined with mine through the art I etched onto their skin. Could I really use this gift Damien had coerced from me to further his own ends? What would become of Crimson Ink if every needle's stroke was shadowed by fear and moral compromise?

A sharp knock on the door shattered my reverie. My heart lurched before settling into a rhythm too fast for comfort. I rose and approached cautiously, knowing that at this hour and with these stakes, visitors were rarely harbingers of good news.

The door creaked open to reveal Evelyn standing there, shrouded in darkness save for the streetlight casting her figure in stark relief against the night.

"You shouldn't be here," I said without thinking, but her presence felt like an anchor in this storm-tossed sea.

"Neither should you," she replied with that same cryptic smile. "But here we are."

I stepped aside and she slipped into the room like a wraith. Her gaze swept over my cluttered space with an air of familiarity that spoke volumes about how much our lives had become entangled since Damien made his play for Crimson Ink.

"You've been quiet since our last... arrangement," she began as she picked up one of my sketches.

I watched her fingers trace over lines that mirrored those racing through my thoughts – intricate patterns woven with care and intention.

"It's been hard to think straight," I admitted.

Evelyn nodded slowly, her eyes never leaving the sketch in her hands. "Damien is ambitious; you know this. He doesn't make offers without expecting significant returns."

I swallowed hard against the knot forming in my throat. "And what does he expect from me? My complete obedience? My soul?"

She laughed softly – not out of humor but as one might when recognizing an unpleasant truth.

"Perhaps not your soul," she said finally. "But certainly your talents."

We stood there in silence for what seemed an eternity until Evelyn placed the sketch back down with deliberate care.

"Alex," she said firmly, her voice cutting through my tangled thoughts like a knife through silk. "Remember who you are and what you stand for."

Her words were like cold water splashed onto my face – bracing and clarifying.

"I'm trying," I said hoarsely.

Evelyn approached me then, close enough that I could see myself reflected in her ageless eyes.

"You must do more than try," she whispered. "Damien is not invincible."

Her touch was light on my arm but carried a weight that spoke volumes.

"He has enemies?"

"Everyone has enemies," she responded cryptically before turning towards the door.

"Evelyn," I called after her before she could disappear into the night once more. "Why are you telling me this?"

She paused at the threshold, half-turned back towards me with shadows dancing across her features.

"Because despite everything," she said quietly, "you're not just another pawn to me."

And then she was gone, leaving me alone with more questions than answers and a resolve slowly knitting itself back together amidst doubts and fears.

I picked up one sketch – a phoenix mid-rise – and studied it until its lines blurred into determination etched onto paper. Maybe it was time for Crimson Ink – for me – to rise from these ashes too.

* * *

I closed the door to Crimson Ink behind the last customer of the night, a silence settling over the shop like dust after a storm. My hands shook as I wiped down the counter, remnants of ink staining my skin, a stark reminder of the day's events. Damien's offer echoed in my head, a tempting call laced with danger. The weight of his amulet around my neck was a constant pressure, a symbol of an alliance I never wanted.

Turning off the lights, I locked up and headed into the city's cool night air. My thoughts were a whirlwind of possibilities and what-ifs. The Mark of Power, its allure and threat, danced at the edges of my consciousness. I needed advice, someone to listen without judgment or agenda.

Tara's place was my refuge, her door always open. As I walked toward her apartment, my footsteps seemed to beat out a rhythm that matched my racing heart. She was a friend who knew nothing of supernatural tattoos or vampire gangs but had always been there for me when life got complicated.

I knocked on her door, the sound too loud in the quiet hallway. When Tara opened it, her face lit up with surprise and concern.

"Alex? What's wrong? You look like you've seen a ghost."

I let out a breath I hadn't realized I was holding and stepped inside her warm, inviting space.

"I need to talk," I said simply.

She nodded and led me to her couch where we both sat down, her cat weaving between our legs in search of attention.

"Start from the beginning," Tara urged, her voice steady and calm.

I hesitated for a moment before diving in. "There's this guy—Damien. He runs... let's just call it an organization with lots of influence in certain circles." I skirted around the truth; she didn't need to know about vampires or otherworldly beings.

"And what does Damien want with you?"

"He wants exclusive rights to my tattoos," I said, choosing my words carefully. "He says he can offer protection and help Crimson Ink flourish."

Tara raised an eyebrow. "But?"

"But it feels like selling my soul," I confessed. "He gave me this amulet that's supposed to protect me, but it feels more like a leash."

She reached over and took my hand in hers, grounding me. "You've always been about freedom—your art is an expression of that. If this feels wrong to you, then maybe it is."

"I know," I sighed, "but there's more at stake than just me and my ethics. There's this design—"

I stopped short. How could I explain the Mark of Power without revealing too much?

"A design?" Tara prompted gently.

"It's complicated," I said evasively. "It has... consequences." The truth was so much heavier than those words implied.

"You've always been careful with your work," Tara observed. "Whatever this is about must be big if it has you this wound up."

I chuckled humorlessly. "You could say that."

"Then why consider Damien's offer at all?" Tara asked pointedly.

I ran a hand through my hair, struggling with the right words to convey the gravity of it all without dragging her into this world of shadows.

"It's not just about what he wants from me; it's about what refusing him means." My voice grew quiet as I considered what Damien and his kind were capable of when crossed.

Tara leaned back against the cushions, thinking for a moment before responding. "Sounds like you're between a rock and a hard place."

"Exactly."

Her eyes held mine for a long moment before she spoke again. "What does your gut tell you?"

"That none of this will end well," I admitted.

"Then maybe you need another perspective." Tara stood up abruptly. "Someone who understands your world better than I do."

She had a point; Jade came to mind immediately—a rival turned ally who knew the stakes involved in our line of work.

"Yeah," I agreed slowly. "Maybe you're right."

Tara hugged me tightly before letting go. "You'll figure this out, Alex. You always do."

Leaving Tara's apartment felt like stepping out from under shelter into an impending storm once again—but with slightly steadier feet.

Jade's studio was on the other side of town, an edgy place that buzzed with energy even at night. As I approached, lights still glowed through the frosted glass door.

I rapped on it lightly before pushing it open.

"Jade?" My voice carried over the hum of tattoo machines still at work in the back room.

Jade emerged from behind a beaded curtain, wiping ink from her hands with a cloth.

"Alex?" She looked surprised but not unwelcoming as she approached me. "What brings you here so late?"

"I need advice—professional advice." It felt strange coming to Jade about this when we'd been competitors not long ago.

She motioned for me to follow her into a private space where designs adorned every inch of wall space—a sanctuary for artists like us.

"What kind of advice?"

"It's about an offer... one that comes with strings attached." My gaze fell upon one of Jade's intricate designs on the wall as if seeking answers within its lines and curves.

Jade leaned against her worktable crossing her arms over her chest as she waited for me to continue.

"It involves exclusive rights to my work... And possibly looking for something very specific and very dangerous." My eyes met hers then flicked away quickly; revealing more might put her in danger too.

She didn't respond immediately but walked over to one of her sketches pinned up among countless others—a phoenix rising from ashes—and traced its outline with one finger thoughtfully before turning back to face me.

"You're talking about being owned," she stated flatly without accusation or judgment—just recognition of what such deals entailed in our world.

"Yes," was all I could muster in reply as anxiety twisted inside me anew at hearing it spoken aloud by someone else.

"And this dangerous thing—does it have anything to do with why everyone seems on edge lately?" Her eyes narrowed slightly as she pieced together rumors and whispers that must have been circulating within our community.

The weight of secrets pressed down on me as heavily as Damien's amulet against my chest.

"It might," I conceded.

Jade nodded slowly then stepped closer.

"Alex..." She began seriously.

And that's when we heard footsteps outside—the distinct sound shattering our bubble of confidences exchanged under hushed tones.

We both turned toward the sound coming from outside Jade's studio—a harbinger perhaps of decisions made manifesting sooner than expected.

* * *

I was wiping down the leather chair when the bell above the door jangled. The sun had dipped below the skyline, and the usual evening crowd hadn't filtered in yet. The figure that entered was hunched, their steps hesitant, like each footfall was a question asked to the creaking wooden floor. They paused at the threshold, their gaze sweeping across Crimson Ink's interior, lingering on the artifacts that clung to the shadows.

"Welcome to Crimson Ink," I called out, keeping my voice steady. "How can I help you today?"

The figure shuffled forward, and as they drew closer, the dim light unveiled a patchwork of bruises marring their skin. Their eyes, bloodshot and desperate, met mine. "I need... protection," they whispered, voice frayed at the edges.

I motioned to the chair. "Have a seat. Let's talk about what you're looking for."

As they sat down, I noticed how their hands trembled, how they kept glancing over their shoulder like fear itself was on their heels. I pulled on my gloves with practiced ease.

"Can you tell me what happened?" I asked gently as I prepared my equipment.

Their story unfolded in broken sentences and ragged breaths. They spoke of debts unpaid and promises broken, of how the vampire gang's cruelty had seeped into their life like a relentless tide. "They... they came for me," they stammered. "Took everything but my skin."

I listened, each word etching itself into my consciousness, heavy with an unspoken plea for salvation.

"And now you're here because you believe a tattoo can protect you?" My hand hovered over a set of inks.

They nodded eagerly, clutching at straws that only I could weave into a lifeline. "I heard... rumors about your work."

The room seemed to close in around us as I considered their request. This person before me bore the marks of Damien's gang — a living testament to the suffering they inflicted upon those who crossed them. If I agreed to help this soul, it would be one more secret to keep from Damien; one more act of rebellion beneath his very nose.

"I can create something for you," I said slowly, carefully not to promise too much too soon. "A symbol of protection."

Relief flickered across their battered face — brief and fragile as a candle's flame in a storm.

As my pen danced across their skin, tracing the outline of an ancient warding sigil, we spoke little. The hum of the tattoo machine filled the silence between us like an incantation — a barrier against outside threats.

"What will happen when they find out?" Their question hung suspended above us.

My focus never wavered from my task as I answered truthfully, "They won't find out from me."

An hour slipped by before I finished — a shield now emblazoned on their skin. As they stood and faced themselves in the mirror, there was a subtle shift in posture; perhaps not confidence reborn but something akin to hope rekindled.

"Remember," I said as they pulled on their jacket with care not to disturb the fresh ink, "this is only part of your armor."

They met my gaze in the mirror's reflection and nodded solemnly before slipping out into the night from whence they came.

Alone again with my thoughts and doubts swirling like smoke around me, I cleaned up my station meticulously. My heart felt heavy with unasked questions: How many more would come seeking refuge? How long could I keep playing this double game under Damien's nose?

The door opened once more; Evelyn stepped inside with her usual grace that seemed at odds with her lethal nature. Her eyes narrowed slightly as she took in my somber expression and the freshly used equipment.

"Busy evening?" she asked casually as she perched on one of the stools.

"Just one client so far," I replied without offering more than necessary.

Evelyn tilted her head ever so slightly. "Damien's getting impatient about that design he asked for." Her words were soft but carried an undercurrent of warning.

I nodded slowly. "I'm working on it." My voice held no trace of hesitation or fear — both emotions firmly locked away behind an impassive facade.

Her gaze lingered on me for a moment longer before she stood up and walked towards one of Crimson Ink's many enigmatic corners where shadows played hide-and-seek with reality. She didn't press further or question why a simple tattoo had taken up an hour of time when no design rested in sight.

I let out a breath I hadn't realized I'd been holding and turned back to my sketchbook where ideas and possibilities swirled within its pages like trapped spirits seeking release. Damien's demand for exclusive designs echoed in my mind like a haunting melody that refused to be silenced.

Each stroke of my pen felt heavier than before — every line drawn with the knowledge that with each piece given to Damien and his gang, part of what made Crimson Ink mine faded into obscurity. Yet with every clandestine symbol of defiance inked onto those who sought sanctuary within these walls — every whisper of resistance against tyranny — Crimson Ink reclaimed its soul piece by piece.

My hand paused mid-sketch; there was still so much left undecided, so many moves yet to be played in this dangerous game where lives hung precariously in balance. A soft sigh escaped me as I contemplated what tomorrow might bring through Crimson Ink's ever-watchful doors.

* * *

The weight of Damien's demand pressed on my shoulders like the thick air before a storm. The silence in the room after his departure was deafening, filled only by the rhythmic hum of the neon sign outside Crimson Ink. I ran a hand through my hair, exhaling slowly as I glanced at the door he had exited through. Damien, with his suave demeanor and piercing gaze, had laid out a future for me that was lined with shadows and whispered promises of power. But it was a future painted in hues I didn't recognize—colors that didn't belong on my palette.

I found myself alone, staring at the array of tattoo machines and ink pots that lined my workstation. The tools of my trade now felt foreign, tainted by the prospect of being bound to his will. The amulet he had given me lay cold against my skin, a shackle disguised as a shield.

A spark of rebellion flickered within me, its warmth cutting through the chill of apprehension. I couldn't—I wouldn't—become an extension of his empire. My craft was mine alone; it was an extension of my soul, not a weapon to be wielded at his command.

I needed a plan, something that could untangle me from Damien's web without tearing apart everything I'd built. Crimson Ink wasn't just my livelihood; it was my sanctuary, a place where magic flowed as freely as the ink from my needles.

I reached for the amulet, its edges biting into my palm as I considered throwing it away. But that would be too easy, wouldn't it? Damien wasn't a man—or vampire—to be dismissed with such simplicity.

My eyes caught sight of a piece of paper on the corner of the table—the sketchbook lay open to a design I'd been working on for weeks: a phoenix in mid-resurrection, its wings unfurling amidst flames and ash. It symbolized rebirth, transformation—a new beginning forged from the remnants of what once was.

The idea struck me like lightning: what if I could reinvent myself under Damien's nose? Remain in plain sight but operate unseen. I could be the phoenix rising from the ashes of his overbearing presence.

With newfound resolve surging through me, I reached for my phone and sent a message to Tara:

"Need to talk. It's urgent."

Her reply came swiftly:

"Come over."

Tara's apartment was only a few blocks away—a short walk in the brisk night air did little to cool the fire burning within me. By the time I reached her door, my mind raced with strategies and contingencies.

She greeted me with concern etched into her features. "Alex, what's wrong?"

I stepped inside, pacing as words tumbled out in a rush. "Damien wants control—over me, over Crimson Ink... He wants to use my tattoos for his own ends."

Tara's eyes narrowed; she'd always been one to see through smoke and mirrors. "You're planning to defy him."

"It's not just defiance," I clarified, stopping to face her squarely. "It's survival—mine and everyone else's who steps foot into Crimson Ink."

We sat down at her kitchen table as she poured two cups of coffee—black as ink—and pushed one toward me. "Tell me your plan," she said.

"I'll play along—for now," I began, cradling the warm mug between my hands. "But behind the scenes, I'll work against him. Maybe even find allies among those who want him gone."

"And what about your clients?" Tara asked pointedly. "People come to you for protection—not to get caught in crossfire."

"I'll keep them safe; that's non-negotiable." My voice held steady with conviction.

We talked into the night, mapping out possible alliances and fallbacks until our words became whispers against the dawn light seeping through her curtains.

By morning we had a semblance of a plan—one that danced on the knife-edge between audacity and insanity.

As I left Tara's apartment with the first rays of sunlight warming my back, I knew what had to be done first: reach out to Jade.

Jade had been in this game longer than most—her network was extensive and her loyalties enigmatic enough to make her an invaluable resource—if she chose to side with me.

I walked back toward Crimson Ink with purpose in every step; if Damien wanted to use my tattoos as conduits for power plays and territorial expansions, then he'd underestimated their true potential—and mine.

The bell above Crimson Ink's door jingled as I pushed it open—the familiar scent of antiseptic mingled with incense greeted me like an old friend. My hand instinctively went to touch the amulet hidden beneath my shirt—a reminder of what was at stake.

I busied myself with preparations for opening hours: cleaning needles, refilling inkwells—each task grounding me further into reality.

Mid-morning arrived without incident; clients came and went, each leaving with more than just ink on their skin—they carried pieces of magic woven carefully into their designs.

It wasn't until later in the afternoon when Jade walked through those doors that time seemed to stand still—a silent acknowledgment passed between us: we were both players in this game now.

Jade's gaze held mine as she approached—one look told me she'd already heard whispers about Damien's proposition.

"You've made waves," she stated simply before glancing around at Crimson Ink's walls adorned with designs that spoke volumes about their creator's dual heritage.

"We need to talk," I said quietly.

Jade nodded once before following me into the back room reserved for private consultations—the same room where Damien had summoned those shadow-beasts not long ago.

The door clicked shut behind us—the rest of Crimson Ink faded away along with its customers' murmurs and laughter; this was our sanctuary within a sanctuary where truths could be laid bare without fear or reservation.

I started at once: "Damien offered protection but at too high a cost—he wants exclusive rights over my talents... over me."

"And you're planning to defy him," Jade surmised—it wasn't a question; she knew too well how this world worked—how people like us worked when pushed too far into corners we didn't belong in.

"Yes." The word tasted like freedom on my tongue—like defiance itself etched into every syllable uttered within these walls meant for creation rather than coercion or control.

* * *

Tara's warning echoed in my mind, a steady drumbeat against the thrum of my pulse. The taste of rebellion was bitter on my tongue, but the tang of fear wasn't far behind. Refusing Damien's offer hadn't just drawn a line in the sand; it had lit a fuse, one that promised an explosion I couldn't yet see but could feel coming.

The shop door creaked open, its bell chiming a tune more ominous than welcoming. My fingers paused above the sketchpad, the image of an ouroboros half-formed, a symbol of rebirth I hoped to embody. The air shifted, grew heavier as if saturated with dark intent. I didn't need to look up to know who had arrived; the atmosphere in Crimson Ink was never so charged unless they were present.

Evelyn glided in, her elegance a sharp contrast to the weight of her presence. Her gaze found mine, locked on it with an intensity that could shatter glass.

"Alex," she began, her voice silk wrapped around steel. "Damien is not a man who takes kindly to... disappointments."

I set my pencil down, a futile attempt at appearing unbothered. "I'm aware," I said, trying to keep my voice steady. "But I have my principles."

"Principles," she repeated, the word rolling off her tongue like an indulgent parent humoring a child. "Such luxury."

Victor loomed behind her, his frame filling the doorway—a silent sentinel whose very silence spoke volumes. The threat didn't need voicing; it hung in the air between us, palpable and poisonous.

"Damien expects loyalty," Evelyn continued. "He offers protection and power in return. Yet you seem intent on... how shall I put it? Charting your own course."

The tension knotted in my shoulders, my hand itching for the comfort of my tattoo machine—the buzz and hum that usually grounded me now seemed distant.

"I chart the course that feels right," I replied, mustering defiance. "I'm not a pawn in Damien's game."

A flicker of something unreadable crossed Evelyn's face before her mask returned.

"You are if he says you are," she stated flatly.

My heart raced at the implication of her words. Damien's reach was long and his grip tight; refusal might mean losing everything I'd built—Crimson Ink was more than a shop; it was an extension of myself.

"I won't be bullied into submission," I declared, though my voice wavered like a candle flame in the wind.

Evelyn took a step closer; Victor remained immobile—a statue save for his eyes tracking every nuance.

"Consider this a friendly warning," she said, her lips curling into something far from friendly. "Refusal is not without consequence."

The door swung open again and Lucas entered, his usual smirk replaced by concern as he caught sight of Evelyn and Victor.

"Is everything okay here?" Lucas asked, his gaze flitting between us.

Evelyn's eyes lingered on me for another moment before she turned to him with practiced grace.

"Just discussing some... artwork," she said smoothly before gesturing for Victor to follow her out.

The bell chimed again as they departed, leaving behind a silence that roared louder than any argument could have.

Lucas approached me cautiously. "You sure you're alright?"

"Yeah," I lied through clenched teeth. "Just another day at Crimson Ink."

He nodded but didn't look convinced. His hand landed gently on my shoulder—a touch meant to comfort but one that couldn't chase away the chill that had settled deep within me.

The day wore on with excruciating slowness—each client's session punctuated by glances toward the door and jumps at shadows. With every hour that passed without incident, my nerves frayed further; dread was a cruel companion.

As night draped itself over the city like a velvet cloak, Tara slipped through the door just as I was locking up. Her expression told me she had heard about my defiance sooner than expected—news traveled fast in our world.

"They're not going to let this go," she said without preamble.

I shook my head, meeting her eyes with what little resolve I had left after a day spent looking over my shoulder. "I know."

"We need to be smart about this," Tara continued. "Damien will retaliate—it's only a matter of when."

The word 'retaliate' sent shivers down my spine; it was one thing to face threats when they were veiled behind pleasantries or promises—it was another entirely when those threats materialized into something you could feel with every sense you possessed.

A sharp knock interrupted our hushed strategy session—three short raps that sounded like thunderclaps in the stillness of Crimson Ink after hours. Tara and I exchanged glances before I moved toward the door with trepidation as my companion.

Peering through the security peephole revealed nothing but shadows until they shifted and coalesced into Trent's familiar form—his face obscured by darkness yet unmistakably tense.

Opening the door cautiously, I kept one hand ready to slam it shut should treachery await on the other side.

"Trent?" I called out softly into the night beyond him.

His response came low and urgent: "They're coming for you."

* * *

The bell above the door jangled a warning, and I glanced up from the tattoo design I was perfecting. Tara stood framed in the doorway, her eyes darting around Crimson Ink like a hawk scouting for threats. Her visit wasn't social; it was a council of war.

"You're sure he's coming?" My voice sounded steady, but my hands betrayed me, the pen quivering ever so slightly against the parchment.

"Damien doesn't take no for an answer," Tara said, crossing the floor to my side. She peered at the design. "Especially not from someone he sees as his."

I pushed the design aside and met her gaze. "We've got to be ready then."

"We?" She raised an eyebrow.

I let out a breath I didn't realize I'd been holding. "Yeah, we. You're not leaving me to face him alone, are you?"

Tara's lips twitched into a smile that didn't quite reach her eyes. "Never."

Lucas came through the back, his usually jovial face drawn tight with concern. "You should know, there's talk on the street."

"What kind of talk?" I asked, bracing myself for more bad news.

"The kind that says Damien's getting impatient. People are scared, Alex." Lucas leaned against the counter, his eyes searching mine. "They're starting to choose sides."

A chill crawled up my spine at his words. The room felt smaller all of a sudden, as if the walls were inching closer with every second that ticked by on the old clock hanging above the door.

Tara laid a hand on my shoulder. "You don't have to do this alone."

But that was just it—I did have to do this alone. My decisions would ripple through lives beyond my own. How many people would suffer if I bowed to Damien's will? How many would suffer if I didn't?

The shop door opened again, and Trent walked in with purpose etched in every line of his frame. He didn't bother with pleasantries.

"Damien's en route," he said bluntly.

My heart skipped a beat, then pounded like a drum in my chest. The sensation reminded me of tattoo needles dancing across skin—urgent, insistent.

"I won't be his pawn," I stated, more to convince myself than inform them.

Trent's expression softened for just a moment before he schooled it back into neutrality. "Sometimes we don't get to choose our battles."

The sound of footsteps outside made us all turn toward the door. The heavy tread was unmistakable; Damien had arrived at Crimson Ink earlier than expected.

I stood up straighter, trying to muster every ounce of courage I had buried deep within me—courage that seemed to be playing an expert game of hide and seek at that very moment.

The door swung open and Damien strolled in as if he owned the place—which he might as well have considering how he commandeered the atmosphere upon entry.

"Alex," he greeted with a half-smile that didn't reach his cold eyes. "We have much to discuss."

My friends flanked me silently—a united front against whatever storm Damien intended to unleash.

"Let's talk in private," Damien suggested—or rather, commanded—with a tilt of his head toward the back room.

Tara's grip on my shoulder tightened briefly before she stepped back, and I walked ahead knowing she'd be right behind me no matter what was said behind closed doors.

The back room felt colder than usual as Damien closed the door behind us with an ominous click. He leaned back against it casually—a predator blocking its prey's only escape route.

"I made you an offer," he began smoothly. "An offer which would've been beneficial for both parties."

"And I made my decision," I replied, standing firm despite feeling like I was being pressed from all sides.

Damien pushed off from the door and stepped closer, each footfall measured and deliberate. "Refusal wasn't what I had in mind when I extended my generosity."

His use of 'generosity' hung heavy in the air between us—taut like a wire waiting to snap.

"You don't control me." My words were a shield even as they felt more brittle than steel.

He chuckled lowly—a sound devoid of any true amusement—and it echoed around us mockingly. "Oh Alex," he said softly but with an undercurrent of steel in his voice, "but that's where you're mistaken."

I felt cornered—literally and figuratively—as Damien's presence loomed over me. There was something about him that seemed larger than life now—more menacing than when he'd first walked through Crimson Ink's doors.

"Your talents are rare," he continued when I didn't respond. "It would be... unwise... for you not to use them under my protection."

The word 'protection' felt like a cage—one lined with velvet perhaps but a cage nonetheless.

"You mean under your control," I corrected him quietly but firmly.

His smile didn't waver as he leaned in close enough for me to see there was no warmth in those dark eyes—only ambition and hunger for power.

"It's all just semantics at this point." His voice dropped lower still—a conspiratorial whisper promising secrets and shadows.

My resolve flickered like a flame caught in drafty room—the instinctual desire for self-preservation wrestling with my sense of autonomy and moral compass.

"And if I refuse?" The question came out steadier than I felt inside where fear and defiance tangled like thorns.

Damien straightened up and looked at me—a long assessing gaze that felt like it could peel layers off my soul—and then shrugged nonchalantly as though discussing something as mundane as weather patterns rather than veiled threats and power plays.

"Refusal isn't really an option anymore Alex." His tone brooked no argument even though every fiber of my being screamed against it. "You're too valuable to be left untethered—and too dangerous to be left unsupervised."

There it was—the crux of it all laid bare between us without pretense or guile: A choice that wasn't really a choice at all; freedom that came shackled with chains; power granted only through surrendering control.

As Damien turned on his heel and left me standing there amid shadows and doubts—his final words echoed mockingly around me setting the stage for an acceptance forced by circumstance rather than genuine acquiescence:

"You'll come around Alex—you'll see things my way eventually."

Chapter 6

G̶uidance in Shadows

I drew the needle across skin with the precision of a master calligrapher, my latest creation taking form. The buzz of the tattoo machine melded with the muted thrum of city life that bled through the walls of Crimson Ink. Each line I etched carried a whisper of power, a silent promise to my client who lay with stoic patience.

The bell above the door chimed, signaling another presence in my sanctuary of ink and magic. I glanced up through the strands of hair that had escaped my ponytail. A figure shrouded in a cloak stood at the threshold, their face obscured by the hood's shadow.

"Give me a moment," I murmured to my client, laying down my tools with care.

The cloaked figure waited as I approached, silent and still as if time held little meaning for them. There was something unnervingly familiar about their posture, an echo of recognition that sent a chill down my spine.

"I know why you're here," I said, my voice steady despite the unease knotting in my stomach. "You've heard about Crimson Ink's specialties."

They nodded slowly, their hands emerging from within voluminous sleeves to lower their hood. A cascade of silver hair spilled out, framing a face that was ageless and otherworldly. Eyes like molten gold met mine, and in them, I saw a reflection not just of myself but of something more—a lineage that stretched beyond human understanding.

"You are Alex," they said, their voice a melodious timbre that resonated within the parlor's walls. "But you are also more than you appear."

I crossed my arms defensively. "And you would know this because?"

Their lips curled into a half-smile. "I've watched you from afar, witnessed your struggle with your dual nature."

My heart raced at their words. Who was this person who claimed such intimate knowledge of me?

"You bear the mark of two worlds within you," they continued, reaching out with a hand adorned with rings that seemed ancient and powerful. "The human realm and that which lies beyond—the realm of entities whose existence is intertwined with magic and myth."

I swallowed hard. No one outside my grandmother had ever spoken to me about my heritage so openly—most people didn't even believe in such things.

"What do you want from me?" I asked.

Their gaze softened. "Guidance," they replied simply. "And perhaps an exchange of services."

The word 'exchange' hung between us like a weighty pendant on a chain.

"You need a tattoo," I guessed, masking my nervousness with professional detachment.

"Yes." They slid back their sleeve to reveal an arm marked with symbols that danced before my eyes, shifting and changing as though alive. "But not just any tattoo—a seal that will help me control the power I possess."

I studied their arm, noting each symbol's intricacy and realizing it was not mere ink but magic woven into their very skin.

"Why come to me?" I pressed.

"Because you are one who can bridge the worlds," they said earnestly. "Your tattoos are more than art; they are conduits for energy both mundane and arcane."

I hesitated before nodding slowly. "Let's talk in private." I gestured toward one of Crimson Ink's secluded rooms reserved for special clients like them—ones who brought whispers of old magic through my doors.

As we settled into the room, its walls adorned with relics and artifacts that seemed to watch us with silent anticipation, they spoke again.

"I know you're wary of your abilities—their source and implications," they said as if reading my thoughts. "You struggle with what you are capable of and what it means for your future."

"How can you possibly understand that?" I asked sharply.

They reached into their cloak and produced an amulet similar to the one Damien had given me—a twin serpent biting its own tail—but theirs was older, wrought from a metal that shimmered like starlight.

"This amulet has been in my keeping for centuries," they explained. "It belonged to someone very much like you—a boundary walker between realms."

My pulse quickened as I reached out tentatively to touch the amulet's cool surface. A jolt surged through me—a connection sparked between our shared heritage and this enigmatic figure before me.

"Who are you?" The question slipped out unbidden.

They inclined their head in acknowledgment. "In time, all will be revealed," they promised. "For now, let us focus on the task at hand."

Withdrawing from the amulet's allure, I pulled out my sketchbook—the same one where ideas often sprang forth unbidden from some deeper wellspring within me—and began to draw. Lines flowed from my pen like water from a spring: symbols of protection interwoven with elements representing balance between light and dark; between known and unknown worlds.

The figure watched intently as the design took shape on paper before finally speaking again.

"You have great potential within you," they observed softly. "It is both your gift and your burden."

I met their gaze squarely then; it was true—I felt it every day—but hearing it acknowledged by another stirred something within me: affirmation mixed with fear.

"We all have burdens to bear," I replied quietly as I continued to draw—the weight of responsibility settling on me like an old familiar cloak.

* * *

I eyed the cloaked figure with a mix of curiosity and wariness. Their sudden appearance in my shop, Crimson Ink, couldn't have been more untimely, considering the shadow Damien and his gang cast over my life. I wasn't just cautious; I was bracing for another wave to crash over me, wondering if this person was another shark in the waters I'd been forced to navigate.

"So, what kind of tattoo are you looking for?" My voice didn't waver; years of dealing with the supernatural had taught me the value of a steady tone.

The figure hesitated before reaching into their cloak. They drew out a small, intricate amulet, its design not unfamiliar to my eyes—a twin to the one Damien had handed me, only this one seemed older, its edges worn smooth by time.

"This amulet," they began, their voice a gravelly whisper that sent a chill down my spine, "belonged to someone who carried the Mark of Power. And you, Alex, are more than what you appear. We could be... valuable to each other."

The Mark of Power again. That cursed design seemed to haunt every corner of my life since it had first been mentioned within these walls. My skepticism wasn't just rooted; it was entrenched.

"And why would I need your... value?" I crossed my arms over my chest, leaning back against the counter lined with ink bottles and tattoo machines.

"Because," they said as they stepped closer, "you are at the center of a storm. You can either be swept away by it or learn to dance in the rain."

I scoffed at their cryptic words. "And what makes you think I don't already know how to dance?"

They nodded slowly as if they had expected my resistance. "Perhaps you do. But even the best dancers can step on a landmine unknowingly."

Their metaphors were starting to irritate me as much as intrigue me. It was like playing chess with someone who refused to move their pieces in any recognizable fashion.

"What's your name?" I demanded.

"You can call me Raven," they said simply.

"Alright then, Raven," I replied with an edge in my voice, "if you know so much about me and this storm you speak of, why not enlighten me on how exactly we could be 'valuable' to each other?"

Raven's hand disappeared into their cloak again and emerged holding a piece of aged parchment. They unfolded it on the counter before me—a map of sorts, but unlike any map I'd seen before. It was a blueprint for a tattoo design complex and compelling in its detail.

"This is more than ink on skin," Raven said quietly. "It's a map of ley lines—magical currents that flow beneath this city."

I studied the design carefully, feeling the pull of something ancient stir within me—my supernatural heritage resonating with the arcane symbols etched on paper.

"And let me guess," I interjected before they could continue their sales pitch, "you want this tattooed on you?"

Raven shook their head slightly. "No, Alex. I want you to have it."

My eyes shot up from the map to meet theirs—a pair of intense eyes visible through the shadow of their hood.

"Why?"

"Because you will need it," Raven replied gravely. "Damien is playing a game that he does not fully understand. The Mark of Power is but one piece on this board—a piece everyone seems to want but no one truly knows how to wield."

I felt the weight of their words press against my chest like a physical force.

"You talk about Damien as if you know him." The suspicion crept into my voice again.

"I know many things," Raven answered cryptically. "And right now, I know that Damien's interest in you is... problematic."

That was one way to put it. Damien's 'interest' felt like a vise around my life—one that tightened with every move he made within Crimson Ink's walls.

"Look," I said sharply, "if you're offering some kind of alliance against Damien and his gang—I'm not interested in making enemies."

Raven chuckled—a low sound that seemed out of place in our conversation.

"I'm not asking you to make enemies or friends," they said. "I'm offering knowledge—a way for you to navigate this storm without becoming its casualty."

I hesitated for a moment before responding; something about Raven felt different from all the other supernatural entities that had darkened my doorstep recently.

"And what do you get out of this?" I asked finally.

"The same thing we all seek—balance." They let those words hang between us like smoke in the air.

Balance—that elusive state that seemed so out of reach lately with every choice teetering between two extremes: submission or defiance.

"I need time to think about this." My words came out slower than intended as I folded up the map and handed it back to them.

Raven nodded once before taking back the parchment and tucking it away into their cloak once more.

"Time is something we both have... for now," they acknowledged with a hint of urgency lingering behind their calm exterior.

As they turned to leave Crimson Ink without another word, I watched them go—the door closing behind them with an almost imperceptible click that sounded oddly final. My heart pounded with a mixture of fear and anticipation—each beat whispering questions about whether Raven's offer was another trap or an unexpected lifeline thrown into these murky waters.

* * *

The map Raven handed me unfurled across my workbench, a web of intersecting lines that seemed to pulse with an energy I could almost feel brushing against my skin. It was as if the city's streets and alleys had been overlaid with a secret, pulsating life force, invisible to the uninitiated. Raven watched me closely, their eyes reflecting the myriad of questions swirling in my head.

"You're more than just a tattoo artist, Alex," Raven began, their voice soft yet carrying an undeniable weight. "Your blood carries the legacy of an ancient line, one that wove the fabric of magic into skin and soul."

I leaned back in my chair, the map blurring before my eyes as I tried to digest Raven's words. "My grandmother used to speak of our family's heritage," I said, memories of her stories creeping into my voice. "But she never mentioned anything about... magic woven into skin."

Raven's gaze didn't waver. "She might've not known, or maybe she chose to keep it from you until you were ready. The tattoos you craft are more than mere designs; they are conduits for the energy that courses through those ley lines." They gestured at the map.

I traced a finger over one of the glowing lines on the parchment, feeling a thrumming sensation against my fingertips. "Conduits," I echoed, the word tasting strange yet fitting on my tongue.

"Yes," Raven continued. "The magic in your blood allows you to tap into these ley lines when you create your tattoos. That's why they're alive with power." They paused, letting the gravity of their words sink in.

A mix of awe and confusion gripped me as I looked at my hands—the hands that had inked countless designs onto trusting skin. Hands that had unknowingly channeled an ancient power. "So all this time, when I thought I was just good at my craft..."

"You were actually practicing an age-old form of magic," Raven finished for me.

I stood up abruptly, pacing across the room. The tattoos I had created over the years flashed through my mind—each one special and now suspect in its origin. The protection amulets, the symbols of strength, even Mariah's piece that came alive on her skin—it all made a twisted sort of sense now.

"But why me?" I asked, stopping in front of Raven again. "Why do I have this ability?"

Raven's eyes held mine steadily. "Because you were born to be a bridge between worlds—the mundane and the mystical. Your lineage is not merely human; it is interwoven with beings who once walked alongside deities and shaped destinies with their art."

I scoffed lightly, trying to deflect the intensity of their statement with humor. "No pressure or anything."

"This is no jest," Raven said sharply. Their tone softened as they added, "Alex, you have a gift that can shape the future—not just for yourself but for all who come into contact with your ink."

The room felt suddenly smaller as if the walls were closing in on me with the weight of this revelation. It was one thing to grapple with being part-human and part-something else entirely; it was another to be told your existence was some sort of cosmic keystone.

"And Damien?" I asked tentatively. "Does he know about this?"

Raven shook their head slowly. "He suspects there's something unique about you—that much is clear from his interest in your abilities and his desperation for the Mark of Power." They leaned forward slightly. "But he doesn't know your true potential."

A shiver ran down my spine at the thought of Damien wielding knowledge like that against me—or worse, using it to further his dark ambitions.

"What am I supposed to do with all this?" My voice barely rose above a whisper.

"Learn," Raven stated simply. "Understand your heritage and harness it before others decide your path for you."

Their words echoed in my mind like a drumbeat urging me forward—a call to action that resonated deep within my bones.

"How? How do I learn about something so... obscure?" Frustration tinged my voice.

Raven reached into their cloak and pulled out an old leather-bound book—its cover etched with symbols that danced before my eyes in recognition or perhaps anticipation.

"This tome has been passed down through generations in your family," they explained as they handed it to me. My hands trembled slightly as I took it—this piece of history that belonged to me yet felt foreign all at once.

"Within its pages are the secrets of your ancestors—the origins and methods behind magical tattooing." Their voice held reverence now—a respect for what lay within the book's time-worn pages.

I opened it gingerly to find drawings and scripts that seemed to leap off the page at me—a language I didn't understand but somehow knew was meant for me.

"This is your legacy, Alex," Raven said solemnly. "And only you can decide how to wield it."

As they spoke those final words, they stepped back into shadow—a silent guardian watching as I began turning pages filled with ancient knowledge—a legacy etched in ink and bound by blood.

* * *

Raven's eyes, twin pools of midnight, locked onto mine with an intensity that seemed to pierce through the facade of Crimson Ink and into the very core of my being. The shop hummed around us, alive with the buzz of needles and the soft murmur of clients delving into their own transformative journeys. But in this quiet corner, it was as if we stood in a separate world, one where the gravity of destiny weighed heavily on my shoulders.

"You're not just a tattoo artist, Alex," Raven said, his voice a low thrum that vibrated with the undercurrents of unspoken truths. "You're a vessel for change. You can inscribe more than skin; you can rewrite fates."

I leaned back against the cool leather of the chair I usually reserved for clients, feeling its familiar comfort against my spine. It offered a silent reassurance as I grappled with Raven's words.

"Rewriting fates is a dangerous game," I replied, folding my arms over my chest. "People come here for ink, not to get tangled in conflicts they don't understand."

Raven chuckled, a sound that seemed to carry the wisdom of ages within its cadence. "Yet you're already entangled, aren't you? Damien and his coven... they see your potential. They fear it."

My jaw tightened at the mention of Damien. The way he'd sauntered into my life, upending everything with veiled threats and false promises of protection, had left a sour taste in my mouth. But Raven was right—I couldn't ignore the pull I felt towards something greater.

"What kind of conflict are we talking about?" I asked, my curiosity piqued despite my apprehension.

Raven moved closer, and the air between us charged with an electric anticipation. "A storm is brewing within our community—the supernatural world isn't as united as it once was. There are factions vying for power, old alliances crumbling under secrets and lies."

"And you want me to... what? Take sides?" The idea sent a shiver down my spine.

"Not sides," Raven corrected gently. "Balance. You have a gift for understanding people—their hopes, their fears. Your tattoos reflect that; they empower and protect. Imagine what you could do if you embraced that on a larger scale."

The thought sent ripples through me. My entire life had been about connection—through art, through ink—but always on an individual level. The prospect of extending that reach was daunting but impossible to ignore.

Raven reached into his cloak and pulled out an aged tome bound in leather that looked as though it had weathered centuries of use. He laid it before me on the glass counter with a reverence usually reserved for sacred relics.

"This is your heritage," he said solemnly. "The knowledge within these pages can help you harness your powers beyond what you've ever imagined."

I traced my fingers over the cover, feeling the etched patterns beneath my fingertips—a language I felt I should know but couldn't quite decipher.

"Why now?" I asked.

"Because there's someone out there who wants to tip that balance," Raven replied darkly. "Someone who seeks to harness power without regard for consequence."

Damien's face flashed in my mind—the smug assurance in his smile that spoke volumes about his disregard for anything but his own desires.

"And you think I can stop him?" The question hung between us like a challenge.

"I think you're one of the few who can." Raven's gaze didn't waver.

I opened the tome slowly, its pages whispering secrets as they turned. Symbols danced before my eyes—ancient runes intermingling with designs that resonated deep within me. It was like looking into a mirror reflecting not just my image but my soul's lineage.

"I'll need help," I murmured almost to myself as I absorbed page after page.

"You have allies," Raven assured me. "Those who stand by you at Crimson Ink—Tara, Jade—they'll be your pillars."

A small smile crept onto my lips at the mention of Tara and Jade—my steadfast friends who'd seen me through both mundane troubles and supernatural strife alike.

"And what about you?" I looked up at Raven. "Where do you stand in all this?"

Raven's expression softened just enough to hint at camaraderie beneath his stoic exterior.

"I am your mentor," he said simply but with conviction that lent weight to every syllable. "I will guide you until you're ready to embrace your role in this conflict."

The responsibility loomed large before me—a call to step beyond the safety of tattoo guns and ink pots into an arena where magic pulsed just beneath the surface of everyday life.

"So what's our first move?" I asked, already feeling the shift within me as I accepted this new path laid out at my feet.

"We fortify," Raven answered without hesitation. "We strengthen your defenses and build upon your knowledge until Damien's shadows can't touch us."

The plan seemed simple enough but carried undertones of war—a silent preparation for battles fought in shadows where every spell cast could turn the tide.

Raven moved towards the door but paused just before stepping out into the chaos beyond our secluded corner.

"Remember this, Alex," he said over his shoulder with an intensity that demanded memorization, "your ink isn't just art—it's power incarnate."

With those parting words hanging in the air like an incantation setting events into motion, he vanished into the throng of patrons leaving me alone with a tome full of ancient wisdom and a heart full of resolve.

* * *

The bell above the door to Crimson Ink chimed, slicing through the hum of conversation and the buzz of tattoo machines. Raven's silhouette filled the doorway, an enigma wrapped in a cloak that seemed to absorb the light around him. I paused mid-stroke on the dragon tattoo sprawling across a biker's back, my hands steady despite the churn of anticipation in my gut.

"Alex," Raven's voice was a whisper yet cut clear across the room, "a moment of your time?"

The biker grunted his approval, and I wiped my inky hands on a cloth before stepping away from my station. Raven beckoned me to the back room, a space that served as my private sanctuary from the demands of the shop floor.

Once inside, Raven turned, his eyes reflecting a seriousness that made my heart skip. "You've been practicing," he stated more than asked, his gaze flickering to my hands which still tingled from channeling magic into ink.

"I have," I admitted. "Every night after closing up, I've been studying that tome you gave me. It's... it's like nothing I've ever seen before."

Raven nodded. "Good. You'll need all that knowledge and more." He reached into his cloak and produced an object wrapped in a cloth that shimmered with threads of silver and gold. "This," he began as he carefully unfolded the cloth, "is something I've safeguarded for many years."

In his palm lay an object unlike any I'd encountered before. It was a compass, but not one meant for navigation by any normal means. Its cardinal points were etched with symbols that resonated within me—a sense of familiarity pulsed through my veins.

"This is an Aethereal Compass," Raven explained, his voice laced with reverence. "It doesn't point north; it points to power—magic power."

My hand hovered over it, feeling the pull of its energy. "How does it work?"

Raven's lips curled into a knowing smile. "It works with you, Alex. Your heritage, your blood—it will guide you to where your power can grow strongest." He pressed it into my palm and closed my fingers around it. "I trust you with this because you need to trust yourself."

The weight of the compass felt like destiny pressing down on my skin.

"Thank you," I whispered, unable to articulate the magnitude of what this gesture meant.

He nodded solemnly before glancing towards the door. "Remember, your art will change lives—save them or doom them." With those parting words, he swept out of the room leaving me alone with the compass.

I studied it for a long moment before tucking it safely in my pocket and returning to finish what I'd started on the biker's back.

The rest of the day passed in a blur of needles and skin; each tattoo completed was another step towards mastery over this strange new realm I found myself in. The Aethereal Compass felt warm against my thigh through the fabric of my jeans—a constant reminder of Raven's faith in me and of the journey ahead.

As dusk fell and Crimson Ink emptied of its last customer, Tara appeared like she often did at closing time.

"You look like someone just handed you Excalibur," she remarked as she leaned against one of the counters.

I chuckled at her comparison but couldn't deny its accuracy. "Not quite Excalibur," I said as I drew out the compass for her to see.

Tara's eyes widened as she examined it from every angle without touching it. "That's no ordinary trinket," she said after a moment. Her tone was hushed as if afraid to disturb its slumbering power.

"It's supposed to help me find where my magic is strongest," I explained.

Tara raised an eyebrow. "And have you tried it out yet?"

"Not yet," I admitted, feeling suddenly foolish for not having thought to do so immediately.

Without another word, Tara grabbed her jacket from behind the counter and gestured towards the door with her head. "What are we waiting for? Let's see what this thing can do."

Together we stepped out into the city night; its energy felt different now—as if each shadow held a whisper and every alleyway was an unturned page in a book of ancient secrets.

I pulled out the compass again and held it flat on my palm under a streetlamp's glow—the hands began to spin wildly before slowing down and pointing decisively towards East.

"That way," I said as much to myself as to Tara.

We followed its direction for blocks until we reached an old park sandwiched between towering buildings like some forgotten slice of greenery—a place where nature had managed to hold its ground against concrete and steel.

The compass led us to an old oak tree in the heart of the park; its branches were gnarled like arthritic fingers grasping at eternity.

"Here," I said as we stood under its canopy.

Tara looked up at the tree then back at me with an expression mixed with awe and concern. "What now?"

"Now," I took a deep breath, feeling both exhilarated and terrified at once, "I think now is when I start truly understanding what it means to be part human, part something... more."

The Aethereal Compass vibrated gently in my hand as if encouraging me on this path—one paved with shadows but also with starlight; one where every decision mattered not just for me but for those whose lives were etched onto their skin in ink—a testament to their stories, their pain, their hopes...and now perhaps their salvation too.

* * *

Tara's hand rested on the bark of the ancient oak, her eyes closed as if she were listening to whispers only she could hear. The Aethereal Compass had led us here, its needle spinning wildly before settling on this very spot. I watched her, the wind playing with strands of her hair, wondering if she felt the pulse of the earth as I did — a rhythm thrumming through the soles of my feet.

"You feel it, don't you?" Tara opened her eyes, a smile tugging at her lips.

I nodded, unable to articulate the blend of awe and fear knotting in my stomach. "It's like the tree's heartbeat syncs with mine."

"Because it does," she replied. "Your magic, your heritage — it's all connected to the life force of this city."

I placed my palm against the rough texture of the oak and felt a surge of energy, a call to the deepest part of my being. It was as if I'd stumbled upon a secret conversation between the ancient roots and the pulsing veins of magic beneath us.

"This is where you draw your strength," Tara continued. "But it's not just about drawing power; it's about understanding it, molding it into something more."

I pulled my hand back and studied it, wondering how many destinies I'd changed with a single stroke of ink. The idea that I could shape more than skin deep designs was exhilarating — and terrifying.

The park around us was empty, save for a few joggers in the distance and birdsong above. It was a sanctuary within the city's chaos, an oasis where magic seemed palpable enough to grasp with outstretched fingers.

"We should get back," Tara said after a moment. "Damien won't be patient forever."

Her words sent a shiver down my spine. Damien — his name was a shackle, his presence a shadow that loomed over every decision I made. Yet here, in this place, his influence seemed diminished, as though the tree whispered promises of freedom.

As we walked back to Crimson Ink, Tara filled me in on her plans — secret gatherings with others who sought to defy Damien's rule. Jade would be there too; she'd always had an uncanny way of sniffing out resistance.

Back at the shop, Raven's words echoed in my mind. "You are at the heart of this conflict whether you choose it or not." The cloaked figure had vanished as suddenly as they appeared but left behind a weight that settled on my shoulders.

Closing up for the night, I lingered by Mariah's chair — where it all began with her tattoo coming alive on her skin. I wondered about every soul who'd sat there seeking transformation through my art. Was there more I could offer them? Could I forge protections not just against physical harm but against darker forces?

My sketchbook lay open on a nearby counter, filled with designs that had yet to find their canvas. A dragon curled around a sword, its scales inked with meticulous care; each one could hold a spell strong enough to bolster courage or shield from deceit.

As I turned the pages, each design felt like a silent vow waiting to be uttered. They were pieces of me laid bare on paper — promises of protection, symbols of strength.

A knock on the shop's front door tore me from my reverie. My heart pounded against my ribcage as I approached cautiously; after hours visitors rarely brought good tidings.

Through the frosted glass paneling I discerned Evelyn's silhouette — elegant and deadly even in shadow.

"We need to talk," she said without preamble when I opened up for her.

The urgency in her voice carried an undercurrent of danger that set every nerve on edge. We sat across from each other in Mariah's chair and its twin, separated by an expanse filled with unspoken tension.

"Damien grows impatient," Evelyn began, her gaze sharp as obsidian shards. "He knows you're capable of more than you let on."

I leaned forward slightly; defiance mustered from depths unknown even to me until now. "I'm not his puppet."

Evelyn studied me for what felt like an eternity before speaking again. "Then prove it."

The air hung heavy between us until she rose and slipped out into the night as swiftly as she'd arrived.

Left alone with my thoughts once more, I pondered Evelyn's challenge — 'prove it.' Prove what exactly? That I wasn't bound by Damien's will? That I could wield power without becoming consumed by it?

The designs in my sketchbook beckoned me once again; they seemed like riddles waiting for answers only I could provide. My gaze fell upon one drawing in particular — an ouroboros encircling a triskele: symbols of eternal cycles and motion that moved forward even as they returned to where they began.

It struck me then; everything was connected — from my tattoos to my lineage to this very city teeming with unseen forces. The supernatural entities prowling its shadows were merely part of an intricate tapestry that had ensnared me since birth.

Tara believed in me; Raven offered guidance and artifacts steeped in ancient wisdom; Jade stood ready to join our cause — these allies forged links stronger than any vampire's command.

A resolve settled within me then; it was time to use what lay at my fingertips for something beyond Crimson Ink's walls or Damien's reach. My gifts were mine alone to command; they didn't belong to him or any other who sought control over what they couldn't understand.

With newfound determination etched into every line on my face, I considered Raven's mentorship and what it truly meant to stand at this crossroads between balance and chaos. This moment marked more than contemplation; it was an awakening.

Perhaps Raven was right; perhaps destiny had always been etched into my skin like one of my tattoos — indelible and full of potential yet realized only through choice and action.

As midnight approached and silence enveloped Crimson Ink once more, I stared at that ouroboros-triskele design long into the night, contemplating this new information and Raven's words...

Chapter 7

A Leap into Darkness

I leaned against the cool glass of the shop front, watching the city's pulse thrum through the streets. A deep sigh escaped me, fogging up the window—a momentary canvas to scrawl my uncertainties. It had come down to this: working for the vampire gang. I'd mulled over every possible path, turned every stone for an alternative, but here I was, cornered by a reality that left little room for choice.

The bell above the door chimed, a sound that once heralded promise, now a harbinger of compromise. They strode in like they owned the place—which wasn't far from the truth now. Damien with his piercing gaze that seemed to look right through me, Evelyn's elegance masking her deadly precision, and Victor's silent bulk that spoke volumes of brute force.

I straightened up, brushing invisible dust from my apron. "Damien," I greeted with a nod. My voice betrayed none of my inner turmoil.

"Alex," he replied with that unnerving smile of his. "Ready to make some magic?"

The words 'magic' and 'ready' felt foreign on my tongue. "As always," I lied smoothly, gesturing towards my workspace.

The walk to my station was short but felt like crossing an endless desert under scrutiny's burning gaze. As I laid out my tools with practiced ease, a part of me mourned the freedom I once took for granted—the freedom to create without strings pulling at my every move.

Damien approached, leaning casually against a counter as if we were discussing nothing more than the weather. "We've got big plans for Crimson Ink," he said, voice smooth as silk but heavy with implication.

I met his gaze squarely. "And what plans might those be?"

He spread his hands wide. "Your talents are... unique," he began, choosing his words with care. "We want you exclusively—your designs, your magic. And in return? Protection, power... whatever you need."

I couldn't help but let out a dry chuckle. "Protection from whom? The dangers you bring to my doorstep?"

His smile never wavered. "A fair point," he conceded. "But think of it as insurance."

I nodded slowly, knowing full well this 'insurance' came with a hefty premium—one that could cost more than just money or peace of mind.

Evelyn watched from across the room, her eyes sharp and calculating. Victor had taken up residence by the door—less bodyguard and more jailer.

"And if I refuse?" The question hung in the air between us like a dare.

"You won't," Damien said simply.

He was right; I wouldn't—couldn't—because what choice did I have? The vampire gang was not known for taking no for an answer. They were patient predators who had finally caught a scent they liked: mine.

So there it was—the crux of it all. Resignation washed over me like a wave over sand, erasing all traces of resistance I had left.

"Fine," I agreed quietly.

Damien's smile widened—a cat that got the canary. He extended his hand and after a brief hesitation, I shook it. His grip was cold and firm; an unspoken contract sealed with flesh rather than ink this time.

The rest of the day passed in a blur—a parade of skin canvases awaiting my reluctant artistry under watchful eyes. Each buzz of my tattoo machine etched not only ink into skin but also further entwined me into their web of dark intrigue.

Tara popped in mid-afternoon under some pretense of needing supplies but shot me a look filled with unspoken questions when she caught sight of Victor by the door.

"Everything okay?" she asked casually as she rummaged through a drawer without really looking at its contents.

"Yeah," I replied with equal nonchalance while continuing my work on a client's arm—a vine pattern that curled and twisted like my current predicament. "Just another day at Crimson Ink."

She didn't push further but left with a tight-lipped nod that told me we'd be having a very long conversation later.

As evening fell and the shop quieted down, only the core members of Damien's gang remained—the Council discussing in hushed tones in one corner while Damien reviewed what looked like old maps sprawled across one of my worktables.

I wiped down surfaces and organized my inks mechanically, each motion allowing me to distance myself from the reality that these were no longer just tools for beauty and expression—they were now weapons in an unseen war where boundaries blurred between art and power.

Evelyn caught my eye as she passed by on her way out, her gaze lingering for just a second too long before she followed suit behind Damien and Victor without a word.

The silence after their departure pressed down on me with weighty significance; it was both suffocating and oddly liberating to be alone again in my own space—even if it was just an illusion now.

Raven had mentioned ley lines—a map to navigate supernatural threats—and now Damien stood over maps as well. Could there be a connection? My hands hovered over my sketchbook filled with half-finished designs and concepts not yet brought to life—symbols and sigils interwoven with deeper meaning than even their wearers understood.

With every line drawn, every shade filled in tonight, I infused each design with silent vows: To navigate this treacherous path laid before me without losing myself completely; to wield this art not just as craft but as shield and sword against those who would use it—and me—for ill; to remember that within these walls, magic still pulsed at its purest—mine to command, mine to protect.

As night deepened outside Crimson Ink's stained-glass windows, shadows played across the floor—reminders that light still existed even when darkness threatened to consume everything around it.

* * *

The weight of Damien's gaze settled on me like a shroud, heavy with expectation and the unspoken threat of consequence. The air in Crimson Ink grew thick, suffused with the scent of old leather and the sharp tang of fear that clung to my skin.

"Alex, your talents are too precious to squander on common flesh," Damien began, his voice a silken thread weaving through the dim light. "I have a task for you—one that requires your... unique abilities."

The edges of the room seemed to blur as he spoke, shadows clinging to the corners like wraiths eager to witness my capitulation. My hand twitched toward my sketchbook, seeking solace in the familiar contours of ink and paper.

"What is it you want from me?" My voice betrayed none of the trepidation that danced along my spine.

Damien's smile didn't reach his eyes. "A simple thing, really. A mark of fealty."

He slid a piece of parchment across the counter, the paper crackling with a quiet malevolence. The design was intricate—a serpent devouring its own tail, Ouroboros, encircled by arcane symbols that whispered of binding and servitude.

"It's a symbol of loyalty," he said. "For one of my... associates. It will link them to me, assure their allegiance is... unwavering."

I studied the design, every line and curve a testament to entrapment. This wasn't just a tattoo; it was a shackle.

"And if I refuse?" The question hung between us like a challenge.

Damien's smile faltered for an instant, a crack in his facade revealing the cold abyss beneath. "You know the terms of our arrangement."

My fingers traced the edge of the parchment as if they could divine some hidden escape within its fibers. There was none.

"Fine," I acquiesced, swallowing back the bile that rose in my throat. "But this doesn't change anything between us."

"Of course not," he replied smoothly. "It's just business."

I turned away from him then, concealing the turmoil that threatened to spill from within. Tara caught my eye from across the room—her expression a blend of concern and defiance.

I beckoned her over as Damien retreated to his shadowed corner with Victor and Evelyn in tow.

"This isn't you," Tara whispered fiercely once she was close enough. Her eyes searched mine for some sliver of rebellion.

"I know," I admitted, allowing myself a momentary lapse into vulnerability. "But sometimes we don't get to choose our battles."

Her hand found mine, squeezing tight enough to ground me in her resolve. "We'll find another way," she said.

I wanted to believe her.

The client arrived under cover of darkness—an unremarkable man whose eyes darted around Crimson Ink as if expecting betrayal from every shadow.

"You're here for the Ouroboros," I stated more than asked as he took his place on the chair.

He nodded, rolling up his sleeve with an eagerness that belied his nervousness. His skin was pale—a canvas untouched by sun or hardship.

My equipment lay ready; needles gleamed under the soft light as I poured black ink into tiny cups. The hum of the tattoo machine filled the silence between us—a steady drone that had always been my harbinger of creation. Now it sounded like an elegy.

As I positioned my hand over his arm, I hesitated—a fleeting moment where choice and consequence warred within me.

"Do it," he urged, mistaking my pause for reluctance.

The needle touched skin and ink began its dance—a meticulous waltz guided by my hand. The serpent took shape beneath my touch—its body a loop without beginning or end.

He didn't flinch as I worked—each symbol woven into flesh binding him tighter to Damien's will. With every line etched into his skin, I felt part of myself erode—the artist within succumbing inch by inch to the enforcer Damien wanted me to be.

"You're doing well," Damien's voice cut through my focus, laced with approval that turned my stomach.

I didn't respond—couldn't trust myself to speak without betraying the storm within me.

Time lost meaning as I completed the tattoo—the serpent's scales shimmering with an unnatural luster as if reveling in its newfound dominion over flesh and soul alike.

"It's done," I announced at last, wiping away traces of blood and ink with clinical detachment.

The man rose, examining my work with a reverence that twisted inside me like a knife. He belonged to Damien now—body and soul entwined in serpentine bonds crafted by my hand.

"Thank you," he murmured before departing into night's embrace—a free man no longer.

As soon as he left, I discarded gloves stained with complicity and turned to face Tara's wordless accusation.

"We'll fix this," she said again, though certainty had fled her tone.

I nodded because it was all I could do—the promise between us hanging fragile as spider silk in morning dew. We were caught in Damien's web now; our struggle against it only tightened its grip around us.

* * *

The buzz of my tattoo machine hummed through the thick, charged air of Crimson Ink. As the needle danced across skin, I etched an Ouroboros, its form a perfect circle of self-consumption. With each line, a part of me winced. This symbol wasn't just ink; it was a shackle for the one who bore it—a binding to Damien's will.

I glanced at the man beneath my hands, his gaze vacant, resigned to his fate. I'd seen that look before—the dawning realization that one's choices had been stripped away, leaving nothing but submission to forces greater and darker than they'd ever imagined.

My shop had become a crossroads for such souls. Damien and his gang didn't just wield power; they were connoisseurs of control, feasting on the helplessness of others. And here I was, their unwilling artist, turning skin into parchment for their dark contracts.

A chime signaled the door opening. The man flinched beneath me. "Easy," I murmured, but my own heart raced. You never knew what—or who—would walk through that door these days.

It was Victor, his presence filling the room like a dark cloud ready to burst. "Alex," he rumbled, "we have a situation downstairs."

I finished the final stroke and wrapped the tattoo. "Give me a minute," I said with a calm I didn't feel.

Downstairs wasn't just storage; it was where the gang conducted their most secretive business. It was also off-limits to me, until now.

I followed Victor down the narrow staircase into a dimly lit room that reeked of old blood and fear. My stomach turned at the sight before me—a circle of beings that shouldn't exist outside of nightmares or fairy tales.

In one corner crouched a creature with skin like molten silver and eyes that wept tears of mercury. Across from it, a woman with vines for hair whispered to flowers blooming unnaturally fast only to wilt seconds later—a cycle as rapid as breaths in panic.

Damien stood in the center, his eyes aglow with unnatural light as he spoke words that seemed to weave around each being like chains.

"This is your world now, Alex," he said without turning to me. "Understand it, and you will understand your place within it."

A shiver ran down my spine at his words—was this an invitation or a threat?

The silver-skinned creature approached me slowly. "Do you see us?" it asked in a voice like liquid metal flowing over stones.

I nodded because how could I not? This being defied all logic yet demanded recognition.

"We are bound by him," it gestured towards Damien with a slender finger that left trails of shimmering air. "He promises us desires fulfilled for services rendered."

Its sadness weighed on me—an anchor pulling at my very soul.

The vine-haired woman didn't speak but her flowers did—a chorus of tiny voices begging for sunlight and freedom.

Victor's hand on my shoulder brought me back to the moment. "They are tools," he said bluntly. "Just like you."

Anger flared within me at his words but died just as quickly. What use was anger when you felt so utterly powerless?

Damien turned then, fixing those piercing eyes on me. "They are proof of what we can offer—and what we can take away."

I understood then that this wasn't just about tattoos or even power—it was about bending reality to one's will.

"And what do they want?" My voice sounded distant even to my own ears.

"Salvation," Damien answered with a sardonic smile. "From themselves mostly."

A cold laugh escaped me before I could stop it—the irony too bitter to swallow silently.

"Let's go upstairs," Damien said abruptly. "We have more work to do."

As I followed him back into the relative normalcy of Crimson Ink's main floor, my mind reeled with what I'd seen—beings powerful and strange reduced to bargaining chips in Damien's game of supremacy.

We settled into our usual places—Damien overseeing everything like some twisted king while Evelyn stood by his side, her face an unreadable mask.

A new client arrived then—a woman whose aura flickered with shadows that spoke of dealings with things best left alone in dark corners of the world.

She wanted a tattoo—a mark that would hide her from prying eyes both mortal and otherwise.

As I worked on her design, transforming her fear into art, I couldn't help but wonder how many others there were like her—caught up in this supernatural underworld where their fates were traded and bartered by creatures like Damien and his gang.

Each drop of ink felt heavy with significance as if by hiding her; I was also hiding parts of myself from Damien's ever-watchful gaze.

But even as I worked, even as I poured every ounce of skill into creating something beautiful out of fear, I knew this was only temporary—that sooner or later Damien would demand more than just my compliance; he would want my soul itself for his collection.

And as if on cue, Damien leaned close as the woman left, satisfaction curling his lips into a smile not meant for mortal eyes. "You do exceptional work under pressure," he murmured. "It makes you valuable."

His words felt like another chain wrapping around me—one forged from reluctant admiration rather than iron or silver—and I knew that this dance we were doing was far from over.

The door chimed again—another client or perhaps another pawn in this endless game? Only time would tell but one thing was certain: Crimson Ink had become more than just a tattoo parlor—it had become a battleground where wills clashed silently beneath the guise of business as usual and where every choice carried weight beyond measure.

* * *

I swept the last of the night's detritus into the trash and flicked off the neon sign that buzzed softly in the window of Crimson Ink. The city's pulse thrummed through the walls, a never-ending rhythm that spoke of life, danger, and secrets hidden in plain sight. My hand hovered over the lock, a sense of foreboding wrapping around me like a cold shroud.

"Closing up?"

The voice slithered through the darkness, its owner concealed by shadows that clung to the alleyway like ink stains. I straightened, muscles tensing.

"I am," I called out, my tone steady despite the adrenaline coursing through my veins. "You looking for some late-night ink?"

A figure emerged from the darkness, tall and cloaked in menace. The air around us grew heavy, electric with unsaid threats. It was Marlon, a rogue sorcerer with a vendetta against anyone who dealt with vampires.

"Not quite," Marlon sneered, his eyes gleaming with malice. "Word on the street is you're cozying up to Damien and his bloodsuckers. Bad move."

I shrugged, feigning nonchalance while my mind raced. "Business is business. You know how it is."

Marlon's laugh was a bark of derision. "I thought you were better than that. Guess I was wrong."

I reached for the door handle, hoping to end this confrontation before it escalated. "If you're not here for a tattoo—"

His hand shot out, slamming against the door and keeping it shut. The wood groaned under his strength.

"You don't get it, do you?" Marlon's voice dropped to a hiss. "You've painted a target on your back."

I glared at him, anger simmering beneath my skin. "And what? You're here to take a shot?"

He leaned in close enough for me to see the fury etched into his features. "Consider this a friendly warning." Marlon's hand sizzled with energy as he pulled back his sleeve to reveal scars that writhed on his skin like living things.

My breath caught at the sight — cursed marks meant to cause pain and subjugation. It was a brutal reminder of what lay at stake when you crossed lines in our world.

"I'll manage," I said quietly, but Marlon wasn't finished.

"You think Damien's protection is worth anything?" He spat on the ground, his expression twisted with contempt. "You're nothing but a pawn to him."

The accusation stung more than I cared to admit.

"Thanks for the concern," I replied coolly while contemplating an escape route. "But I don't recall asking for your advice."

Marlon stepped back abruptly as if struck by an unseen force. His eyes narrowed.

"You'll regret this," he warned before melting back into the shadows from which he'd come.

I released a breath I hadn't realized I'd been holding and waited several heartbeats before daring to unlock and open the door again. Inside Crimson Ink's sanctuary, my pulse began to slow, but my mind wouldn't stop racing.

The door closed behind me with a soft click as I made my way toward my private studio at the back of the shop. Every step felt heavier than the last; every shadow seemed to hold whispered threats.

In my studio, surrounded by designs and drawings that held pieces of my soul within them, I sank into my chair and let out a long sigh. Marlon's words echoed in my head — pawn, target, regret — each one chipping away at my resolve.

A knock at the door startled me from my thoughts.

"Alex? You okay in there?" Tara's voice filtered through with concern lacing each syllable.

"Yeah," I called out as I rose to open the door. Tara stood there, her brow furrowed in worry.

"I saw Marlon skulking around outside," she said as she stepped into my space — our space — where we'd shared dreams and fears alike.

"He was just leaving," I replied while avoiding her gaze.

Tara crossed her arms over her chest. "And?"

"And nothing." The lie tasted bitter on my tongue.

She studied me for a moment longer before speaking again. "Alex, you can't let Damien or any of these thugs scare you into submission."

My laugh held no humor. "It's not just about being scared anymore."

Tara approached and placed her hands on my shoulders — grounding me as she always did when chaos threatened to sweep me away.

"You have friends," she reminded me softly but firmly. "We won't let Damien or anyone else push you around."

Her confidence was infectious; it seeped into me like warmth from a fire on a cold night.

"Thanks," I managed before pulling her into an embrace that spoke volumes more than words ever could.

As we parted ways for the night, leaving Crimson Ink behind us like a beacon in the dark cityscape, Tara's presence at my side reminded me of what true loyalty felt like — something Damien would never understand nor possess.

The streets were empty as we made our way down them; even the usual nocturnal creatures seemed to sense an undercurrent of danger and kept their distance.

It wasn't until we rounded a corner toward our respective homes that Tara broke the silence between us.

"What are you going to do?" Her question hung in the air like mist over water.

I stopped mid-stride and looked up at the sky above us — void of stars yet full of possibilities both wondrous and terrifying alike.

"I'll find a way out of this mess," I declared with more certainty than I felt deep down in my bones where fear still lingered like poison waiting to strike.

Tara nodded once before heading off toward her own place with just one backward glance that told me she believed in me even when doubt clouded every thought I had about tomorrow and all its unknowns.

Alone again under an indifferent sky, I forced myself to keep moving forward even as uncertainty gnawed at me from within because giving up wasn't an option — not now when so much hinged upon choices yet unmade and paths yet untrodden by ink-stained hands like mine.

* * *

I wiped the last trace of ink from my client's arm, the whir of my tattoo machine subsiding into silence. A sense of accomplishment filled me as I admired the fresh design—a raven in flight, its wings laced with symbols of freedom and strength. My client, a young woman with eyes that spoke of seen horrors, gazed at the reflection of her new tattoo with a mixture of awe and relief.

"Thank you," she whispered, her voice a thread of silk in the cool air of Crimson Ink. "I feel like I can finally start over."

As she left, clutching the aftercare instructions I handed her, the bell above the door jangled softly. The brief moment of peace shattered like glass against stone. Victor stormed in, his imposing figure filling the doorway, flanked by two others whose names I never bothered to learn. They had that look—shadows beneath their eyes that told stories of centuries lived and blood spilled.

"Damien wants to see you," Victor grunted, his voice a low rumble that sent a chill through the parlor.

The pit of my stomach knotted as I followed them through the back, where the pulsing heart of Crimson Ink's dark side lay hidden. The vampire gang's true lair—a stark contrast to the front's facade of creativity and healing—was an underground chamber lit by flickering torches and filled with an air thick with power and old earth.

Damien stood at the center, his presence commanding even in stillness. His eyes met mine as I approached, their depths holding centuries of secrets and unspoken threats.

"We have a problem," he announced without preamble. His fingers danced over an open grimoire, its pages ancient and curling.

Evelyn was there too, her elegance doing nothing to soften the calculating glint in her eye. She watched me closely as Damien continued.

"A rogue necromancer has been disrupting our operations," he said, his voice even but heavy with displeasure. "Tonight we remind this city who truly rules its shadows."

My breath caught as Damien lifted his hand. The air seemed to thicken; shadows twisted and stretched across the walls like living things hungry for light. With a single word from Damien's lips—a word that felt older than time—the shadows surged forward, merging into forms both grotesque and mesmerizing: shadow-beasts born from nightmare and malice.

Victor smirked as he watched them prowl around the chamber before disappearing through walls that could not contain them.

"This is what we are capable of," Evelyn said softly beside me, her voice a silken threat. "Do not forget it."

I swallowed hard, feeling the weight of their power press against me like a physical force. It was one thing to know about their influence—it was another to witness it firsthand. The gang wasn't just a group of vampires conducting shady business; they were a force that could bend reality to their will.

I returned to my station in silence, trying to shake off what I'd seen as clients trickled in for their appointments. With each buzz of my machine, I fought to focus on my art rather than on what lurked beneath it all—the web of control and dark intentions spun by Damien and his followers.

Hours passed in a blur until nightfall crept through the windows, casting long shadows across Crimson Ink's floors. That's when she walked in—a woman cloaked in an aura that spoke volumes without uttering a single word. Her gaze locked onto mine with an intensity that rooted me to the spot.

"I need your help," she said quietly once we were alone in my booth. "They're coming for me."

The way she said "they" didn't need clarification—I knew exactly who she meant.

"What did you do?" I asked while setting up my station for another session.

Her lips twisted into a rueful smile as she rolled up her sleeve, revealing scars that snaked around her arm like vines seeking sunlight.

"I saw too much," she admitted. "And now I know too much."

Her request was simple: A tattoo to shield her from prying eyes—both mortal and otherwise. As I sketched out the design—a lattice of protective runes intertwined with symbols of concealment—I couldn't help but feel we were kindred spirits bound by our brushes with darkness.

"You have power," she murmured as my needle worked its magic on her skin. "But it comes with great risk."

Her words echoed in my head long after she left into the night—another soul adrift amidst the tumultuous tides controlled by creatures like Damien.

As midnight approached, I prepared to close shop when Evelyn swept in without warning. Her gaze lingered on me with an unreadable expression before settling on an empty chair near my workbench.

"We have someone who requires your special touch," she stated flatly.

A young man stepped forward from behind her—pale, visibly shaking—with fear etched into every line on his face.

"He betrayed us," Evelyn explained coldly while Victor loomed behind him like death's shadow. "You will mark him so he cannot hide."

I felt sick as realization dawned—the tattoo they wanted wasn't just for identification; it was a brand for betrayal, a permanent reminder etched into flesh by my unwilling hand.

As I readied myself for this distasteful task, trying not to look into the young man's desperate eyes or think about what would become of him after tonight...

* * *

The hum of the tattoo gun blended with the tense silence in the room. I traced the lines on the young man's arm, the design a mix of thorns and chains, a symbol of his betrayal and his new bond to Damien's gang. He flinched under the needle, but I worked with steady hands, my mind a whirlwind of conflict and strategy.

"You're doing the right thing," Evelyn whispered from her corner, her voice a silken thread laced with steel. "It's about survival, Alex."

I finished the last loop of the chain and set down my gun, wiping away excess ink. The design was complete—a permanent reminder of his choices and mine. I wrapped his arm with a professional detachment that belied my inner turmoil.

"Keep it clean and dry," I instructed, meeting his gaze for a moment. His eyes were wide, haunted. He nodded mutely and stood to leave.

As the door closed behind him, I sank into my chair, exhaustion creeping into my bones like an unwelcome guest. Tara slipped in quietly, her presence a balm to my frayed nerves.

"You can't keep doing this," she said softly.

I looked up at her through strands of hair that had fallen loose from my ponytail. "What choice do I have?"

She leaned against the counter, her face etched with concern. "There's always a choice, Alex."

Her words hung in the air as I considered them. Yes, there was always a choice—between submission and defiance, between fear and courage. I could feel Damien's grip tightening around Crimson Ink like ivy strangling an oak tree.

The evening waned as we talked, plotting quietly while Damien's influence cast long shadows across my shop. Tara reminded me of the power in my lineage—of Raven's faith in me and Jade's counsel to remain unowned.

When she left, the night pressed against the windows of Crimson Ink with inky fingers. I flipped through my sketchbook to a blank page and began to draw—pouring every ounce of defiance and hope into each line.

A knock at the door jarred me from my reverie; it was Evelyn again, this time alone.

"He won't stop," she said without preamble. "Damien is determined to have you under his thumb."

I closed my sketchbook with a snap. "Then he doesn't know me very well."

Evelyn's lips twitched into what might have been a smile or a snarl—I couldn't tell which. "Be careful," she warned before disappearing back into the night.

Alone again, surrounded by ancient texts and whispered secrets, I took stock of where I stood—caught between worlds in a city that never truly slept.

My fingers traced over patterns inked onto my own skin—reminders of where I came from and what I was capable of. A quiet determination settled over me as if my tattoos themselves whispered encouragement.

Raven's Aethereal Compass lay next to me on the desk. It pulsed faintly, its glow a heartbeat syncing with mine. With it came the knowledge that ley lines coursed beneath this city like veins under skin—full of power waiting to be tapped.

I had always known that Crimson Ink was more than just a tattoo shop; it was an extension of me—a place where magic met flesh and ink could change lives.

Now it had become something else—a battleground where destinies were written in blood rather than ink.

I rose from my desk and walked over to where Damien had summoned those shadow beasts earlier. The room felt colder than usual, shadows clinging to corners like cobwebs.

In that space between heartbeats, where silence was a living thing, I made my choice—a vow cast in steel rather than words.

I would not be Damien's pawn or his puppet master's marionette. My tattoos would not become shackles for others or myself; they would be keys—keys to freedom and shields against darkness.

The night deepened as I cleaned up after another day marked by quiet battles and silent victories—each client leaving with more than just ink under their skin.

The weight of responsibility settled onto my shoulders—a mantle woven from threads of magic and humanity alike.

Tomorrow would bring new challenges—I knew that as surely as ink knew skin—but for now, there was peace in purpose; solace found within the sanctuary of these walls that bore witness to so much more than anyone could imagine.

And so I turned off the lights one by one until only moonlight spilled across hardwood floors stained with history and sacrifice—the shop silent but for the echoes of promises made to myself: to navigate this dangerous world on my own terms; to wield power not as a weapon but as an artist's tool; to be neither hero nor villain but simply Alex—a tattoo artist caught in a dance with destiny.

Crimson Ink may have been ensnared by vampire games and supernatural threats but within its walls pulsed a heart that beat defiantly against all odds—a heart that belonged solely to me.

As I locked up for the night, every shadow seemed filled with potential allies or hidden enemies—it was impossible to tell which—but one thing was certain: no matter how treacherous this path became or how many twisted turns it took, my resolve would remain unbroken; for when you wield magic on your skin and destiny at your fingertips...what is there truly to fear?

Chapter 8

Hidden Realms Revealed

The door to Crimson Ink swung open with a gust of wind that seemed to carry whispers of forgotten lore. I stood behind the counter, needles and ink at the ready, but the figures that entered weren't here for tattoos—at least not the usual kind.

Damien led the procession, his presence like a shroud of velvet darkness that quieted the room. Behind him trailed a menagerie of entities I had only read about in the musty pages of my grandmother's journals. A woman cloaked in emerald flames, a being whose shadow writhed and twisted independent of its owner, and a creature with eyes that mirrored the starless night sky.

"Alex," Damien's voice cut through the stillness like a blade, "your education begins now."

I swallowed hard, nodding. My heart hammered against my ribs, an anxious prisoner within its bone cage.

Damien gestured to the flame-cloaked woman. "Meet Lysandra, a phoenix in human guise. Her fire is rebirth and destruction intertwined." The heat from her presence licked at my skin, a caress that promised both comfort and annihilation.

The shadow-being stepped forward next. Its form flickered, as if undecided between man and monster. "And this is Mordecai, a shadowmancer bound to the umbra between worlds." The shadows around us seemed to lean toward him, drawn by an unseen force.

Lastly, Damien turned to the creature with abyssal eyes. "Here stands Orion. He is what you might call an astrologer—though his craft reaches far beyond reading stars."

Orion nodded at me; his gaze felt like falling into infinity.

Damien's gaze held mine captive. "They're part of our world—the hidden threads in the tapestry you've only begun to unravel."

I looked at each of them, trying to match confidence with curiosity. "I'm honored," I managed to say, though it sounded more like a question than a statement.

Lysandra stepped closer, her fiery aura dimming slightly. "You possess gifts that align with our practices," she said, her voice a melodic hum that resonated with warmth. "We wish to see them honed."

Mordecai remained silent; his very essence was an enigma wrapped in whispers and darkness.

Orion spoke next, his voice carrying the weight of eons. "Your art is potent; it shapes destinies. We seek your alliance in charting new fates."

The weight of their expectations bore down on me as I processed what stood before me—an offer to delve deeper into realms where my art could transcend ink and skin.

"What exactly would you have me do?" I asked tentatively.

Damien smiled; it didn't reach his eyes. "You will learn from each," he said simply.

My shop suddenly felt like foreign territory—transformed into an academy of arcane mysteries under Damien's decree. This wasn't what I had envisioned for Crimson Ink or myself, yet intrigue tugged at my spirit.

Lysandra approached first. She held out her hand; from it rose a small flame that danced between her fingers—a mesmerizing waltz of fire and air.

"Your tattoos can be more than mere marks," she said as I watched the flame twirl. "They can be conduits for rebirth, vessels for purging old wounds and igniting new strengths."

She motioned for me to take her hand; hesitantly, I did so. The flame leaped onto my palm but didn't burn—it was warm and soothing instead.

"Feel the energy," she urged.

I closed my eyes and focused on the sensation—the ember in my hand sparked images of mythical birds soaring through cycles of death and life.

Next came Mordecai. The darkness around him gathered and formed shapes at his command—a raven here, a coiling serpent there—all made from pure shadow.

"Your lines can bind or liberate," he said as he manipulated the darkness effortlessly. His gaze fixed on mine; it was an invitation to dance with shades and whispers.

I reached out tentatively into the gloom he conjured; it enveloped my fingers like cool silk. In that moment, I felt secrets flow into me—hidden knowledge that yearned for expression through ink.

Orion waited patiently for his turn; when it came, he placed before me an ancient astrolabe made of silver and sapphires that seemed to hold captured stars within them.

"The heavens influence all," Orion explained as he guided my hands over celestial charts etched into metal and gemstone. "Your art can channel these cosmic energies—aligning mortal flesh with astral forces."

I peered into the device; constellations spun beneath my fingertips as if alive. A rush filled me—the thrill of connecting dots across space and time through my craft.

Throughout these introductions, Damien observed with keen interest—a puppet master watching his marionettes perform.

"We'll start small," he finally said after Orion finished demonstrating how celestial alignments could enhance tattoo magic. "You'll practice under their guidance until you master these new facets of your talent."

There was no mistaking it—I was now under their tutelage whether I wished it or not. The gang's operations spanned wider than blood trades and dark dealings—it delved into practices ancient and powerful beyond common understanding.

My hands trembled slightly as I looked at each supernatural entity standing in my shop—my new mentors in arts both wondrous and terrifying. Damien expected me to absorb their knowledge—to weave fire, shadow, and stars into my tattoos—but at what cost?

As they dispersed throughout Crimson Ink, setting up strange artifacts on workstations once reserved for mundane tattooing supplies, I felt a shift within myself—a mixture of dread and excitement for what lay ahead in this world far beyond what I had imagined.

***

I perched on the worn leather stool at the back of Crimson Ink, needle in hand, etching an intricate pattern of intertwining vines across a client's shoulder. The hum of the tattoo machine blended with the soft murmur of conversations drifting from the front of the shop. It was business as usual, or so it seemed until the bell above the door jangled with a sense of urgency that cut through the calm.

I glanced up. Victor stormed in, his face set in a grim line, flanked by two of Damien's loyal followers whose names never stuck with me. Their presence alone set my nerves on edge. I paused, wiping away a bead of ink from my client's skin. The man beneath my needle tensed, sensing the shift in atmosphere.

"Alex," Victor called out, his voice low and demanding. "Damien needs you."

The client looked up at me with wide eyes. "Should I—"

"Stay," I instructed, patting his shoulder gently. "Almost done here." My voice betrayed none of my trepidation as I laid down my tools and followed Victor to Damien's lair below the shop.

The air grew colder as we descended the narrow staircase into a space that seemed a world apart from the creative sanctuary above. Damien sat at an ornate desk that could have belonged in another century, surrounded by tomes that whispered of dark secrets and power.

"Evelyn tells me you're learning fast," Damien said without looking up from his book. His tone was casual, but I could feel tension coiling in the room like a waiting serpent.

I nodded, unsure how much he knew about my reluctance to embrace these lessons in darkness. "I've had good teachers," I replied cautiously.

He finally raised his eyes to meet mine, and I felt a chill skitter across my skin. "Good," he said simply before shifting his gaze to Victor. "Bring them in."

Victor nodded and exited the room briefly, returning with two figures—a man bound by magical restraints and a woman whose defiant gaze never wavered even as she was pushed forward.

My heart pounded against my ribs as I recognized her—the woman who had come to me for a tattoo not long ago, seeking protection from entities like Damien.

Damien rose from his seat with a grace that belied his lethal nature and circled around to stand before them. The man looked beaten, bloodied; his eyes held a defeated glint that spoke volumes of the torture he must have endured.

"This is what happens when loyalty falters," Damien announced, addressing not just me but anyone who dared cross him. His hand hovered over the man's head as he spoke an incantation that made my skin crawl.

I watched, frozen, as shadows slithered from Damien's fingers and wrapped around the man like tendrils of smoke—squeezing tighter until his screams filled the room.

The woman remained stoic even as tears brimmed in her eyes—a show of strength I couldn't help but admire.

"You see," Damien continued, turning toward me while maintaining control over the shadows that tormented the traitor before us. "Power requires discipline. And discipline sometimes demands... examples."

The man's screams subsided into whimpers as Damien released him from his shadowy grip; he crumpled to the floor like a marionette with its strings cut.

My stomach churned with revulsion at this display of cruelty—cruelty I had somehow become complicit in by standing here and doing nothing.

"And you," Damien addressed the woman now. "You sought protection from powers beyond your understanding." His voice held an edge sharper than any blade in my shop.

She lifted her chin defiantly. "Better to die free than live under your yoke."

A murmur of surprise rippled through Damien's followers—her courage was unexpected.

Damien chuckled darkly, stepping closer until he towered over her. "Bold words for someone so... vulnerable."

I couldn't help but interject; her bravery struck a chord within me—a reminder of why I fought so hard for autonomy within this twisted game of power. "She came to me for protection," I said evenly, locking eyes with Damien.

He turned slowly to face me, a smile playing on his lips that didn't reach his eyes. "And did you provide it?"

My pulse raced as I weighed my words carefully. "I did what was asked of me."

The room held its breath as Damien considered this before nodding once, almost imperceptibly. He stepped back from the woman and turned toward Victor. "Take her away," he commanded with casual indifference. "She'll be useful in negotiating with her friends."

Victor motioned to the others who quickly seized her arms and dragged her away; her gaze lingered on me—a silent plea or perhaps an accusation.

Once they were gone, silence descended upon us like heavy cloth smothering all sound.

Damien finally broke it with a clap of his hands as if brushing off invisible dust from his palms. "Let's not let today's unpleasantness distract us from our goals," he said smoothly as if torture were nothing more than an inconvenient interruption to his day.

"Of course," I replied automatically while my mind raced with conflicting emotions—horror at what had transpired mingled with relief that it wasn't worse.

I returned upstairs feeling like a ghost haunting my own life—going through motions that once brought joy now tainted by knowledge of what lay beneath them: power struggles played out through pain and fear where people like that brave woman were mere pawns sacrificed without hesitation or remorse.

The buzz of tattoo machines greeted me—a stark contrast to screams still echoing in my ears—and I forced myself back into routine: finish this tattoo, help this client, keep moving forward despite everything inside screaming at me to run far away from this madness enveloping Crimson Ink and everything it once stood for.

* * *

The weight of the standoff with Damien clung to me like the remnants of a nightmare, refusing to dissipate even as I opened Crimson Ink for another day. Each ring of the doorbell, each shadow that crossed the threshold, set my heart pounding with a mix of anticipation and dread. Today was no different.

She entered as the clock struck the late morning hour, her presence slicing through the hum of daily routine like a blade. Tall and shrouded in a coat that swept the floor with each deliberate step, her face remained hidden beneath a hood so deep it seemed to swallow light. The air around her shimmered with an energy that raised every hair on my arms—a sure sign of someone steeped in the supernatural.

"Can I help you?" My voice emerged steadier than I felt.

Her silence stretched out before she finally spoke, her tone low and melodic, almost hypnotic. "I seek the artist whose ink transcends mere flesh."

I motioned toward my work station, taking note of her measured movements. She carried herself with an unnerving grace, each motion calculated and precise. I readied my tools as she settled into the chair, her eyes finally meeting mine as she drew back her hood.

A rush of recognition hit me—the angular face marked by scars that told tales of battles fought and won; eyes that flickered with inner fire. This was no ordinary client; this was a warrior from the supernatural community, a being whose very essence vibrated with untold power.

"I'm Alex," I said, offering my hand which she regarded for a moment before taking it. Her grip was firm, her skin cold to the touch.

"Call me Rowan." Her voice wove through the air, carrying an accent I couldn't place—a blend of ancient cadences.

"And what brings you to Crimson Ink?"

Rowan's gaze shifted from mine to survey the parlor's walls adorned with designs both mundane and mystical. "I require your particular skills," she said cryptically. "A tattoo that is more than art; one that serves as a ward."

I nodded slowly. A ward wasn't unusual in my line of work but given her nature, this was bound to be no simple charm against bad dreams. "What are you warding against?"

Her lips pressed into a thin line as she contemplated whether to trust me with more information. "There are forces aligning in the shadows," she murmured. "Ancient entities that hunger for resurgence."

Chills traced down my spine at her words. I'd felt those shadows creeping closer each day since Damien's threats became part of my reality.

"Let's design something powerful then." I reached for my sketchbook and pencils.

Rowan watched me intently as I sketched lines and symbols, each stroke guided by intuition honed over years steeped in magic and ink. The design took shape—a shield interwoven with sigils of protection and strength, rooted in both my heritage and knowledge gleaned from ancient texts.

Rowan studied the design closely before giving a single nod of approval. "Begin."

As needle met skin, Rowan's story unfolded between bouts of silence and shared glances in the mirror's reflection.

"I am one of the last guardians of an ancient grove," she confessed softly after a time. "But there are those who would see it razed for their own gain."

My hands remained steady even as my mind raced with questions about this grove and its significance within the supernatural world.

"Why come to me?" I asked, focusing on infusing each line with potent magic.

"Your reputation extends beyond human clientele," Rowan said cryptically. "And there are few who can weave protection into their art as you do."

The flattery didn't escape me but neither did the undercurrent of desperation in her voice—Rowan needed an ally and had taken a risk seeking me out.

We continued in relative silence until I completed the last line. The ink shimmered on her skin, charged with energy that pulsed like a heartbeat against my fingertips.

"It is done." I wiped away excess ink to reveal the finished ward—dark lines etched with precision against her pale skin.

Rowan examined my handiwork, rotating her arm to view it from every angle before allowing herself a small smile—a rarity among those who lived life braced for battle.

"This will serve well." She stood, pulling out a pouch heavy with coins that clinked softly against each other—payment more than sufficient for my services rendered.

But instead of taking it, I hesitated—a thought taking root in my mind.

"Information is more valuable to me than gold," I ventured cautiously.

Rowan arched an eyebrow at that but didn't seem displeased by the notion.

"What do you wish to know?"

I leaned back against my workbench considering how much to reveal about Damien's interest in me or about the Mark of Power—each piece of knowledge could expose vulnerabilities or create new enemies if not handled carefully.

"How do these ancient entities tie into ley lines?" It was broad enough not to betray too much yet specific enough to address current concerns—my concerns since Raven's visit had hinted at their importance.

Rowan regarded me with newfound curiosity; evidently satisfied by my request's nature—or perhaps its intelligence—she nodded slowly.

"The ley lines are conduits," she began. "Channels through which energy flows beneath our city streets like veins filled with lifeblood."

I listened intently as Rowan explained their significance—to both our world and those realms beyond our sight—and how they could be used or corrupted by those with knowledge and intent. As she spoke, pieces fell into place within my mind: maps studied under Damien's scrutiny suddenly held new meaning; rumors whispered amongst allies coalesced into coherent theories.

My focus on Rowan only sharpened when she leaned closer, lowering her voice further still.

"There are places where these lines intersect," she confided, "nodes of immense power coveted by many."

She reached into another pocket and produced a folded piece of parchment—a map marked by symbols familiar yet arcane.

"Guard this knowledge well," Rowan warned as she handed it over.

My fingers brushed hers as I took possession—a transaction far more significant than any exchange of coin could ever be.

With Rowan's departure came a sense of cautious optimism mingled with apprehension; potential alliances had always been double-edged swords within our world.

Yet as dusk fell upon Crimson Ink once more and shadows lengthened across its floors—the map concealed securely within my grasp—I knew this encounter had opened doors previously barred: avenues ripe for exploration amidst dangers known and unknown alike.

And despite everything—despite Damien's suffocating presence—I felt ready to walk those paths.

* * *

The map Rowan left with me sprawled across my workbench, a labyrinth of lines that pulsed with an energy only I seemed to feel. I traced a finger over the intersections, each a beacon of potential magic, a wellspring for my tattoos. It wasn't just ink and skin anymore; it was about channeling the raw essence of the city, the power coursing beneath its concrete veins.

My gaze lifted to the shop around me, Crimson Ink. Once a sanctuary for my art, now it was a battleground of shadows where I played a dangerous game. Damien's game. Every day, his gang brought their politics and their plots into my space, and I had to weave through them like a ghost—seen, yet apart.

I learned early on that in this world of fangs and power, it wasn't just about surviving; it was about understanding the unspoken rules that governed us all. Damien, Evelyn, Victor—they were the triumvirate that held Crimson Ink in an iron grip. And then there were the others: The Council with their old-world machinations and The Acolytes with eyes full of hunger for status.

"You're quiet today," Tara's voice cut through my reverie as she stepped into the shop.

"Just thinking," I replied, folding the map away from prying eyes.

"About what they want from you?" She followed my gaze to where Victor loomed by the door like some dark sentinel.

"Among other things," I admitted.

I had to play this smart. Every move I made had to be calculated, every word measured. With Tara at my side—a friend who saw beyond the supernatural taint that colored my world—I felt braver than I might have admitted.

"You can't let them see you sweat," she whispered.

I nodded, rolling down my sleeves to cover the tattoos that snaked up my arms—marks of power that I wouldn't let Damien exploit any further than he already had. My skin prickled with awareness as I turned to face Victor. He nodded once, his gesture both an acknowledgment and a command. Time to get to work.

Evelyn sauntered in not long after, her presence demanding attention without a single word spoken. She slid onto one of the tattoo chairs with grace that belied her lethal nature.

"Damien wants to see new designs," she said coolly.

I hesitated but kept my expression neutral. "Of course."

Her eyes narrowed slightly as if trying to peer into my thoughts. "Remember who provides for you here."

I nodded again because what else could I do? Yet defiance smoldered within me like a banked fire ready to ignite at any moment.

I spent hours drawing under Evelyn's watchful gaze, each line an act of rebellion etched in secret defiance. When she finally left, satisfied with what she'd seen—or perhaps simply bored—I let out a breath I hadn't realized I'd been holding.

"You're getting good at this," Tara remarked from her perch on the counter where she'd been thumbing through one of my sketchbooks.

"Good at what?" My hands paused over a design featuring an ouroboros devouring its tail—an endless cycle of power and betrayal.

"Hiding in plain sight." She closed the book gently and hopped down next to me. "But remember why you're doing this."

I nodded once more, thinking about Rowan's map hidden away beneath stacks of paper and ink pots. It was about more than just staying safe within these walls; it was about keeping one step ahead of whatever game Damien thought he was playing with me as his pawn.

Over the next few days, whispers filled Crimson Ink like smoke—rumors of unrest among The Council and whispers of disloyalty from The Acolytes. Power struggles within vampire hierarchies were nothing new, but they were treacherous waters for a human—or part-human—to navigate.

One evening as I locked up for the night, Lucas approached me hesitantly. He was one of The Acolytes but always seemed different—less predatory than his counterparts.

"Alex," he said in a hushed tone that suggested he wanted neither eavesdroppers nor recognition for our conversation. "Not everyone is as they seem."

His words hung between us like a puzzle missing its final piece.

"What do you mean?" I asked carefully.

"Some here respect what you do," he continued cryptically before vanishing into the night without another word.

Respect? In this den? It was as foreign a concept as sunlight in their cold lives—but it was something to consider as I turned over his words in my mind long after he'd gone.

It became clearer each day that not all ties within Damien's gang were forged from loyalty or fear; some were tenuous alliances waiting for an opportunity to break free or change sides. The thought offered no comfort; if anything, it made everything more precarious—a misstep could mean disaster not just for me but for those who dared stand with me in whatever small ways they could muster.

One afternoon found me drawing up an intricate pattern when Mordecai strode into Crimson Ink without preamble—a Council member whose wisdom was as sharp as his fangs.

"You're caught in webs more tangled than your art," he remarked casually while inspecting my designs sprawled across various surfaces.

"And if I am?" I kept my tone neutral even as adrenaline coursed through me at his scrutiny.

"Then know which strands to pull...and which will unravel you completely." His cryptic advice left me more alert than ever before he departed with a nod that might have been approval or warning—it was hard to tell with him.

The game grew more complex by the hour: allies hidden among enemies and friends cloaked in shadows—the politics of survival never-ending and always evolving. Damien might think he held all the cards, but he didn't know about Rowan's map or about ley lines that whispered secrets only I could hear—secrets that could shift the balance ever so slightly in my favor if played right.

As night descended on Crimson Ink once more, with only the hum of neon lights for company, I pondered Mordecai's words and Lucas's warning. Trust was a currency too valuable to squander carelessly here—yet without it, how could any alliance stand?

My mind raced with possibilities as Tara returned from running errands, her arrival grounding me once again in reality—the reality where magic and danger intermingled so closely that it was impossible to tell where one ended and the other began.

* * *

The hum of the tattoo machine vibrated through my fingertips, a steady pulse that usually calmed my nerves. Not today. The ink flowed onto skin, but the design I etched felt like a betrayal to every line I'd ever drawn. Damien leaned against the doorframe, arms folded, a dark silhouette against the dim light.

"Make sure it's exactly as I specified, Alex," his voice was velvet wrapped around steel.

I nodded without looking up, focusing on the intricate pattern that would bind this person to Damien's will. Every line felt heavy with consequence. The client, a young man with fear etched deeper into his eyes than any tattoo I could place on his skin, lay still, his breathing shallow.

Tara stood just outside the room, her presence a silent protest. Her eyes met mine in a silent conversation we'd had too many times. *You can't keep doing this,* they said.

But what choice did I have? Damien's protection came at a cost, and that cost sat heavy in my stomach, an anchor dragging me down into depths I'd never wanted to explore.

The design took shape – an Ouroboros consuming its own tail – but in this context, it was no symbol of eternal renewal. It was a shackle.

The needle dipped into the crimson ink as I shaded the final touches. *This isn't you,* Tara's eyes reminded me from across the room.

She was right; this wasn't me. But neither was being powerless against Damien and his kind. My hand hesitated for a fraction of a second before continuing its work.

I glanced at the young man beneath my needle. "Why did you agree to this?" My voice was barely above a whisper, meant only for his ears.

He closed his eyes tightly for a moment before reopening them with resignation. "My sister... she's sick. Damien promised he'd help her."

His words were a punch to my gut. Damien had woven his web of promises and debts so intricately that even those who sought to escape found themselves more entangled.

"Done," I said finally, setting aside the machine and wiping away the excess ink to reveal the completed tattoo.

Damien pushed off from the doorframe and approached, examining my work with an unreadable expression. "Excellent," he murmured, but there was no warmth in his praise.

The young man sat up slowly, examining the mark now part of him forever. There was gratitude there, yes – but also horror at what he had become: a pawn in Damien's game.

I could see Tara's reflection in the mirror across the room; her disappointment mirrored my own self-loathing.

Damien turned his gaze to me as he escorted the client out of the room. "You've done well today," he said casually as if he hadn't just forced me to brand another soul with servitude.

Once they left, Tara stepped in, her brow furrowed with concern. "How long can you keep doing this?" she asked softly.

I shook my head, unable to meet her gaze. "I don't know."

We sat in silence for a moment before she spoke again. "You're not just your magic or your tattoos, Alex."

Her words stirred something within me – a flicker of defiance that refused to be snuffed out no matter how much darkness Damien cast over me.

I stood up abruptly, knocking over my stool in haste. "I need some air."

Outside Crimson Ink, I took deep breaths of city air – tainted as it was – and let it fill my lungs with something other than tension and dread.

The sun had begun its descent behind towering skyscrapers; its dying light painted everything in shades of gold and shadow. This city with its hidden magic and darker corners had always been home – now it felt like a prison.

I walked without direction until I found myself by an ancient oak in that forgotten park where Tara had once led me – where we discovered that source of power rooted deep within both the earth and ourselves.

Leaning against its rough bark, I let out a sigh that seemed to carry every burden I'd shouldered since meeting Damien.

"What are you willing to sacrifice?" The question wasn't new; it echoed through every decision I made these days. But tonight it bore extra weight because tonight there might be an answer waiting within reach if only I dared to grasp it.

Closing my eyes, I imagined not what Damien wanted from me but what I wanted for myself – for Crimson Ink – for every soul who sought sanctuary under my needle.

Survival had always been paramount – an instinct hardwired into every fiber of my being since childhood days spent tracing lines on paper while grandma whispered stories of our lineage laced with both wonder and warning.

But survival without principle was hollow existence; if I lost myself completely in this fight for power among creatures of night and shadow – what would be left worth saving?

My hand went to the amulet hanging around my neck – cold metal against warm skin – reminder of ties binding me tighter than any ink ever could.

As night fell around me and stars blinked into existence above city lights, determination solidified within me like ink setting into skin: I would not be complicit in this corruption any longer.

There had to be another way – one that didn't force me to trade pieces of my soul for fleeting safety or uncertain allegiance. And whatever that path might be – however treacherous or hidden from sight – it started with one step away from fear and toward something resembling hope.

* * *

The oak tree's ancient roots had always provided a sanctuary, a place where the city's noise faded into a hushed whisper, allowing my thoughts to unfurl. But as I stood there, Damien's latest demand weighing on my conscience, the serenity I sought eluded me. I couldn't shake the image of his cold, piercing eyes as he ordered me to ink yet another soul into servitude.

Tara's voice echoed in my mind, a stark reminder that I was edging closer to becoming what I despised. The night was still, save for the rustling leaves above me. Their dance seemed to mock my indecision.

I closed my eyes and let out a long breath, trying to center myself. The air carried the scent of damp earth and the faint trace of something else—a metallic tang that tingled at the back of my tongue. It was an aroma that didn't belong in this natural haven.

"Alex?" Tara's voice cut through the stillness.

I opened my eyes to find her approaching, her expression a blend of concern and determination. She held out her phone, its screen glowing with urgency.

"I think you need to see this," she said, pressing it into my hand.

On the screen was an article from one of those fringe websites that delved into supernatural conspiracies—the kind most people laughed off as fiction. But I knew better. The headline screamed about a recent spike in mysterious disappearances across the city, all linked to those bearing magical tattoos.

My stomach knotted as I read on. The article speculated about a vampire gang using these tattoos as trackers—binding their victims to them not just in service but in location too. A chill crept up my spine as I realized this could be Damien's true intention behind his insistence on me tattooing his symbol on people.

Tara watched me closely. "It can't be a coincidence, right? The tattoos you've been forced to make..."

I shook my head slowly, trying to piece it together. If Damien could track anyone through these tattoos... "It's like he's playing chess with lives as pawns."

We stood there for a moment, the gravity of our discovery sinking in. It wasn't just about control anymore; it was about domination on a scale I hadn't imagined.

"We need more than assumptions," I finally said. "We need proof."

With determination fueling our steps, we made our way back to Crimson Ink under the cloak of nightfall. Damien wouldn't be there at this hour; he preferred to conduct his business when the sun dipped below the horizon and shadows grew long.

The shop felt different as we entered—what once was a sanctuary for art and expression now seemed like a lair where dark schemes were hatched. We went straight for Damien's private room—the one place I'd always avoided out of fear of what I might find.

The door creaked open with our tentative push, revealing shelves lined with ancient texts and artifacts that thrummed with power. My gaze fell upon an ornate chest that sat atop a pedestal in the corner—a chest I had never seen before.

With Tara keeping watch at the door, I approached it cautiously. The chest bore symbols that resonated with an energy that felt familiar—like they were related to the tattoos I had been crafting under duress.

"Be careful," Tara whispered as I reached out to open it.

Inside lay a map marked with various locations across the city—locations that matched up with those mentioned in the article about disappearances. My breath hitched as I traced my finger over one particular spot—an area where several lines converged.

"It's a nexus," I murmured, more to myself than to Tara.

"A what?"

"A nexus—a point where multiple ley lines intersect," I explained quickly. "It amplifies magical energy."

"And if Damien is placing trackers on people…"

I nodded grimly. "He could be using them to harness energy from these nexuses… or worse."

Tara peered over my shoulder at the map, her brow furrowed in thought. "There's got to be something here we can use against him."

As we scanned through Damien's private documents—tomes filled with dark rituals and lists of names marked with cryptic symbols—I stumbled upon something unexpected: a series of letters between Damien and an unknown correspondent discussing something called "The Ascension Protocol."

My hands trembled slightly as I read through them. The letters spoke of a grand plan coming to fruition—a plan involving not just control over individuals but over entire supernatural factions within the city.

"They're planning something big," Tara said softly, having read over my shoulder. "Bigger than just tracking people."

It clicked then—the Mark of Power wasn't just about bestowing abilities or asserting dominance; it was about ascension—Damien's rise to unparalleled power among both humans and supernaturals alike.

The final piece fell into place when we found correspondence detailing a ritual tied to an upcoming celestial event—a lunar eclipse that would occur in just three days' time.

"He plans to use the eclipse...and the Mark..." My voice trailed off as horror washed over me.

"We have three days," Tara said firmly, snapping me out of my shock.

Three days to unravel Damien's scheme and prevent whatever catastrophe he intended to unleash upon our city—and potentially beyond its borders.

As we prepared to leave with all we could carry of Damien's hidden knowledge, an icy resolve settled over me. With every fiber of my being tingling with both fear and purpose, I knew what needed doing: it was time for Crimson Ink—and its artist—to fight back with every magical mark at our disposal.

Chapter 9

Allies in the Night

A chill brushed my neck as I locked the front door of Crimson Ink. The street, a normally vibrant artery of the city's nightlife, lay deserted under the cloak of midnight. I glanced around, a habit born from weeks of looking over my shoulder, feeling the weight of Damien's amulet against my chest—a constant reminder of the pact I never wanted.

The whisper came from the shadows, as soft as silk sliding across skin. "Alex."

I stiffened, turning to find a figure detached from the darkness of an alleyway. A hood obscured their face, and instinct told me to reach for the protection spells etched in ink on my forearms.

"Easy," they murmured, a hand emerging in a placating gesture. "I'm not here for trouble. Quite the opposite."

"Who are you?" My voice barely carried over the hum of distant traffic and the far-off wail of sirens.

"A friend," they replied, taking a cautious step forward. "Or at least an ally."

The moon peeked from behind a veil of clouds, casting enough light to reveal a glint in their eyes and a subtle nod toward the amulet at my neck. The Resistance—those who stood against Damien's rule and his ilk—was more than myth and rumor after all.

"Walk with me," they said.

I hesitated for only a heartbeat before falling into step beside them. We moved in silence, away from Crimson Ink and deeper into the labyrinthine heart of the city. Every footfall echoed like a heartbeat racing with trepidation and curiosity.

"You know who I am," I ventured as we turned down an alley lined with refuse bins and graffiti that told stories in coded signs only some could read.

"I do," they acknowledged. "And I know about Damien's leash on you."

The word 'leash' tightened around my throat like a noose, but I swallowed it down along with my pride. "So you've come to what? Offer me an out?"

"In a manner of speaking." They stopped before an unmarked door set into a wall that had seen better days. "What if I told you that you could use your gifts without being someone's pawn?"

I studied their silhouette, trying to discern their sincerity. "What's the catch?"

"No catch," they assured me. "Only mutual benefit."

"And if I say no?"

"The door remains open." They gestured toward the entrance beside us. "But opportunities like this don't linger."

With a creak that spoke volumes about its age and secrets, the door opened inward, spilling dim light onto cracked pavement. I hesitated on the threshold, feeling the divide between my known hell and this new uncertainty.

"Your choice, Alex."

Taking a breath that tasted of dust and diesel, I stepped inside.

The room was sparse—a single bulb hung from the ceiling, casting more shadows than light across concrete and exposed brick. A table sat at its center with two chairs opposite each other as if waiting for clandestine players in this game of chess.

"Sit," they invited.

I did so, keeping my senses alert for any hint of deception or danger while they remained standing like a sentinel against unknown threats.

"We're not so different," they began, pulling back their hood to reveal features sharpened by resolve and eyes that had seen too much yet refused to look away from what was necessary. Their face remained shrouded in darkness—security through anonymity.

"And yet we are," I countered softly.

"You bear your power on your skin; we carry ours in our hearts." They leaned forward slightly as if sharing a secret meant only for those who dared defy oppressive forces. "You seek balance; we fight for it."

"And what exactly does your resistance need from me?"

Their gaze held mine—a mirror reflecting shared battles fought in different arenas but with equal stakes at risk. "We need an artist whose ink can protect those who stand on the front lines against creatures like Damien."

I felt something shift inside me—the first fluttering beats of wings long caged by fear and obligation.

"You realize what you're asking?" My words hung between us like smoke in cold air.

"We do." They straightened again, resolute as stone but not without empathy—a duality that resonated with my own inner turmoil. "And we wouldn't ask if we didn't believe you capable."

The weight of their faith pressed against my chest—a burden or perhaps an armor against what loomed ahead; it was hard to tell which just yet.

"What would be expected of me?"

"To continue your craft," they said simply. "But for those who fight back."

The offer was seductive in its simplicity—a chance to wield my heritage not as a weapon for tyrants but as a shield for rebels.

"And Damien?" The name tasted bitter on my tongue—a poison I had no choice but to swallow each day under his thumb.

"We have plans for Damien." Their voice was steel wrapped in velvet—a promise or perhaps a warning; it was difficult to discern through the thumping pulse in my ears.

I leaned back in my chair, running ink-stained fingers through hair damp with sweat born not from heat but tension coiled tight as springs within me.

"I need time to think." It was both truth and stalling—a lifeline thrown into tumultuous waters where sharks circled beneath deceptively calm surfaces.

"You have until sunrise." The finality in their tone left no room for negotiation—an ultimatum served with precision that allowed no misinterpretation.

They turned then, cloak billowing behind them like dark wings unfurling against encroaching dawn's light creeping through fissures meant to keep daybreak at bay but failing just enough to remind us that time was both enemy and ally depending on one's position in this war hidden beneath veneers of normalcy we both understood were nothing more than fragile illusions waiting to shatter under truth's relentless pressure.

* * *

The moon, a pale eye in the sky, cast a weak glow over the city as I stood at the edge of the rooftop, pondering the stranger's offer. The Resistance — an elusive group I'd only heard whispers about, their existence like a shadow you can't quite catch sight of. And now, they'd stepped out of the dark, offering me a chance to join their fight against Damien and his iron grip on the city's supernatural underbelly.

My mind raced with questions as I waited for the promised meeting. Could I trust them? Could they trust me, given my forced allegiance to Damien? The amulet hanging heavily around my neck was a constant reminder of my bond to him. How could I explain that without sounding like a double agent?

The appointed hour arrived with the soft rustle of footsteps. Three figures emerged from the darkness, cloaked in anonymity. They stopped a few feet away, forming a loose semi-circle. I could feel their eyes on me, sizing me up — calculating my worth or threat.

"Alex?" The one in the middle stepped forward slightly, voice tinged with suspicion.

"That's me," I replied, my tone steady despite the unease knotting in my stomach.

"We're part of the Resistance," she said. "You can call me Lynx." Her hand rested on something beneath her jacket — likely a weapon or an artifact of some sort.

"And you came alone?" I asked, squinting to make out any hint of deception in her stance.

"Just like you did," another said from her left — a guy with a voice that seemed too calm for someone meeting a potential adversary.

"We know about your... situation with Damien," Lynx continued. "We also know about your gifts."

I took a deep breath. "And what exactly do you want from me?"

"Your skills," she said plainly. "Damien is planning something big. We need to counteract it before it's too late."

I could feel their mistrust as tangibly as the night air against my skin. But then again, my own suspicion mirrored theirs. If I was going to align myself with these people, I needed assurances — solid ground amidst this swamp of uncertainty.

"And what makes you think I won't turn you in to Damien?" My question hung between us like smoke, waiting for a wind to disperse it.

Lynx chuckled dryly. "Because if you were loyal to him, we wouldn't be having this conversation."

The third figure spoke up for the first time. "We've been watching you for some time now," she said with a hint of respect underlying her words. "You've managed to keep your core intact despite everything he's thrown at you."

My gaze shifted between them as they spoke. It was true; Damien had tried to shape me into his instrument — but at every turn, I had infused my work with subtle rebellions. Maybe they had seen that.

"How can I be sure this isn't some test of his? A way to gauge my loyalty?" My question was genuine; Damien had played such mind games before.

"You can't," Lynx admitted, and for a moment, her face softened under the hood. "But we're taking just as big a risk meeting you here."

Silence fell upon us again — heavy and expectant.

"Say I agree to help you," I ventured cautiously after what felt like an eternity. "What happens next?"

"We'll give you all we've got on Damien's plans," Lynx replied quickly as if she'd anticipated my conditional acceptance all along.

The man added, "We operate in cells; no one knows too much about the others."

"Compartmentalization," I nodded understandingly; it was smart given Damien's reach and resources.

"And how do we communicate? You must have some secure way?"

The third figure handed me a small device resembling an old pager. "Encrypted messages only," she explained briefly. "Only we have access to this channel."

I weighed the device in my hand, feeling its significance press into my palm — this was real now.

"You need to decide quickly," Lynx said after a pause that felt charged with urgency.

I looked at each of them in turn; they were warriors fighting for freedom while I had been caught in a web woven by fear and power plays. But here was an opportunity — not just for rebellion but redemption too.

"I'll help you," I stated firmly but kept going before they could react with either relief or joy. "On one condition: No one gets hurt because of me."

Their nods were curt and synchronized; our temporary alliance sealed by shared goals and mutual caution.

"We'll be in touch soon," Lynx said before turning away with her companions disappearing into the night just as silently as they'd arrived.

Left alone once more on that rooftop with nothing but thoughts and stars for company, I couldn't shake off the feeling that everything had changed yet again. The Resistance might have accepted me tentatively into their fold, but our initial encounter left no doubt that trust would have to be earned on both sides — through actions more than words.

For now, though, there was little else to do but wait for their signal and prepare myself for what lay ahead: learning their ways while keeping up appearances at Crimson Ink and planning how best to use my inked artistry against Damien's dark designs without tipping him off that his tattoo artist had just inked an alliance with his enemies.

* * *

The weight of the encrypted device in my pocket felt like a promise, a token of trust—or perhaps a reminder of the precarious edge on which I now balanced. The resistance had approached me with an offer I couldn't refuse, yet as I made my way through the labyrinth of streets to the designated meeting spot, a dilapidated warehouse at the edge of town, doubts gnawed at me. The place had a certain aura, one that whispered of clandestine gatherings and revolutions born from whispers.

I stepped inside, my senses immediately attuned to the scent of damp concrete and the faint hum of anticipation. A group huddled around a makeshift table laden with maps and photos. Among them was Lynx, their gaze sharp as ever.

"Alex," Lynx greeted with a nod, gesturing for me to join them. "Glad you could make it."

I pulled up a chair, the device in my pocket now burning against my thigh. "You know why I'm here," I started, cutting straight to the chase. "But before we dive into anything, I need to know more about what you're fighting for—and what's at stake."

Lynx exchanged looks with the others before speaking. "The vampire gang's grip on this city has to end," they began firmly. "They're not just feeding off people anymore; they're enslaving them—through fear, through magic, through tattoos that do more than just sit on your skin."

A woman with scars tracing her arms like vines chimed in. "They've got their fangs in every facet of life here—politics, businesses... no one's safe."

"And it's not just humans they control," added a man whose eyes held stories no words could fully capture. "Other supernatural beings suffer under their rule too."

My hand unconsciously traced the outline of the amulet beneath my shirt as I listened to their accounts—the corruption, the violence, the exploitation that seeped like poison through the city's veins.

"So where do I fit into all this?" I asked after a heavy silence fell upon us.

"You have a gift," Lynx said plainly. "One that could tip the scales in our favor. Damien knows it too—that's why he wants you on his leash."

The word 'leash' made my skin crawl, but I nodded for Lynx to continue.

"We've been looking for ways to counteract their magic," Lynx explained. "To protect our people from being marked by their control. Your tattoos... they could be our shield."

A shield... The idea resonated within me—a chance to use my art as a bastion against tyranny rather than an instrument of it.

"And how do you plan on taking them down?" I probed further.

A map spread across the table became the focus as another member stepped forward, her finger tracing lines that snaked across the paper—the ley lines I knew all too well.

"We've been monitoring their movements," she said. "They're planning something big for the lunar eclipse—something that involves those ley lines you're so familiar with."

"The Ascension Protocol," I murmured, remembering Tara's words and feeling a chill despite the stuffiness of the room.

"Yes," she confirmed. "We don't know exactly what it entails yet, but we suspect it's going to give Damien unprecedented power."

"We need to stop it before it starts," Lynx added gravely.

The conversation flowed like water—ebbing and weaving as we discussed strategies and shared knowledge. For every piece of information they offered, another puzzle piece clicked into place in my mind—the breadth of Damien's ambition was staggering.

As we talked through plans and contingencies, I found myself caught up in their fervor—a far cry from the hesitation that had shadowed my steps on the way here. These people were not soldiers by any conventional definition; they were survivors who had seen enough to take a stand.

One resistance member leaned back in his chair, eyeing me thoughtfully. "You know," he mused aloud, "it's funny how fate works sometimes—puts you right where you need to be."

I allowed myself a small smile at that. Maybe he was right; maybe there was some strange serendipity at play here.

"Can you tell me about those who have suffered under Damien's rule?" I asked after some time had passed—a part of me needing to understand more deeply whom we were fighting for.

The room grew quiet as if each person was sifting through countless tales of woe. Then slowly, stories began pouring out—tales of loved ones taken in the night never to return; children marked with symbols that left them hollow-eyed and obedient; communities torn apart by fear and mistrust sown by dark whispers.

Each account was like a shard of glass pressing against my heart—the cruelty they described was unbearable but also igniting an anger within me that was fierce and clear-cut.

As time ticked by unnoticed by us all, our gathering became more than just an exchange of plans—it transformed into something binding us together: common ground forged through shared outrage and hope.

And so we continued talking long into the night—the hum of determination never wavering—as if our very words were weaving together a new future—one where freedom wasn't just an abstract concept but something tangible we were willing to fight for with every breath in our bodies.

* * *

Lynx's words hung in the air like the scent of rain on concrete, potent with possibility and fraught with danger. The resistance had been nothing more than whispers, stories told in hushed tones behind closed doors. Now here they stood, tangible and fervent, extending a hand to pull me from the depths of my entanglement with Damien.

"We know you've got one foot in their world and one out the door," Lynx said, eyes sharp as the blade of a knife. "You're valuable to us, Alex. Not just for your ink."

The clandestine warehouse was cold, a vast space filled with the echo of our conversation. The Resistance members around me were an assortment of humans and beings whose auras shimmered with hidden strengths, their gazes assessing me with a mix of suspicion and hope.

I crossed my arms, ink-stained fingers tapping an anxious rhythm against my biceps. "I get why you'd think that," I began, my voice steady despite the tumult inside me. "But let's not pretend this isn't risky. Damien's not blind to betrayal."

"Neither are we," Raven interjected, stepping forward from the shadows. Their presence was a comfort and a reminder of the power coursing through my veins—a power that could tip scales or draw blood.

Lynx nodded at Raven's words, then refocused on me. "Risks? Sure, they're part of any game worth playing. But we're not playing games here, Alex. We're fighting for our lives—and yours."

Their conviction stirred something within me. The same spark that had ignited when I first felt the thrum of magic beneath my skin; it flared now with renewed vigor.

"And what exactly do you need from me?" I asked, trying to keep my voice neutral.

"We need your eyes and ears inside Crimson Ink," Lynx said, laying it bare. "Information is our ammunition."

The warehouse seemed to close in around us as I considered their proposal. Damien had always been two steps ahead—could I really manage to gather intel without tipping him off? The idea was daunting; it was like dancing on the edge of a knife.

"And what about protection?" I questioned. "If Damien gets wind of this..."

"We've got measures in place," Lynx assured me, but their words didn't quite reach my gut where fear gnawed at me like a hungry animal.

A sigh escaped me before I could cage it. I glanced around at the faces watching me—hopeful faces, hardened by loss and struggle.

"Say I agree to this," I said slowly. "What's your endgame? How does this all play out?"

Lynx exchanged looks with Raven before responding. "The Ascension Protocol—it's more than just a power grab. It's an anchor for Damien to exert control over every being in this city."

My stomach dropped at the revelation—Damien's ambition knew no bounds.

"So we stop him," I said quietly. "We stop the Protocol."

"That's right." Lynx's voice was steel wrapped in velvet.

I took a deep breath and released it slowly, feeling the weight of the amulet under my shirt—a constant reminder of Damien's hold over me.

"All right." The words tasted like metal on my tongue as I spoke them into existence. "I'm in."

A collective exhale rippled through the group like leaves in a gust of wind—relief mingled with resolve.

"We'll keep communication open," Lynx said, handing me a small device that fit snugly into my palm—a lifeline or perhaps a leash.

"Use it wisely," Raven added with an inscrutable look.

I nodded, pocketing the device as if it were just another tool of my trade. But we all knew it was more than that—it was a declaration.

The meeting disbanded soon after, leaving me alone with Raven under the dim warehouse lights.

"You did good," Raven said softly.

"I just hope I did right," I replied.

Their hand found my shoulder in a reassuring squeeze before they melted back into darkness—ever-present but always just out of reach.

The night air hit me like a splash of cold water as I stepped outside into the desolate alleyway that bordered the warehouse. The city sprawled out before me—my canvas and my cage—a place where shadows held secrets and every street corner could be a crossroads or a dead end.

As I walked back towards Crimson Ink, each step felt deliberate—like setting pieces on a chessboard where every move could be checkmate or catastrophe. My mind spun scenarios like spiderwebs—delicate but deceptively strong—their threads weaving together strategy and subterfuge.

Crimson Ink loomed ahead, its familiar gothic facade both welcoming and warning. Within its walls lay both sanctuary and snare; now more than ever, it was both home and battleground.

The bell above the door chimed as I entered—a sound that usually signaled beginnings but now felt like an omen.

Evelyn was there, her eyes meeting mine with an unreadable expression as she polished glasses behind the bar—an act so mundane amidst our secret war it bordered on absurdity.

"Late night?" she asked casually as if she didn't already know every step I took within these walls was monitored by unseen eyes—Damien's eyes.

"Just taking care of some personal business," I replied evenly while heading towards my workspace—a sanctum where ink flowed like truth and lies alike.

Evelyn nodded but said nothing more as she returned to her task—a silent sentinel whose loyalties were shrouded in shades of gray as deep as her vampire nature allowed.

* * *

I stood at the threshold of Crimson Ink, the tattoo parlor that was my refuge and now, my prison. The scent of ink and antiseptic hung in the air like a promise or a threat, depending on who walked through that door. The weight of Damien's amulet against my chest was a constant reminder of the tightrope I walked. As I arranged my tools for the day, the encrypted device Lynx had given me buzzed to life.

"Alex, we need to talk," Lynx's voice crackled through the static. "Meet us at the old textile factory on Fifth. Midnight."

The rest of the day passed in a blur of skin and ink. I marked people with symbols that meant freedom or bondage—never just ink on skin, not anymore. Each line I drew was a word in a story I didn't want to tell but had no choice but to narrate.

Midnight found me outside the derelict factory, shadows playing tricks with my mind. The building loomed like a specter from a bygone era, its broken windows like eyes watching me with suspicion.

Inside, the Resistance had set up a temporary base, shrouded in darkness except for the flickering lights casting long shadows across their faces. They gathered around a makeshift table strewn with maps and photos.

Lynx gestured for me to sit down. "You want to prove you're not under Damien's thumb? Here's your chance."

The task was simple yet daunting: create a magical tattoo for one of their own—a symbol that would allow them to move undetected by Damien and his gang. But it wasn't just any symbol; it was an ancient sigil that required channeling power from ley lines, something I'd never attempted outside the safety of Crimson Ink.

I swallowed hard, feeling my heartbeat drumming in my ears. "You realize this is new territory for me," I said, trying to keep my voice steady.

"We wouldn't ask if we didn't believe you could do it," Raven spoke up from the darkness, her voice both reassuring and commanding.

The Resistance member who needed the tattoo was introduced as Cipher—a man whose face was hidden beneath a hood. He stepped forward into the light, and as our eyes met, I saw desperation mingled with hope.

I nodded slowly. "When do we start?"

"Now," Lynx said. "Time is something we don't have much of."

The location chosen for this clandestine operation was an abandoned subway station beneath the city—neutral ground where ley lines converged. It felt like descending into Hades' realm as I followed Cipher down into the bowels of the earth.

The air grew cooler as we ventured deeper underground until we reached an open platform where graffiti murals waged silent wars on decaying walls. Here lay the pulse of magic that flowed unseen beneath the city's skin.

I unpacked my tools—needles, inks, and gloves—and then took out my sketchbook where I'd been designing and refining symbols for weeks now. Symbols that held power if drawn correctly... if channeled correctly.

Cipher removed his hood and shirt, revealing his back to me—a canvas marred by scars but ready for transformation. As he lay down on an improvised table made from wooden planks and crates, I traced the sigil onto his skin with practiced precision.

"Ready?" I asked.

He nodded without speaking.

The hum of my tattoo machine filled the silence between us as I began etching lines into Cipher's skin—the sigil slowly taking form under my hand while I focused on drawing power from the ley lines around us.

It wasn't easy—the energy resisted like a wild horse refusing to be tamed—but bit by bit, I coaxed it into Cipher's skin alongside ink infused with herbs and whispered spells. Sweat beaded on my forehead; each line demanded concentration beyond what any normal tattoo required.

The sigil began to glow faintly with each pass of my needle—an eerie light in the darkened subway station that felt like victory and danger all at once.

Cipher clenched his teeth but didn't make a sound as magic infused his very being. And then it was done—a glowing symbol upon his back that pulsed softly with its own life force.

I slumped back in exhaustion, watching Cipher rise and examine his new mark in a shard of broken mirror. His eyes met mine in reflection—gratitude there but also something else... resolve?

"You've done well," Lynx's voice echoed around us as she stepped out from where she'd been observing silently in the shadows. "But there's more at stake than just evading Damien."

I knew she was right; this wasn't just about slipping past one vampire gang leader's notice—it was about claiming back our city from those who sought to control it through fear and magic bound in flesh.

"You'll need rest," Raven advised as she approached us both with a concerned gaze. "But know this: you've taken your first step towards something greater than any of us imagined."

As we emerged from underground with dawn's first light painting streaks across the sky, there was no fanfare or cheers—only silent nods between those who now shared more than secrets; we shared a bond forged in ink and magic.

Lynx handed me back my encrypted device before departing with Cipher into the morning haze—promises of contact soon to come whispered on their lips.

Walking back toward Crimson Ink, fatigue weighed heavy on my limbs but inside surged an unfamiliar sense of purpose—an ember of defiance stoked into flame by my own hands. And yet uncertainty shadowed every step because even as one battle ended tonight... another loomed just over the horizon.

* * *

The Resistance's abandoned factory was cold, the kind of cold that seeped into your bones, reminding you of the grave. Lynx paced before me, their eyes alight with a fire that spoke of battles past and the promise of skirmishes to come. Cipher leaned against a concrete pillar, their newly inked sigil beneath their shirt—a silent sentinel guarding secrets not even I fully understood.

"You're in, then?" Lynx's voice cut through the stillness like a knife.

I glanced at the device they'd given me—compact, unassuming, a lifeline in a sea of treachery. "I'm in," I said, feeling the weight of my words. "But if we're doing this, we need to be smart. Damien's got eyes and ears everywhere."

Cipher nodded, pulling out a map littered with scribbles and markers. "We've got intel on some of his operations—places where they gather, routes they take."

I took the map, studying it as if it were one of my tattoo designs. The ley lines I knew so well snaked across it, intersecting with points marked by Cipher's careful hand.

"We need to hit them where it hurts," I murmured, tracing a line from Crimson Ink to an area marked as a frequent haunt for Damien's acolytes.

Lynx arched an eyebrow. "And how do you propose we do that?"

"Information is power," I replied. "We gather intel on their movements, their plans. We find out where they're vulnerable."

"And how do we get this information?" Cipher asked skeptically.

I couldn't help but smile. "We use what I know best—tattoos." I pulled out my sketchbook, flipping through pages until I found what I was looking for—a design that could easily be passed off as a new trend but was laced with magic that would make anyone wearing it more inclined to share secrets.

Lynx's eyes widened. "You can do that?"

"It's risky," I warned them. "But if we can get these tattoos on some key people without raising suspicion..."

"It could give us the edge we need," Cipher finished.

"We start small," I suggested. "A few tattoos here and there—nothing that'll make Damien suspect a thing."

The three of us huddled over the map and my designs as plans began to take shape—the start of our strategy to undermine the vampire gang's operations without drawing unwanted attention.

Hours slipped by as we plotted and planned. My fingers grew cramped from sketching potential tattoo placements and sigils; my mind raced with possibilities and dangers alike.

Lynx stood abruptly, breaking our concentration. "We'll need allies—people on the inside who can help spread these tattoos."

"I might know someone," I admitted hesitantly.

Cipher raised an eyebrow in question.

"Jade," I said simply. My old friend had her own reasons for despising Damien's influence over the city.

"Can she be trusted?" Lynx asked pointedly.

"With my life," I assured them without hesitation.

"Then it's settled." Lynx extended their hand toward me. "We work together to bring down Damien and his gang."

I clasped their hand firmly, feeling the pulse of shared resolve between us. We were more than individuals now; we were a collective force rising against the shadows.

I stood there with Lynx and Cipher in that desolate warehouse, feeling like the hero in some grand tale—except this was no storybook legend; this was my reality, fraught with peril at every turn.

The first rays of dawn crept through cracks in the walls as we finalized our initial steps. A sense of camaraderie warmed me against the lingering chill as we agreed to meet again under cover of nightfall to initiate our plan—one tattoo at a time.

Chapter 10

The Cost of Power

The neon sign of Crimson Ink buzzed like a dormant wasp waiting for the right moment to sting. I flicked it off, the silence afterward feeling heavier than the sound itself. Inside, the air clung to my skin, saturated with the metallic tang of ink and the residual magic that seemed to seep from the walls. As I tidied up after a long day of needling skin and weaving spells, I couldn't shake off the feeling that each tattoo I crafted under Damien's orders left a darker imprint on my conscience.

I pulled out the broom to sweep away the day's debris when something caught my eye—a glint of something beneath one of the plush client chairs. I bent down, sweeping aside loose hairs and scraps of paper until my fingers brushed against something cool and hard. It was a pendant, shaped like an eye, its center a polished black stone that seemed to drink in the light. I knew this pendant; it belonged to one of Damien's clients who had come in last week for an enchanted tattoo.

Curiosity nudged me deeper as I turned it over in my hand, remembering how that same client had left with more than just fresh ink—a look of subdued terror had lurked in their eyes as they exited through the door. That same fear now reflected back at me from the polished stone.

The bell above the door jingled and in came Jade, her expression grim. "We've got a problem," she said without preamble.

"What kind of problem?" My voice was steadier than I felt.

"Follow me," she urged.

We navigated through darkened alleys until we reached an apartment complex that had seen better days. Jade led me up a narrow staircase to room 307 and knocked softly. The door creaked open, revealing a gaunt figure with sunken eyes that darted nervously behind us before gesturing us inside.

I didn't need an introduction to recognize one of my canvases—Markus. His arms were etched with tattoos I had inked under duress, each symbol a shackle linking him to Damien's will.

"Show him," Jade whispered.

Markus rolled up his sleeve, revealing one of the tattoos—a serpent coiled around his forearm. The scales shimmered with an eerie light that wasn't just from the dim bulb overhead.

"It burns," he rasped. "It feels like it's... alive."

My heart sank as he described sensations no ink should cause: whispers at night filling his head with commands, an incessant itch beneath his skin where the serpent lay. The magic imbued in his tattoo was supposed to grant strength, not subjugate him to madness.

"Can you do anything?" Jade asked, her voice taut with concern.

I examined Markus' arm closely. The enchanted ink radiated a malevolent aura that shouldn't have been there if done properly—this was a perversion of my art. It dawned on me then; these tattoos weren't just marking territory or showing loyalty—they were meant to dominate mind and body alike.

"We have to get these off him," I said resolutely, already mentally sifting through counter-spells and salves that might soothe the cursed ink.

But it wasn't just Markus—there were others like him out there, branded by my hand at Damien's behest, suffering in silence or unaware of their slow descent into thrall-dom.

"We'll need help," Jade said as if reading my thoughts. "This is bigger than just one or two unfortunate souls."

Back at Crimson Ink, I couldn't sit still. The pendant weighed heavily in my pocket like a leaden secret as Jade and I poured over old grimoires and texts on magical tattoos for any mention of reversal or purification rituals.

There had to be something we could do—some way to undo what had been done—but as hours slipped into night without any concrete answers, doubt crept into every crack in my resolve.

Then Lynx called; they needed another batch of espionage tattoos for the Resistance by tomorrow night. They didn't know about Markus or what these tattoos could really do—how they could turn someone into nothing more than a puppet writhing on unseen strings.

I bit back a sigh as I took down their order—each tattoo now felt like an ethical minefield where one wrong step could spell disaster for someone else's life.

"I've got some ideas," Tara whispered when Lynx's call ended. She'd been quiet all evening, her eyes scanning pages until they were red-rimmed and tired. "But we're going to need time... and trust."

Trust—the very thing Damien had shredded when he forced me into his service—the thing I was asking these people marked by pain and fear to give me as I tried desperately to untangle them from his web.

Tara laid out her plan: we'd start with Markus, using some untested spells combined with good old-fashioned tattoo removal techniques—a mix of science and sorcery that made me anxious yet hopeful.

We worked through the night until dawn painted faint streaks across the sky. With every piece of evidence we gathered—the physical scars left by enchanted ink gone rogue, the psychological toll on those who bore them—it became clearer that Damien wasn't just building an army; he was forging chains with every drop of ink spilled in his name.

I sat alone as Tara left to get some rest, staring at my own hands—these hands that held so much power yet felt so helpless against this tide of darkness we were facing.

The weight of responsibility settled on my shoulders like an unwelcome cloak as I pondered our next move. How many more were out there suffering because of these tattoos? How many lives had been altered—twisted—by promises etched in ink?

This was no longer just about defying Damien or protecting Crimson Ink; it was about salvaging souls from his insidious grasp—one painstaking stroke at a time.

* * *

The clock ticked past midnight, the neon sign of Crimson Ink bled red into the murky darkness. A clandestine hush blanketed the shop as I prepped my station for a procedure I wished I could refuse. Damien had ordered an enchanted tattoo for one of his underlings—a symbol of loyalty that ran deeper than ink in skin. It was dark magic, a realm I ventured into with trepidation.

A hulking figure slouched into the chair across from me, his eyes a pair of hollow pits, seeking either salvation or doom—I couldn't tell which. "Just make it quick," he grumbled, a tinge of fear lacing his voice.

I nodded, my hands steady despite the storm raging in my gut. The design was intricate, an ouroboros consuming its own tail—an endless cycle of servitude and rebirth. With each line I etched, the tattoo needle buzzed like a harbinger of the sinister pact being forged. I felt the power of ley lines coursing through me, converging at the point of my needle to imbue this man with a curse disguised as allegiance.

The room's air grew dense as if reality itself thickened to witness this unholy sacrament. My hand moved with practiced precision, but my heart raced against it—this was not what my art was meant for.

The man's skin rippled with each stroke, and shadows gathered around us like spectators drawn to a spectacle of horror. With every completed loop of the ouroboros, his muscles tensed, his breath grew ragged—a physical manifestation of his spirit being shackled.

As I filled in the scales of the serpent, a faint glow began to emanate from beneath its inked flesh. It was as if I had opened a vein and instead of blood, there flowed an ethereal luminescence. The light twisted and writhed within the confines of my artistry, seeking escape or perhaps dominion over its new host.

He clenched his jaw, veins bulging on his forehead as if fighting an internal battle against an invading force. A low growl escaped his lips, primal and pained—a sound no human throat should ever make.

"Don't fight it," Damien's voice slithered into the room from where he leaned against the doorway, eyes gleaming with cruel satisfaction. "The more you resist, the more it'll hurt."

I wanted to protest, to scream that this wasn't protection but subjugation. Yet words clung to my tongue like traitors too cowardly to leap into battle.

As I drew the final curve to complete the circle, an invisible force slammed into us. The man arched his back in agony as though unseen talons dug into his flesh to claim their due. A twisted symphony of whispers filled the air—promises or threats? I couldn't discern.

The glow intensified until it blazed like a star born from darkness—a perverse beacon heralding submission and power entwined in one. Then just as suddenly as it had flared up, it dimmed and disappeared beneath his skin which now bore only a stark black tattoo.

He slumped forward, sweat drenching his brow and breathing labored as if he had run through every nightmare that ever plagued him.

"Welcome to the fold," Damien murmured with a cold smile that didn't reach his eyes.

I stood back from my workbench feeling like an accomplice in something unforgivable—a puppet whose strings had been pulled to dance on command.

"Is it done?" The man's voice was weak but edged with newfound resolve—or perhaps resignation to his fate.

"Yes," I confirmed with reluctance heavy on my tongue.

His eyes met mine for a moment—no longer hollow but alight with an ember that wasn't there before—an ember that flickered with Damien's essence rather than his own fire.

As he left my chair and staggered out of Crimson Ink, shadow seemed to cling to him like a second skin—one that whispered secrets and strategies known only to those who dwelt in darkness.

Damien approached me then; our gazes locked in silent confrontation—a test of wills between jailer and reluctant jailbird.

"You've outdone yourself tonight," he said flatly. But behind those words lurked something unsaid—an acknowledgment that even though he held sway over me now, there might come a time when I'd be beyond even his reach.

With nothing left to say—or perhaps too much held back—I watched him leave before collapsing into my chair; the exhaustion wasn't just physical but etched deep within my soul. My hand trembled slightly—not from exertion but from dread for what lay ahead.

Tara entered then; her presence always seemed to cut through chaos like sunlight piercing clouds. "You okay?" Her question was simple yet loaded with layers that reached far beneath surface wounds.

"No," I admitted because lying would only add another layer of shadow where light was needed most. "But we'll get through this."

Her nod was solemn; together we'd face whatever twisted roads lay before us—with ink and will as our weapons against encroaching night.

* * *

The weight of the ouroboros tattoo bore down on me long after the ink had dried and the underling had left Crimson Ink. The symbol, meant to represent eternal cycles, now twisted in my mind into a shackle, binding another soul to Damien's sinister will. As I cleaned my tools, the metallic scent of blood mixed with the sterile tang of disinfectant, a ritual that usually calmed me only heightened my anxiety.

Tara stood by the door, her eyes a mirror to my turmoil. "Alex, you can't keep doing this. You're not just putting ink on skin—you're chaining them."

Her words echoed in my head as I scrubbed harder. I knew she was right. Each line I etched became a link in an invisible chain, and Damien held the other end. It was as if I was stitching them into his tapestry of control with every drop of ink that penetrated their skin.

But what choice did I have? Damien's amulet, heavy against my chest, served as a constant reminder of our bargain—my protection for my compliance. Yet protection felt more like imprisonment with each passing day.

I took a deep breath and looked at Tara. "I'm aware, but if I refuse..."

She cut me off with a raised hand. "I know the risks, but this—this is changing you."

Was it? My mind flashed back to my grandmother's teachings—how tattoos were more than art; they were connections to the soul. And here I was, abusing that sacred bond for fear of what might happen if I didn't.

That night at home, I sat amidst piles of ancient texts and sketches that littered my floor like autumn leaves around an old oak tree. The room was silent except for the scratch of my pen and the occasional turn of a page. Research had always been a refuge for me—a way to escape into history and lore—but not tonight. Tonight it felt like digging through the remnants of who I used to be before Damien's shadow fell over Crimson Ink.

A soft knock at the door broke my concentration. It was Jade, her face etched with concern.

"Alex, we need to talk," she said as she stepped inside.

She didn't wait for an invitation; Jade never did. Her presence was a gust of fresh air in the stifling confines of my predicament.

"What is it?" I asked, already bracing myself for more bad news.

"It's about the tattoos—the ones you're giving out under Damien's orders." She paused as if searching for words that wouldn't wound me further. "They're doing more than just binding people to him."

My heart sank. "What do you mean?"

Jade took a seat across from me and sighed. "I've been tracking some of your clients—those who've received those tattoos—and they're changing, Alex."

I frowned, not following her train of thought.

"They're becoming aggressive, erratic... It's like their free will is eroding away."

The revelation hit me like a punch to the gut. Not only was I marking people for Damien's cause, but now it seemed that these tattoos were altering them fundamentally.

I buried my face in my hands. This was beyond moral dilemmas; this was a question of humanity—of what made us who we are.

"Can we reverse it?" My voice was muffled by my palms.

Jade reached out and gently pulled my hands away from my face. "Maybe," she said softly. "But we'll need time and resources—things we don't have much of."

The idea sparked something within me—a flicker of rebellion that had been smothered under fear and obligation.

"We'll find a way," I said with more conviction than I felt.

Jade nodded and stood up to leave. "I'll do what I can from my end."

Alone again, surrounded by arcane knowledge that suddenly felt alien to me, I pondered our next move. How many people had I marked? How many lives had I unknowingly damaged? The thought made me sick.

Tara's warning rang clear now: 'This is changing you.' But perhaps there was still time—to change back or to change course entirely.

Over the next few days at Crimson Ink, each client that came in for one of Damien's tattoos weighed heavily on me—a moral anchor dragging me down into dark waters where guilt and responsibility churned relentlessly.

One afternoon as I prepared my station for another one of these sessions, Evelyn sauntered in with her usual air of indifference masking something sharper underneath.

"You're quiet today," she remarked casually as she leaned against the counter where rows of ink bottles glinted under harsh fluorescent lights.

"I'm focusing," I lied without looking up from arranging my needles.

Evelyn chuckled darkly. "On your art or your conscience?"

Her question struck too close to home, sending ripples through the calm façade I struggled to maintain.

"Both," I admitted after a pause heavy enough to drown words unsaid between us.

Evelyn studied me for a moment before pushing off from the counter and strolling toward one of Damien's waiting underlings—a canvas prepped for another binding symbol.

"You should be careful," she said without turning back to look at me. "Damien doesn't take kindly to hesitation."

I watched her walk away and turned back to my workbench where empty skin awaited its mark—the mark that would draw another person into our dark dance with destiny.

Each drop of ink became a question: What price am I willing to pay? Each line drawn asked: How far am I willing to go?

The hum of the tattoo machine filled the silence between client breaths and thoughts too loud within my own head—a symphony playing out in shades of black and gray.

And so there I stood at a crossroads within myself—the artist versus the accomplice—while outside forces moved pieces in a game where human lives were currency.

It was in this tangled web that another figure entered Crimson Ink—a stranger with an offer that promised redemption or ruin in equal measure.

***

The bell above the door jangled, slicing through the buzz of my tattoo machine. I glanced up, wiping ink from my fingers. A young woman stood in the doorway, her eyes darting around Crimson Ink like a cornered animal. She looked familiar, but her name escaped me in the haze of faces I'd inked over the years.

"Can I help you?" I called out, setting aside my tools.

She approached my station with hesitant steps. "I... I think I have one of your tattoos," she murmured, voice trembling like a leaf in the wind.

Her sleeve rolled up with a quiver, revealing an ouroboros writhing around her forearm – not just an image, but a living shadow that seemed to pulse with a dark life of its own. My heart sank; it was one of Damien's designs. One meant to bind and control.

"That's... one of mine," I admitted, my throat tight with guilt. "What's happening to you?"

She bit her lip, struggling with words as if each one was a shard of glass. "It's like... like I'm not myself anymore. I do things—terrible things—without thinking. It whispers to me, promises power but takes everything."

Her eyes met mine, brimming with silent pleas for salvation. The shop felt suddenly colder, as if her despair had seeped into its bones.

"I'm sorry," I whispered, knowing how inadequate it sounded.

"I know you're caught up in this too," she said with surprising clarity. "But you can stop it, can't you? You have to."

The weight of her expectation bore down on me like an anchor to the soul. She saw me as more than an artist – a liberator, perhaps – and that shook me to my core.

"I'll do what I can," I promised, though the path ahead was shrouded in uncertainty.

She nodded and pulled down her sleeve as if covering the tattoo could silence its siren call. "Thank you," she said before turning away, leaving me with a reflection of what my work had become – chains rather than freedom.

As she left, Tara entered through the back door, her expression somber. "That was Emily," she said softly as if reading my thoughts. "She was in your chair three months ago."

Recognition dawned on me; Emily had been vibrant then, full of life and laughter. Now she was a husk haunted by shadows.

"What are we going to do?" Tara asked.

I looked down at my hands – these hands that had brought art to life and now bound souls to darkness.

"We fight back," I declared with newfound resolve.

Tara nodded firmly and together we turned toward the battle ahead.

* * *

The evening swallowed the day whole, the kind of darkness that blankets the city in a hush. The neon sign of Crimson Ink buzzed like a lone firefly against the night. Inside, my hands shook as I cleaned my equipment, each clink of metal a reminder of the tattoos I'd etched that bound souls to Damien's will.

I had to talk to someone, get this weight off my chest that was crushing me from the inside out. I picked up my phone and dialed Lynx, my voice a mere whisper when he answered.

"Meet me at The Roost? It's urgent."

His reply came quick and sharp. "Ten minutes."

The Roost was our code for the rooftop where we first plotted against Damien. The city stretched out below it, an expanse of secrets and lives intertwining like the threads of a tapestry.

Lynx was there when I arrived, his silhouette carved against the skyline. He turned, his face coming into view as I approached.

"You look like hell," he said without preamble.

I exhaled a laugh that held no humor. "Feel like it too."

We sat on the edge, our legs dangling over the side as we shared the silence for a moment. Then I let it all spill out—the ouroboros tattoos, Emily's desperation, Tara's concern—and how every stroke of ink felt like a betrayal to my own soul.

Lynx listened, his gaze fixed on the city below. When I finished, he spoke, his voice soft but fierce.

"Damien's been playing god with people's lives for too long."

I nodded. "And I've been his unwilling disciple." The admission tasted bitter on my tongue.

"But you've got power too," Lynx reminded me. "Your ink doesn't just bind; it can protect, empower... free."

A shiver ran down my spine as his words stirred something within me—a glimmer of hope amidst the dread.

"I want to use my abilities for something good," I said, more to myself than to him. "But every time I try to push back..."

"He pushes harder," Lynx finished for me.

I looked at him then, really looked at him. The resolve in his eyes mirrored my own—the same fire that had driven us both into this resistance.

"We'll find a way," he said with certainty. "We're going to hit Damien where it hurts most—his pride and his power."

"How?" The word was a lifeline thrown into turbulent waters.

"We've got people everywhere—inside his operations, in places he thinks are under his thumb." Lynx's mouth curved into a wry smile. "He's not as untouchable as he believes."

The thought of turning the tables on Damien sparked something rebellious within me—a surge of defiance against the fear that had been gnawing at my insides.

"And what about Emily? And all those like her?" My voice broke on their names.

Lynx reached into his jacket and pulled out a small vial filled with a luminescent liquid—the color of moonlight captured in glass.

"We think this is the key—an antidote to counteract Damien's dark magic." He rolled it between his fingers before offering it to me. "Jade's been working on it; she believes in its power."

I took it from him, feeling its coolness seep into my palm.

"Can it really free them?" The question was barely audible over the thrumming of blood in my ears.

"We have to believe it can." Lynx stood up and offered me a hand. "Are you with us?"

Taking his hand, I pulled myself up to stand beside him—unsteady but resolute.

"I'm with you," I said, tucking the vial safely away. "But we need more than hope; we need a plan."

Lynx nodded toward the labyrinthine streets below us. "We're gathering intelligence—every scrap we can get our hands on about Damien's next move."

"And then?"

"We strike at The Ascension Protocol—disrupt whatever he has planned for this lunar eclipse."

A shudder ran through me at the mention of Damien's mysterious scheme.

"What do you need from me?" My question was an anchor grounding me amidst the storm brewing within.

"Keep doing what you're doing at Crimson Ink." Lynx turned to face me squarely now. "But infuse your work with countermeasures—symbols of rebellion and freedom hidden in plain sight."

My heart pounded at the audacity of it—to deceive Damien under his very nose.

"Will it be enough?" Doubt clawed its way back into my throat.

"It has to be." Lynx clasped my shoulder with an assurance that felt solid and real—a stark contrast to everything else teetering on uncertainty.

He checked his watch then, signaling our time was running short.

"I have to go; they'll be expecting me soon." His tone left no room for questions about where 'they' might be or what dangers awaited him there.

"One more thing," I called after him as he began to retreat toward the stairwell access door.

He paused, half-turned toward me.

"Thank you," I said simply because gratitude was all I had left to offer amidst this chaos we were wading through together—a beacon flickering faintly in the dark.

Lynx gave a nod that seemed both acknowledgment and farewell before disappearing down into the stairwell, leaving me alone with the city and its secrets once more.

* * *

The heavy door to Crimson Ink closed with a soft click, sealing off the night's chill. Damien and his entourage had left, their departure as enigmatic as their presence. In the silence that followed, the hum of the neon sign outside seemed to grow louder, a buzzing reminder of the turmoil that had just vacated the space.

I stood there for a moment, letting the quiet wash over me, feeling the weight of the amulet against my chest—a constant reminder of the bind I was in. The night had been a torrent of coded conversations and veiled threats, each interaction with Damien's gang like a chess move in a game I barely understood. But as I wiped down the counter for the last time that evening, my thoughts began to crystallize into something resembling determination.

I was done being a pawn.

Tara lingered by the shop's entrance, her eyes scanning mine for signs of my internal tempest. "Alex," she said softly, her voice cutting through my reverie.

I met her gaze and offered a weary smile. "It's alright," I lied. It wasn't alright—far from it—but admitting vulnerability wasn't an option when you were in my shoes.

She crossed her arms and leaned against the wall, skepticism written all over her face. "We can't keep going like this," she murmured. "You can't keep going like this."

She was right. The tattoos I'd been crafting under duress were not just marks on skin; they were chains binding souls to Damien's will. Each one was a stain on my conscience, a deviation from the craft I loved and respected. And while each session with Damien's minions left me feeling more trapped, it also stoked a fire within me—a burning need to reclaim control over my art and my life.

"Then we won't," I said with more confidence than I felt. "We're going to fight back."

Tara straightened up, hope flickering in her eyes like the first light of dawn breaking through darkness. "What do you have in mind?"

I began to pace around the room, my thoughts racing as I tried to piece together a plan from the fragments of possibilities that lay scattered in my mind. "Damien thinks he's got me cornered," I started, "thinks that he can use my tattoos as his personal brand of control."

"And?" Tara prompted when I paused.

"And he's underestimating what these tattoos can really do." My voice grew stronger as conviction took hold. The tattoos weren't just emblems of servitude; they could be vessels of liberation if wielded correctly.

"We know he's planning something big with this Ascension Protocol—something tied to the ley lines and the lunar eclipse." The words tumbled out now as ideas began connecting like dots in one of my intricate designs. "If we can find out exactly what he's aiming for, we might be able to throw a wrench in his plans."

Tara nodded slowly, absorbing each word. "You think you can alter the tattoos? Make them work against him?"

"Not just alter them." A smile tugged at my lips—a genuine one this time—as an audacious idea took shape. "We could create new ones—tattoos that empower instead of enslave."

My hands itched for my sketchbook; ideas for designs were already blooming in my head like night-blooming flowers reaching for moonlight. Tattoos imbued with subtle magic that could shield minds from Damien's influence or enhance strength without succumbing to his control.

Tara watched me closely, trying to follow where my train of thought was headed. "But how are you going to do that without him noticing?"

"That's where it gets tricky." My fingers traced over the countertop as if they were drawing out plans on invisible parchment. "I'll have to be careful—craft them during regular appointments, maybe even pretend they're part of Damien's orders."

Tara's eyes narrowed in thought before she added, "And we'll need allies—people who can wear these tattoos and stand against Damien when the time comes."

"Allies..." The word resonated with me; it wasn't just about standing up to Damien anymore—it was about building something bigger than myself or Crimson Ink.

"We've got Lynx and Cipher from the Resistance," Tara continued, "and Jade's always been reliable."

"Jade..." My mind flickered back to earlier conversations with her—the concern in her voice when she spoke about Damien's growing influence and her unwavering support for what Crimson Ink stood for.

"Yeah," I said slowly, a plan starting to take solid form in my mind. "Jade has connections throughout the city—artists and clients who trust her."

"We need someone on the inside too," Tara added cautiously. "Someone who knows Damien's operations intimately."

The name sprang forth unbidden: Evelyn. She'd been there from the start, always lurking at Damien's side but never fully committed to his cause—or so it seemed from her veiled warnings and ambiguous loyalties.

"She could be our wildcard," I murmured aloud.

"Are you sure we can trust her?" Tara's brow furrowed.

I shook my head slightly—not in disagreement but in acknowledgment of the risk involved. "We don't have much choice."

There was silence then as we both considered what lay ahead—a daunting undertaking fraught with danger at every turn.

I picked up my sketchbook and flipped it open to a blank page; it was time for new beginnings—for symbols that spoke not just of defiance but of hope too.

"I'll start tonight," I declared with resolve as I began sketching out rough outlines on paper—the beginnings of an insurrection inked into existence.

As dawn approached and exhaustion tugged at every fiber of my being, there was no turning back now; I had made my choice—to stand against oppression and fight for freedom through every line etched into skin by Crimson Ink.

Chapter 11

Temptations of the Mark

T he day bled into evening as I closed the last book on the Mark of Power. I'd read every volume that whispered its name, traced every symbol associated with its legend. It was a tattooist's myth, an artist's holy grail – and I had thought it nothing more than a tale to awe aspiring inkers. Yet, as the day waned, I found myself sitting in the dim light of my apartment, surrounded by ancient texts that confirmed its existence.

My hands trembled slightly as I placed the last dusty tome back onto the shelf. The air felt thick with knowledge, and the weight of it pressed down on me, heavier than Damien's amulet that hung around my neck. My mind spun with images of the Mark - an intricate design, its lines flowing like water yet sharp as a blade's edge.

The sound of a knock broke my reverie. I opened the door to find Raven standing there, his cloak billowing slightly as if caught in a wind that wasn't there.

"I see you've done your homework," he said, his voice echoing a calm that didn't reach his eyes.

I stepped aside to let him in, feeling the air shift as he crossed my threshold. He walked straight to my desk and spread out a parchment - one I hadn't seen before - marked with symbols and diagrams.

"This is what you're looking for," he said, tapping the paper with a long finger.

The parchment detailed the Mark of Power in ways no book had described. It wasn't just an amulet or a tattoo; it was a convergence, a living spell woven into ink and skin. According to the parchment, the Mark could amplify one's innate abilities to unfathomable levels, bending elements, summoning creatures from other planes, even warping time and space at its bearer's will.

Raven pointed to each symbol explaining their function and how they connected to form the Mark's full potential. "It's not just power that it grants," he murmured. "It binds you to the very fabric of magic itself."

My head spun with each revelation. The potential was unimaginable – but so were the dangers. Each symbol carried risks: madness from too much knowledge; destruction wrought from uncontrolled power; a life force drained by continuous use.

"It's incredible," I breathed out, unable to tear my gaze away from the parchment.

Raven nodded. "Yes, but it's also a curse as much as it is a blessing." His voice was solemn now. "The Mark feeds on your essence; it can consume you if you're not careful."

I looked up at him sharply. "Consume me?"

He nodded again. "Your life energy becomes part of the Mark – part of its power source. The more you use it, the more it demands."

I swallowed hard, trying to process what that meant for me – for anyone who bore this tattoo. To hold such power and yet be held by it...it was both enthralling and terrifying.

"We need to ensure Damien never finds this," I said after a moment of heavy silence.

"That's why I'm here," Raven replied. "You have the skill to create it but also the wisdom to understand why you never should."

My heart raced at his implication. "You want me to make sure no one can complete this Mark?"

"Exactly." Raven folded up the parchment carefully and tucked it inside his cloak.

"But how?" I asked, panic edging into my voice. The idea of carrying such responsibility was daunting.

"You'll find a way," he said with confidence that seemed misplaced in me.

His belief in me was unnerving; did he not understand how fragile my control over my own fate felt? Yet there was something empowering about being entrusted with such a task.

We spent hours discussing strategies – how to protect the knowledge without wielding its power directly – until Tara knocked on my door.

"Hey," she greeted us with a concerned frown as she took in our serious faces and the strewn-about books. "What's going on?"

Raven looked at me, giving me a silent nod before vanishing into thin air - his usual dramatic exit leaving Tara wide-eyed in surprise.

I cleared my throat. "It's about Damien and his search for something...dangerous."

Tara stepped closer, her expression turning grave as she caught on to my meaning without another word spoken between us.

"We have work to do," she said simply.

And work we did – through nights that turned into mornings and back into nights again. We poured over every text related to magical tattoos and wards against dark enchantments until our eyes burned from fatigue.

Then came breakthroughs - subtle alterations within traditional designs that could counteract some effects of Damien's dark magic without revealing our hand too soon; glyphs hidden within mundane tattoos capable of safeguarding their bearers from Damien's reach; each discovery like a piece of armor forged for an unseen war brewing beneath city lights and shadowed alleys.

Every tattoo I etched from then on became both shield and sword - symbols disguised within dragons' wings or roses' petals but holding powers that even Damien would struggle against should he ever attempt to wield the Mark through someone else's skin.

But amidst this quiet rebellion bloomed fear – fear of what might happen if Damien discovered our plans or if we failed altogether; fear that maybe we were playing with forces too vast for us to comprehend or control.

Yet there was no turning back now - not when every stroke of my needle held promises whispered through ink: promises of protection, promises of defiance…promises of hope for those caught between light and dark in this ever-twisting dance between power and those brave or foolish enough to seek it out.

* * *

I leaned back in my chair, the sketchpad resting on my knees, a labyrinth of lines and shapes sprawling across the page. My fingers, stained with ink, twitched as I pondered the Mark of Power that now consumed my thoughts. The weight of its potential pressed against the walls of my mind, tempting me with visions of what could be.

The city outside hummed with life, a stark contrast to the stillness within Crimson Ink. In this moment of quietude, my imagination unfurled like the wings of a dark phoenix, soaring through possibilities that could change not only my life but also the fabric of the supernatural world itself.

What if I claimed the Mark? Would it sear into my skin like a brand of fire, endowing me with powers that would dwarf those of any vampire or sorcerer I'd ever encountered?

The thought alone sent a thrill racing through me. I could elevate my artistry to realms uncharted, etch tattoos that didn't just mimic life but were life itself—creations that could breathe, think, even love.

I pictured myself walking through the city, invisible threads of influence extending from my fingertips. With a mere touch, I could shift the tide of power, dismantle hierarchies that had stood unchallenged for centuries. I could build sanctuaries for those hunted by creatures like Damien and his gang, shield them with tattoos woven from the very essence of protection and defiance.

My mind danced with visions of grandeur—a hero in the shadows championing the downtrodden. Yet another voice whispered seductive promises of personal gain. With such power at my disposal, who would dare cross me? Who would not bend to my will? The allure of control was intoxicating.

I saw myself draped in opulence, no longer lurking on the fringes but reigning supreme over this clandestine world. My name would be whispered in reverence and fear; none would dare question my authority. Every supernatural being would seek out Crimson Ink, not as customers but as supplicants begging for a sliver of the might contained within my ink.

The fantasies spiraled further—Damien kneeling before me, stripped of his arrogance. Evelyn and Victor watching from afar with eyes wide in awe or perhaps envy. The Vampire Gang's dominion crumbled to dust at my feet as I carved out an empire governed by art and magic combined.

A knock on the door jarred me from my reverie. Tara stood there, her gaze holding a depth that pulled me back to reality. She didn't need to say anything; her presence alone reminded me of who I was—Alex, an artist caught between worlds, striving to uphold integrity in a city teeming with darkness.

I cleared my throat and tucked away those dangerous dreams like secret weapons beneath a cloak. "Tara," I greeted her warmly, "what brings you here?"

Her lips pursed in concern as she crossed the threshold into my sanctuary. "I heard you were alone with your thoughts—dangerous territory for someone like you."

I offered her a wry smile. "Just contemplating future designs," I lied smoothly.

She raised an eyebrow but let it slide as she pulled up a chair beside me. "We don't have much time before Damien's next move," she said softly. "We need to focus on our plan."

Our plan—a resistance built not on might but on cunning and unity. It was our beacon in this storm that threatened to swallow us whole.

Tara laid out blueprints on the table before us—a network of ley lines crisscrossing beneath the city like veins pumping lifeblood into its heart. My fingers traced over them lightly; they hummed with potential.

"We can use these," I murmured more to myself than to Tara.

"Yes," she agreed eagerly. "But we must be careful not to draw too much attention."

Attention—the last thing we wanted from Damien or his ilk.

As we poured over maps and schematics late into the night, plotting our silent rebellion against forces that had ruled from shadowed corners for too long, a part of me clung to those grandiose fantasies where power flowed through me unchecked.

But deep down, past ambition and pride, lay something purer—a resolve not just to thrive but to protect what mattered most: freedom for myself and for all those ensnared by this supernatural web we called home.

The clock ticked on as Tara and I delved deeper into our strategies for using ley lines to amplify our efforts against Damien's Ascension Protocol. With every passing hour, I felt myself drawing closer to an inevitable crossroads where dreams would clash with duty.

But until then... until then...

* * *

The clock's relentless ticking matched the thumping of my heart, a constant reminder that time was slipping through my fingers. In the dim light of my apartment, the city's pulse resonated in the air, thrumming with the life of the unknowing masses and those like me, caught between worlds. My eyes flitted across the room, lingering on the Mark of Power's intricate design etched into my sketchbook.

It was a dangerous dance, toying with the idea of harnessing its power. With every line and curve of the Mark, I felt its seductive pull—a quick route to strength, an answer to my predicament with Damien. But at what cost? The Mark didn't just bestow power; it consumed those who bore it. Could I risk becoming what I sought to defeat?

A knock on my door snapped me out of my thoughts. With a hesitant step, I opened it to find Tara, her eyes wide with urgency.

"We need you, Alex," she said, her voice a whisper lost in the cacophony of the night.

I stepped aside to let her in, closing the door behind her. "What's going on?"

"It's Damien," she began, pacing back and forth like a caged animal. "He's got someone—someone important to us. He knows we won't act against him as long as he has leverage."

I swallowed hard. The stakes were higher than ever. "And you think using the Mark could give us an edge?"

Tara stopped and faced me squarely. "You know it could. It could shift everything in our favor."

My fingers brushed against the sketchbook's edge as I considered her words. The temptation was palpable—the Mark of Power was right there, within reach.

"I've seen what it does to people," I countered, my voice barely above a whisper. "It devours them from the inside out."

"But you're different," Tara insisted. "Your heritage—"

"Doesn't make me immune to corruption." I cut her off more sharply than intended.

We stood in silence for a moment that stretched between us like an untraversable chasm.

"Damien is going to make his move soon," Tara said at last, breaking the stillness. "The lunar eclipse is in three days."

"I know." The words came out heavier than lead.

She looked at me with desperation that clawed at my resolve. "We can't afford to play it safe anymore."

A lump formed in my throat as I turned away from her gaze and walked over to my desk where lay my tools of trade and magic—ink pots and needles arrayed like soldiers ready for battle.

"I've spent my life mastering this craft," I murmured more to myself than to Tara, "creating tattoos that can protect or empower without demanding one's soul as payment."

"And now you have a chance to use that mastery for something bigger," Tara said from behind me.

I ran a hand through my hair and let out a shaky breath. Every instinct screamed against using the Mark—it went against everything I stood for as an artist and as a person who straddled two worlds yet belonged fully to neither.

"We'll find another way," I declared with more confidence than I felt.

"Alex..." Tara began but stopped short when she saw my expression.

The conviction in my eyes must have spoken louder than words because she nodded slowly, her shoulders slumping ever so slightly.

"We trust you," she said finally. "But if there's any part of you that believes in taking this risk—"

"There isn't." The lie tasted bitter on my tongue.

Tara hesitated but then moved toward the door without another word. Before she left, she turned back to me with a solemn look.

"Remember why we're doing this," she implored softly before disappearing into the night.

I sank into my chair once she was gone, feeling both relieved and trapped by my decision. My gaze fell upon the Mark again—the power it promised mocked me from its paper prison.

Was it cowardice or wisdom holding me back? The line between them blurred more each day.

For hours I sat there wrestling with myself until fatigue dragged me into restless sleep right at my desk.

Morning light spilled into the room when I jerked awake at another knock on the door—a more insistent one this time.

I opened it to find Raven standing there with an unreadable expression etched across his face.

"Alex," he greeted solemnly before glancing over his shoulder as if expecting shadows to leap at him any moment. "We need your help."

"What happened?" My heart rate picked up again—the same rhythm of dread drumming within me.

"It's Lynx," he said quietly but urgently. "Damien has him."

My stomach dropped like a stone into water—Lynx was key to our resistance efforts; without him...

Raven stepped closer and lowered his voice even further. "We need that Mark now more than ever."

My hands trembled slightly as I weighed his words against every moral fiber within me. To save Lynx would mean stepping over a line from which there might be no return.

"We don't have much time." Raven's gaze held mine—a silent plea for action when every moment mattered.

I closed my eyes for just a second—a brief reprieve from reality—and when they opened again, they met Raven's expectant stare head-on.

"We can't use it," I stated firmly despite everything inside me warring against itself. "The cost is too high."

Raven studied me for a moment before nodding slowly in acceptance—or perhaps resignation—and turned away without another word.

As he walked off down the hallway, his footsteps echoed like a death knell for Lynx—and maybe for all of us—and yet somewhere deep inside where fear mingled with hope, I clung onto the belief that we'd find another way—one that didn't require surrendering our souls for power.

***

I stood before the ancient oak, its roots entwined with the city's pulse, the whispers of the ley lines humming beneath my feet. I felt it—the pull of power, a siren's call that both terrified and beckoned. The Mark of Power, a design fraught with danger and temptation, lay heavy in my thoughts. It promised strength, but at what cost?

As the sun dipped below the skyline, painting the clouds in fiery hues, I realized I needed counsel—someone who understood the weight of power and its consequences. I sought out Orion, my mentor in astrology and magic, whose wisdom had always been a beacon in times of uncertainty.

The door to his bookshop creaked open, chimes announcing my arrival. The scent of aged parchment and smoldering incense wrapped around me like a comforting embrace. Books towered in precarious stacks, their spines etched with gold and secrets.

Orion emerged from behind a curtain of cascading beads, his eyes reflecting knowledge as deep as the night sky. "Alex," he greeted, his voice a melody of warmth and concern. "I sensed your turmoil."

"I'm at a crossroads," I admitted, clasping my hands together to still their shaking. "Damien has captured Lynx, and now more than ever, the Resistance needs strength to fight back. But I'm scared... scared of what using the Mark might make me become."

Orion led me to a pair of worn leather chairs nestled among the books. He poured two cups of tea from an ornate pot; steam rose like spirits being freed. "Power," he began as he handed me a cup, "is like fire. It can warm a home or raze it to ash. The Mark is no different—it amplifies what is already within you."

I sipped the tea; it tasted like liquid courage infused with mint.

"But how do I wield it without being consumed by it?" My voice trembled with the weight of responsibility.

Orion's gaze held mine—a lighthouse in stormy seas. "By remembering who you are and why you fight. You are not Damien; your heart beats to a different rhythm."

"But isn't using the Mark playing into Damien's hands? Doesn't it make me just like him?" My hands clenched around the cup as if it were my resolve hardening.

"The ethical dilemma you face is one many have stumbled upon." Orion leaned forward, his eyes never leaving mine. "To wield power responsibly is to understand its nature—its ability to corrupt absolutely."

I considered his words—a puzzle demanding to be solved.

"Damien seeks control," Orion continued, "to bind others to his will. But you seek freedom—not just for yourself but for all those ensnared by his darkness."

A spark ignited within me—the flame of defiance that had flickered since Damien first crossed my threshold at Crimson Ink.

"And what if I lose myself to it?" The question hung between us like an unsheathed sword.

"Alex," Orion said with an intensity that bordered on fervor, "the very fact that you question this shows your heart's true compass."

He stood up and walked over to an old oak cabinet that seemed as timeless as he was. With care, he opened a drawer and retrieved an object wrapped in velvet—a compass not unlike Raven's Aethereal Compass but older somehow.

"This has been passed down through generations of those who've walked between worlds." He handed it to me with reverence.

I unwrapped it delicately; it felt alive in my hands.

"It will guide you," Orion assured me, "not just in space but in spirit."

As I gazed upon its intricate face, realization dawned on me—the path I chose would define not just my fate but also that of others caught in Damien's web.

"Thank you," I murmured, tucking the compass safely away.

Orion smiled—a small gesture that carried the weight of galaxies. "Remember this: every choice has ripples that reach farther than we can see."

With newfound determination mixed with caution forged from Orion's advice, I left his sanctuary for the city's shadows that beckoned me onward.

The night embraced me as I walked toward where Lynx was being held captive—a place darkened by more than just the absence of light. The Resistance depended on me; their hopes intertwined with my own fears and resolve.

I stopped beneath a streetlamp whose flickering light struggled against the encroaching darkness—a mirror to my own conflict within. The compass throbbed with energy against my chest; its presence reassured me as much as Orion's words did.

Lynx's capture wasn't just about them; it was about all those who dared stand against tyranny—those who refused to bow before Damien's might.

I couldn't allow fear to dictate my actions any longer; Lynx had taken risks for our cause—it was time for me to do the same. Not with blind ambition but with clear purpose: to use power responsibly and ethically.

The road ahead was fraught with shadows and unknowns—a labyrinth whose exit lay shrouded in mist. But as I moved through the cityscape that held both danger and sanctuary within its veins, I felt a clarity that had eluded me before speaking with Orion.

Each step was measured; each breath a silent vow—I would not let Damien define my legacy nor would I allow fear to anchor me in place while others suffered under his reign.

The city pulsed around me—its heartbeat echoing mine—and within that symphony of life and struggle, I found strength not just from Orion's wisdom or from Raven's guidance but from within myself—a conviction tempered by time and trials.

As I neared Lynx's prison—an abandoned warehouse repurposed for darker designs—I readied myself for what lay ahead. With each stride forward, doubts shed from me like leaves in autumn wind—my resolve firming into iron will.

The night grew deeper around me as if sensing my purpose—whispering secrets only those attuned could hear—and amidst those murmurs, one truth rang clear: power wielded without conscience was no power at all—it was enslavement masquerading as strength.

With Orion's teachings echoing through time like ancient chants—and Raven's tools secured close—I prepared to face whatever darkness awaited inside the warehouse walls...

...for though power might seduce or scare—it was ultimately mine to shape and share.

* * *

In the dusky corners of Crimson Ink, the air hung thick with the scent of ancient parchment and dried ink. The shop, once a haven for my artistry, now felt like a cage lined with veiled threats and Damien's pervasive influence. It was during these long, uncertain days that a figure stumbled through the door, their presence slicing through the stillness like a shard of moonlight piercing the night.

The man's skin bore the labyrinthine etchings of tattoos far more intricate and volatile than any I had ever dared to conjure. They writhed across his flesh like living things, whispering of power... and ruin. His eyes, once bright with promise, now flickered with the shadows of corruption.

"Help me," he rasped, voice a mere echo of strength squandered.

I ushered him into my private sanctum, away from prying eyes and ears that hungered for secrets not theirs to claim. His name was Dorian—a name that resonated with an ominous familiarity. A sorcerer who'd once been revered for his gift to weave enchantments into ink, now reduced to a cautionary whisper among those who dared dabble in the arcane.

"What happened to you?" I asked, my hands steady as I helped him onto the worn leather chair that had borne witness to countless transformations.

Dorian's laugh was a hollow sound, devoid of humor. "The same thing that could happen to you if you're not careful," he warned, his gaze cutting through me. "Power is an alluring mistress. She embraces you, whispers promises of grandeur... but she never lets go."

I studied the chaotic tapestry etched into his skin—the result of giving in to temptation. Each tattoo pulsed with its own sinister energy; some clashed against others, vying for dominance in a silent war waged upon his very soul.

"You were consumed by your own creations," I surmised.

"Aye," he confirmed with a nod that seemed to take all his remaining strength. "The Mark... it calls to those like us—those who can tap into its wellspring of power. But it doesn't come without cost."

His warning rang true within me; echoes of Orion's counsel whispered through my thoughts. The ethical balance teetered precariously on the edge of a blade—one wrong step could send everything crashing down into chaos.

"Can you be saved?" The question lingered between us like a fragile thread threatening to snap under the weight of truth.

Dorian's gaze held mine as he reached out with a trembling hand—a gesture seeking connection or perhaps absolution. "Once you've tasted such power... it changes you. I am beyond salvation."

The silence stretched taut as I considered his plight. Here before me sat a man—a mirror reflecting what could become of me should I lose myself to ambition and greed.

"I will try," I whispered, not just for him but for myself as well—for the part of me that still clung fiercely to hope and redemption.

Dorian closed his eyes as if summoning memories from deep within. "I was approached by someone much like Damien," he began, voice barely above a whisper. "He offered me everything: protection from those who would see my talents shackled, resources beyond measure... but most importantly, he offered me freedom."

His words hung heavy in the air as he continued. "But freedom is an illusion when bound by chains of your own making." He opened his eyes then—eyes that bore into mine with an intensity that spoke volumes more than words ever could.

"And what did you give in return?" My voice trembled slightly despite my efforts at composure.

Dorian lifted his shirt slightly to reveal an ouroboros tattoo similar to those I had been forced to ink under Damien's command—a snake devouring its own tail in an eternal cycle of consumption and rebirth.

"This was my first step towards damnation," he admitted with no trace of pride—only resignation laced with regret. "Each tattoo thereafter only drew me deeper into darkness until I became more shadow than man."

I absorbed his story in silence; every word felt like another weight added onto my already burdened shoulders. The parallels between our paths were stark and undeniable—a reminder that even though our intentions may differ, our fates could easily align.

Dorian shifted uncomfortably in his seat; it seemed even sitting was an ordeal for him now—his body no longer fully under his command but rather at the mercy of the magic coursing through him unchecked.

"You seek control over your destiny," Dorian stated rather than asked—as if reading my very thoughts laid bare before him. "But control is fleeting when faced with forces greater than oneself."

I nodded silently; understanding dawning within me like dawn breaking over a somber night sky.

As we sat there—sorcerer and tattoo artist bound by more than just our shared craft—I pondered on how close I stood on that precipice where power beckoned seductively from beyond. Dorian served as both warning and testament; a reminder that succumbing to temptation could lead one down a path from which there was no return.

And so we continued our discourse deep into the twilight hours—two souls seeking solace in shared burdens and unspoken understandings while around us, forces gathered like storm clouds on the horizon threatening to unleash their fury upon us all.

* * *

The air crackled with tension, a silent symphony that hummed along the ley lines beneath the city. I stood at the threshold of my shop, Crimson Ink, a sanctuary that had become a battleground of wills. My fingers brushed over the cool metal of the amulet that hung heavy around my neck—a reminder of Damien's reach and my own burgeoning resolve.

A fresh canvas awaited me inside, skin eager for ink and magic. The client was a young woman with eyes that carried the weight of knowing too much. She wanted a tattoo to remind her of her strength—a phoenix rising from ashes.

As I prepped my tools, the sterile clink of metal and buzz of the tattoo machine were meditative, drowning out the whispering doubts. The design came to life under my steady hand, each line infused with care and an undercurrent of defiance. This was no mere image; it was a shield wrought from conviction, an emblem of rebirth much like my own journey.

The woman's gaze met mine in the mirror as I worked, her eyes welling with gratitude. "You don't just give tattoos," she murmured. "You give pieces of hope."

Her words echoed in my heart, fanning the embers of purpose that had been smoldering within me. It was easy to lose oneself in Damien's shadow—to see only darkness and forget the light that cast it.

"You're right," I replied with a nod, focusing on shading the phoenix's wings. "Hope is what we all need—a reminder that no matter how dark it gets, we can rise again."

The bell above the door jangled, and I glanced up to see Tara stepping inside. Her presence was a balm to my fraying nerves—a touchstone to who I was before Damien's grasp tightened around Crimson Ink.

She leaned against the counter, watching me work with an intensity that spoke volumes. "Damien's growing impatient," she said quietly, her voice barely carrying over the buzz of my tattoo machine.

I kept my focus on the design, letting muscle memory guide me as I navigated our precarious reality. "Let him wait," I responded evenly. "I'm not his puppet—never have been."

Tara's lips curved in a smile tinged with pride. "That's why we're going to win this thing," she affirmed.

The shop door opened again, admitting Jade into our little haven. Her presence was always a catalyst—her energy transformative. She surveyed the room with sharp eyes before her gaze landed on me.

"We've got movement on Damien's end," Jade reported, crossing her arms over her chest. "He's getting ready for something big."

The final lines of the phoenix took shape under my hand—the last vestiges of ink marking skin and sealing intent. I nodded at Jade without missing a beat.

"Then we'll be ready too," I declared as I cleaned my needle for sterilization.

Tara stepped closer to Jade as they huddled over a map strewn across one corner of the counter. Ley lines intersected across it like veins—pulsing with potential and danger alike.

My client rose from her seat, her eyes lingering on her new tattoo in the mirror—a mix of awe and newfound courage reflecting back at us.

"Thank you," she whispered, touching the bandage lightly.

I offered her a soft smile in return, understanding unspoken between us—this was more than ink; it was armor for her soul.

After she left, Jade approached me with a serious expression. "We can't let Damien get what he wants—not without consequences."

I knew she was right; every fiber of my being screamed it. But knowing and acting were two very different beasts—a lesson learned in fire and etched in ink.

Tara joined us, her hand finding mine in silent solidarity. We stood there together—three souls intertwined by fate and choice alike.

"The Resistance needs you to step up," Jade said firmly but not unkindly. "Your talents... they could turn the tide."

I felt their weight—their belief in me—and it bolstered my spirit like nothing else could.

"I'll do what must be done," I vowed, conviction steeling within me despite the whispers of temptation that danced like shadows at the edge of consciousness.

The sun dipped low outside, casting long shadows across Crimson Ink's floor—a mosaic of light and dark that mirrored our reality all too well.

"I won't become what Damien wants," I continued as we sat amidst scattered designs and whispered plans—the remnants of battles past and those yet to come. "My abilities are not weapons for his war but tools for our freedom."

Jade nodded, her expression softening just so—a warrior acknowledging another's mettle.

"And when this is over?" Tara asked quietly as night embraced us in its cool shroud.

I met her gaze squarely—two souls alight against encroaching darkness.

"When this is over," I began slowly, every word etched with certainty as if spoken into existence by will alone, "Crimson Ink will be a place where people come not just for tattoos but for sanctuary—for magic that binds us together rather than tears us apart."

The commitment settled within me like an anchor amidst tumultuous seas—an unyielding point amidst chaos' dance.

Tara squeezed my hand gently—a gesture laden with unspoken understanding—and Jade looked on with respect shining in her eyes.

As night claimed its dominion outside Crimson Ink's walls, we three guardians sat resolute against whatever tides may come—a triad bound by shared resolve and unfaltering compasses guiding us through storms yet unseen.

Chapter 12

Betrayal's Sting

The sun had long since dipped below the horizon, but the night felt anything but peaceful. I leaned against the cool counter of Crimson Ink, my fingers tracing the grooves in the wood, each one a reminder of the countless clients who had sat here seeking transformation. But tonight was different. Tonight was about uncovering deceit within the shadows.

A frantic knock shattered the silence, echoing off the walls like a prelude to chaos. I glanced up to see Jade, her face pale and her eyes wide with urgency.

"Alex, you need to know—there's been a betrayal," she gasped, barely catching her breath as she pushed through the door.

I straightened up, my heart pounding against my ribs. Betrayal was a poison few in our line of work could survive.

"Who?" I demanded, my voice steady despite the turmoil brewing inside me.

"It's Victor," she whispered, and that single word felt like a blade slipping between ribs. "He's turned against Damien."

Victor—the enforcer, Damien's right hand—the thought of him switching sides was as shocking as it was dangerous. He knew too much; he was too deep within their ranks. What could have possibly driven him to such an act?

"Why?" I probed further, knowing that understanding his motives might be key to navigating the chaos that was sure to follow.

Jade leaned in closer, lowering her voice even though we were alone. "He's been feeding information to a rival faction for months. They caught him tonight—Damien is furious."

I exhaled slowly, processing this new thread in an already tangled web. If Victor had truly betrayed Damien, there would be no forgiveness—only swift and brutal retribution. But it also meant there were cracks within the gang's armor—cracks that could be exploited.

"Damien doesn't know we're aware of this yet," Jade continued, glancing nervously towards the door as if expecting it to burst open at any moment.

"We need to act fast then," I said, my mind racing with possibilities. This betrayal could be our opportunity to weaken Damien's hold on us all—but it also meant walking on a razor's edge.

Tara entered just then, her expression grim as she caught the tail end of our conversation. "I heard about Victor," she said simply, joining us at the counter.

"What do you think this means for us?" I asked them both. The 'us' wasn't just Tara and Jade now—it was every soul who had found themselves ensnared by Damien's ambitions.

"It means chaos," Tara replied without hesitation. "And chaos can be good for us if we're careful."

Careful and cunning—I had learned those lessons well under Damien's relentless gaze. We needed a plan—one that would shield us from whatever storm Victor's betrayal would unleash upon the supernatural underbelly of our city.

"I'll need to talk to Lynx," I mused aloud. "The Resistance needs to know about this—they might want to move up their timeline."

Jade nodded in agreement while Tara reached out and squeezed my hand—a silent promise of support.

"I'll gather more information," Jade said resolutely. "We need eyes and ears on this; we can't afford to be blindsided."

"And I'll reach out to our other allies," Tara added. "If things go south with Damien, we'll need all the help we can get."

As they set out on their tasks, I turned my attention back to my sketchbook—my sanctuary amidst this brewing storm. The pages were filled with designs imbued with hope and rebellion; now more than ever, they felt like weapons in a war where ink was as powerful as blood.

The bell above the door jangled harshly as it swung open again—too soon for either Tara or Jade to have returned with news. My pulse quickened; only trouble came calling at this hour without warning.

In strode Evelyn—her elegance marred by an undercurrent of tension that pulled tight at her features. She moved like danger personified—a panther clad in silk and secrets.

"Alex," she greeted me with a nod, her gaze searching mine for signs of weakness or deceit.

"Evelyn," I replied with equal measure, refusing to show any trepidation at her sudden appearance.

"We need to talk," she said crisply—a statement rather than a request.

I gestured towards the back room where privacy could be guaranteed—for now—and led the way. Once inside, Evelyn wasted no time.

"You've heard about Victor," she stated flatly—it wasn't a question but an acknowledgment of shared knowledge in this twisted game we played.

"I have," I confirmed, watching her closely for any hint of her true intentions.

"He was careless—and now he will pay for his mistake." Her words were cold; they carried the weight of inevitability that came with crossing Damien.

"And what does Damien plan for him?" I asked cautiously, aware that his decision could ripple through all our lives like a stone cast into still water.

"That is not your concern." Evelyn fixed me with a look that brooked no argument—a reminder of where power truly lay within Crimson Ink's walls.

I inclined my head slightly—a subtle concession—but my mind whirred with questions unanswered and plots unspun. Victor's betrayal might have been careless or calculated; either way, it shifted things in ways we couldn't yet fully grasp.

Evelyn stepped closer now, her presence imposing even in silence. "Damien expects your loyalty now more than ever," she warned softly yet sharply as if each word were honed steel. "Don't forget where your allegiance lies."

But allegiance was a fickle thing when survival hung by a thread—as frayed and fragile as trust within our ranks had become since Victor's fall from grace had come to light.

* * *

Evelyn's words hung in the air like a guillotine's blade, poised and ready to sever any sense of security I'd clung to. Victor's betrayal, while a ripple in Damien's ocean of schemes, had become a maelstrom threatening to pull me under. The implication of my involvement, however innocent, cast shadows across my shop—shadows that slithered along the walls and whispered treachery.

I met Evelyn's gaze, her eyes cold and unyielding as the steel of a blade. "Victor's actions are his own," I said, my voice steady despite the tempest within. "My loyalty to Damien has been unwavering."

A ghost of a smile flickered on Evelyn's lips. "Loyalty is not just about action, Alex. It's about perception. And right now, the perception is... muddy."

She left with those parting words, leaving a chill that crept into my bones. No sooner had the door closed behind her than panic began to snake its way into my heart. My mind raced—could Victor have implicated me in his betrayal? Was this some twisted game where I was the pawn set to take the fall?

The bell above the door jingled and my body tensed, ready for confrontation. But it was only Tara, her face etched with concern.

"Alex, what happened? You look like you've seen a ghost."

I forced a smile that didn't reach my eyes. "Just the usual vampire politics."

Tara arched an eyebrow. "Evelyn looked serious. What did she want?"

"To remind me that loyalty is more than skin deep," I replied cryptically.

She frowned but didn't press further, sensing my reluctance to divulge the details of my entanglement with Damien's gang.

The rest of the day passed in a blur—a series of tattoos etched on skin, each line drawn with precision but marred by my inner turmoil. Every time the bell rang, my heart skipped a beat, fearing it was retribution come calling.

Night fell over the city like a shroud and with it came an ominous silence to Crimson Ink. The usual nightlife buzz was absent tonight; even the supernatural elements seemed to hold their breath.

I was cleaning up when shadows danced across the frosted glass of the front door—a foreboding sign that sent shivers down my spine. Three figures entered—two I recognized as members of Damien's gang, flanking a third I didn't know.

The unfamiliar face was gaunt, eyes hollow as if life had been drained from him—an emissary bearing bad news or worse intentions.

"Damien wants to see you," he rasped.

My mouth went dry. "Now?"

His nod was slow, deliberate.

Tara stepped forward protectively. "He can't just summon Alex whenever he pleases."

The man's stare shifted toward her for an uncomfortable moment before returning to me. "It's not up for debate."

With one last look at Tara, whose eyes blazed with silent fury, I followed them out into the night.

Damien's lair was beneath Crimson Ink—a subterranean chamber lined with ancient texts and artifacts that reeked of dark magic. He sat on his throne-like chair, flanked by his loyal council members who watched me with predatory interest.

"Alex," Damien greeted me with mock warmth as I approached. "There are whispers... rumors that you've been consorting with traitors."

I felt anger rise within me at his accusation but kept it leashed behind a calm facade. "You know better than to listen to whispers."

His laugh was humorless. "But when whispers turn into screams? What then?"

I held his gaze; it felt like staring into an abyss.

"Victor made his choices," I said carefully. "And I make mine—my loyalty has never wavered from Crimson Ink."

Damien stood up and descended the steps toward me slowly—each footfall measured and heavy with intent.

"And yet here we are," he murmured as he circled me like a predator sizing up its prey. "A predicament where your innocence is tainted by association."

"I've done nothing wrong," I asserted.

Damien stopped in front of me, his proximity oppressive. "Perhaps," he conceded after a pause heavy enough to drown in. "But perception is reality in our world."

He returned to his seat and waved his hand dismissively at his men who advanced on me like wolves closing in for the kill.

"Search him," Damien commanded coldly.

Hands rougher than any tattoo machine I'd ever held patted me down while I stood rigid as stone. The emissary from earlier produced something from my jacket pocket—a small vial filled with ink-black liquid—and held it up for Damien to see.

"That's not mine," I protested immediately, recognizing it as one of Victor's concoctions.

Damien took the vial and held it between slender fingers as he contemplated it with an inscrutable expression.

"Interesting," he mused aloud before fixing his gaze back on me with renewed interest—or perhaps suspicion would be more apt a word for it.

"Someone plants contraband on you and you expect me to believe there's no connection?" His voice held an edge sharper than any needle could provide.

"I swear on Crimson Ink itself," I began passionately before catching myself; swearing on something so dear felt like sacrilege even under duress.

Damien watched me for what felt like eternity before speaking again.

"You'll stay here tonight—under watch." His decision was final; an edict no one dared question.

I glanced at Tara who'd followed discreetly at a distance; she met my gaze with equal parts worry and resolve—an unspoken promise that she wouldn't let this lie unchallenged.

As Damien's enforcers escorted me deeper into his domain's bowels—a prison cloaked in velvet darkness—I wondered how long before perception became my new reality—one crafted by others' treachery rather than my own actions or truth.

* * *

The clink of the lock snapping shut echoed through the room, the finality of it reverberating in my chest. Damien's parting sneer still clawed at my mind as his henchmen escorted me out of his sight. I was under watch, a prisoner in my own shop, the irony not lost on me. This sanctuary of ink and skin, once a place of freedom and creativity, had become my cage.

My heart hammered against my ribcage as I scanned the parlor for an escape. Evelyn's eyes followed me, sharp as daggers, her earlier warnings now a haunting premonition. The air was thick with tension; every breath felt stolen, every movement watched.

A whisper of fabric drew my attention to the back door — Tara. She stood just outside the threshold, a silent promise of salvation in her eyes. The resistance. The memory of Lynx's offer to join their fight flickered in my mind like a beacon. I had until sunrise to decide, but dawn had come early.

With a discreet nod to Tara, I feigned calm and turned toward the restroom. "Gotta wash up," I muttered to the thug positioned by the door — Victor's replacement — a burly man with eyes as vacant as a cloudless sky.

He grunted an acknowledgment without moving from his spot. My fingers grazed the cool handle of the restroom door as I slipped inside, locking it behind me with a soft click that belied my frantic pulse.

The small window at the top of the wall beckoned me with its sliver of freedom. With no time to spare, I climbed onto the sink, ignoring its protests under my weight. I pried at the window with desperate fingers until it gave way with a creak that sounded too loud for comfort.

The alleyway outside was a tight squeeze, shadows clinging to its walls like conspirators. My escape would have to be swift and silent — any clatter or misstep could betray me.

I heaved myself up and through the opening, my body protesting each contortion required to slip through that narrow passage. Once outside, I dropped into the alleyway with more force than grace, wincing as I felt the impact jolt through my legs.

The chill morning air bit at my skin as I straightened up and scanned my surroundings for any sign of pursuit. Nothing stirred save for a stray cat slinking away into obscurity.

Tara emerged from her hiding spot, her presence both reassuring and alarming in its urgency. "We need to move," she hissed, grabbing my arm and pulling me down the alleyway toward an uncertain future.

Our footsteps were hushed whispers on the damp pavement as we navigated through a labyrinth of backstreets and narrow passageways known only to those who sought invisibility in plain sight.

Tara led me toward an area unfamiliar even to me — parts of this city still shrouded in mystery despite years of tracing its veins with ink and magic. We reached an unremarkable door nestled between two graffiti-laden buildings; it was here that Tara finally halted.

She knocked thrice in quick succession followed by two slower thuds against the weathered wood — a code that seemed as much a plea as it was a signal.

Seconds stretched into eternity before locks clicked and bolts withdrew from within. The door creaked open just enough for us to slip through before shutting once again with silent finality.

The space beyond was dimly lit; shadows clung to corners like cobwebs. Before us stood Lynx — their features obscured beneath their hood — but their posture exuded authority and an unspoken understanding of our plight.

"You're cutting it close," Lynx said in that voice which never quite revealed their thoughts completely.

I shrugged off Tara's grip, stepping forward on unsteady legs. "Damien's patience ran out faster than expected."

Lynx regarded me for a moment before nodding toward another door deeper within our hideaway. "We have little time," they murmured. "Damien will not stop until he has what he wants."

As if on cue, distant sirens wailed their nocturnal lament — or perhaps they sang an overture for what was to come; either way, they underscored our precarious situation.

We moved deeper into our temporary refuge — walls adorned with relics of rebellion and determination — until we reached what could only be described as Lynx's inner sanctum: maps sprawled across tables illuminated by candles flickering like captive stars.

"You need rest," Lynx said softly but firmly as they motioned toward a cot tucked away in one corner beneath shelves heavy with books and artifacts from battles long past or yet to come.

I sank onto it gratefully yet restlessly; sleep was an indulgence far beyond reach when fear clawed at every shadow, transforming them into threats lurking just beyond sight.

"Keep watch," Tara volunteered quietly while Lynx simply nodded before turning back to their maps strewn across tables like tapestries woven from secrets and strategy.

There we were: three souls bound together not by ink but by necessity and defiance — each one acutely aware that sanctuary was merely borrowed time within walls that whispered tales of others who had fought...and those who had fallen before us.

I lay back on the cot with eyes wide open even as exhaustion pulled at every muscle like relentless tides eager to drag me under into oblivion's embrace; yet surrender eluded me amidst this taut symphony of anxiety playing its discordant melody within my chest where once there thrummed only passion for art now intertwined irrevocably with purpose forged from danger's crucible.

This is where I found myself: caught between breaths held tight in anticipation...waiting...waiting for whatever came next in this precarious dance along fate's razor edge where one misstep could spell ruin or perhaps...just perhaps...redemption.

* * *

The hideout's air, thick with tension, seemed to compress against my skin as I surveyed the huddled forms of the resistance. Lynx paced like a caged animal, muttering plans under his breath. Tara sat cross-legged in the corner, her eyes closed in meditation or maybe prayer. I leaned against a cold concrete wall, trying to etch into my mind the map of ley lines that might soon serve as our battleground.

It was Cipher who approached me, his face etched with lines of worry that hadn't been there when we first met. He was our strategist, the one who could play three moves ahead in our game against Damien and his gang. I needed his insight.

"You're holding up okay?" he asked quietly, his voice not betraying the concern that flickered in his eyes.

"As well as one can be when their choices might decide the fate of a city," I replied, trying to offer a wry smile but only managing a tight grimace.

Cipher nodded, understanding all too well. "We need to talk about Victor."

I straightened up at the mention of the name. Victor's betrayal had sent ripples through our ranks. His position as Damien's enforcer had always been ironclad—or so we thought.

"Victor always struck me as loyal to a fault," I began, "Why would he risk everything? Damien's retribution will be merciless."

Cipher sighed and glanced around before speaking again, "It's not just about loyalty. Victor has always been ambitious. Maybe too ambitious for his own good."

"And that led him to betray Damien?" I questioned, trying to piece together the puzzle.

Cipher moved closer, lowering his voice even further. "Victor didn't see a path forward within the gang. He's been passed over too many times for positions that should've been his. Damien has a tight grip on power and doesn't share the spotlight willingly."

I pondered this new information, the image of Victor as an enforcer starting to crumble and reveal something more complex underneath. "So he seeks power," I mused aloud.

"Exactly," Cipher confirmed. "But there's more. Victor has always been wary of your presence in Crimson Ink."

I raised an eyebrow at that. My own role within Damien's web had always felt like that of an outsider—an oddity tolerated for my abilities rather than truly accepted.

"Why? What threat could I possibly pose to him?" I asked.

Cipher hesitated before answering, "You represent something uncontrollable to him—a wildcard that could upset the balance he's trying to establish for himself."

I let out a breath I didn't realize I was holding. "So in his eyes, by aligning with Damien's enemies..."

"You become a piece on his chessboard instead of Damien's," Cipher finished for me.

We fell into silence, each lost in thought about the implications of Victor's actions and what it meant for us moving forward.

"Alex," Cipher said after a moment, breaking the silence with urgency in his tone. "There's something else you should know."

I met his gaze squarely, bracing myself for more unwelcome truths.

"Victor's not alone in this," he revealed. "There are others within the gang who share his discontent with Damien's rule."

I felt a flicker of hope at that—cracks within the gang could be advantageous to us—but it was quickly tempered by caution.

"Who else?" I pressed.

Cipher shook his head slightly, "Names aren't important right now; just know that Victor's betrayal might just be the tip of an iceberg."

My mind raced with this new information—the idea that we weren't alone in our fight against Damien's tyranny offered a glimmer of potential allies but also painted a target on our backs for those seeking their own advantage.

"We need to tread carefully," Cipher warned. "Damien will be watching for any signs of treachery within his ranks now more than ever."

I nodded solemnly. The game had changed once again; new players emerged from shadows while others shifted allegiances behind veils of deceit.

Suddenly Lynx appeared beside us, cutting through our exchange with sharp focus in her eyes.

"Alex," she addressed me directly, "we have word from Jade—she's made contact with someone inside who might be willing to help us."

I looked between Lynx and Cipher, feeling both wariness and resolve stir within me.

"Who is it?" I asked cautiously.

Lynx exchanged a glance with Cipher before responding. "Evelyn."

The name struck me like a bolt—Evelyn had always been Damien's shadow; her loyalty was beyond question—or so it seemed.

"She wants to meet," Lynx continued. "Says she has information critical to our cause."

My pulse quickened at the prospect; Evelyn's knowledge could change everything. But it also meant walking into what could very well be a trap set by one of the most dangerous vampires in the city.

Lynx must have read my hesitation because she placed a firm hand on my shoulder and said, "We'll plan this out carefully; you won't go alone."

A thousand scenarios played out in my mind—all with different endings but few promising safety or success. This was it: another crossroads where choices were few and stakes were life itself.

Cipher leaned closer and murmured just loud enough for me and Lynx to hear: "Trust is rare currency these days—spend it wisely."

His words resonated deep within me as I contemplated meeting Evelyn—a woman enshrouded in as much mystery as menace—with only one certainty clear amidst swirling doubts: whatever path we chose now would irrevocably shape what came next.

* * *

The weight of Victor's betrayal hung heavy in the air, an unspoken signal that the landscape of power within the city was shifting beneath our feet. The shop's usual hum of needles and soft chatter had faded into a silence punctuated only by hushed conspiracies and wary glances. As I cleaned my station, the scent of antiseptic couldn't mask the lingering stench of fear and treachery.

Lynx's message still burned in my pocket, a reminder that the next move would define not just my fate, but also that of the Resistance. With every stroke of the broom, I swept away not just debris but also remnants of any delusion that life could return to what it once was.

Evelyn's words replayed in my mind, a loop of caution and veiled threats. Her offer to divulge information had come at a price—one I wasn't sure we could afford to pay. But with Damien's gaze turned inward, seeking out disloyalty in his ranks, opportunities arose from the shadows like serpents ready to strike.

I locked up Crimson Ink for the night, ensuring each click of the bolt was firm—a futile attempt at control when every decision felt like a gamble. Tara met me outside, her face set in determination.

"We need to plan," she said without preamble as we walked briskly toward our rendezvous with Lynx.

"Damien's distracted with Victor's mess," I mused aloud. "This might be our chance to gather more intel or even sway some of his followers."

Tara nodded, her eyes scanning our surroundings for unseen threats. "We need more than information. We need leverage—something to tip the scales when Damien decides to make his move."

As we turned into an alley shrouded in darkness, I couldn't help but feel the stirrings of something dormant within me—a sense of power I'd long neglected. It whispered promises of strength and protection but demanded a steep price in return.

We arrived at a nondescript door guarded by Cipher, who nodded us through with a solemn expression. Inside, Lynx waited, surrounded by maps dotted with colored pins and strings that formed a web of strategy and intent.

"Alex," Lynx greeted me with a nod as Tara and I took our seats at the battered table. "We've got little time and much to do."

I spread my hands on the table, palms down as if feeling for the pulse of our plans through the wood grain. "We need allies," I began. "Those within Damien's circle who are disillusioned or scared enough to turn."

"And how do you propose we find them?" Lynx asked skeptically.

"We use what we have," Tara interjected before I could speak. "Alex's tattoos can be... persuasive."

A murmur went around the room as eyes turned toward me—some filled with hope, others with doubt.

I let out a slow breath. "We could create tattoos imbued with subtle influences—confidence for those too afraid to stand up, clarity for those blinded by loyalty."

"And trust?" Lynx pressed.

"Trust is harder," I admitted. "But there are ways to enhance empathy—to forge connections where none exist."

Lynx considered this for a moment before giving a decisive nod. "Do it. But we must also think defensively."

I knew what he meant before he continued—the Mark of Power loomed over us all like an omen. The temptation to wield it clawed at me from within, yet its dangers were not lost on me either.

"I won't use it," I said firmly. "There has to be another way."

Lynx leaned back in his chair, studying me as if seeing me for the first time. "You've grown stronger than when we first met," he observed.

"Or more desperate," I replied wryly.

The conversation shifted then, from tactics to logistics. Jade would be instrumental in spreading our tattooed influence—her network was extensive and her loyalty unwavering.

As we planned into the early hours, my mind kept drifting back to Evelyn's promise—information that could change everything or nothing at all.

"We meet her tomorrow night," Lynx finally said as if reading my thoughts. "But Alex—you're staying behind."

"What?" The word shot out before I could temper it with reason.

"It's too risky," Lynx continued firmly. "If this is a trap..."

"I can handle myself," I interrupted him, my voice more steady than I felt.

"You're not expendable," Tara said softly beside me.

I met her gaze and saw not just concern but fear—a fear that mirrored my own about what lay ahead for all of us.

"I'll stay behind this time," I conceded after a moment, knowing that this battle required more than just bravery—it needed wisdom too.

With roles assigned and plans laid out like pieces on a chessboard, we dispersed into the dawn's early light—a band of rebels each carrying their own quiet resolve against an enemy that thrived in darkness.

Back in my apartment above Crimson Ink, I found solace in my sketchbook—the pages filled with designs that held power beyond ink and skin. Here was where rebellion took shape under my pen—a phoenix rising from ashes, chains breaking under muscle and willpower...

My thoughts wandered back to Damien's amulet—its weight now more oppressive than protective—and to Raven's tome that lay hidden beneath loose floorboards. Each offered paths diverging toward salvation or ruin; each demanded choices I never thought I'd have to make.

As sleep eluded me and sunlight began to creep across ink-stained floors, I embraced this new reality: A tattoo artist caught between worlds not just by birthright but by choice—a choice now bound by ink and blood and an unyielding resolve to reclaim what was ours by right: freedom from tyranny disguised as protection; power wielded not for domination but for unity; magic infused not with malice but with hope—a hope as enduring as the very art that pulsed through my veins.

***

The air in the hideout hung heavy, a mix of anticipation and dread knitting together like the tight stitches of a wound. Lynx paced the concrete floor, the rhythm of his boots a drumbeat to the silent symphony of our anxiety. Tara stood by the makeshift table, her fingers tracing over maps scattered with scribbles and symbols that only we could decipher.

"Alex, you can't seriously be considering Evelyn's offer," Tara said, her eyes never leaving the map but her voice cutting through my thoughts.

I perched on the edge of an old sofa, a relic in this place of shadows and secrets. The cool metal of Damien's amulet pressed against my chest through my shirt, a constant reminder of the noose around my neck. "We need every advantage we can get," I replied, weighing the cold fact that we were outmatched.

Lynx stopped pacing and turned to me. "If it's a trap—"

"It might not be," I cut in. "Evelyn's smart. She knows playing both sides could save her skin if Damien's ship sinks."

Tara sighed, exasperation lacing her breath. "Or she could be leading us right into Damien's fangs."

I stood up, stretching my legs, feeling the coiled tension like a spring ready to snap. "We don't have to walk in blind. We take precautions."

Lynx crossed his arms, his brow furrowed as he considered it. "And what precautions would those be?"

A plan started to form in my mind, a risky gambit that danced on the edge of folly and genius. "We'll meet her on our terms—neutral ground, public place. Somewhere Damien wouldn't dare start trouble."

"And if he does?" Tara asked.

"Then we'll give him a show he won't forget," I said with more confidence than I felt.

Lynx nodded slowly. "I'll arrange it. But Alex, this is your call. If things go south..."

"They won't," I assured him, though the butterflies in my stomach betrayed my bravado.

The hours ticked by as we prepared for the meeting with Evelyn. Tara insisted on accompanying me as backup; I didn't argue—the more eyes we had watching for a double-cross, the better.

As night fell like a curtain over the city's sins, we chose an old café that still bore the marks of better times—a place humming with life where supernatural dealings were masked by mundane chatter and clinking cups.

Evelyn arrived fashionably late, sliding into the booth across from me with a grace that belied her lethal nature. Her eyes flickered to Tara standing off to the side before settling on me with an unreadable expression.

"I appreciate you coming," I began cautiously.

She waved off my gratitude with a gloved hand. "Let's skip pleasantries. You want information; I want insurance."

I leaned forward slightly. "Insurance against what? Damien?"

Her lips twitched into something that could've been mistaken for a smile in another life. "Against uncertainty."

Tara tensed beside me; she smelled treachery like bloodhounds sniffed out fear.

"And what do you have for us?" I asked.

Evelyn slid an envelope across the table; inside were photos—Damien's hideouts, his associates, plans written in codes that whispered secrets only to those who spoke their language.

"This is good," I murmured after inspecting them briefly.

"It's more than good—it's your lifeline," Evelyn countered smoothly.

"So what's your price?" I asked bluntly.

"Protection when this all goes down," she replied without hesitation.

Tara shifted uneasily behind me. It was one thing to take down Damien; it was another to shelter one of his top lieutenants.

"I'll consider it," I said noncommittally as I pocketed the envelope.

Evelyn stood up smoothly, her eyes locking onto mine with an intensity that left no room for doubt. "Don't take too long deciding."

She left as quietly as she had come, leaving behind an echo of power plays and hidden agendas.

Back at our hideout, Lynx dissected Evelyn's information with surgical precision while Tara watched him like a hawk ready to pluck out lies from truths scattered on paper wings.

"Can we trust this?" Lynx finally asked me after hours of analysis.

"We don't have much choice." My reply came from somewhere deep inside me—a place where caution fought against desperation and often lost.

Tara placed her hand on my shoulder—a silent vow that she'd follow me into whatever hell I was leading us toward.

It was then that it hit me—the weight of every decision resting squarely on my shoulders and the lives intertwined with mine. The choice wasn't just about whether or not to trust Evelyn; it was about how far I was willing to go to end Damien's reign over us all.

The answer came to me like lightning searing through fog—I would do whatever it took, even if it meant walking into fire and letting it forge me anew or burn me to ash.

"We use Evelyn's information," I declared with newfound resolve. "But not just defensively."

Lynx raised an eyebrow in silent question while Tara waited for me to continue.

"We've been hiding in shadows for too long," I said as power thrummed beneath my skin—a melody of ink and magic waiting for release. "It's time we bring this fight into the light—use our tattoos not just as shields but as weapons."

A collective breath filled the room—a prelude to chaos or victory; only time would tell which melody fate would favor.

Tara's grip tightened around my shoulder—solidarity or steadying herself against what was to come? Perhaps both.

I looked each of them in the eye before continuing: "We tattoo every ally we have with symbols of rebellion and strength—turn them into living beacons of our resistance."

Murmurs of agreement rose around us—a chorus ready for battle's song.

"We strike during The Ascension Protocol," I said firmly. "When Damien is most vulnerable—when he thinks he has already won."

Tara nodded fiercely while Lynx clenched his fists—resolute.

"We will turn his eclipse into our dawn."

Chapter 13

Gathering Shadows

The air hung thick with the stench of damp concrete and rust as I entered the dimly lit basement that served as our makeshift war room. Shadows clung to the walls, and in their midst, the key members of the Resistance huddled around a battered table, their faces etched with lines of worry and determination. Lynx, his eyes sharp as ever, nodded to me as I approached. Tara stood close by, her arms folded across her chest, a storm brewing in her gaze.

"Thanks for coming, Alex," Lynx said without preamble. "We don't have much time."

I took my place among them, feeling the weight of my decisions like a shroud around my shoulders. "Let's get to it then," I replied.

Cipher, her hair tied back in a no-nonsense ponytail, unrolled a map across the table. It was marked with various symbols and notes that traced the ley lines beneath the city like veins. "We've identified several weak points in Damien's network," she began. "His reliance on these lines for power could be his undoing."

"Could be?" Tara interjected, skepticism lacing her voice. "We need more than 'could be' if we're going up against him during The Ascension Protocol."

I leaned over the map, tracing a finger along one of the lines that converged at an old cemetery on the outskirts of town. "We disrupt the flow here," I suggested, tapping the spot decisively. "If we can sever his connection to this line during his ritual, it might just give us the edge we need."

Lynx considered this for a moment before nodding slowly. "It's risky," he admitted. "But high risk might bring high reward."

I could feel everyone's eyes on me as I straightened up, and I knew they were waiting for more than just suggestions—they were waiting for leadership. A leadership that I had reluctantly embraced since Damien had marked me as his own.

"Alright," I said, mustering more confidence than I felt. "Let's talk about how we can make this happen without tipping our hand."

Tara spoke up first. "We need diversions—lots of them. We have to spread Damien's forces thin if we want to stand any chance at taking out that ley line connection."

"Agreed," Lynx added. "We've got people who can create chaos where it counts." He looked at me with a question in his eyes.

"I can help with that," I confirmed. "I've been working on something—a series of tattoos designed to amplify emotions." A murmur of interest went around the table.

"You mean like an emotional contagion?" Cipher asked.

"Exactly." The tattoos were my latest innovation—ink that could spread feelings like wildfire through a crowd.

"It's brilliant," Tara said with grudging admiration. "But it'll take precision timing."

"We'll have to coordinate with other cells across the city," Lynx added.

My thoughts drifted briefly to Evelyn's role in all this—our clandestine informant from within Damien's ranks. Trusting her was like playing with fire; she was as dangerous as she was valuable.

"And what about Evelyn?" I asked, voicing my concerns aloud. "She's our wild card."

Lynx exchanged a glance with Tara before responding. "Evelyn will get us inside intel—we need to be ready to act on it immediately."

The room fell into contemplative silence as we all considered our next moves. We were outgunned and outnumbered but driven by something much stronger than fear—hope.

"We'll need contingencies," Cipher pointed out pragmatically. "If anything goes wrong—"

"When it goes wrong," Tara corrected grimly.

"—we need fallback plans." Cipher finished unfazed by Tara's interruption.

"And those plans start with us right here," I declared firmly, locking eyes with each member of our group in turn.

The weight of responsibility bore down on me heavier than ever before, but I refused to let it crush me—I couldn't afford to.

As we delved deeper into our strategy session, plotting each move like chess pieces in a game where every decision was life or death, time seemed to blur around us until only our mission remained clear and sharp.

In every shadow that flickered across the walls of our bunker, in every hushed conversation that passed between us under cover of darkness, there lay our resolve—a silent vow etched in ink and blood—to bring down Damien and free our city from his grasp once and for all.

* * *

In the hollowed quiet of our makeshift war room—a repurposed backroom in Jade's tattoo studio—my allies and I gathered around a table strewn with maps, arcane tomes, and the digital glow of Cipher's laptop. The air was thick with the scent of incense and determination. We were a motley crew: tattoo artists, a tech wizard, an ex-gang member, and even a sorcerer. Our collective goal? To undermine Damien's Ascension Protocol.

"We've got less than 48 hours," Lynx announced, his eyes scanning over the network of ley lines we'd mapped out across the city. "We need to finalize our strategy."

I nodded, my fingers tracing over the pathways that pulsed with hidden power, energy lines that intersected beneath the very streets where mundane life carried on oblivious to the supernatural undercurrents. "These ley lines are our lifeline. If we can disrupt Damien's connection to them, we can weaken his control."

Cipher leaned in, pointing to a cluster of lines that converged near Crimson Ink. "This is where Damien's hold is strongest. He'll be channeling energy from here during the eclipse."

Jade tapped a stack of papers beside her. "I've compiled every bit of lore on ley line disruption we could find." Her gaze met mine with unspoken understanding—we both knew the depth of magic contained within these ancient scripts could be our salvation or our downfall.

Tara pulled out a collection of small jars filled with pigments that glimmered unnaturally in the low light. "These are the enchanted inks I've been working on," she said. "Each one is keyed to amplify emotions—hope, courage, defiance."

My own contribution lay next to Tara's—a series of designs I'd painstakingly created, each imbued with protective charms and empowerment sigils. These weren't just tattoos; they were wearable talismans designed to shield and strengthen our allies.

Lynx rapped his knuckles on the table, drawing our attention back to him. "We need to know more about Damien's movements on the night of the eclipse. Evelyn?" he prompted.

Evelyn shifted uncomfortably, her usual confidence waning under the weight of her betrayal to Damien. "He's planning something big at Crimson Ink," she admitted. "But I don't have specifics."

"You think you can get us more intel?" I asked.

She hesitated for a fraction too long before nodding. The trust between us was as thin as rice paper—easily torn and just as transparent.

"Victor's still feeding us information from inside," Jade added quickly, sensing tension in the air. "He might be able to give us more."

I couldn't help but feel a twinge of bitterness at Victor's name—the same man who'd been so quick to peruse my collection of ancient texts for Damien's benefit now played double agent.

Cipher cracked his knuckles and swiveled his chair toward us. "I've hacked into the city's surveillance system," he announced proudly. "We'll have eyes everywhere."

The room hummed with potential energy as each piece of our collective puzzle slotted into place—a tapestry woven from threads of skill and desperation.

Tara scooted closer to me and whispered, "You sure about this? Once we start, there's no going back."

I met her gaze squarely, my resolve hardening like ink setting into skin. "We have no choice," I said quietly. "Damien won't stop until he controls everything—or destroys it trying."

The plan was audacious—during The Ascension Protocol, we would deploy teams across key ley line intersections armed with Cipher's tech and my tattoos to disrupt Damien's connection while sowing chaos among his forces with emotionally charged symbols.

It wasn't just about throwing a wrench into Damien's machinations; it was about igniting a spark within those under his thrall—a beacon for those who'd lost their way in his darkness.

As we dispersed to our respective tasks—the clock ticking down with relentless certainty—I couldn't shake off the feeling that this was more than just a battle for control or survival. It was a fight for our very souls.

With each brushstroke of ink onto skin, I wove spells of protection and rebellion—a silent resistance etched into flesh that would resonate with every heartbeat of those brave enough to stand against tyranny.

The weight of responsibility bore down on me like a physical force as I prepared my equipment for what would undoubtedly be my most crucial session yet at Crimson Ink.

There was no room for doubt now; only action.

"Let's get to work," I said, rolling up my sleeves as Tara nodded beside me. We had resources pooled and knowledge shared; now it was time to put them into play—to craft an uprising one tattoo at a time.

* * *

I could feel the tension in the air, thick as the scent of ink and magic that always lingered in Crimson Ink. We huddled around a crude map of the city, marked with lines that traced the hidden pulse of power beneath our feet—the ley lines. Lynx pointed to various spots on the map, each a node of energy that Damien sought to exploit.

"We hit him where it hurts," Lynx said, her voice low and steady. "The ley lines. If we disrupt his access during The Ascension Protocol, we throw off his entire plan."

Jade nodded, her hands tracing over the marked intersections. "We'll need more than just a disruption. We need a multifaceted plan—one that not only cuts off his power but also sows confusion within his ranks."

Cipher leaned back against a stack of crates, arms folded across his chest. "And how do you propose we do that without getting caught? Or worse?"

I took a deep breath, feeling the weight of responsibility settle on my shoulders. "We play to our strengths," I said. "Each of us has skills that can contribute to this plan. It's about coordination and timing."

Tara brushed her hair back from her face, eyes scanning over us all. "Alright then, let's hear it. What's the game plan?"

"We split into teams," I began, feeling the blueprint of our strategy take shape in my mind. "Team one focuses on the ley lines. They'll use the enchanted inks I've prepared to tattoo symbols at each intersection—symbols that will draw out and nullify the energy Damien's trying to harness."

"That's where I come in," Jade interjected with a confident smile. "I know a few runes that'll scramble any magical signal Damien tries to send out."

"Perfect," I replied. "You'll lead team one with Cipher and a few others from the resistance who are skilled in stealth and diversion."

Lynx's eyes were sharp as she spoke next. "Team two will handle internal disruption. That's my territory." She tapped on various locations on the map—Damien's known hideouts and places where his followers gathered. "We spread rumors, plant doubts among his followers, make them question Damien's leadership."

Tara chimed in, her voice determined. "I'll take team three for protection and quick response." She gestured to herself and two others who were adept at combat magic. "If anyone gets into trouble or if Damien sends his goons after any of you, we're there to provide backup."

"And Evelyn?" I asked cautiously.

Lynx nodded solemnly. "She's our inside woman. She'll feed us real-time information on Damien's movements during The Ascension Protocol." Her gaze met mine with unspoken understanding—the risk Evelyn was taking by aligning with us.

The final piece fell into place as I considered my own role in this intricate dance of deception and defiance. "I'll be moving between teams," I said resolutely. "Ensuring our tattoos hold their power and offering support wherever it's needed most."

"Sounds like you've got yourself spread thin," Cipher remarked.

I shrugged slightly but felt my resolve harden like ink setting into skin. "It's what needs to be done."

Jade placed her hand on my shoulder briefly—a silent message of solidarity—before turning back to the map. "We have 48 hours until The Ascension Protocol begins." Her finger stabbed down on one of the nodes pulsing ominously on our makeshift chart.

"That gives us two days to finalize our plans and get into position," Lynx added.

"We'll need to work fast then," Tara said as she stood up, rolling her shoulders back as if readying herself for battle.

"And carefully," Cipher added.

The group nodded collectively—an unspoken oath binding us together.

For hours we drilled down into specifics—routes, timing, fallback points—until every member knew their part like a verse from an old song.

As night descended upon us like a cloak woven from shadow and silence, I looked around at this band of rebels—their faces set with determination, their eyes alight with purpose—and felt an unfamiliar sense of camaraderie stir within me.

With final nods exchanged and hands clasped briefly in solidarity, we dispersed into the darkness of the city that waited beyond our secret haven's walls.

The next day dawned gray and heavy—a mirror to my mood as I made my way through deserted alleys towards Crimson Ink. The weight of Damien's amulet around my neck felt colder than usual as if it sensed my betrayal and disapproved.

Inside Crimson Ink, everything appeared normal—the buzz of tattoo machines a comforting drone beneath the undercurrents of fear and anticipation swirling within me.

I busied myself preparing pigments and needles—tools of my trade now turned weapons against an enemy who was both formidable and familiar.

Clients came and went—a canvas of skin bearing silent witness to their stories etched in ink—a reminder that amidst this brewing storm lay lives untouched by our hidden war.

Yet with each client that left satisfied with their new tattoos—a blend of artistry and protection—I could feel our plan inching forward like a silent predator stalking its prey.

As dusk approached once more, wrapping its velvet arms around the cityscape outside my windows, I paused—a momentary lull before tomorrow's storm—and closed my eyes.

Images danced behind my lids—flashes of what might come—the risks we were taking... The lives we were putting on line...

But beyond fear lay something else—a glimmering thread weaving through every vision—the hope for freedom... For a future unmarred by Damien's dark ambitions...

With a deep breath drawn from wellsprings of courage I never knew I possessed, I opened my eyes once more—to face whatever tomorrow would bring—together with those who had become more than allies... They had become friends... Comrades... Family...

And together—we would rise or fall—as one.

* * *

In the cavernous heart of the abandoned subway station, I could feel the thrum of the city's pulse vibrating through the walls, a rhythmic echo of anticipation. This derelict place had become our sanctuary, our command center against Damien and his tyrannical grip. Lynx had said it was shielded from prying eyes, cloaked in spells woven by Cipher's deft hands. But it wasn't just a hideout—it was my crucible, where I'd forge my skills into weapons of defiance.

The Resistance had gathered around makeshift tables littered with maps and notes. Amidst them, I set up my station: inks infused with magic, needles that seemed to hum with potential, and parchment spread out like wings ready to take flight. These weren't just tools; they were extensions of my will.

"Ready to become the artisan of rebellion?" Lynx's voice cut through my focus.

I looked up, meeting his gaze squarely. "I've been ready. Let's turn this art into an arsenal."

He nodded, gesturing to Cipher who approached with a thick tome under her arm—the same one Raven had given me, filled with ancient knowledge about magical tattoos. Its pages held secrets that stretched back centuries, linking my heritage to the mystical energies that flowed beneath the city.

Cipher opened the book to a marked page. "This chapter details sigils that amplify emotions. If we can stir enough unrest within Damien's ranks—"

"Chaos from within," I finished her thought, already envisioning the designs taking shape on skin.

For hours we pored over the text, Cipher guiding me through complex symbols and incantations while Tara ensured we weren't interrupted. Jade checked in periodically, bringing updates and fresh supplies. The sense of urgency never waned; it seeped into every line I drew, every rune I memorized.

We moved on to practical application as dusk settled outside our clandestine walls. On a volunteer from the Resistance—a burly man named Knox—I began etching a sigil designed to heighten awareness and sharpen instincts. The ink sank into his skin, shimmering slightly as my magic mingled with his life force.

"You're not just giving him a tattoo," Jade remarked from behind me, her tone tinged with awe.

"No," I said without breaking my rhythm. "I'm giving him eyes in the back of his head."

The tattoo came alive under my touch, a network of lines and shapes interlocking around Knox's shoulder blade like a spiderweb laced with dew at dawn. It wasn't just about aesthetics; it was functionality woven into form.

Jade whistled softly as she watched the sigil pulse faintly with an inner light. "Damien won't see him coming."

As night enveloped us completely, I moved on to more intricate designs—ones meant to protect against psychic attacks and manipulation. These would be for Tara and Lynx; they were taking risks far greater than any of us by stepping directly into Damien's shadow during The Ascension Protocol.

Tara sat before me first, rolling up her sleeve with determined eyes that held a storm within their depths. As I worked on her arm, crafting barriers in every stroke of my needle, she spoke softly.

"We're changing things, Alex," she said with conviction strong enough to carve canyons into existence. "We're shaping our own destiny."

Her words were fuel to my flame as I continued working late into the night, my fingers steady even as fatigue tugged at their edges.

When dawn broke through the cracks in our fortress of solitude and rebellion, we emerged different—stronger. Our tattoos were not just marks upon our skin; they were emblems of our cause.

We practiced moving as one unit in syncopated rhythm through drills led by Lynx—a dance between shadows designed to keep us safe and undetected when we struck at Damien's forces. With each movement etched in muscle memory and magic-infused ink coursing through our veins like liquid fire, we became something more than ourselves: a singular force bent on fracturing an empire built on fear and subjugation.

But practice wasn't enough; we needed to test our newfound abilities outside these walls where reality awaited with sharp teeth bared.

With Tara at my side like an anchor against the stormy sea ahead, we ventured out under Lynx's watchful eye to scout one of Damien's lesser-known outposts—a small tattoo parlor that served as a front for his nefarious dealings.

As we slipped through the alleys like whispers on the wind, Tara brushed her fingers against her new tattoo—a touchstone amidst uncertainty—and gave me a nod that said more than words ever could.

The outpost was dimly lit and reeked of blood mixed with disinfectant—an abattoir masquerading as a place of artistry. It sickened me to think how many souls had been bound here under Damien's command.

We didn't have long before risk turned into recklessness; so with quick but thorough glances exchanged between us three infiltrators, we mapped out escape routes and noted guard placements—all while feigning interest in mundane designs displayed on cracked walls lined with yellowed wallpaper peeling at its corners like secrets desperate for daylight.

Our tattoos held strong—Tara's senses razor-sharp as she picked up hushed conversations between gang members boasting about recent conquests; mine providing an aura of inconspicuousness that let us pass unnoticed like ghosts drifting through their midst; Lynx's imbuing him with charisma that saw him schmoozing information from an unwitting artist about troop movements on eclipse night.

It was exhilarating—each successful evasion felt like another crack in Damien's façade—and terrifying all at once because each step forward brought us closer to a precipice from which there would be no return.

When we regrouped back at base camp after our reconnaissance mission—unscathed but hearts pounding hard enough to rival any drum—I couldn't help but feel a sense of pride swelling within me for what we'd accomplished together in such little time.

Our plan was coming together piece by piece—every tattoo another stitch in a tapestry of revolution—and for once since this nightmare began... I dared hope that maybe... just maybe... we stood a chance against the darkness threatening to engulf us all.

* * *

The flickering light of the subway station cast an eerie glow over our huddled forms, maps sprawled out before us like the scattered pieces of a puzzle we were desperate to solve. The sharp tang of metal and the distant rumble of trains long gone formed the backdrop to our whispered strategizing. Lynx's eyes were alight with determination, Cipher's hands steady as he marked out positions, and Tara... Tara was the rock we all clung to in this maelstrom.

Yet, as I dipped my brush into the pot of ink infused with magic, I couldn't shake the coil of dread that wound tighter around my heart. The weight of responsibility bore down on me, each stroke of my brush a potential difference between life and death. Could these tattoos truly protect us from Damien's wrath? Could we really shatter his plans and liberate our city?

A chill crept up my spine, unbidden, as I etched the symbols onto Tara's skin. The designs came alive under my touch, glowing faintly with a power that was part ancient rite, part desperate hope. Tara met my gaze, her confidence unwavering, but it did little to still the tremor in my hands.

"I know that look," she murmured once the others had moved away to finalize their parts in our plan. "Talk to me."

I hesitated, unwilling to voice the fears that might unravel the fragile threads of courage we'd woven together. But Tara knew me too well; she could read the unspoken dread like a book.

"It's just..." I began, then paused, searching for words that wouldn't sound like defeat. "What if it's not enough? Damien is more than just a man; he's a force we've barely scratched the surface of understanding. What if these tattoos can't protect you all? What if I can't..."

"Alex," Tara interrupted gently but firmly. "You're not alone in this. We're all carrying our share of doubts, but we trust you—your skills have already saved lives."

Her belief was a balm, yet it couldn't fully ease the knot in my stomach. Every scenario I'd run through ended with some loss, some failure that could trace its roots back to me.

I shook my head slightly. "I just can't help thinking about what Damien is capable of—what he'll do if he finds out about us before we're ready."

Tara reached out and took my hand, her grip warm and grounding. "Then we won't let him find out until it's too late for him to do anything about it."

Her words were meant to comfort, yet they sparked another round of what-ifs in my mind. If Damien discovered our plans too soon... The image of Crimson Ink overrun by his shadow-beasts flashed before my eyes—a nightmare I'd lived through once already.

"We've been careful," Lynx called over from his position by the map. "We have contingencies for every contingency."

But even as he spoke with such conviction, I saw it—the same shadow of doubt that flickered behind his eyes. It was there in Cipher's tense shoulders as he pored over ley line charts and Jade's clenched jaw as she checked her equipment one last time.

We were a band of misfits and mavericks bound together by a common enemy—an enemy whose reach extended further than any of us could truly comprehend.

"Contingencies don't account for everything," I said softly, almost to myself.

Tara squeezed my hand again before releasing it. "Maybe not," she conceded with a sigh that told me she understood all too well. "But Alex, think about how far you've come—how far we've all come since Damien first tried to ensnare you with his amulet."

Her words were a thread leading back through time—to moments of defiance against Damien's cruelty and small victories snatched from the jaws of defeat.

She was right; there had been growth amidst the fear—a resilience forged in fires I never would have willingly walked into alone.

A sudden surge of determination welled up within me—the same surge that had compelled me to create Crimson Ink in the first place. It wasn't just about survival anymore; it was about reclaiming what Damien had tried to take from us—our wills, our lives... our city.

"I won't let him win," I declared with newfound resolve. My voice carried across the station—a declaration more than an assurance—and heads turned toward me.

"That's the spirit," Lynx said with a nod.

Cipher smiled grimly but approvingly.

Jade approached then, her expression serious but not without hope. "We believe in you," she said simply.

Their faith bolstered me; it became a shield against the onslaught of doubt trying to breach my defenses once more.

And so we continued—planning and preparing for what would either be our greatest triumph or our most devastating defeat. Each moment spent in quiet collaboration steeled us against what lay ahead—each whispered plan and shared glance binding us closer together.

But even as I stood there among friends who had become family—each one ready to face down darkness beside me—I couldn't escape the creeping tendrils of fear that whispered incessantly in my ear: Was it truly possible for us to succeed against such formidable odds?

It was a question without an answer—a riddle whose solution lay shrouded in shadows not yet cast by an enemy who remained steps ahead.

So there we stood—in limbo between hope and despair—with only our shared resolve and each other to light the way forward into an uncertain future where nothing was guaranteed except the promise that we would face it together.

* * *

A shiver raced down my spine as I surveyed the collection of faces huddled around the dim glow of the subway station's flickering lights. This ragtag group of rebels, friends, and newfound allies all bore the weight of our impending confrontation with Damien. Lynx, Cipher, Jade, Tara — each one etched with tattoos of my making, symbols of our unity and shared purpose.

"We've got one shot at this," Lynx's voice cut through the murmur of the underground hideout. "When Damien initiates The Ascension Protocol, we strike. Alex's tattoos will be our edge."

Nods rippled through the crowd. I felt their eyes on me, some filled with hope, others with skepticism. Could they sense the tempest of doubt swirling within me? Did they know how heavily Damien's amulet weighed around my neck, a constant reminder of his dark influence?

I pushed those thoughts aside and focused on the map spread out before us. Ley line intersections marked in crimson, each a pulsing vein of potential power that Damien sought to exploit. Our plan was etched around them, a strategy as intricate as any tattoo I'd ever designed.

Jade leaned over the map, her finger tracing a path from one intersection to another. "Team One will block these points," she said confidently. Her team would use enchanted tattoos to create emotional barriers, an ingenious twist on my art.

Lynx nodded at Cipher and then at me. "Team Two will spread confusion among Damien's ranks," he stated firmly. His eyes held a fire that kindled my own determination.

"And Team Three," Tara chimed in, her hand resting briefly on my shoulder, "will be ready to step in with protection and backup."

Evelyn's role was crucial; she would be our insider feeding us information while staying hidden within Damien's shadow. It was a risk — trusting her — but it was one we had to take.

As plans were solidified and roles assigned, a tightness gripped my chest. This was more than just rebellion; it was a war for freedom from Damien's tyrannical grip on our supernatural community.

The hours passed in a blur as we prepared our enchanted inks and protective tattoos. My hands moved with practiced precision, drawing power from the ley lines into each drop of ink that would soon adorn skin.

I had given Tara and Lynx tattoos designed to shield them from psychic attacks — symbols that hummed with energy against their skin. We tested them at an outpost, and they worked flawlessly, extracting information without leaving so much as a ripple in the psychic landscape.

The night air was thick with tension as we left our subterranean refuge and moved through the city's shadowed streets. Time was running out; The Ascension Protocol loomed like a storm cloud over us all.

We split into our teams at the designated rendezvous point — an old church with stained glass windows that danced with colors even under the moonless sky.

"I'll be right here if you need me," I assured them all before they departed into the night. I could feel their determination matching mine; it pulsed like a heartbeat beneath my fingers as I touched each shoulder in silent farewell.

Alone for a moment, I allowed myself to breathe — really breathe — feeling the night air fill my lungs. Then I unfurled the map once more, my fingers tracing ley lines that sang with power just beneath this city's skin.

It was then that something unexpected happened: The amulet around my neck grew warm against my chest. A warmth that spread through me like sunlight piercing clouds.

I drew it out from under my shirt and watched as it began to glow softly in my palm — not just reflecting light but emanating it. And there was something else; it vibrated gently as if responding to an unheard call.

That's when I heard it — or rather felt it: A thrumming beneath my feet, a resonance within the earth itself. The ley lines were responding not just to Damien's ritual preparations but also to something within me.

Was this what Raven had hinted at? That there was more to my heritage than even I knew? That within me lay not just the power to create but perhaps also to command?

I turned back toward where Team One had vanished into darkness and made a decision: If Damien sought to use these ley lines for his Ascension Protocol, then I would use them too — but for our liberation.

The warmth from the amulet spread up through my arm and settled into my heart space like an ember ready to ignite into flame.

That ember burst forth then, not as fire but as clarity — an understanding so profound it took away what little breath I had left: I wasn't just a pawn in Damien's game or even simply a tattoo artist with magical lineage; I was someone who could shape destinies — not just on skin but across this city and beyond.

This revelation solidified something within me: resolve hardened like ink setting into skin — permanent and unyielding. With every piece of myself that Damien had tried to claim or control came an equal measure of strength that he could never touch because it lay deep within me where only truth resided.

As I clasped the amulet back around my neck, its glow subsided but its warmth remained like courage made manifest against my skin.

"I'll see this through," I whispered into the night air which seemed to hold its breath along with me. "For Crimson Ink... for all of us."

With newfound resolve coursing through me like lifeblood through veins, I strode forward into darkness not as prey but predator — ready for whatever lay ahead because now I knew: Whatever power Damien thought he had over me paled in comparison to what truly lay within.

Chapter 14

The Path to Power

The city's heartbeat thrummed beneath my feet, a rhythm I felt in my bones as I stood at the threshold of an abandoned bookstore that had seen better days. The windows were boarded up, the sign faded, but the ley lines whispered secrets through the cracks in the pavement, guiding me here. It was a hunch, a tug in my gut that led me away from the subway station and my allies.

I pushed open the door with a creak that echoed through the musty air. Dust motes danced in the shafts of light piercing through the wooden planks. The scent of old paper and forgotten stories filled my lungs. Rows upon rows of books loomed like silent sentinels guarding knowledge lost to time.

A voice shattered the silence. "Looking for something specific, or just browsing?"

Startled, I spun around to find an old man emerging from the shadows, his eyes gleaming with an intensity that belied his frail appearance. He leaned on a carved cane, its top shaped like an ouroboros—the very symbol that haunted my dreams and marked those bound to Damien.

"I... I'm not sure," I admitted. My voice sounded strange in this place of quietude. "There's something I need to find."

The old man chuckled, a sound like rustling pages. "Isn't there always?" He gestured with a gnarled hand toward the back of the store. "Come with me."

He moved with surprising agility between aisles crammed with books until we reached a table blanketed with dust. On it lay a book bound in leather so dark it seemed to swallow the light around it. My heart skipped a beat as he opened it carefully, revealing pages filled with symbols that sang to my soul.

"This is what you're here for," he said softly.

I stepped closer, peering at the ancient text. The script was indecipherable but familiar—like a song heard in childhood and half-remembered.

"How do you know?" My question was barely above a whisper.

The old man tapped his temple with a crooked finger. "When you've lived as long as I have, you learn to listen to the whispers of magic."

I glanced at him sharply. "Who are you?"

He smiled enigmatically. "A friend of your grandmother's," he revealed.

A chill ran down my spine at the mention of her—a woman who'd straddled two worlds just as I did now.

"The Mark of Power..." His voice drew me back to the present, "is more than just a design or a tool for control." He flipped through pages until he stopped at an illustration that took my breath away.

There it was—the Mark—drawn in intricate detail with symbols that seemed to shift even as I stared. It wasn't static; it was alive, changing subtly just as Raven had described.

"It's a living entity," he continued, confirming what Raven had warned me about. "It chooses its bearer and imparts not just power but wisdom... or madness."

My hands trembled as I reached out but didn't touch the page. "Where is it?" I asked, fearing the answer.

"Lost," he said simply. "But not unreachable."

I frowned, confused and anxious. Damien couldn't get his hands on this—if he did...

"You're thinking too narrowly," he chided gently, as if reading my thoughts. "The Mark isn't about granting power; it's about balance."

"Balance?" I echoed.

"Yes." He nodded solemnly. "Our world teeters on the edge of chaos and order, light and shadow. The Mark exists to maintain that equilibrium."

My mind raced as pieces fell into place—a puzzle half-solved but still veiled in mystery.

"And Damien?" I pressed on.

"A disruptor," he answered gravely. "He seeks to tip the scales for his gain."

"So how do I find it? The Mark?"

The old man closed the book and looked up at me with eyes like pools of ancient wisdom.

"Follow your lineage," he instructed cryptically. "Your blood will guide you."

Frustration clawed at me—more riddles when clarity was what I needed most.

"Can you be more specific?" My tone edged on pleading.

He stood then, moving past me toward a shelf obscured by shadows. From it, he retrieved an object wrapped in velvet so deep blue it was nearly black.

"This," he said as he handed it to me, "will help you see."

I unwrapped it carefully to reveal an orb made of crystal clear enough to be mistaken for water yet hard as diamond—a scrying sphere?

"It will show you what you need," he explained before adding sternly, "but be warned: knowledge comes at a price."

"I understand." Though truthfully, fear twisted inside me—a knot tight with potential consequences.

"You must go now," he urged suddenly urgent.

"Why? What's happening?"

But he didn't answer; instead, his gaze fixed on something behind me—an unseen presence that raised every hair on my neck and sent adrenaline coursing through my veins.

Turning slowly, heart pounding in dread anticipation, I faced the unexpected sight of Tara bursting through the door, her expression taut with alarm.

"We need to leave—now!" she gasped out between breaths. "Damien's enforcers are sweeping the area!"

Panic gripped me as reality crashed down—there was no time for more questions or answers; survival took precedence over curiosity.

With one last look at the old man who nodded gravely as if this was all part of some grand design beyond my understanding—I tucked the sphere into my jacket and followed Tara into the maze-like alleys behind the bookstore.

We ran under a bruised sky threatening rain while lightning crackled distantly—nature mirroring our urgency—and yet amidst chaos's impending descent upon us all a calm certainty settled within me: armed with this scrying sphere and fueled by newfound purpose from ancestral whispers...

* * *

The scrying sphere felt cool and heavy in my palm, its surface a swirl of mist and shadow. I clutched it tight, as if it could anchor me to my resolve. The old man's words lingered in my mind, a siren's call to embrace the heritage I'd spent so long tiptoeing around. The Mark of Power wasn't just a symbol; it was a legacy, a balancing force intertwined with my bloodline.

I slipped the sphere into my pocket just as Tara burst into the bookstore, her eyes wide with urgency. "Damien's sent his scouts out," she hissed, her breath coming in short bursts. "They're sweeping the city for you."

We left the bookstore with haste, blending into the evening throng that filled the streets. My heart raced not just from fear of Damien's pursuit but from the weight of the task ahead. To uncover the secrets of the Mark of Power, I'd have to venture deep into his territory.

The Red Quarter – that's what they called it. A part of the city where neon signs bled into the night like open wounds and shadows moved with predatory grace. It was Damien's playground, his kingdom of concrete and steel where he ruled unchallenged.

Tara walked beside me, her hand on the small of her back where she kept her knife hidden. We didn't speak much; words seemed trivial when weighed against the gravity of our mission.

"I'll be with you every step," she promised as we approached the invisible boundary that separated Damien's dominion from the rest of our world.

I nodded, swallowing hard. The Red Quarter wasn't just a place; it was a statement—a declaration that here, darkness reigned supreme.

We ducked into an alleyway as a pair of vampires sauntered past, their laughter echoing against the walls like a chilling melody. I pressed myself flat against the cold brick, feeling its rough texture bite into my skin through my shirt.

Tara gave me a look, one that said we weren't turning back now.

The scrying sphere pulsed in my pocket—a heartbeat urging me forward.

As we ventured deeper into the Red Quarter, I couldn't help but feel like I was walking through a gallery of Damien's conquests. Each tagged wall, each whispered rumor added to his mythos—a vampire lord whose influence seeped into every crack and crevice.

The address given to me by the old man led us to an old apartment building nestled between two neon-lit bars. Its façade was worn by time and neglect; its windows stared out like blind eyes onto the street.

"This is it," Tara whispered, casting a wary glance over her shoulder.

The lobby was empty save for a flickering lightbulb that did little to chase away the darkness. We took the stairs two at a time, reaching the third floor where a single door stood at the end of a long corridor.

Number 307 – this was where I'd find what I sought: information on my lineage and possibly even clues to finding the lost Mark itself.

My hand hovered over the doorknob, hesitating. What lay beyond this threshold? Answers? Or another trap set by Damien?

Tara nudged me gently, and I turned the knob.

The apartment was shrouded in shadows save for moonlight spilling through a crack in heavy curtains. Dust motes danced in its silver beam like tiny spirits lost in time.

"Alex," Tara murmured from behind me.

I took a step forward and felt something shift beneath my feet—a rug pulled taut across a trapdoor.

A chill ran down my spine as I bent down and pulled back the rug to reveal an iron ring set into wooden planks. This had to be what I was looking for—a hidden archive or sanctum where secrets of my ancestry lay buried.

Tara helped me pull open the trapdoor; hinges groaned in protest as if they hadn't moved in ages. A ladder descended into darkness below us.

"Be careful," Tara warned as I placed my foot on the first rung.

The air grew colder as we descended into what felt like another world—a space untouched by time where magic hung thickly in silence broken only by our breathing and distant sounds from above filtering through cracks in floorboards.

Shelves lined with ancient books towered around us while artifacts from bygone eras rested on pedestals covered in dust and cobwebs. This place was a tomb of knowledge waiting to be awakened by those brave enough—or desperate enough—to seek its wisdom.

My fingers brushed over leather-bound spines until one book caught my attention. It pulsed with energy that resonated with mine—an energy connected to my very soul.

I pulled it from its resting place; its cover depicted an intricate mark—the same symbol that haunted my dreams since childhood—the Mark of Power etched into leather like destiny calling out to me.

Tara stood guard at my side as I opened it carefully. Pages filled with arcane symbols and cryptic text fluttered under my touch while whispers filled my ears—voices from within or perhaps echoes of those who'd once wielded this knowledge?

We were so engrossed in our discovery that we didn't hear them until it was too late—the sound of footsteps descending rapidly towards us...

* * *

My heart hammered against my ribs as the rhythmic thumping of footsteps approached. Tara and I exchanged a glance that spoke volumes; we were cornered in this clandestine archive, our sanctuary potentially breached by forces unknown. I slipped the book with the Mark of Power symbol into my bag and whispered an incantation under my breath, hoping to veil us from sight.

The footsteps ceased, just inches from the door. A pause, pregnant with tension, then the door creaked open. We held our breaths, cloaked in my hastily conjured magic. A shadow loomed in the doorway, spilling into the room like dark ink. But it wasn't one of Damien's thugs—it was a hulking creature, eyes glinting with otherworldly malice.

"Damn," I muttered. My protection spells were meant for human threats, not this.

The creature sniffed the air, its nostrils flaring as it scanned the room. It was a hellhound, I realized—Damien's supernatural bloodhounds. I motioned for Tara to stay still and silent as the beast prowled closer.

"You can see it too, right?" Tara whispered.

I nodded and reached into my bag, fingers grazing the tools of my trade. Ink and needles wouldn't stop a hellhound, but magic might. Drawing on my heritage, I visualized a binding sigil in my mind's eye—a tattoo without skin to hold it.

The hellhound growled low in its throat as it edged closer to our hiding spot. It could sense us, even if it couldn't see us. I thrust my hand forward and released the sigil into the air. The glowing emblem shot toward the beast and wrapped around its form like ethereal chains.

The hellhound snarled and snapped at the air where the sigil bound it but could not break free. It was contained for now.

"We need to move," I said to Tara, urgency lacing my voice.

We slipped past the bound creature and into the labyrinthine corridors of the Red Quarter—Damien's turf crawling with vampires and worse.

The Red Quarter was a trap in itself; every alleyway seemed to breathe danger. We darted from shadow to shadow, avoiding streetlights like they were spotlights on a prison wall. Every noise made me twitch—every hiss of steam from a pipe sounded like a vampire's hiss.

It wasn't long before we hit our first barrier—a wall that hadn't been there moments before. It rose seamlessly from the cobblestones, bricked with what looked like obsidian stones that absorbed all light around them.

"A glamour," Tara murmured beside me.

I placed a palm against it; it felt colder than ice, colder than death itself. A shiver ran down my spine as I channeled warmth from within me into my fingertips—a warmth born from my human side—and pressed it into the cold stones.

They resisted at first but then shuddered under my touch as if rejecting an infection. Slowly, light began to seep through cracks in the barrier until it crumbled away like ash in a strong wind.

We didn't have time to celebrate; another presence made itself known—a wraithlike figure emerging from a nearby alleyway.

It drifted toward us without feet, its hollow eyes fixed on mine.

"You should not be here," it moaned, its voice echoing from some hollow cavity within its spectral form.

I swallowed hard but stood my ground. "We seek knowledge—not conflict."

"The Mark... you carry it..." The wraith extended a finger that blurred in and out of existence.

I tensed but didn't back away. "We mean to use it for good."

"Lies!" The wraith's howl sliced through the air like ice shards. "All seek power... all fall..."

Tara stepped forward, her voice steady despite her fear. "We're different."

The wraith paused then floated closer until I could feel its unearthly chill brush against my skin.

"Prove it," it demanded.

I dug deep into myself for something pure—something untouched by Damien's dark world—and found an image of Crimson Ink as it once was: a place of art and sanctuary before Damien's stain corrupted it.

I projected this image towards the wraith with all the sincerity and resolve I could muster—the vision of Crimson Ink restored to its former glory under my hand alone—a beacon against darkness rather than an instrument of it.

The wraith cocked its head as if considering what lay before its vacant gaze then dissipated without another word—leaving us free to press onward but chilled by its cryptic test.

Our path twisted deeper into vampire territory where streetlamps flickered erratically and shadows seemed animated by their own sinister wills—not quite alive but certainly not lifeless either.

At last we reached what had to be our final obstacle: an ancient iron gate etched with runes that hummed with magical energy—a gate that led to Damien's most closely guarded secrets if rumor held true.

It stood tall and ominous between two buildings that leaned inward as if conspiring together against intruders.

"I've seen these runes before," I said quietly, tracing one with a fingertip—the sensation like tracing scar tissue on skin long healed yet still sensitive.

"These are wards," Tara added softly behind me.

And they were powerful ones at that—wards designed not just to keep people out but also ensnare those who dared try their luck.

But luck had little to do with what came next—it was skill honed by heritage and necessity.

Drawing once more upon everything I'd learned—from grandmother's stories to Raven's tome—I visualized an unbinding sigil specific for these wards.

My hand moved on its own accord then—as if guided by some ancestral instinct—and traced symbols in the air before me: each motion deliberate each line connected by purpose rather than chance.

As I completed the final stroke—a release rather than an end—the gate responded first with resistance then acceptance until at last it swung open soundlessly revealing darkness beyond yet promising light ahead if only we dared enter...

* * *

The gate swung open with a low, resonant groan that echoed through the musty air of the Red Quarter, and Tara and I stepped into a room that was a stark contrast to the decay outside. Here, inside Damien's hidden vault, was a collection that would make any museum curator weep with envy. There were artifacts that pulsed with arcane energy, books bound in otherworldly materials, and scrolls that shimmered with enchantments. Yet, amidst all this supernatural splendor, my eyes fixed on a single pedestal in the center of the room.

On it lay an ancient tome, its cover embossed with a symbol that seemed to dance before my eyes – the Mark of Power. I felt an irresistible pull toward it, as if all my magical heritage converged on this singular point. My fingers twitched with anticipation as I moved closer, Tara's cautious footsteps behind me a soft patter in the otherwise silent chamber.

I hovered my hand above the book, not daring to touch it just yet. The air around it was charged, heavy with expectation. "This is it," I whispered, more to myself than to Tara.

"Yeah," she replied, her voice laced with awe and a tinge of fear. "But be careful, Alex. We don't know what kind of protections Damien might've put on it."

Her warning came too late. As my fingertips grazed the cover, a shockwave of energy blasted outward, throwing both of us back against the wall. Pain lanced through my body as if I'd touched a live wire. My ears rang, and for a moment, all I could see were spots dancing in my vision.

Tara was at my side in an instant, her hand on my shoulder. "Are you okay?" she asked urgently.

"Yeah," I gasped out once I found my breath again. "Just... electrified."

My gaze returned to the book. It remained on its pedestal, untouched and unopened. The symbol on its cover glowed faintly before fading back into the leather binding. It was mocking me, or so it felt.

"Damien's protections," Tara muttered darkly. "We need to find another way."

Frustration boiled within me. To come so close and still be so far – it gnawed at me like hunger pangs. The Mark of Power was there, within arm's reach, but sealed away behind invisible barriers that I had no key to unlock.

"We can't just give up," I said firmly as I pulled myself up to stand again.

"Of course not." Tara's eyes gleamed with determination in the dim light. "We'll figure this out."

We began searching the room for anything that could give us insight into bypassing Damien's magical safeguards – books on ancient wards, scrolls detailing protective spells – but each one seemed more cryptic than the last.

As we scoured through piles of knowledge that spanned centuries, if not millennia, my mind kept returning to the pedestal and its infuriatingly elusive prize.

"Alex!" Tara's voice cut through my thoughts like a blade. She held up a dusty scroll with trembling hands. "This might be something."

I joined her side and unrolled the parchment carefully between us. It depicted an intricate pattern of lines intersecting at various points – ley lines – with annotations scrawled in a language I couldn't read but somehow understood deep within my bones.

"The key is not just magical," I murmured as realization dawned on me. "It's geographical too."

Tara nodded excitedly. "These intersections... they're power nodes where ley lines cross. Maybe we need to be at one of these specific points to break through Damien's defenses."

A plan began forming in my head; it was bold and fraught with danger but holding onto caution hadn't gotten us anywhere thus far.

"Tara," I started hesitantly but she cut me off with a knowing look.

"You want to go now? To one of these intersections?"

I nodded grimly.

She didn't argue or try to dissuade me; she knew as well as I did that time wasn't on our side.

"Then let's go," she said instead, rolling up the scroll and tucking it into her jacket.

Leaving Damien's vault behind felt like stepping away from destiny itself – retreating when every fiber of my being screamed to push forward. But this wasn't giving up; this was strategizing.

We moved swiftly through the Red Quarter's deserted alleys towards one of the locations marked on our stolen scroll – an old cathedral now lying in ruins after years of neglect and conflict between supernatural factions.

The moon hung low in the sky by the time we arrived at our destination – a haunting silhouette against clouds that whispered promises of rain yet withheld their tears.

The ruins were desolate; crumbled stone walls whispered stories of ancient prayers and long-forgotten sermons as we stepped cautiously over scattered debris towards what had once been an altar.

Tara pulled out the scroll again and consulted it under the moonlight while I closed my eyes and extended my senses outward – feeling for the hum of energy beneath us where ley lines met.

And there it was – faint but unmistakable – like threads woven together by an invisible hand guiding fate itself.

"This is it," Tara confirmed quietly beside me.

The sensation was different here; there was power thrumming underfoot waiting to be harnessed or perhaps unleashed. With every breath I drew in this sacred space marked by both gods and monsters alike over eons past, determination hardened within me like steel tempered by fire.

I reached out again toward that power source using every bit of magical intuition passed down through generations coursing through my veins until finally... connection!

A surge raced up from deep within earth straight into heart igniting something primal long dormant until now... The air crackled around us charged particles dancing before our eyes as ley line energy responded to call...

Yet even as strength flowed through me newfound understanding blossomed alongside sobering truth - whatever lay beyond Damien's protections wasn't going be easy acquire nor safe wield...

As moment passed tension grew heavy air pregnant anticipation future events yet unfold ... We stood there united purpose despite uncertainties ahead knowing full well challenges we'd face journey just beginning...

* * *

Charged with power beneath the cathedral's ruins, I could feel the pulse of the city's ley lines coursing through me like a heartbeat. My skin tingled with potential, and my tattoos hummed with an energy that resonated with the ancient stones. Tara watched me, her eyes wide with a mix of fear and awe. "Alex, are you sure about this? Damien will feel it if you tamper with his network."

"I have to be," I replied, the words barely above a whisper. The connection to the ley lines was intoxicating, filling me with a sense of invincibility I'd never known. But it was more than that – it was clarity. For the first time, I felt like I wasn't just reacting to Damien's moves; I was ahead of him.

Taking a deep breath, I focused on the network of energy beneath us. If we were going to stand any chance during The Ascension Protocol, we needed an edge – and this was it. I let my consciousness drift along the ley lines, seeking out the points where Damien had anchored his dark magic.

Suddenly, a voice broke through my concentration. "Looking for something?"

I snapped back to reality and spun around. Victor stood at the entrance of the ruins, his imposing figure silhouetted against the dim light filtering in from above. Tara instinctively moved in front of me, her hands raised defensively.

"What do you want?" she demanded.

Victor raised his hands in a placating gesture. "Easy now," he said calmly. "I'm not here to fight."

My mind raced as I assessed our options. Victor was Damien's enforcer; if he was here without backup, he either came with a message or a mission – neither of which boded well for us.

"I need to talk to Alex," Victor continued, his gaze locking onto mine.

Tara glanced at me uncertainly but stepped aside, giving me space to approach him. "Talk then," I said cautiously.

He looked around before speaking in a hushed tone. "Damien's lost it," he began, and something in his voice made me believe him. "He's obsessed with finding that Mark of Power and using The Ascension Protocol for his own gain. It's not just about control anymore – it's about supremacy."

"And you disagree with his methods?" I asked skeptically.

"It's not just that." Victor shifted uncomfortably. "He's going too far. He doesn't see that this... power play of his is going to burn everything down – including us."

"So what? You want out?" Tara interjected sharply.

"No." He met my eyes with an intensity that took me by surprise. "I want to stop him."

I studied Victor closely, searching for any sign of deceit. His expression was earnest, almost desperate.

"Why should we trust you?" I pressed.

Victor sighed and pulled something from his jacket – an amulet similar to mine but cracked down its center, dark energy seeping from it like smoke. "Because I've been under his thumb too long," he said quietly. "And because I believe you can actually change things."

Tara and I exchanged a glance before she nodded slightly at me – a silent agreement that we should hear him out.

"What do you propose?" I asked.

Victor explained that Damien had become careless in his pursuit of power and had neglected certain protections within his network of influence on the ley lines – protections Victor himself had been responsible for maintaining.

"I can show you where they are," he offered. "You could use your tattoos to disrupt them... weaken his hold."

It was an opportunity too good to pass up – inside knowledge from one of Damien's own lieutenants could give us the upper hand we so desperately needed.

"Alright," I said after a moment's hesitation. "Show us."

We gathered around an old map Victor produced from inside his coat, detailing the intricate web of ley lines under the city. He pointed out several key locations where our efforts would have maximum impact.

"Hit these spots," he instructed, marking each one with an X. "It'll cause enough chaos in Damien's ranks for you to do whatever it is you're planning."

I nodded thoughtfully, already visualizing the tattoos that would serve as catalysts for disruption.

"Thank you," Tara said grudgingly as Victor prepared to leave.

"Don't thank me yet," he replied grimly. "If this doesn't work..."

His voice trailed off as he turned away from us and disappeared into the shadows of the ruins.

As soon as he was gone, Tara turned to me with urgency in her voice. "We need to move fast before Damien catches on."

I agreed wholeheartedly but paused as a sudden warmth enveloped my chest – the amulet Damien had given me pulsed softly against my skin as if responding to my resolve.

"Let's get back to Lynx and Cipher," I suggested quickly. "They need to know about this development."

We made our way out of the ruins stealthily, avoiding any unwanted attention from Damien's patrols or other supernatural entities lurking in the shadows.

Once safely back at our hideout, we shared Victor's intel with Lynx and Cipher who listened intently before discussing how best to integrate this new information into our plans against Damien's Ascension Protocol.

Lynx was skeptical at first but eventually conceded that Victor's betrayal could be genuine considering how high stakes had become for all involved parties within Crimson Ink's sphere of influence.

As discussions continued late into night surrounding how we could exploit these new-found weaknesses in Damien's defenses, tension hung thick air among us all knowing what failure would mean not only ourselves but also for entire city held under vampire gang's control.

With each moment passing by ticking closer towards lunar eclipse's zenith hour when Ascension Protocol would commence full force leaving little room error margin or second chances should our plans go awry during confrontation ahead.

* * *

The city's underbelly pulsed with secrets, the hum of magic from the ley lines weaving a restless energy that I could almost taste on my tongue. Crimson Ink stood as a beacon amidst this chaos, my own fortress of solitude, where ink and magic danced under my skin, yearning for release. Tara and Victor flanked me, their presence a reminder of the delicate thread we all dangled from—puppets to some, rebels to others.

We had gathered in the back room of my shop, pouring over the ancient scroll Victor had swiped from Damien's vault. It detailed ley line intersections throughout the city, points where power converged like rivers meeting in an endless ocean. My fingers traced the lines, feeling them resonate with the Mark of Power etched into my mind's eye.

"We need to be precise," I murmured, tapping a spot on the map where several lines intersected. "Damien's defenses are weakest here."

Victor leaned in closer, his eyes scanning the symbols that flanked the intersection. "Damien always thought these points were merely wellsprings of power," he said. "But they're more than that—they're conduits, channels."

Tara crossed her arms, her gaze skeptical yet curious. "Channels for what?"

I hesitated. My knowledge of the ley lines was intimate but incomplete. The Mark's connection to them remained an enigma—one I was desperate to unravel.

"The Mark," I began slowly, piecing together whispers of lore and gut instinct, "is not just a reservoir of power. It's a key."

"A key to what?" Tara asked, her brow furrowed.

"That's what we need to find out." I exhaled sharply. We were playing with fire, with elements beyond our understanding. But what choice did we have? Damien wouldn't hesitate to use whatever means necessary to achieve his ends.

As we delved into the arcane text further, a pattern emerged—a motif repeated throughout history in various cultures and myths but always associated with immense power and great peril. The Mark wasn't merely a tool; it was a living entity that sought balance between forces: light and shadow, order and chaos.

"It's not just granting power," I said softly, almost afraid to voice my revelation. "It's maintaining equilibrium."

Victor nodded slowly, absorbing the weight of my words. "And Damien upsets that balance with every move he makes."

Tara stepped back, her eyes wide with realization. "So if he gains control over it..."

"He doesn't just tip the scales," I finished for her. "He risks collapsing everything."

The room fell silent as we contemplated this new understanding of the Mark of Power. It was not merely a weapon or shield but a guardian at its core—a protectorate over the natural order.

The plan had to change; we couldn't allow Damien even a whisper of control over something so vital.

"I have an idea," Victor said after moments heavy with thought hung between us like fog. He laid out his strategy: using the ley line intersections not only to disrupt Damien but also to reinforce the balance threatened by his Ascension Protocol.

"We'll need everyone," Tara added determinedly. "Lynx and Cipher can rally our allies on the ground while Jade secures more support."

I nodded in agreement; it was a sound plan—dangerous but our best shot at halting Damien without invoking the Mark directly.

With roles assigned and hearts weighed down by the gravity of our task, we parted ways under cover of nightfall—the city's darkened silhouette an ominous backdrop to our clandestine operations.

The following hours were a blur as we set about preparing for what was coming—a storm brewing on the horizon that promised either salvation or ruin.

Lynx orchestrated movements through encrypted channels while Cipher wove spells into tattoos that would shield our allies from Damien's mental intrusions.

Jade worked her contacts tirelessly, securing aid from those who shared our cause or simply opposed Damien's reign.

And there I stood in Crimson Ink's shadowed corners, channeling energy through ink into symbols etched upon willing skin—each one a promise of protection and defiance against tyranny.

Our movements remained undetected until the night air crackled with anticipation—the lunar eclipse approaching like an ominous drumbeat signaling war's commencement.

The Resistance gathered at our chosen intersection—a place where ancient cobblestones met modern asphalt—hidden from prying eyes by magic and sheer willpower.

We stood ready when darkness enveloped us—not just absence of light but a thick blanket woven from shadows stretching across dimensions—an abyss threatening to swallow us whole if we faltered.

Then it happened—the moment we had all been waiting for yet dreading in equal measure: The Ascension Protocol began.

Damien emerged atop a nearby rooftop bathed in an eerie glow—a silhouette against celestial events unfolding above us—his voice thundering across spaces both physical and metaphysical as he invoked ancient rites designed to bind and bend reality itself.

His followers echoed his chants—voices merging into a cacophony that sought to overpower us—to crush resistance beneath waves of discordant sound.

But we held firm—our resolve strengthened by newfound knowledge that this was not merely a battle for control but one for balance itself—the very fabric of existence hanging delicately in balance as forces clashed invisibly around us.

It was then—midst incantations and arcane energies swirling like tempests—that my understanding deepened further still: The Mark sought its bearer—a chosen one whose spirit resonated with its purpose—who could wield its power without succumbing to corruption or hubris.

My hands shook as realization dawned upon me—a truth so potent it threatened to unravel me: I wasn't just connected to this ancient design; I was its destined keeper—its steward chosen by fate or perhaps by bloodline's call echoing through ages long forgotten.

I looked around at those who had become family through strife—each face etched with determination—and knew what must be done: To accept this mantle thrust upon me—to guide rather than dominate—to preserve rather than destroy—to be beacon rather than conqueror amidst encroaching darkness threatening all we held dear.

Chapter 15

Ordeal of the Mark

I stood in the dim light of the back room at Crimson Ink, the weight of centuries pressing down on my shoulders. The Mark of Power sprawled across the page before me, its lines and symbols an intricate dance of ancient knowledge and latent energy. The air buzzed with anticipation, thick with the scent of ink and magic.

Tara watched me from across the table, her eyes a mix of concern and unwavering support. Victor leaned against the doorframe, arms folded, his presence a silent reminder of the treacherous path that had led us here.

My fingers hovered above the Mark's design, hesitant. To recreate it was to invite power into one's life—power that could heal or destroy, uplift or corrupt. It wasn't just a tattoo;

it was a testament to my heritage, my abilities, and now, it felt like an albatross around my neck.

"You sure you're ready for this?" Tara's voice sliced through my apprehension.

I exhaled slowly, feeling the familiar tingle in my fingertips—the call of my dual nature. "I have to be," I replied. "Damien won't stop until he controls everything... or destroys it trying."

Victor pushed off from the doorframe and approached. "Remember," he said, his voice low, "the Mark is more than a weapon against Damien. It's a symbol of balance—the balance you've always tried to maintain."

His words were a cold splash of reality. The Mark wasn't just about confronting Damien; it was about preserving that delicate equilibrium between light and shadow—a balance that seemed to fray with each passing moment.

I dipped the needle into the enchanted ink—a concoction Tara, Jade, and I had perfected over countless trials. Its color shimmered with an otherworldly sheen, ready to be transformed into something far greater than mere pigment on skin.

My hand moved with practiced precision as I began to draw the Mark onto a piece of parchment for practice. The design came alive under my touch, each stroke imbued with purpose and intent. This wasn't just another tattoo; it was a conduit for raw power.

Tara paced behind me as I worked, her energy a mixture of nerves and adrenaline. "When Damien realizes what we're doing—"

"We'll be ready," I interjected without lifting my gaze from the parchment. I couldn't afford doubt—not now.

Victor joined in our silent vigil over the Mark's recreation. His betrayal of Damien had been risky, but necessary. He'd seen firsthand what unchecked power could do and had chosen a different side—a side where his sins might find redemption.

Hours slipped by unnoticed as I poured myself into the design. The symbols began to pulse with an ethereal glow, responding to my touch like a living creature stirring from slumber. The room itself seemed to hold its breath.

And then it was done—a flawless replica of the ancient Mark on parchment. But this was only preparation; soon enough, I would need to transfer it onto skin—my skin—and bind its power within me.

Tara let out a whistle as she examined my work. "Alex... it's perfect."

"It has to be," I muttered. "Anything less could mean disaster."

Victor nodded solemnly. "We don't have much time left before the lunar eclipse—the zenith of Damien's Ascension Protocol."

A chill ran down my spine at his words. Time was our most relentless enemy; we had plans in place for sabotage and resistance but they hinged on this moment—on me accepting this immense power.

The three of us gathered closer around the table as if our shared resolve could fortify us against what lay ahead. The Mark glowed softly on its paper canvas as if sensing our unity.

"Are we sure about this?" Tara's question hung in the air like mist—tangible yet impossible to grasp.

My heart pounded in rhythm with my thoughts—a drumbeat marching toward an unknown fate. The fear that I might lose myself to this power gnawed at me relentlessly.

But then there was Lynx's unwavering determination; Cipher's quiet strength; Jade's cunning intellect—all counting on me not just as a tattoo artist but as someone who could make a difference in this fight against tyranny.

"No," I admitted finally, locking eyes with both Tara and Victor. "But certainty is a luxury we don't have right now."

Victor clasped his shoulder in solidarity while Tara nodded grimly.

We knew what needed to be done—the Mark had to be brought forth from parchment to flesh—but none of us were naive enough to ignore the risks involved.

I glanced at my reflection in a nearby mirror: young yet aged by battles unseen by most—a duality not unlike the supernatural blood coursing through me—a heritage that granted me such extraordinary gifts yet constantly tested my humanity.

As night encroached upon our cityscape beyond Crimson Ink's walls—a city unaware of how close it teetered toward chaos—I felt an unspoken promise rise within me: whatever darkness might come from wielding this Mark, I would face it head-on for those who stood beside me—for those who still believed in light amid shadows.

"Let's begin," I declared with newfound resolve echoing in each word—a resolve born from acceptance of both sides of who I am—the human and supernatural entity intertwined within me forevermore.

The room held still as history breathed through its walls while destiny awaited on bated breath for ink to meet skin—to mark me not only with power but also with purpose... responsibility... consequence...

* * *

The Mark's design lay before me on parchment, a tapestry of lines and symbols that seemed to dance and shift before my eyes. It was alive in a way that no other tattoo I'd ever crafted had been. Tara and Victor stood by my side in the cathedral's ruins, the silence between us heavy with unspoken fears and unasked questions. The moon hung high, casting an ethereal glow through the shattered stained glass, as if giving its silent blessing—or perhaps its warning.

My hand hovered over the Mark, trembling not from fear of the needle but from the gravity of what I was about to undertake. The ink, already prepared with an infusion of my own blood, waited patiently for its purpose. As I dipped the needle into the dark liquid, it felt as though I was signing an invisible contract with fate itself.

I pressed the needle to my skin, and with each puncture, a whisper of power hummed through me. It was a symphony of potential, of paths yet to be chosen. The Mark could be a beacon of hope or a harbinger of destruction. And there I was, in the eye of that storm, clutching onto my ethics like a lifeline.

The sensation wasn't painful; it was transcendent. The Mark bonded with me, sinking deeper than flesh and blood—it touched upon my soul. Each line etched onto my skin carried with it the history of those who had borne this power before me. They were keepers of balance who had stood at this very precipice.

"Alex?" Tara's voice cut through my concentration, laced with concern. "You're shaking."

I paused, looking up into her eyes. "I'm okay," I lied.

Victor paced behind us, his gaze fixed on the Mark. "You know what you're doing is right," he said with conviction that I wished I could mirror.

"Is it?" I whispered more to myself than to them.

This wasn't just about Damien or his twisted aspirations anymore; it was about every choice that would come after this moment. It was about power—the kind that could mend broken systems or shatter them entirely.

With each segment of the Mark completed, a new weight settled onto my shoulders—a burden growing heavier with every drop of ink that melded into my being. Was I ready to be a guardian? A protector? Could I trust myself to wield such power without succumbing to its seductive call?

Tara knelt beside me, her hand finding mine and squeezing gently. "You've always used your gifts for good," she reassured me.

But doubt gnawed at me like a relentless beast.

A rustle echoed through the ruins—a reminder that time was fleeting and Damien's threat loomed ever closer. Yet here I sat, frozen by introspection while the world outside teetered on the brink of chaos.

I resumed my work, each line drawn now a silent vow: I would not falter; I would not become what I feared most. The Mark took shape—a convergence of power and promise—on my skin and within my spirit.

As the final touch connected end to beginning, sealing the design in an unbroken loop, energy surged through me like a lightning strike hitting bare earth. My breath caught in my throat as visions flickered behind closed eyelids—of places steeped in shadow and light intertwined; faces unknown yet achingly familiar; battles fought in silence between heartbeats.

Then all at once it ceased—the torrent receding into a trickle—leaving behind clarity sharper than any blade.

"I'm done," I announced to Tara and Victor as they watched me rise to my feet. The Mark pulsed on my arm with a life all its own—beautiful yet terrifying in its potential.

"You are more than this Mark," Victor stated firmly as if he could sense the turmoil within me.

I nodded but couldn't shake off the lingering apprehension that clung like cobwebs to my thoughts.

A soft glow emanated from beneath my sleeve where the Mark resided—a glow that matched the luminescence of Orion's scrying sphere which lay nearby atop an ancient tome. It was as though both objects recognized their kinship in purpose and power.

"We need to test it," Tara suggested cautiously. "Before we face Damien."

The weight of her words settled over us like a shroud; this wasn't merely practice—it was preparation for war.

We ventured deeper into the cathedral's shadowy embrace until we found ourselves within its once-sacred heart—an altar now barren save for echoes of prayers long since silenced.

"Focus on something simple," Tara instructed as she set up makeshift targets from debris scattered around us—crumbled statues and fallen pillars repurposed for our grim rehearsal.

Simple? There was nothing simple about this—about any of it—but nevertheless, I reached within myself where the Mark thrummed eagerly against my willpower.

Drawing upon its strength felt like dipping into an endless wellspring; power surged forth at my command—controlled but eager to expand beyond confines set by flesh or fear.

My first attempt sent shockwaves rippling through air thick with anticipation; stone targets cracked under invisible pressure while dust danced around us like specters awakened from slumber by our audacity to challenge fate itself.

Tara clapped her hands together with delight at our success but beneath her excitement lurked caution—an understanding that this display was but a whisper compared to screams we'd soon have to confront head-on against Damien's malice and ambition.

As we continued testing our limits under cover of nightfall's embrace, doubts still shadowed every move I made—a relentless reminder that for every action there would be consequence whether borne by intention or accident. The power within me felt both ally and adversary—an echo of battles fought across time where lines blurred between salvation and ruin based on choices made by those who dared hold dominion over forces beyond mere mortal kenning.

This dance between light and shadow played out across cathedral floors—an ancient ballet witnessed only by remnants of piety lost amidst rubble remains—a silent testament to dualities faced when one wields might enough to shape destinies other than their own...

* * *

The Mark of Power seared my skin, a living emblem that pulsed with every heartbeat. Its weight was both a comfort and a curse, an assurance of strength and a harbinger of the war that brewed beneath the city's deceptive calm. I stood at the precipice of choice, the Mark an anchor and a sail in the tempest that was Damien's ambition.

I'd barely had time to grow accustomed to the feel of ancient magic coursing through my veins when the door to Crimson Ink swung open, casting a long shadow across the parlor floor. Damien entered, his presence as commanding as ever, flanked by Evelyn and Victor. Their eyes found mine, unspoken threats glinting in their cold stares.

"You've been busy," Damien remarked, his voice smooth as silk and just as ensnaring. "I trust you're not having second thoughts about our... partnership?"

His use of the word 'partnership' twisted in my gut. There was no partnership here, only coercion—a velvet glove over an iron fist. The amulet he'd given me lay heavy against my chest, a constant reminder of the invisible chains that bound me to his will.

"I'm just doing what's necessary," I replied, careful to keep my voice steady despite the drumming fear that threatened to betray me.

Evelyn stepped forward, her movements predatory and graceful. "We've noticed an uptick in resistance activity lately. You wouldn't know anything about that, would you?" Her eyes narrowed ever so slightly, searching for any sign of deceit.

I met her gaze squarely, allowing none of my trepidation to surface. "My focus is on tattoos and ink. Politics aren't my forte."

Damien chuckled, a low sound that didn't quite reach his eyes. "Alex, let's not dance around pretenses. You are far more than just a tattoo artist—and we both know it." He gestured to the Mark etched into my flesh. "With such power at your disposal, you could sway the tides of this city."

Victor grunted his agreement, arms folded across his massive chest as he loomed beside Evelyn like a silent sentinel.

"I could," I conceded with a nod. "But power doesn't interest me."

"Lies," Damien said softly, taking another step closer until I could feel the chill of his presence. "Power interests everyone—especially those who claim otherwise."

He circled me then, like a vulture eyeing its next meal. His proximity sent shivers down my spine despite my resolve not to show weakness.

"The Ascension Protocol is fast approaching," he continued as he paced around me. "We can't afford distractions or... betrayals." He let the word hang between us like a guillotine blade poised to fall.

Evelyn's gaze never wavered from mine; she was waiting for any flicker of rebellion, any whisper of dissent. The room felt smaller with each second that passed—a cage with bars made of shadows and threats.

"And what do you want from me?" I asked when Damien paused before me once more.

His smile was razor-sharp as he replied, "Your loyalty—unquestioned and unwavering." He reached out and placed a hand on my shoulder; it felt like a shackle being tightened.

"The Mark of Power must remain our secret," Evelyn added with a pointed look at the arcane symbol on my arm. "If it falls into the wrong hands..."

Her words trailed off ominously; she didn't need to finish for me to understand the gravity behind them.

Victor stepped forward then; despite his brutish appearance, there was an intelligence in his eyes that many underestimated—including myself at times.

"You're playing with fire," he growled lowly. "Don't get burned."

I held their gazes one by one—Damien's calculating stare, Evelyn's ice-cold scrutiny, Victor's brute force warning—all instruments in their symphony of intimidation.

"I've never been one to play games," I said quietly but firmly. The lie tasted bitter on my tongue—I was entangled in more games than I cared to admit—but it was necessary.

Damien removed his hand from my shoulder but remained close enough for me to feel his breath against my skin.

"Good," he murmured before turning on his heel and heading toward the door with Evelyn and Victor following suit.

As they left Crimson Ink, their presence lingered like fog over water—opaque and suffocating. Alone now with only my thoughts for company, I exhaled slowly; it had taken all my willpower not to reveal the storm within me—the plans forming beneath each word spoken tonight.

I knew I had precious little time before Damien enacted whatever machinations he'd concocted with this Ascension Protocol. The Resistance counted on me now more than ever; Tara's determined face flashed in my mind along with Lynx's steadfast resolve and Jade's unwavering support.

There was no turning back now; I couldn't afford hesitation or doubt. With each tattoo I crafted from this moment forward—whether it be sigils of protection for those brave souls fighting alongside me or bindings meant to ensnare—I would weave defiance into every line and shade.

The Mark pulsed once more—a call to arms from within—and I knew then that despite Damien's pressing threats and reminders of stakes higher than skyscrapers... there was no safety in surrender.

I rolled down my sleeve over the Mark; it was time to prepare for what lay ahead—to ready myself for whatever darkness awaited beneath the looming eclipse's shadow.

* * *

The buzz of the tattoo machine in my hand blended with the steady thrum of my heartbeat, each pulse echoing the Mark of Power inked into my skin. As I etched a protective sigil onto a young woman's wrist, her eyes shut tight against the sting, my own eyes glazed over—not with pain, but memory.

Her wrist under my fingers became a time-worn page, flipping back to when Crimson Ink was just a shop and not a battleground. Damien hadn't yet cast his shadow over my life; the tattoos I created were born from free will, not coercion or fear. How simple it had been, that notion of choice.

I recalled the way Evelyn's eyes had narrowed, her voice low and insidious as she warned me about Damien's offer. It was supposed to be an opportunity, a chance for protection and power. Yet even as she spoke those words, her face twisted with something like pity. She knew what it meant to be caught in his web—she'd been ensnared long before I was.

The machine's whir went on uninterrupted as another image flashed before me: Victor perusing those ancient texts with a reverence that bordered on obsession. He'd once mentioned the dangers of wielding too much power—how it could twist and corrode the soul. Was he speaking from experience or cautionary tales? Either way, his warning now ricocheted around in my skull like a siren call.

A shiver ran down my spine, and the young woman flinched beneath my hand. "Sorry," I murmured automatically, though I wasn't sure if it was for the momentary slip or for all the ways in which I'd become entangled in this dark tapestry.

I couldn't shake the memories—Lysandra's voice as she spoke of fire, how it could cleanse or consume depending on one's control. Mordecai's shadow lessons were always shrouded in enigma, urging me to look beyond what was visible to the naked eye. And Orion's starry wisdom reminded me that every person is part of a larger constellation, their actions rippling out into eternity.

Their advice wasn't just about harnessing supernatural abilities; it was about understanding consequences—knowing that every action leaves an imprint far deeper than ink on skin.

The faces of those affected by Damien's cruelty flickered in my mind like ghostly apparitions. There was Mariah, whose skin crawled with ink come alive at my touch—a gift that should have been miraculous but now felt like a burden. And Emily, who came to me desperate for release from an ouroboros tattoo that sought to devour her essence from within.

Each face bore silent testament to the gravity of what I did next. My choices were no longer just about survival; they held the weight of all these lives in balance.

With every line drawn and every drop of ink infused with magic, I knew I was carving out more than just images—I was sketching out destinies. It had become clearer with every passing day that there would be no walking away from this path I'd been forced onto. The Resistance needed me—the city needed me—to stand against Damien's Ascension Protocol.

As the tattoo took shape under my hands, I thought back to that first encounter with Raven. He had seen something in me before I saw it in myself—a potential for greatness or ruin. His words were always cryptic but laden with truth: "Your bloodline is your greatest strength and your deepest challenge."

And then there was Lynx from the Resistance—how we'd sat across from each other in mutual distrust before realizing our goals aligned more than we cared to admit at first. We were both soldiers in our own right, fighting an unseen war where every move could tip the scales irrevocably.

Tara... dear Tara... Her unwavering belief in me often felt like a lifeline amidst the chaos swirling around us. She saw through Damien's illusions and recognized his threats for what they were—a desperate grasp at control.

Each flashback fortified my resolve like steel under fire. The sting of betrayal by Victor—that moment when trust shattered into countless sharp fragments—served as a reminder that even those closest to us could become ensnared by power's allure.

My hand steadied as clarity washed over me anew. These weren't just recollections; they were signposts guiding me towards an inevitable confrontation—one that would determine not only my fate but that of everyone touched by Crimson Ink's magic.

The young woman opened her eyes as I finished her tattoo—a shield interwoven with runes—and sat up to admire it in the mirror. Her smile reflected none of the darkness behind its creation; instead, it held hope—a beacon shining against an encroaching night.

"You're so much more than a tattoo artist," she said softly.

I offered her a smile but didn't voice what we both knew—that these days, 'artist' was perhaps the smallest part of who I'd become.

As she left Crimson Ink with her newfound protection etched into her skin, Tara walked in, urgency etched into every line of her face. Her arrival pulled me back from memory's depths into the present's stark reality—the now where decisions had to be made and actions taken.

"We've got movement," she said tersely. "Damien's called a meeting."

I nodded once; there wasn't time for hesitation anymore—not when every choice carved out futures yet unseen.

We moved towards our next act in this unfolding drama—one where I held not just a needle but destinies between my fingertips—and with each step forward, we wrote not just history but our very selves into legend's ink-stained pages.

* * *

The buzz of the tattoo gun in my hand was like a swarm of determined bees, each one buzzing a mantra of rebellion into my skin, into my soul. The Mark of Power lay sketched out on the table before me, a design so potent with ancient magic it seemed to dance beneath the fluorescent lights of Crimson Ink. The shop was empty except for me. Damien had demanded privacy for this act, not out of respect, but to assert control. His cronies loomed in the shadows beyond the door, a reminder of the leash they thought they had on me.

The Mark was supposed to be a tool for them, a means to an end that I couldn't stomach. It was meant to elevate Damien to heights unseen, a god among vampires and all those who cowered beneath his shadow. But as I dipped the needle into the ink—a blend I'd prepared under moonlight and with a heart full of intent—I knew I could not let this come to pass.

My hand hovered over my forearm, where the Mark would find its home. A drop of ink fell, splattering on my skin like a sign from the fates. The decision loomed over me like the blade of a guillotine—once dropped, there was no going back.

The door creaked as Evelyn slipped inside, her presence an icy draft in the warm room. "Time is precious, Alex," she whispered. "Damien grows impatient."

Her eyes flicked to my arm and then away, but not before I caught the flicker of fear that she couldn't quite hide. Evelyn knew what this Mark meant—knew what it could do. She wasn't here just as an observer; she was here as Damien's insurance policy.

I nodded at her without words and pressed the needle to my skin. The sting was sharp and immediate, but it was nothing compared to the weight of consequence that each line carried. As I worked, I felt something ancient stir within me—a power from my lineage that Damien sought to chain for his own purposes.

"You understand what this will do to you?" Evelyn's voice cut through my focus like a knife through silk.

"I know," I murmured back.

And I did know—the Mark would change me, enhance me, maybe even consume me if I wasn't careful. But as I continued the design, a secret unfolded within my mind like a dark blossom blooming at midnight. A variation in the pattern, something only someone with my heritage could conceive—a safeguard hidden within its lines.

I etched into my flesh not just a symbol of power but also one of defiance—a tweak so subtle it would be indistinguishable from the original unless you knew where to look. It was an act of rebellion against Damien's vision—a chance for me to assert control over what was quickly becoming uncontrollable.

Evelyn leaned closer, her gaze sharp as shards of glass. "What are you doing?"

"Just concentrating," I replied through gritted teeth as another line formed—a line that wasn't in Damien's book or any other tome he'd ever seen.

With each stroke, I could feel power coursing through me—power that would soon be Damien's unless I acted swiftly and decisively. My mind raced with possibilities, with outcomes both terrifying and exhilarating.

As I worked on the final strokes of the Mark—the ones that would seal its magic—I paused. The moment hung suspended like a single drop of rain clinging to a leaf before falling to earth. Here lay my true choice: complete the Mark as intended or alter its purpose and risk everything in one defiant breath.

I thought about Tara and Lynx; their faces flashed before me like ghosts in the night. They were fighting for something bigger than any single one of us—for freedom from tyranny and oppression.

A bead of sweat dripped down my brow as Evelyn's impatience became palpable—a pressure that demanded submission and compliance.

I leaned back for just a second—just long enough to catch my reflection in the mirror across from me—and there it was: determination etched into every line on my face.

My hand moved before I could second-guess myself any further, finishing off with an embellishment that altered its intent—turning what would have been an amplifier for Damien into a beacon for resistance; turning what would have been his ultimate weapon into potentially his downfall.

As soon as it was done—as soon as the last trace of ink settled into place—I felt it: an alignment within myself and within the energies that swirled around us all unseen.

"What did you do?" Evelyn's voice cut through again, sharper now with an edge that spoke volumes of her allegiance and her fear.

"Finished it," I replied evenly while masking the thunderous beat of my heart against my ribs.

She scrutinized me closely then nodded once before turning away. "We should show him."

I wrapped up my arm carefully concealing the still fresh tattoo beneath layers of bandages—my secret shielded from prying eyes for now.

The door opened again and this time Damien himself stood there—an imposing figure whose smile never reached his eyes.

"Let's see it then," he commanded smoothly while fixing me with his cold gaze—a gaze that seemed to pierce right through me seeking out lies and treachery.

I rose slowly every movement calculated every breath measured under his scrutiny. My fingers grazed over the bandages feeling their rough texture against my fingertips feeling too the thrumming energy beneath them—the energy of change hope resistance all wrapped up in one little mark.

This was it—the pivotal moment when paths diverged when futures were forged when choices made indelible marks not just on skin but on destinies themselves.

* * *

I let the needle hum to a stop, pulling back to admire the intricate web of lines and shades that had just sprung from my hands. The tattoo, a mix of geometric shapes and ancient symbols, wrapped around Damien's forearm a request he'd made with that unnerving smile that didn't quite reach his eyes. It was supposed to be a talisman of power, an amplifier for his already formidable abilities.

But I'd changed it—subtly. The smallest shifts in the pattern could alter its purpose. This tattoo wouldn't empower him; it would sap his strength, bit by bit, and funnel it to the Resistance. My heart raced at the thought of what I'd done. This was an act of defiance that went beyond anything I'd dared before.

Evelyn leaned against the doorframe, her gaze flickering over my work. "Is it done?" Her voice cut through the silence that had settled in the room like a dense fog.

"Yeah, it's finished." I wiped Damien's skin clean and applied a bandage with hands that didn't tremble—years of practice hiding my nerves.

Damien rose from the chair, flexing his arm and examining the tattoo with an unreadable expression. "Excellent work as always, Alex." He said it casually, but there was a weight to his words—a veiled threat reminding me of what was at stake.

I nodded, keeping my expression neutral as I packed away my tools. The Mark of Power on my own arm pulsed beneath my sleeve—a silent reminder of the responsibility I shouldered.

As Damien exited Crimson Ink with Evelyn in tow, their shadows seemed to linger ominously in the room long after they'd left. I took a deep breath, allowing myself a moment of respite before cleaning up.

The shop felt different now—like a battleground where invisible wars were fought with ink and needles instead of swords and shields. Every client who came through that door could be an ally or an enemy in disguise. My tattoos were more than art; they were weapons in a war where the line between right and wrong often blurred.

The bell above the door jingled as another figure stepped into Crimson Ink. A cloaked man whose face was obscured by shadows—another player in this dangerous game. He approached me with purpose in his stride.

"Alex," he began, his voice low and urgent, "I need your help."

My instincts screamed caution as I eyed him warily. "What kind of help?"

"A tattoo," he replied, pulling back his cloak to reveal a jagged scar across his collarbone—a mark left by dark magic if I had to guess. "One that can protect me from... certain influences."

The implication hung heavily between us. He wasn't just talking about any influence; he meant Damien's influence.

I weighed my options quickly. Helping him could expose me further to Damien's wrath if he found out—or worse yet, if this man was a trap sent by Damien himself to test my loyalty. But if he was genuine...

"Sit down," I gestured toward my workstation with feigned confidence that belied the churning uncertainty within me.

As he took a seat, I prepared my station with practiced efficiency—ink pots lined up neatly, fresh needles gleaming under the harsh light. My fingers moved on their own accord while my mind raced with possibilities and potential outcomes.

I started on his design—a shield interwoven with sigils of warding and strength—a protective emblem designed to resist external control. With each line etched into his skin, I infused a little magic drawn from the Mark on my arm, hoping it would be enough.

Time slipped away as I worked; only the rhythmic buzz of the tattoo machine filled the room—a meditative drone that allowed me to focus solely on my task at hand.

When it was finally done, I stepped back to inspect my work once more—the shield looked impenetrable on his skin; it felt impenetrable too. The man examined it with an approving nod.

"Thank you," he murmured as he stood up and fastened his cloak once again.

I nodded curtly—no words needed—and watched him leave Crimson Ink with cautious steps that echoed softly against the floor.

The moment he left, a shiver ran down my spine—an instinctual reaction warning me that things were about to change drastically.

Alone again in the quiet shop, doubt crept in like unwelcome company—the nagging thought that perhaps this time I'd pushed too far; maybe this act would be what finally tipped Damien off to my betrayal.

The consequences of empowering Damien's enemies while weakening him were vast and unpredictable—but necessary risks for what we hoped to achieve: freedom from his tyranny for everyone caught in his web.

Still... fear gnawed at me as I considered what could happen if Damien discovered what I'd done—not just to myself but to Tara, Lynx, Jade... all those who had put their trust in me. We were all entangled now, woven together by shared secrets and common goals.

The sun dipped below the horizon outside as evening fell over the city—a reminder that time was running out before Damien's Ascension Protocol came into play during the lunar eclipse three days hence.

I steeled myself for what was coming next because there was no turning back now; not after everything we'd set into motion together as a resistance against him.

Cleaning up after another day at Crimson Ink felt different this time—each sweep of cloth over counter surfaces felt like wiping away evidence; every click of lock tumblers sounded like sealing away secrets within these walls until they would burst forth in defiance once more when we made our stand against Damien during The Ascension Protocol.

My heart raced faster with each beat—adrenaline mixing with anxiety—as uncertainty about our future loomed large over us all like storm clouds gathering on an otherwise clear night sky...

Chapter 16

A Twist of Fate

In the dim light of Crimson Ink, my hands moved with a precision that felt like second nature. The needle hummed against skin, sketching out the intricate lines of a design that had haunted both my dreams and waking hours. The Mark of Power's ancient symbols danced beneath my fingertips, each stroke heavy with the burden of history and the electric thrill of potential.

Damien had been clear about what he wanted—the unadulterated Mark, etched into his skin to wield its untamed strength. But as I worked, a voice whispered through the sinews of my being, a call to conscience that refused to be ignored. My moral compass wouldn't allow me to give him—or anyone—unrestricted access to such formidable power. The

Mark was not just a tool; it was a legacy, an entity that commanded respect and demanded balance.

The shop was silent save for the persistent buzz of the tattoo machine and Damien's occasional shifts in the chair. Evelyn stood guard by the door, her eyes an unwavering sentinel on every move I made. I couldn't let them see the conflict raging within me or catch even a hint of my intent to alter the Mark.

So, with every ounce of subtlety I possessed, I began to deviate from the original pattern. The alterations were minute—nearly imperceptible deviations in line work, small additions disguised as aesthetic flourishes. Each change was an act of rebellion, a silent scream against the tyranny Damien sought to enforce with this symbol of power.

I couldn't shake off the awareness that this act could spell my doom if discovered. The fear sent adrenaline coursing through my veins, but it was outweighed by something stronger—a conviction that rooted me firmly in place despite the danger.

As I worked, memories of those touched by my art filled my mind. Their faces reminded me why I wielded this power—for protection, for connection, for empowerment without oppression. The Mark as Damien envisioned it would be none of these things; it would be a shackle for all who fell under its sway.

"Almost there," I murmured, focusing on the sound of my voice to steady my nerves. It was crucial now more than ever to maintain composure; any sign of hesitation could raise suspicion.

Damien's reply was a low grunt that barely registered above the tattoo machine's drone. His confidence fueled my determination; he was so certain in his conquest that he couldn't fathom betrayal from his own chosen artist.

With each passing minute, I felt more like an alchemist than a tattooist—transmuting one form of power into another, crafting a safeguard where there had been none. In this new version of the Mark, I wove protections against misuse and malintent. It was designed to amplify strengths but also to bind aggression and curb the impulse for domination.

Evelyn shifted her stance by the door, her gaze momentarily flickering away from me. In that brief window of distraction, I channeled energy into the Mark through the ley lines beneath us—the same energy that coursed through me since Raven's revelation and Orion's counsel.

My heart pounded against my ribs as if trying to break free from its cage. With each additional symbol hidden within the grand design, I reinforced my intention: This Mark would not be an instrument of subjugation but rather one of equilibrium.

"You're unusually quiet today," Evelyn remarked suddenly, her voice slicing through my concentration like a blade.

I met her gaze in the reflection of a nearby mirror and forced a smile onto my lips. "Just focused on delivering quality work," I said casually before returning my attention to Damien's skin.

Time slipped by like sand through fingers—each grain another secret sewn into flesh. As I neared completion, doubt flickered at the edges of my resolve like shadows at dusk. Was it enough? Could these small changes truly hold back the tide Damien intended to unleash?

A bead of sweat traced its way down my temple—a traitorous sign of inner turmoil. I wiped it away quickly with the back of my hand before continuing.

Finally, after what seemed both an eternity and a mere moment had passed, I pulled back to survey my work. To any onlooker—including Damien himself—it was impeccable: The Mark stood proud on his skin, commanding and formidable as intended.

Yet beneath its surface lay alterations known only to me—hidden threads in a tapestry that could unravel Damien's plans from within if he dared misuse its power.

"There," I said with feigned satisfaction as I cleaned away excess ink and applied a bandage over his new tattoo. "Let it heal properly before you start testing its limits."

Damien rose from his seat and examined himself in the mirror with an air of arrogance that made me clench my jaw tight enough to hurt. He nodded approvingly before turning his sharp gaze toward me.

"Excellent work as always," he said smoothly while pulling on his shirt over fresh gauze.

Evelyn opened her mouth as if to speak but paused when Damien raised his hand slightly—a silent command for silence.

"We'll see soon enough how well you've done," he continued cryptically before striding out with Evelyn trailing behind him like a shadow tethered to its source.

Alone at last in Crimson Ink's hallowed space turned battlegrounds turned sanctuary once more—I allowed myself a breath steeped in relief and apprehension alike.

This secret alteration was either a stroke of genius or folly incarnate; only time would tell which one would come to pass. But one thing was clear: No matter how things unfolded from here on out, surrender wasn't written in any line or curve upon my skin—not now nor ever would be.

* * *

The moment Damien handed me the original design of the Mark of Power, my stomach twisted into knots. Its intricate patterns seemed to dance and shift before my eyes, a testament to the untold might it possessed. As much as its beauty captivated me, the terror of what it could do – what Damien wanted it to do – set my resolve in stone. I would alter this mark. The risks be damned; if I didn't, the city would fall into darkness under Damien's rule.

I locked myself in my apartment that night, the only sounds the hum of the city and the scratching of my pencil against paper as I copied the Mark's design. My hand moved with practiced precision, yet I paused every so often to let my gaze sink into each swirl and line, committing every detail to memory. The power it held wasn't just in its aesthetics; it was in its intention, its construction. And that was what I needed to understand – to unravel and then weave back together into something safer.

Hours slipped by like shadows as I dissected the Mark. Each element had a purpose: a line for strength, a curve for control, a dot for longevity. I knew that even the slightest alteration could render it useless or worse, volatile. My hands were steady but my heart raced, for this wasn't just any tattoo – it was a catalyst that could either save or destroy lives.

The alteration had to be subtle yet effective, hidden within the Mark's own complexity. I found myself drawing from ancient texts and whispered lore, pieces of knowledge gathered over years of study and practice. The key lay in balance – ensuring that whatever power the Mark wielded didn't tip into domination or aggression.

As dawn broke, casting a pale light through my window, inspiration struck like a lightning bolt. A series of minuscule symbols, derived from protective runes and sigils for temperance, could be interwoven with the existing design. They would be almost invisible to anyone who didn't know exactly what they were looking for – especially someone like Damien, who was blinded by ambition and hunger for power.

My fingers worked tirelessly, sketching out these new elements until they felt like second nature. By weaving them into the foundation of the Mark's design, they would act as regulators without dampening its overall potency – hopefully enough to keep whoever bore it from becoming another one of Damien's puppets.

With every change made on paper, I practiced on scraps of pigskin I kept for testing ink and needle depth. It wasn't enough to know the design; I had to execute it flawlessly when the time came to transfer it onto skin.

Tara dropped by in the afternoon with coffee and furrowed brows. "You sure about this?" she asked as she glanced over my shoulder at my work.

"Have to be," I replied without looking up from my sketchbook.

She lingered by my side in silence before placing a reassuring hand on my shoulder. "Just... be careful."

I gave her a nod; words weren't needed between us anymore.

For days I continued this ritual – study, sketch, practice – until every line of defense was embedded in both my mind and muscle memory. The closer we got to the night of The Ascension Protocol, the heavier the air felt around Crimson Ink.

On the eve of our confrontation with Damien's forces, Lynx visited me at the shop after hours. His presence alone could put us all at risk but his concern was clear as he scanned my face for any sign of doubt.

"You ready?" he asked in his usual no-nonsense tone.

"As ready as one can be when they're about to dance with devils," I answered while securing my sketchbook in a safe beneath one of the workstations.

Lynx nodded once sharply before handing me a small object wrapped in cloth – an amulet he claimed would shield me from prying eyes while I worked on Damien's tattoo.

"You pull this off..." he began but trailed off as if hesitant to hope too much.

"When," I corrected him firmly because doubt was a luxury we couldn't afford right now. "When I pull this off."

He left me with that steely look that always made me believe we might just have a fighting chance against whatever nightmare Damien planned to unleash upon us all.

That night as I lay awake in bed staring at the ceiling above me, every possible outcome played out behind closed eyes. If discovered mid-alteration or afterward... Well, Damien wasn't known for his mercy or understanding. But if successful... The Mark could become an instrument not just of balance but resistance too.

When morning came with its golden hue spilling over buildings and streets alike, Crimson Ink awaited me like an old friend ready for battle. My hands didn't shake as they usually did before an important piece; they were calm because everything hinged on today – not just for me but everyone involved in this fight against darkness.

As hours ticked away toward evening and towards our destiny intertwined with ink and blood alike, there was no room left for fear within me; only focus remained sharp as a blade poised for action.

With every preparation checked and rechecked again until there was nothing left but to wait for Damien's arrival at Crimson Ink – wait and hope that our plan would not unravel at its seams before we even had chance begin weaving rebellion into reality itself.

And so there beneath buzzing fluorescents above tattoo stations prepped and ready lay fate's threads between fingers skilled enough twist them into future we dared dream might still exist beyond tonight's veil uncertainty danger alike...

* * *

The hum of the tattoo machine mingled with the thrum of my pulse as I worked. Under the guise of concentration, I kept my focus narrowed to the skin beneath my hands, etching in the protective runes into the Mark of Power. Every line I drew was a delicate balance between empowerment and safeguarding against misuse. It had to be perfect, indistinguishable to the untrained eye, yet potent enough to derail Damien's plans.

I was alone with one of the Acolytes, a young vampire named Seth who hadn't been turned long enough to have lost all semblance of his humanity. His job was to watch me, to ensure I remained on task and didn't stray from Damien's orders. He stood by the door, a silent sentinel whose gaze I could feel boring into my back. But it was Evelyn's warning that echoed in my mind: "They may not look like much, but these fledglings have eyes that miss nothing."

The shop was quiet at this hour, save for the low murmur of voices from the front where Tara and Lynx strategized in hushed tones. They knew what I was doing; they were part of this rebellion. The air crackled with a current only those privy to our plot could sense.

A bead of sweat traced a path down my temple as I continued the meticulous work. Each rune I embedded into the design was a small act of defiance—a tiny revolution in ink and blood.

"You're awfully focused today," Seth commented from his perch by the door. His voice startled me, but years of practice kept my hand steady.

"Just ensuring quality," I replied without looking up. My heart pounded against my ribcage like a caged bird desperate for freedom.

"Can I see?" His sudden interest sent a jolt through me.

"Not yet," I said quickly. "It's bad luck to reveal a work in progress."

He shrugged, disinterested once more, and leaned against the door frame. I let out a breath I didn't realize I'd been holding and continued with renewed urgency.

The clock ticked away minutes that felt like hours as I wove magic and resistance into every stroke. This tattoo would be my masterpiece or my undoing.

A noise at the front caught my attention—footsteps approaching. Panic flared within me as Victor's unmistakable presence filled the shop. His heavy boots echoed ominously as he made his way toward us.

Seth straightened up as Victor entered the room, his eyes immediately fixing on me and my work.

"What's taking so long?" Victor demanded, his voice low and threatening.

"Perfection takes time," I said, masking my nerves with feigned nonchalance.

Victor loomed over me, peering at the design taking shape on Damien's back. "I hope for your sake it is perfect."

I nodded curtly, refusing to meet his gaze as he scrutinized my work with a predator's intensity. The tension hung heavy in the air—a tangible thing that wound its way around us.

As Victor leaned closer, his shadow fell across Damien's skin and for one heart-stopping moment, I feared he'd notice the subtle changes—the additional lines that weren't part of Damien's original request.

But then his attention shifted as Lynx appeared at the doorway behind him.

"Victor," Lynx called out with calculated casualness. "We need you up front."

Victor gave me one final look before straightening up and heading out of the room with Lynx trailing behind him like a shadow detaching itself from its master.

I exhaled slowly once they were gone, allowing myself a brief moment to regather my composure before resuming my work with even greater care than before.

The close call had heightened every sense; every flicker of movement made me tense up, ready to defend or explain away my actions if necessary. But no further interruptions came, and Seth remained blissfully oblivious as he scrolled through his phone, likely more interested in social media than whatever dark designs Damien had planned for our city.

As hours passed and evening bled into night, Damien remained still beneath my needle—a statue awaiting animation through dark arts or through mine—a subtler magic meant not for control but for liberation.

My hand never wavered as line after line took shape under its command. My resolve crystallized with each rune—this tattoo would not bind but protect; it would not enslave but empower those who stood against tyranny.

As I neared completion of the Mark, every nerve ending screamed for rest but also vibrated with adrenaline—a heady mix that fueled my determination despite exhaustion nipping at its heels.

Then came the moment—the final rune etched into place with precision borne from desperation and hope intertwined like lovers' fingers clasped tightly together in defiance of an uncertain future.

There it was: The Mark of Power altered by an artist who had once believed her only gift was beauty made manifest on skin but now knew better—now understood that her art could shape destinies just as it shaped flesh.

A soft chime from outside announced midnight's arrival—an hour when dark things roamed freely under moon's silver gaze—an hour when Crimson Ink stood quiet except for those within who conspired against darkness with light made tangible through ink and willpower.

Seth glanced up from his phone as if sensing something amiss—an unspoken shift in atmosphere—but found nothing out of place; just an artist leaning back to admire her work on Damien's skin—a work now done but whose true test lay ahead in how it would perform when called upon during The Ascension Protocol's unfurling drama soon to unfold beneath an eclipse-darkened sky.

* * *

The needle hummed in my hand, a familiar vibration that grounded me as I etched into Damien's skin. The room was thick with tension, the kind that stifled breath and made every moment stretch out like taffy. Seth's hawk-like gaze never left my back, his presence an oppressive shadow over my workspace. Every now and then, Victor leaned in, his eyes scanning the intricate lines and curves of the Mark of Power as I recreated it on Damien's arm.

I focused on my breathing, keeping it even, keeping the tremor from my hands. This was it—the moment that could define or destroy everything I had worked for. Every stroke of the needle carried a silent rebellion, a hidden defiance against the darkness that Damien embodied.

The design I inked onto him held my secret alterations—minute changes in the pattern that only a true master of magical tattoos would detect. These weren't just artistic flourishes; they were alterations to the very essence of the Mark's power.

I had infused protective runes within the filigree, balancing the potency of the original Mark with curbs on aggression and domination. It was a delicate operation, akin to defusing a bomb while the timer ticked down. If I made a single misstep or if Victor noticed something amiss, it would all be over—not just for me but for the entire Resistance.

But fortune favored me today, or maybe it was skill—years of honing my craft until I could make ink dance to my will. With each line and shade, I imbued it with intentions of freedom and resilience rather than submission and control.

The shop was quiet save for the buzz of my tattoo machine. Seth stood rigid as a statue by the door while Victor perched close by like a vulture awaiting its meal. I could feel their eyes on me as I worked, but I couldn't let that distract me.

Damien was oblivious to my treachery, lost in whatever dark reverie he entertained as he lay prone on my table. His trust in his own infallibility was his weakness—a crack in his armor that I exploited with every twist of my wrist.

My heart beat in sync with the rhythm of my machine—a steady drumming that seemed to whisper courage into my veins. There were moments when Victor's scrutiny made me falter, but Lynx's distraction was perfectly timed—a sudden commotion outside that drew Victor's attention just long enough for me to conceal a crucial protective sigil within a thorn of the design.

The minutes dragged into hours until finally, I pulled back to survey my work. It was done. The Mark of Power lay embedded in Damien's skin, its appearance unchanged to an untrained eye but fundamentally altered in ways that only someone like me could understand.

Seth finally moved from his post by the door, coming closer to inspect my work. His face was impassive as stone as he studied the Mark—his eyes flicking over every line and shade. A bead of sweat trailed down my spine despite the coolness of the shop.

Victor returned from investigating Lynx's disruption and joined Seth in examining Damien's new tattoo. My breath hitched as they conferred in low tones—words I couldn't quite catch over the pounding of blood in my ears.

Damien finally stirred, rising from his prone position to gaze at his arm with an expression akin to reverence—or perhaps it was greed; with him, it was hard to tell.

"It is complete then?" His voice rolled through the room like distant thunder.

"Yes," I replied evenly, masking any hint of triumph or anxiety from creeping into my tone.

Damien flexed his arm, turning it this way and that as if feeling out its new power. He met my gaze then—his eyes sharp as shards of obsidian—and for a moment, I wondered if he knew what I had done.

But he simply nodded once—a curt gesture—and said nothing more about it.

As they left Crimson Ink that night—the gang members one by one disappearing into shadows—I felt both exhaustion and elation weigh on me equally. The room felt suddenly vast and empty without their presence—an echo chamber for my racing thoughts.

I wiped down surfaces mechanically; every motion felt surreal as if I were watching myself from afar. My mind kept replaying every second spent under their scrutiny—the razor-thin line between success and disaster.

It wasn't until Tara slipped into the shop that reality snapped back into place—the here and now solidifying around her concerned frown and steady hands as she helped me clean up without a word.

"You did it," she finally whispered once we were alone amidst disinfectants and bandages—a statement rather than a question.

"I did," I confirmed quietly while stripping off gloves stained with ink and latent magic.

We didn't celebrate; there wasn't time for relief or revelry—not yet anyway. This was just one victory in what promised to be a long campaign—one fraught step toward an uncertain future where freedom teetered on a knife-edge against tyranny.

And as we stepped out into the cool night air together—Tara's hand resting lightly on my shoulder—I knew this: no matter what came next or how dark things might seem...with every mark I made upon this world—I'd fight for hope over fear...for liberation over dominion...for life over shadow...always.

* * *

The door closed behind Damien and his crew, and the heavy silence in Crimson Ink felt like a shroud. I stared at my hands, stained with ink and laced with lines of weariness. Had I truly made the right decision? I altered the Mark of Power—a symbol that could tilt the world on its axis—and here I stood, second-guessing my intentions.

Tara leaned against the counter, her gaze searching mine for certainty. "You okay?" she asked, her voice a lifeline in the storm of my thoughts.

"Yeah," I lied. "Just tired." My eyes flicked to the door, half-expecting it to burst open and for Damien to stride back in, his dark eyes narrowing with suspicion.

I wiped my hands on a cloth, watching the ink bleed into the fabric—a stark reminder of the mark now etched onto Damien's skin. It was supposed to empower him, but the runes I'd woven into its design carried my silent rebellion. They were subtle—enough to pass Victor's scrutiny—but they altered the essence of what Damien sought: absolute control.

Tara didn't press further; she knew me too well. We both understood that if Damien discovered what I had done, it wouldn't just be my life at stake. It would be everyone connected to me—Tara, Lynx, Jade—all those brave souls who fought in the shadows against Damien's looming tyranny.

I wandered over to my sketchbook and flipped through pages filled with designs—each one a testament to my struggle between two worlds. The sketches seemed to whisper of possibilities and risks, reminding me that every choice bore its own consequence.

"Alex," Tara said softly, breaking through my reverie. "Whatever happens, we'll face it together."

Her words should've been comforting, but they felt like chains—bindings that linked us all to an uncertain fate. What if I had just signed our death warrants? Or worse—what if my actions led not only to our downfall but also fed into Damien's ascent?

I nodded but couldn't voice my fears aloud; they were too monstrous to take shape in words. Instead, I busied myself with cleaning up the parlor, the rhythmic motion allowing me a semblance of control.

As night fell and Crimson Ink dimmed to darkness save for a few scattered lights, I couldn't shake off the weight pressing on my chest. I knew what needed to be done next; we had planned every step meticulously. But as I traced the lines of energy crisscrossing beneath the city—the ley lines that thrummed with power—I questioned whether our efforts would be enough.

I felt like an imposter in my own skin—a tattoo artist who dabbled in forces beyond comprehension. The Mark on Damien was proof of that—a beacon of rebellion that could ignite or extinguish hope depending on its wielder.

"You should get some rest," Tara said, interrupting my spiraling thoughts. "Tomorrow's another day."

She was right; rest was essential. But as I left Crimson Ink for the solitude of my apartment above, sleep felt like an elusive dream.

In bed, I stared at the ceiling as shadows played across it—the byproduct of streetlights filtering through half-closed blinds. The silence was heavy with unspoken questions: What if Damien sensed something amiss? What if he tested the Mark and discovered its true nature?

And then there was Victor—a man whose allegiance teetered on a knife's edge. His betrayal could unravel everything we had worked toward if he decided to align with Damien fully once more.

The hours ticked by slowly as scenarios played out in my mind—each one ending in catastrophe or triumph without any certainty which would come to pass.

Eventually, exhaustion claimed me and pulled me under into a restless slumber where dreams mingled with reality—where magic and fear danced together in a relentless waltz.

Morning came too soon—a gray light filtering through clouds heavy with unshed rain. As I made coffee in silence, Tara joined me in the kitchenette.

"We should check in with Lynx," she said while reaching for a mug.

I nodded absently, sipping coffee that tasted bitter on my tongue despite the sugar I had added. "Yeah," I replied. "We need to know if anything's changed overnight."

She watched me closely as if she could see through the façade of calmness I tried to maintain.

"You're worried about Victor," she stated rather than asked.

"Among other things," I admitted finally. My concerns were like threads woven tightly around me—Victor's loyalty being just one strand among many.

"Victor knows what's at stake," Tara assured me as she poured herself coffee. "He won't turn his back on us now."

Her confidence should've bolstered mine, but instead it highlighted how little control we truly had over people and their choices—even those who seemed committed to our cause.

"We need every ally we can get," I murmured before setting down my cup with more force than necessary. It wasn't just allies we needed; it was assurance—an impossible guarantee that our plan would succeed against odds stacked high as skyscrapers around us.

We finished our coffee in silence before heading downstairs to open Crimson Ink for another day—one filled with ordinary tasks masking extraordinary plans that churned beneath the surface like an undertow waiting to pull us under or carry us away toward victory.

As clients came and went throughout the day—each one leaving with a piece of art forever etched onto their skin—I kept wondering whether any mark could truly encapsulate what we hoped to achieve or whether our ambitions were nothing more than ink spilled across canvas without form or function.

And when evening came again with no word from Lynx or any sign from Victor indicating where his true loyalties lay—I felt doubt clawing at me once more like thorns drawing blood from flesh already too worn and too tired from battles fought in shadows rather than sunlight.

* * *

The shop's door chimed its usual melancholic tune as the last client of the day slipped out into the growing dusk. Crimson Ink was quiet now, save for the faint hum of neon signs and the gentle scratch of my pen as I doodled absentmindedly on a scrap of paper. My mind wasn't on the ink or the designs that spilled from my fingertips—it was on the weight of Damien's eyes, dark pools that could drown me if I wasn't careful.

Tara stood at the threshold of my private studio, her arms folded across her chest, a shadow of concern etched onto her face. She knew as well as I did that what I had done today was not just a mere act of defiance; it was a declaration of war.

I set down my pen and met her gaze. "It's done," I said simply, but those two words carried the weight of our shared struggle against Damien's tyranny.

She took a step forward, her eyes searching mine for any sign of regret or fear. "And the alteration?"

A wry smile tugged at the corner of my lips. "Hidden in plain sight. If Damien knows his skin as well as he claims, he'll feel something's off. But he won't find it—not unless he knows exactly what to look for."

Tara nodded, her lips pursing in thought. She knew the risks, how finely I had to tread this line between subterfuge and outright rebellion. "You're sure it'll work?"

I shrugged, a nonchalant gesture that belied the meticulous planning that had gone into every stroke of my needle. "As sure as I can be without seeing it in action. But it's more than just hoping it works; it's about taking back control, about making sure we're not just pawns in his game."

She stepped closer still, her eyes softening with something akin to pride. "You're braver than you give yourself credit for, Alex."

A laugh escaped me before I could stop it—a bitter sound that filled the empty shop. "Bravery has nothing to do with it," I said, but even as I spoke, I knew it wasn't entirely true.

Tara reached out and placed a hand on my shoulder—a gesture that grounded me to the here and now. "We need to tell Lynx and the others," she said firmly. "They deserve to know what you've done."

I nodded and grabbed my jacket from where it hung on a hook by the door. Together, we stepped out into the cool night air, leaving behind us a day's work and stepping into a future uncertain and fraught with peril.

The city's pulse beat beneath our feet as we made our way through dimly lit streets to our meeting place—an abandoned subway station that had become our haven against Damien's ever-watchful gaze. The graffiti-stained walls were a stark contrast to the pristine surfaces of Crimson Ink but held a certain beauty all their own.

Lynx was there already when we arrived, his face obscured by shadows that seemed almost like an extension of his being. Cipher leaned against one wall, her eyes closed as if she were listening to secrets whispered by ghosts only she could hear.

"We've done it," Tara announced without preamble as we approached them.

Lynx straightened up at her words, his attention immediately focused on us. "Done what?" he asked cautiously.

I met his gaze evenly, letting him see the resolve in my own eyes. "The Mark," I said simply. "It's been altered."

Cipher's eyes snapped open at that, her expression one of disbelief tinged with hope. "Altered how?" she asked quickly.

"With protective runes," Tara explained before I could speak. "Subtle changes that will undermine Damien's control without alerting him to our interference."

Lynx regarded me for a long moment before nodding slowly—a gesture that conveyed both his approval and understanding of what this meant for us all.

"It was risky," he finally said, his voice low and measured.

"But necessary," I added firmly.

He considered this before speaking again. "This changes things—for all of us." There was weight behind his words—a recognition of what we had set into motion today.

Cipher pushed off from the wall and came to stand beside Lynx, her gaze flickering between Tara and me. "This means we're closer than ever to stopping him," she said quietly.

"Yes," Lynx agreed solemnly.

We stood there together in silence for a moment—four souls bound by a common cause and an unspoken understanding that there was no turning back now.

"It won't be easy," Lynx finally broke the silence. "But with this... We stand a chance."

"We do more than stand a chance," I said firmly, feeling something within me stir—a mixture of hope and determination that had been too long buried beneath fear and uncertainty.

Lynx offered me a rare smile then—a flash of teeth in the darkness that somehow felt like sunlight breaking through clouds.

"We'll need to move quickly," Cipher said pragmatically, always one step ahead in her thoughts.

"And carefully," Tara added pointedly with a glance in my direction—a reminder of what we were up against.

I nodded in agreement before looking around at each member of our makeshift family—each one strong in their own right but stronger still together.

"Let's plan our next move then," Lynx said decisively as he led us deeper into the station where maps and plans lay waiting for us on makeshift tables illuminated by flickering candlelight.

We gathered around them—each one voicing thoughts and ideas freely as we pieced together our strategy against Damien's Ascension Protocol—the Mark alteration serving as both catalyst and anchor for our resistance efforts.

And as we talked long into the night—our voices mingling with those whispered by ghosts—there was an unshakable sense of unity among us; a bond forged by shared secrets and commitment to a cause greater than ourselves.

Chapter 17

Hunted

The walls of Crimson Ink seemed to close in around me, the dim light casting elongated shadows that danced like specters of my own treachery. Damien stood at the center of it all, his back to me, as he examined his new tattoo in the large, ornate mirror that had witnessed countless transformations but none so duplicitous as this.

Evelyn's gaze bore into me from across the room, her eyes narrow slits of suspicion. The air crackled with a tension so thick it could rival the heavy incense that clouded the parlor. It was the calm before a storm I had knowingly summoned.

I wiped my hands on a cloth, stalling, watching Damien's expression shift from satisfaction to puzzlement. He ran a pale finger over the intricate design etched onto his skin, feeling for something unseen but undeniably present. His lips parted in a silent curse.

"Something isn't right," he murmured, his voice as smooth as the velvet curtains framing the shop's storefront. "This isn't what I requested."

I swallowed hard, forcing my voice to steady. "It's exactly as we discussed," I lied. My hand trembled slightly as I set aside the cloth. "The Mark of Power, in all its glory."

Damien turned then, his piercing gaze locking onto mine. "Is it, Alex?" He strode towards me with predatory grace, each step measured and lethal. "Or is there more to this design than meets the eye?"

Evelyn moved to flank him, her own anger a silent undercurrent beneath her poised exterior. Victor loomed near the door like a gargoyle poised for attack, his bulk a clear reminder of the physical threat that accompanied any displeasure from Damien.

"You've always been an artist with secrets," Damien continued, his voice laced with dark amusement that did not reach his eyes. "But if you think you can play games with me—"

"I assure you, there are no games here," I interrupted with false confidence.

Damien was close enough now that I could feel the chill emanating from his undead body. "Then you won't mind if Evelyn takes a closer look," he said with deceptive calmness.

Evelyn stepped forward and I fought to keep my face impassive as she scrutinized my work. The silence stretched between us like a tightrope I balanced upon with bated breath.

Her fingers traced the lines of ink, her touch feather-light yet laden with an unspoken threat. I knew she was searching for the protective runes hidden within the Mark—a safeguard against Damien's ambition and a spark for rebellion.

Seconds ticked by like hours until finally Evelyn straightened up and locked eyes with Damien. She gave a nearly imperceptible shake of her head.

"There's something... different," she said quietly.

Damien's expression hardened into something feral and dangerous. "Different how?" His voice was low and even, belying the fury simmering just beneath the surface.

Evelyn glanced at me then back at Damien. "It feels... restrained."

A cold laugh escaped Damien's lips as he returned his attention to me. "And what have you restrained, Alex? My power? Or your own cowardice?"

I bristled at his words but kept my composure under his scrutiny. The Mark had been my gambit—a way to tip the scales without inciting outright war—but now it teetered on the brink of exposure.

"I've done nothing but follow your instructions," I insisted once more, hoping my facade would hold against their combined acumen.

Damien leaned in closer until we were nearly nose to nose; his breath smelled of ancient tombs and forgotten things best left buried. "Do not take me for a fool," he whispered venomously.

Victor shifted by the door and Tara stepped discreetly behind me—a silent show of solidarity and readiness for whatever might unfold next.

"Perhaps we should test it," Evelyn suggested coldly.

A bead of sweat trickled down my temple as I realized that any demonstration would likely reveal my betrayal—and unleash consequences I wasn't sure we could withstand.

Damien regarded me for a long moment before nodding slowly at Evelyn's proposal. He rolled up his sleeve further and extended his arm towards her. Her fingers danced over his skin once more before she began chanting in an ancient tongue known only to those steeped in vampire lore and dark magic.

The air grew thick with power as she spoke each syllable; I felt it press against my skin like an impending doom eager to break free from its shackles.

Then came the moment of truth—the moment where everything I had worked for either came crashing down around me or stood firm against their probing magic.

Evelyn's chant reached its crescendo and there was a palpable surge in energy—a flash of light that made everyone except Damien flinch away.

And then... nothing happened.

No explosion of power, no surge of dominance from Damien—just an empty anticlimax that left confusion in its wake.

Damien's eyes flickered between surprise and realization; Evelyn looked equally perplexed yet undeterred as she repeated her spell once more to no avail.

I barely contained my relief; my subterfuge had held—for now—but how long before they pieced together what I had done?

As they conferred in hushed tones too low for human ears—forgetting momentarily that mine were not entirely human—I stole a glance at Tara whose expression mirrored my own mixture of triumph and trepidation.

The game had changed; we had drawn our line in the sand against Damien's encroaching darkness. But at what cost?

We were playing with fire—and in our world—that meant dancing on a knife-edge between survival and annihilation.

* * *

I etched the last swirl of the tattoo onto Damien's skin, the ink seeping into his flesh like a dark promise. As I pulled away, my heart pounded against my ribs, a drumbeat of impending doom. The room, once filled with the hum of conversation and the clink of glasses, had fallen eerily silent.

Evelyn's gaze locked onto mine, her eyes narrow slits of suspicion. "What have you done, Alex?" she asked, her voice a low hiss that cut through the silence.

"Nothing," I replied, my voice steady despite the fear coiling in my gut. "Just what was asked of me." I wiped away the excess ink and stood back, presenting Damien's arm as if it were a masterpiece.

Damien rose from the chair, flexing his newly marked arm with a smirk. "Feels powerful," he murmured, his eyes meeting mine for a fleeting second before turning to Evelyn. "Does it look right to you?"

She leaned closer to inspect my work, her finger tracing the outline of the design. My heart skipped as she lingered over one particular spot where I'd embedded a protective rune within the larger pattern—a silent rebellion against Damien's tyranny.

"It looks... different," she said after a pause, her tone sharpening with each word. "There's an addition here that wasn't in the original design."

Damien's eyes flickered with something dark and dangerous. He turned to me slowly, his expression shifting from satisfaction to suspicion. "Alex," he began, his voice low and menacing, "you better have a good explanation for this."

I swallowed hard. The walls of Crimson Ink seemed to close in around me as I realized my subterfuge was unraveling before my eyes.

"I... must have misunderstood the instructions," I stammered, hoping to feign ignorance.

Damien wasn't buying it. He stepped closer, towering over me like an ominous cloud ready to burst. "Misunderstood?" His voice dripped with disbelief. "Or intentionally altered?"

The air in the room grew heavy with tension as everyone waited for my response.

"No," I insisted, trying to keep my voice from shaking. "It was an honest mistake."

Evelyn moved between us, her hand on Damien's chest as if to hold back an impending storm. "This isn't like Alex," she said cautiously. "Perhaps we should test the tattoo's power before jumping to conclusions."

Damien nodded curtly and extended his arm towards one of his acolytes—a young vampire named Marcus who stood trembling in the corner.

"Touch it," Damien commanded.

Marcus hesitated only a moment before reaching out and laying his hand on Damien's arm. A shiver ran through him but nothing more; no surge of power or visible reaction from either party.

I let out a breath I didn't realize I'd been holding. My secret alteration remained just that—secret.

Damien's gaze remained fixed on me though; mistrust etched into every line of his face. He knew something was amiss; he just couldn't prove it—yet.

"You're playing a dangerous game," he warned me before turning to leave with Evelyn at his heels.

The moment they were gone, Tara rushed over to me, her face pale with worry.

"Are you okay?" she asked in a whisper meant only for my ears.

I nodded but couldn't shake off the feeling that I'd just signed my own death warrant. My betrayal might have gone undetected this time, but it wouldn't stay hidden forever—not with Damien's paranoia and Evelyn's sharp intuition.

"We need to get out of here," Tara urged, glancing nervously towards the door where Damien had exited moments ago.

I knew she was right—the walls of Crimson Ink were no longer safe for me; they were closing in fast and threatening to crush me under their weight.

"I can't leave yet," I said quietly, my mind racing through all the possible outcomes. "There are still people here who need protection from him."

Tara grabbed my arm urgently. "Alex, if they find out what you've done—"

"They won't find out." The confidence in my voice didn't reach my heart.

We both knew it was only a matter of time before Damien discovered my treachery; when that happened, there would be nowhere in this city—or any other—that would be safe for me.

For now though, there were still tattoos to ink and destinies to shape—even if mine seemed more certain than most.

I cleaned up my station mechanically while Tara watched me with anxious eyes that mirrored my own fears back at me.

"We'll figure this out," she said finally breaking our silence with a determination that belied her fear. "We always do."

Her words were meant to comfort but they felt hollow in light of what we were up against: Damien's wrath was not something easily evaded or overcome.

But Tara was right about one thing—we always figured things out somehow even when everything seemed stacked against us.

I glanced around Crimson Ink one last time knowing it might be for the last time if things went south from here—which they inevitably would given how close Evelyn had come to unraveling everything tonight...

"Let's go then," I said taking Tara's hand in mine feeling its reassuring warmth as we stepped out into the night air ripe with possibility—and peril—knowing full well that every step took us further down a path from which there might be no return...

* * *

The air in Crimson Ink felt thick, laced with an energy that buzzed against my skin. I leaned against the wall in the back room, its once comforting shadows now a cloak I wished to shed. Damien's warning echoed in my mind, a relentless tide that threatened to erode my resolve. But resolve was all I had left.

Tara stood beside me, her presence a beacon of solidarity. We shared a glance, no words needed. The plan was clear; we had gone over it countless times. It was now or never.

I rolled up my sleeve, revealing the Mark of Power on my arm. It hummed with a subtle vibration, an undercurrent of energy from the ley lines beneath the city. The plan hinged on this – using the Mark not just as a tool of protection but as a means of escape.

"I'll create a diversion," Tara whispered, her eyes darting toward the door.

Before I could protest, she vanished into the shop's main area. I could hear her voice rise, arguing with Victor about a non-existent appointment. Victor's growl of frustration was my cue.

I focused on the Mark, envisioning the back alley behind Crimson Ink. The power surged within me, and I felt as though I were being pulled apart and stitched back together all at once. The walls of the room blurred as I stepped through the shadows and into the narrow passage beyond.

The escape should have been seamless, but it wasn't. The alley was not empty as I had hoped; two of Damien's acolytes stood smoking by the dumpster, their eyes widening in shock at my sudden appearance.

"What in hell—" one began, but he never finished his sentence.

With a flick of my wrist, I etched an air displacement sigil in the space between us. A gust of wind slammed into them like an invisible battering ram, sending them sprawling against brick and trash cans.

I didn't wait to see if they would get up; instead, I sprinted toward the street. My heart pounded in my chest like a drumbeat urging me forward. The chill night air clawed at my throat as I gasped for breath.

The sounds of pursuit rose behind me – shouts and footsteps that echoed through the empty streets like a hunting call. Panic threatened to take hold; every corner I turned could be a trap, every shadow a hidden enemy.

A figure stepped out from an alcove ahead, blocking my path – Seth, his eyes glowing faintly in the dim light. He had always been quick, his reflexes honed by centuries of survival.

"Seth," I panted, skidding to a stop. "Please."

His gaze narrowed on me, considering. For a moment there was silence – just two souls weighing each other in the balance.

"Go," he said finally and stepped aside.

I didn't question it; gratitude would have to wait. Instead, I dashed past him and continued down the labyrinthine alleys that crisscrossed this part of town.

The sounds of pursuit faded as I wove through streets and passages only known to those who called this concrete jungle home. Every turn was calculated; every choice led me further from Crimson Ink and closer to freedom – or so I hoped.

An ambush lay in wait around one such corner – three vampires from Damien's gang materialized out of nowhere with movements too fast for human eyes to follow.

There was no time for sigils or elaborate magic now; instinct took over. A simple rune flashed across my mind – light – and suddenly brilliance exploded from me like a supernova.

They recoiled from the light that seared their night-adapted vision, hissing curses as they shielded their eyes.

I seized the momentary advantage and bolted past them before they could recover their senses. My lungs burned with exertion; adrenaline flooded my veins like fire.

Another turn brought me face-to-face with Evelyn herself. Her expression was unreadable – anger? Betrayal? Both?

"Alex," she said coolly as she moved to intercept me.

My breath came out in ragged gasps as I braced myself for whatever came next.

"Evelyn," I replied warily, backing away step by step until my spine pressed against cold brickwork.

Her gaze flickered to my arm where the Mark lay hidden beneath fabric and ink. She knew what it meant – what power it held – but she hesitated.

"Why?" Her single word cut through our standoff like a blade seeking truth amidst lies.

"For freedom," I managed to say through clenched teeth.

She studied me for what felt like an eternity before stepping aside much like Seth had done earlier.

Freedom's scent was intoxicating; it urged me forward even as caution screamed for restraint.

But then came Victor's unmistakable voice echoing off the buildings around us – "There!"

Panic surged anew as Victor rounded a corner flanked by more gang members than I could count at first glance. He pointed directly at me with unerring certainty; there would be no talking him down or escaping his clutches without confrontation.

I took off again, feet pounding against pavement as if they alone could distance me from danger's reach. An old fire escape ladder loomed ahead; without hesitation, I leaped for it and began climbing with desperation fueling every move upwards towards rooftops that promised respite from relentless pursuit below.

* * *

The clang of my frantic footsteps echoed off the metal rungs as I ascended the fire escape. Heart pounding, I risked a glance over my shoulder. Below, Victor and his goons were a snarling mass of shadows, climbing after me with vampiric agility. I'd barely put any distance between us, and my breath came in sharp, ragged pulls from the exertion and fear.

As I reached the rooftop, the cold night air hit me like a wall. My lungs ached for reprieve, but there was no time to rest. I darted across the gravel-topped expanse toward the opposite edge, searching for another route of escape.

That's when I heard it—the unmistakable sound of leather soles hitting the roof behind me. I whipped around, half-expecting to see Victor ready to pounce. Instead, it was Rowan, the supernatural warrior who had sought my help weeks before.

"Rowan?" My voice was an incredulous whisper.

He nodded curtly, his expression grim. "No time to explain. Follow me."

I didn't hesitate. Rowan led me toward a section of the roof lined with dormant air conditioning units. He pulled one aside to reveal a narrow hatch that seemed to lead into darkness.

"Inside," he urged.

I clambered down after him into what appeared to be a maintenance corridor—a stark contrast to the open night sky I'd just left behind. The confined space seemed to press in on us as we moved with urgency through the dimly lit tunnel.

Rowan's unexpected presence threw me for a loop. "How did you find me?"

"I've been keeping tabs on you since our last encounter," he said without looking back. "The Resistance has eyes everywhere."

His admission made me wonder about his allegiance and whether his previous quest for a protective tattoo had been part of something larger—a web of resistance that even now continued to ensnare Damien's machinations.

We emerged from the corridor into an abandoned building, its walls stripped bare and windows boarded up. It was like stepping into a different world—a silent sanctuary amid chaos.

"This place," I began but Rowan cut me off.

"It's safe for now." His eyes scanned our surroundings before settling back on me. "They won't think to look for you here."

"Why are you helping me?" I asked, struggling to catch my breath.

Rowan sighed heavily, a shadow passing over his face in the dim light from a cracked windowpane. "Our goals align, Alex. You want freedom from Damien's grasp; so does the Resistance."

I knew he was right; our enemies were one and the same. Yet trust didn't come easily—not in this city, not in this life where betrayal lurked at every corner.

We moved deeper into the building until we found an old office space with a heavy door that Rowan insisted we barricade from inside.

As we worked to move an old filing cabinet against the door, Rowan glanced at my arm—the Mark of Power shimmered faintly under my sleeve—and his gaze lingered with a mix of respect and concern.

"That Mark..." He hesitated as if choosing his words carefully. "It makes you valuable—but also vulnerable."

I felt its warmth against my skin, an ever-present reminder of power and peril interwoven through each intricate line.

"It's also what saved us tonight," I pointed out quietly.

Rowan nodded solemnly before turning away to peer through the slats in the boarded-up window.

Silence enveloped us again until he broke it with a sudden intensity that made me startle. "We need to move again soon."

"Where?" The question felt heavy on my tongue; every step forward was another step into uncertainty.

"Somewhere Damien wouldn't dare follow," Rowan replied cryptically as he turned back toward me with an unreadable expression.

A knot formed in my stomach at his words—a mixture of anticipation and dread that seemed all too familiar lately. It seemed every decision led down paths riddled with shadows and whispers of danger.

As if reading my thoughts, Rowan stepped closer and placed a hand on my shoulder—a surprising gesture that somehow felt grounding amidst the swirling chaos of our reality.

"We will stand against him together," he said firmly. "You're not alone in this fight."

The resolve in his voice steeled something within me—the flicker of defiance that refused to be extinguished no matter how dark things got. With allies like Rowan at my side, perhaps there was hope yet for us all.

We didn't linger long in our makeshift haven; there was too much at stake and too many eyes that might be prying into our sanctuary's shadows at any moment. So we continued our flight through forgotten passages and derelict rooms—silent specters haunting spaces left behind by those who had fled or fallen before us.

Eventually, we emerged onto another rooftop under cover of darkness—a different vantage point from which we could survey our surroundings and plot our next move without immediate fear of discovery.

Rowan pointed out key landmarks—places where we might find temporary refuge or resources needed for whatever lay ahead—and shared whispered plans whose details danced dangerously close to rebellion and uprising.

And as I stood there beside him—my pulse still racing but now more from adrenaline than fear—I realized how far I'd come since first etching ink into skin beneath Crimson Ink's watchful gaze: from tattoo artist to reluctant pawn in Damien's games; from survivor scraping by on wits alone to resister poised on brink of revolution; from solitary figure shrouded in doubt to someone who might just hold key needed turn tide against encroaching darkness once and for all.

* * *

I'd been running for what felt like an eternity, the city's labyrinthine alleyways and shadow-drenched rooftops blurring into a dizzying montage of escape. My breath came in ragged gasps, a stark contrast to the rhythmic pounding of my heart that hammered against my ribs like a caged beast desperate for release. I clutched the Mark on my arm, feeling its power pulse beneath my skin, a silent beacon guiding me through the night.

The chase had begun at Crimson Ink, where Victor's gaze had burrowed into me like a drill, suspicion etched deep into his furrowed brow. I knew it was only a matter of time before he pieced together the truth of the tattoo I'd given Damien – a truth laced with defiance and subtle sabotage.

The streets were a treacherous terrain, crawling with Damien's lackeys who scoured every corner for me. But it wasn't just the foot soldiers I feared; it was the feeling that Damien's eyes were upon me, that his wrath was but a shadow's breadth away.

I darted into an alleyway, its narrow confines choked with refuse and lined with the back entrances of grimy establishments. The scent of stale grease mingled with fear as I wove between dumpsters and discarded crates. The alley spilled out onto a wider street bathed in the sickly yellow glow of streetlights.

I pressed myself against the cold brick wall, heart sinking as footsteps echoed close behind. The amulet around my neck, given to me by Lynx for protection, thrummed against my chest—a small comfort as Victor's voice snarled threats from the darkness.

A door to my right creaked open. Through the sliver of light, an arm reached out, beckoning me with urgency. Without hesitation, I slipped through the opening and found myself pulled into an embrace of shadows.

"Quickly," whispered a voice I recognized as Raven's. The resistance member had appeared like a specter at just the right moment—a harbinger of either salvation or another trap. But at that instant, his presence was all that stood between capture and freedom.

He shut the door with silent precision and ushered me down a narrow hallway lined with peeling wallpaper and the faint aroma of mothballs—an olfactory relic from times long past. We descended stairs that groaned under our weight until we reached what seemed like an underground bunker.

The room was sparsely furnished: a table laden with maps and various arcane instruments; chairs huddled together as if sharing secrets; shelves brimming with books whose spines whispered tales of magic and lore. The air was thick with anticipation—this was a sanctuary where strategies were born and fates decided.

Raven motioned for me to sit at the table before he began securing bolts on doors and windows—measures against unwanted guests or sudden assaults.

"We don't have much time," he said as he joined me at the table. His eyes were like flint, sparking determination. "Damien's influence grows by the hour; we must act."

My fingers traced over one of the maps spread before us—a tapestry of streets and symbols marking ley line intersections where power converged in unseen rivers beneath our feet.

"We'll need more than just tattoos to fight him," I said, voice steady despite my inner turmoil.

Raven nodded in agreement. "True, but your artistry is our ace in the hole—the key to unlocking potential in our ranks and destabilizing Damien's hold."

I considered this—the gravity of responsibility resting on my shoulders like an invisible mantle. The Mark on my arm seemed to thrum in agreement; it yearned for purpose beyond mere decoration or claim to power—it craved balance.

"I'll need supplies," I said after a moment's pause. "Inks infused with elements from these ley lines—ones that resonate with liberation rather than oppression."

Raven rose from his seat and walked over to one of the shelves where jars filled with vibrant liquids sat like potions awaiting an alchemist's touch.

"These are what you seek," he said, handing me several jars whose contents glowed faintly even in the dim light of our refuge.

The colors danced before my eyes—crimson for strength, azure for clarity, emerald for growth—all waiting to be woven into symbols upon willing skin.

"We have allies ready to bear these marks," Raven continued as he returned to his seat. "People who believe in our cause and your role within it."

My hand closed around one of the jars—a weight both literal and metaphorical—as resolve solidified within me. This wasn't just about fighting Damien; this was about defending who we were as individuals—our right to choose our own paths without fear or manipulation.

The bunker fell silent save for our breathing and distant sounds muffled by earth and stone above us. It was in this stillness that I realized we were not alone—a figure emerged from shadows near a bookcase: Tara.

Her eyes met mine—pools reflecting concern but also fierce loyalty—and she nodded once before taking her place beside us at the table.

"Are you ready?" she asked softly yet firmly—a question meant for both Raven and me.

I met her gaze with equal intensity before looking down at the map spread before us—the city's veins laid bare as if pleading for relief from Damien's tightening grip.

With newfound purpose coursing through me as palpable as ink through needle tip, I replied without hesitation: "Let's begin."

* * *

I slumped into a rickety chair, the room around me buzzing with the subdued energy of rebellion. It was a makeshift space, hidden beneath the city's pulsing streets, where shadows clung to the corners like silent guardians. Raven had brought us here after the narrow escape, a sanctuary for those who dared to defy Damien and his gang. My fingers tingled with residual magic, the Mark on my arm a constant reminder of the power I harbored and the peril it invited.

Tara leaned against a graffiti-covered wall, her gaze fixed on me. "You okay?" she asked, her voice low and steady.

I nodded, though my mind was anything but still. "Yeah, just processing everything."

She crossed the room and handed me a bottle of water. "Take a minute. You've earned it."

The cool liquid was grounding as it flowed down my throat. Around us, others from the Resistance moved with purpose, but I could sense their unease—a reflection of my own inner turmoil.

Cipher sat at a nearby table littered with maps and tech gear, tapping away at a laptop with a furrowed brow. Lynx paced by the door, every so often peeking through a sliver in the boards that covered the windows.

"We're not safe here for long," Lynx finally said. "Damien's going to turn this city upside down looking for us."

I sighed and set the bottle down. "Then we need to be one step ahead."

Raven pulled out several vials of ink from his bag—inks I'd infused with magic strong enough to rival Damien's dark influence. He placed them on the table with a sense of reverence.

"We use these wisely," he said, his eyes meeting mine. "Your tattoos have already begun shifting the tide."

The weight of his words pressed upon me like a leaden cloak. The tattoos were more than art; they were symbols of resistance, etched into skin as acts of defiance.

Tara sat beside me and took my hand in hers—an anchor in a sea of chaos. "You've changed lives tonight, Alex," she said softly.

I wanted to believe her, but doubt gnawed at me from within. Damien was cunning and ruthless; he wouldn't take this betrayal lightly. The thought sent shivers through me despite the warmth of Tara's touch.

Lynx joined us at the table, pulling over another chair. "The gang's network is shaken up; that much we know," he started. "Your little alteration to Damien's tattoo—it's got them all on edge."

"Good," I muttered more to myself than anyone else.

Cipher looked up from his screen. "They're paranoid—questioning each other's loyalty left and right." He paused, allowing a wry smile to flicker across his lips. "It's causing chaos in their ranks."

I glanced down at my arm where the Mark thrummed with latent energy beneath my sleeve. It was a tool—a weapon—but it wasn't without its risks.

"We need to keep hitting them hard," I said firmly. "Keep them off balance while we gather our strength."

Raven pulled out a map of the city's ley lines and spread it across the table. Lines intersected and wove across paper like threads in an intricate tapestry—a blueprint of magical potential that coursed beneath our very feet.

"Here," he pointed to several spots marked with red Xs, "are where they're weakest—where we hit them next."

We leaned over the map as Raven traced routes with his finger—paths that wound through shadows and secrets only we knew.

Tara squeezed my hand tighter as we planned our next moves—our strategy against an enemy who had eyes everywhere and malice as deep as the night itself.

The door cracked open slightly; Jade slipped in silently like smoke under a doorframe.

"They're scouring every nook of this city," she reported breathlessly. "But so far, they haven't picked up your trail."

A collective sigh rippled through us—relief mingled with tension.

Lynx locked eyes with me then—a silent exchange heavy with unspoken thoughts before he spoke aloud: "This is bigger than any of us now."

He was right—the stakes had soared beyond personal vendettas or quests for power; they touched every life in this city caught between light and shadow.

A plan began forming—a daring play against Damien's dominance that hinged on every skill I possessed and every ally we could muster.

"We'll need everyone we can get," I said after explaining what brewed in my mind—a scheme audacious enough to either free us or bind us forever in darkness.

Tara nodded resolutely while Lynx folded his arms across his chest—a glint of resolve sparkling in his eyes.

Cipher closed his laptop with a snap—the signal that he too was all in for whatever came next.

The energy shifted then—from desperation to determination—as if our very spirits had been tattooed with indelible ink marking us as warriors in this clandestine war against an ancient evil that lurked just beyond sight.

We huddled closer around the map—the room now charged with an electricity that buzzed through each one of us—a current fed by hope as much as fear.

The consequences loomed large—I knew that better than anyone—but as I looked into each determined face surrounding me, I also knew retreat wasn't an option anymore. We'd chosen our path—steeped it in ink and blood—and now there was only forward into whatever darkness awaited us beyond Crimson Ink's doors.

Chapter 18

Return to the Fray

Blood pounded in my ears as I darted through the narrow alley, the brick walls on either side of me nothing but blurs. The stench of decay and the city's underbelly filled my nostrils, a stark reminder of the grim reality I found myself in. The night air sliced against my skin, but it was nothing compared to the razor-sharp tension slicing through my mind.

I could hear them—Damien's lackeys—mere footsteps behind me, their hisses like whispers of death. I had thought myself clever, thought that my magical tattoos could keep me one step ahead. But they were closing in, and my tricks wouldn't last forever.

A surge of panic propelled me forward. I reached into the wellspring of power within me, to the Mark of Power pulsing on my arm. The tattoo thrummed with energy, an energy I had been too hesitant to fully embrace until now. My mind reached out, searching for a glyph that might aid my escape.

In a fleeting moment of clarity amid the chaos, I drew upon a symbol from memory—a rune for obfuscation—and pushed its magic outward. A mist began to form around me, a visual echo of my desperation to remain unseen. I didn't dare look back as the fog enveloped me.

The mist thickened behind me, sounds becoming muffled. For a moment, there was silence—sweet, precious silence—before the shouts resumed, farther away now. They had lost me, if only temporarily.

I rounded a corner sharply, nearly losing my footing on a slick patch of grime that coated the cobblestone. Ahead lay an open street bathed in the sickly yellow glow of street lamps. Too open, too exposed. My breath came in ragged gasps as I considered my options.

Then it hit me—a plan wild enough that it just might work.

I sprinted toward an old service door I knew was rarely locked—the back entrance to an abandoned tenement that bordered Damien's territory. The metal handle was cold under my grip as I yanked it open and slipped inside.

The door closed with a thud behind me and I leaned against it for a moment, willing my heart rate to slow. The musty air of neglect filled my lungs as darkness enveloped me. The tenement was silent except for the sound of water dripping somewhere in the distance—an eerie symphony to accompany my racing thoughts.

The gravity of what I'd just done began to settle on me like dust on old furniture. In altering Damien's tattoo, I'd committed an act of rebellion that would not go unpunished if discovered. The stakes were higher than ever; there was no turning back now.

I shook off the paralyzing fear that threatened to take root and started navigating through the dark interior by memory alone. Each step felt heavy with consequence—each creaking floorboard might announce my presence to anyone or anything lurking within these forsaken walls.

This building had once been a sanctuary where those who sought protection from Damien's reach could hide away from prying eyes and piercing fangs. Now it stood empty—a monument to false hope and failed resistance efforts.

My mind raced as much as my pulse had moments ago. Was there anywhere truly safe left in this city? Anywhere beyond Damien's long shadow? My own shop, Crimson Ink, once a haven for expression and magical artistry, had become little more than another chess piece in his twisted game.

I pressed onward until I reached what used to be an apartment on the second floor—a place where secret meetings had taken place before betrayal left us scattered like leaves in the wind.

Here in this forgotten room with its peeling wallpaper and cracked windows did reality truly sink its claws into me. I was alone—not just physically but emotionally too—as if every tie that bound me to others was fraying under Damien's relentless ambition.

It wasn't just about survival anymore; it was about identity—about not losing myself to this world that demanded so much and offered so little in return.

A noise startled me from my reverie—a scurrying that seemed too deliberate for any rodent or ghost of days past. Instinctively, I pressed myself against the wall next to what remained of an old fireplace mantle and held my breath.

"Alex?" A voice called out—a voice I recognized but couldn't quite place in the disorienting dark.

I hesitated before answering—a lifetime's worth of caution wrapped up in that split second.

"Who's there?" My own voice sounded foreign in this place stripped bare by time and turmoil.

"It's Victor." The reply came with an edge of urgency that sent a new kind of shiver down my spine—one born not out of fear but potentiality.

Victor—Damien's former enforcer turned uneasy ally—stood before me now as a testament to how quickly alliances could shift in this supernatural underworld we inhabited.

"What do you want?" My words were tinged with suspicion despite our shared interests against Damien's looming tyranny.

"I need your help," he said simply yet earnestly—an admission that carried weight given his past reluctance to show vulnerability or seek assistance outside his own formidable capabilities.

The emotional exhaustion from tonight's close call mixed with wariness at Victor's unexpected appearance made it difficult for me to process his request right away. Still reeling from my narrow escape and bracing myself for what might come next, part of me wanted nothing more than to disappear into the night—to leave behind this constant struggle between dark and light, between oppression and freedom.

But another part—the part marked by ink and magic and a stubborn refusal to give up—recognized an opportunity when it presented itself even under such strange circumstances.

Victor stepped into what little light filtered through the grimy windows—the pale illumination painting him as both ghostly apparition and flesh-and-blood man desperate for change.

"What kind of help?" The question lingered between us like smoke from extinguished candles—an echo of past battles fought together against common enemies.

He took a deep breath before speaking again—a man gathering courage from places he might once have feared to tread.

"We need to stop him," he said with conviction strong enough to cut through doubt "We need you."

* * *

Victor's eyes met mine, a silent plea echoing in the depths of his gaze. Once Damien's enforcer, he now stood before me, a man teetering on the brink of rebellion. The ink-black night cloaked us both as I listened to his hurried whispers, the clamor of the city's supernatural undercurrents fading into a distant hum.

"I need your help, Alex," Victor said, urgency lacing his words. "Damien... he's gone too far. We have to stop him."

I hesitated, memories of our past encounters swirling in my mind like dark ink in water. Victor had been a threat once, a danger to me and to Crimson Ink. Yet here he was, stripped of his arrogance, seeking my aid. Could I trust him? My heart pounded with the weight of decisions that stretched before me like shadows at dusk.

"I'll help you," I finally uttered, the words carving themselves into the cool air between us. "But we do this my way."

Victor nodded, a new alliance forged in the face of a common enemy. As he slinked back into the night from which he came, I knew what I had to do next.

I needed guidance—someone who understood not just my heritage but also the implications of wielding the Mark of Power that now thrummed beneath my skin. The only person who could provide such insight was Orion.

I made my way through the city's labyrinthine streets, each step bringing me closer to Orion's secluded haven. It was an antiquarian bookshop by day, a front for the vast knowledge he held within its walls. By night, it transformed into a sanctuary for those seeking enlightenment—or in my case, guidance.

The bell above the door jingled softly as I entered. The musty scent of old paper and leather enveloped me like a familiar embrace. Shelves lined with ancient tomes reached toward the high ceiling, and I found Orion nestled among them like an owl perched in its nest.

"Alex," he greeted me without surprise, as if he'd been expecting my visit all along. His eyes glimmered with otherworldly wisdom beneath the brim of his hat.

"Orion," I began, my voice steady despite the turmoil within me. "I need your help."

He motioned for me to follow him into the back room where countless scrolls and artifacts lay scattered across tables and pedestals—a cartographer's dream mapped out in celestial charts and arcane symbols.

"I sensed you'd come," Orion said while pouring two cups of tea from an iron kettle that seemed as old as time itself. "The Mark has awakened something in you... something powerful."

I took the cup he offered and sat down across from him. The tea was fragrant with herbs and spices that tickled my senses—a subtle reminder that even here, magic was at play.

"It has," I admitted, rolling up my sleeve to reveal the Mark etched upon my arm—the intricate design that held so much promise and peril.

Orion studied it intently, his fingers tracing lines invisible to my eyes as if reading braille inscribed by ancient forces.

"The Mark of Power is not just an amplifier of abilities; it is a vessel for balance between light and shadow," he explained solemnly. "It requires a guardian who understands this delicate equilibrium."

"And you believe I'm that guardian?" The question lingered between us like smoke from extinguished candles.

"You are more than you know," Orion replied with certainty that bordered on prophecy. "But with such power comes great responsibility—and risk."

Risk—I knew it all too well. The weight of Damien's amulet around my neck served as a constant reminder of the danger I faced every day.

"How do I wield this power without succumbing to its darker temptations?" The plea spilled from me like ink from an overturned bottle—desperate for direction.

Orion leaned forward, his eyes locked onto mine with an intensity that felt as though he were peering into my very soul.

"You must listen not only to your lineage but also to your heart," he said quietly. "The magic within you is ancient, but it is guided by your choices—by your will."

My hand instinctively went to my chest where my heart beat a steady rhythm beneath flesh and bone—a reminder that despite everything, I was still human.

"The ley lines," I murmured thoughtfully. "They are part of this balance you speak of?"

"Indeed." Orion rose from his seat and unfurled a map upon the table—a web of lines crisscrossing over an old blueprint of the city. "They are conduits for magical energy—the lifeblood of this world."

My gaze traced over the intersections marked on the map; nodes pulsing with potential power—power that Damien sought to exploit for his Ascension Protocol.

"We must disrupt his connection to these lines," I declared with newfound resolve.

Orion nodded approvingly. "You have allies—those who will stand by your side in this battle." He glanced toward a shadowed corner where Raven stood silently watching—a steadfast sentinel in our fight against tyranny.

"We'll need more than just strength; we'll need strategy," Raven added as he stepped forward into the light.

I looked between them both—my mentor and my ally—and felt something stir within me: hope amidst darkness.

"What do we do first?" My voice was steady now—calm despite everything hanging in the balance.

Orion placed a hand on my shoulder—a gesture both comforting and empowering—as Raven laid out blueprints across the table.

"We strike at dawn."

* * *

Dawn painted the sky with strokes of crimson and gold as I trudged up the cobbled path leading to Orion's bookshop. The weight of the Mark on my arm felt like a shackle, heavy with the burden of power and the looming responsibility it entailed. I'd been skirting around the edges of my fears for too long, and now, like ink spreading on parchment, those fears darkened my resolve.

The bookshop's bell chimed an ominous welcome as I stepped inside. The scent of aged paper and musty leather enveloped me, a stark contrast to the fresh air outside. Orion was perched behind his counter, his eyes piercing through the dim light like twin lanterns in the fog.

"I need to talk," I blurted out before he could greet me. My voice cracked with urgency.

Orion regarded me silently for a moment, then nodded toward the reading nook nestled between towering bookshelves. "Speak your mind, Alex."

I paced back and forth on the worn rug, each step punctuating my growing agitation. "You've seen what this Mark can do—the power it holds." I gestured to my arm where the symbol lay dormant yet alive beneath my skin. "But have you ever felt its weight? Have you ever been haunted by the sheer force of what you carry within?"

Orion folded his hands atop an open grimoire. "Power is a relentless companion, Alex. It does not ease its grip nor lighten its load for anyone."

"That's just it!" My voice rose as frustration bubbled up inside me. "I didn't ask for this. Every decision now comes with consequences that reach far beyond myself." I paused, catching a glimpse of my own wild eyes reflected in a nearby mirror—eyes that seemed to belong to someone else.

"And yet," Orion interjected calmly, "you wield it with an instinctive grace that belies your uncertainty."

"Grace?" The word tasted bitter on my tongue. "What grace is there in being forced into a corner? In having to choose between lesser evils?"

"You forget," Orion said softly, "that power also grants you choices that others may never have—the choice to defend, to protect, to change the course of events."

I stopped pacing and faced him squarely. "But at what cost? Every time I tap into the Mark's energy, I feel it gnawing at me, demanding more." My hands clenched into fists at my sides. "How do I bear this without becoming like Damien—corrupted by the very thing I'm trying to fight against?"

Orion's gaze held mine with an unwavering steadiness. "You bear it by remembering who you are and why you fight." He rose from his chair and approached me slowly. "Alex, you were chosen not for your lineage alone but for your heart—for your ability to empathize and connect with others."

"But how can I be sure?" Desperation crept into my voice as fear wrapped its cold fingers around me. "How can I trust myself when every use of this power risks tipping the balance?"

"Because you question it," he replied without hesitation. "Because you fear it."

My breath hitched as his words sank in.

"Damien never doubted his right to wield power over others," Orion continued. "He embraced it without regard for consequence or cost." He reached out and placed a hand on my shoulder—a gesture grounding me amidst my tempest of emotions.

"And what if I fail?" The question emerged as a whisper—a confession of my deepest dread.

"Then you will have failed trying to do what's right," Orion said firmly. "And there is honor in that effort."

A silence stretched between us, filled only by the quiet creaking of bookshelves and distant murmurs from outside.

"Come," Orion said after a while, leading me toward a secluded corner where a heavy tome lay open on a stand illuminated by a single shaft of light.

He traced his finger along an intricate diagram depicting ley lines converging at a focal point—the heart of our city.

"This is where we make our stand," he declared with resolve.

My eyes followed his movements as he outlined our strategy—the use of ley lines to amplify our resistance against Damien's encroaching darkness.

"And here—" He pointed to a series of symbols bordering the diagram. "—are your allies."

Raven's silhouette was etched among them—a reminder that I wasn't alone in this fight.

"Your strength lies not only in your power but also in those who stand beside you," Orion said, meeting my gaze once more.

The truth of his words washed over me like rain cleansing away layers of grime from old stone—refreshing yet eroding at the same time.

As we delved deeper into plans and contingencies, discussing every possible outcome from victory to defeat, something shifted within me—a subtle realignment like tectonic plates settling after an earthquake.

By the time Tara slipped into the room quietly—her presence both comforting and fortifying—I felt fortified enough to confront what lay ahead.

She joined us by the tome, her expression etched with concern but her posture resolute.

"We've got work ahead," she stated simply.

Nodding in agreement, we gathered around Orion's table—a triad bound by common purpose—as we prepared for battle against not just Damien but also against our own doubts and fears.

The morning sun climbed higher in the sky outside as we huddled together inside that sanctuary among books and ancient wisdom—readying ourselves for whatever darkness awaited us beyond those walls.

* * *

Dawn filtered through the dusty windows of Orion's bookshop, casting a soft light on the myriad of ancient texts that lined the walls. I stood there, amidst the knowledge of ages, feeling both anchored and adrift. The Mark on my arm pulsed gently, a constant reminder of the power I now wielded and the choices that led me here.

Orion moved about the room with a grace that belied his age, pulling volumes from shelves with purposeful intent. His eyes, though worn with the wisdom of years, sparkled with an energy that seemed to dance in step with the morning light.

"Alex," he began, his voice steady and reassuring, "the tattoos you create are more than mere symbols etched in skin. They are conduits for your will, manifestations of your spirit."

I nodded, absorbing his words. I'd known the tattoos were powerful—that much was clear from the changes I'd seen in those who bore them—but Orion's words hinted at a depth I hadn't fully grasped.

He handed me a book, its cover worn but enchanting, embossed with symbols that resonated within me. "This tome," he continued, "speaks of the Aetherial Weave—the fabric that binds all magic. Your tattoos tap into this weave, pulling threads to form new patterns."

I opened the book cautiously, as if afraid its secrets might spill out and scatter like leaves in the wind. The pages were filled with intricate diagrams and script in a language that felt familiar yet unknown. It was as if I understood it on an instinctual level—a language spoken by my blood rather than my mind.

"The choices you've made," Orion said softly, drawing my attention back to him, "they've shaped not only your path but also the weave itself. Every tattoo you've imbued with intent has altered reality's fabric ever so slightly."

I pondered his words. Each client I had worked on carried a piece of my magic—my choice—within them. I'd altered destinies without fully realizing it.

"Consider Damien," Orion pressed on gently. "Your defiance in altering his tattoo... You've chosen to weave protection over domination into his fate."

A shiver ran down my spine at the mention of Damien's name. That act of rebellion was perhaps the boldest stroke I had painted upon the Aetherial Weave. It was done out of necessity but not without fear of repercussions.

"But how can I be sure," I asked hesitantly, "that my choices are right? That in seeking to protect, I do not inadvertently bind or harm?"

Orion placed a hand on my shoulder—a gesture that felt as grounding as it was comforting. "Alex," he said earnestly, "certainty is a luxury seldom afforded to those who bear great power. But remember this: your empathy and your desire to help rather than harm have been your guiding stars."

His words washed over me like waves upon sand—reshaping thoughts and smoothing jagged doubts. He was right; my intentions had always been to shield and empower.

"And what of the Mark?" I inquired, glancing down at the arcane symbol etched into my flesh.

"The Mark is ancient—older than any vampire or witch you know," Orion explained. "It holds power over creation and destruction alike. Your lineage makes you its guardian; how you choose to use it will determine its nature."

I let out a breath I hadn't realized I'd been holding. The responsibility was immense but so was the opportunity for change—for good.

"Your connection to the ley lines," he continued while tracing a line across an old map spread out on a table nearby, "it's unique. You can channel their energy through your tattoos directly into the Aetherial Weave."

The map showed intersections marked in various places across the city—the heartbeats of magical energy that pulsed beneath concrete and steel.

"And Damien?" Tara asked as she joined us at the table, her presence a welcome strength beside me.

"He seeks to harness these ley lines for The Ascension Protocol," Orion replied gravely. "If he succeeds..."

He didn't need to finish; we all knew what was at stake—the subjugation of wills and souls under Damien's thrall.

"We'll need allies," Tara stated firmly.

"And we have them," Raven added from behind us—his arrival silent as shadow.

He placed before us several vials filled with luminescent ink—the kind that shimmered with promise and purpose.

"These are infused with essences from various magical beings—each willing to stand with us against Damien," Raven announced.

My eyes widened at his revelation. The Resistance had grown beyond what I'd imagined—each vial represented another thread in our tapestry of defiance.

"You will need to understand each essence deeply," Raven said as he handed me one of the vials—a liquid fire that seemed to dance within its glass prison.

"To imbue your tattoos with their full potential," he continued, "you must connect with their source—embrace their nature as part of your own."

The task seemed daunting—to take on such power required more than skill; it demanded an openness of spirit that left one vulnerable.

"Start with fire," Raven suggested with a knowing smile. "It purifies and renews."

I took the vial gingerly between my fingers and felt its warmth seep into my skin—a sensation both exhilarating and intimidating.

"You're not alone in this," Tara reminded me gently.

"No," Orion agreed softly, "you never were."

As we stood there among ancient texts and new allies—with magic both old and new coursing through our veins—I realized our choices had indeed shaped our world thus far. But it was our unity that would determine its future—a future we would face together.

* * *

The musty scent of ancient tomes filled Orion's bookshop as I stepped into the familiar haven. The dim light from the windows bathed the room in a warm, golden hue, casting shadows that seemed to dance with the wisdom contained within these walls. Orion, with his usual enigmatic presence, greeted me from behind a pile of books, his eyes reflecting the same light that flickered in the fireplace.

"You look troubled, Alex," he said, his voice soft yet penetrating. "Sit. It's time we spoke of things beyond spells and sigils."

I sank into a leather chair opposite him, the weight of my recent actions and decisions pressing heavily on my chest. Orion studied me for a moment, his gaze both kind and discerning.

"Reflect on your journey," he urged. "Think about the choices you've made, who you've become in this process. The power you wield is not just in your hands; it resides in your heart."

His words nudged open a floodgate of memories—clients whose skin I had marked with magic that changed their lives; allies I had empowered; enemies I had defied; and the Mark of Power that now pulsed on my own skin, a constant reminder of the delicate balance I must maintain.

I traced my fingers over the Mark, feeling its energy resonate through me. It was a part of me now, an indelible symbol of my heritage and potential. But with it came questions that gnawed at me: Was I wielding this power responsibly? Was I using it to create or to control?

"The decisions you've made..." Orion continued, pulling me back from my reverie. "They were necessary steps on your path. But every choice carries consequences."

I knew he was right. Every tattoo I'd inked had altered someone's fate. Every alliance had shifted the balance of power in this hidden world we inhabited. Even my defiance against Damien—each act was a stitch in the tapestry of my existence.

"But who do you want to be, Alex?" Orion asked pointedly.

That question hit hard. Who did I want to be? The artist whose work was feared and respected? A pawn used by others for their own ends? Or something more—a beacon of hope in a world shrouded in shadows?

I had begun this journey thinking only of my craft, my shop—Crimson Ink—a place where magic and artistry intertwined. But somewhere along the way, it became more than that. It became about protecting those who couldn't protect themselves, standing up to forces that sought to use power for their own selfish gains.

I let out a breath I hadn't realized I'd been holding and met Orion's unwavering gaze.

"I want to be someone who uses their gifts for good," I confessed. "I want to be true to myself and my abilities without succumbing to darkness."

Orion nodded slowly, as if he'd expected this answer all along.

"And what have you learned about yourself so far?" he asked.

I closed my eyes, letting the warmth from the fireplace seep into my bones as I pondered his question. Images flickered behind my eyelids—the faces of those I'd helped and those I'd hurt.

"I've learned that power is seductive," I began, opening my eyes to look at Orion again. "It can corrupt even the best intentions if not checked by conscience."

Orion's lips twitched in what might have been approval or amusement—it was hard to tell with him.

"Go on," he encouraged.

"And," I continued, "that despite everything—the danger, the fear—I'm not alone." Tara's steadfast support flashed through my mind; Raven's shared vision; Jade's camaraderie; even Victor's unexpected alliance—they were all threads woven into my life now.

"I've learned that trust isn't given lightly but earned through actions," I said firmly.

Orion nodded again as he rose from his seat and approached one of the towering bookshelves. He selected an old leather-bound volume and handed it to me.

"This book contains stories of those who walked paths similar to yours," he explained as I took it reverently into my hands. "You'll find both warnings and inspirations within its pages."

As I leafed through the ancient pages filled with tales of magic and moral struggles, something within me settled—a sense of belonging to a lineage much greater than myself.

"You're at a crossroads," Orion spoke again as he returned to his chair across from me. "The path ahead is fraught with challenges that will test your character."

I absorbed his words like ink into skin—a permanent imprint on my consciousness.

"And no matter how dark it gets," he added with a hint of sternness breaking through his usually calm demeanor, "remember who you are and who you strive to be."

Our eyes locked in silent understanding—a mentor guiding his pupil toward self-realization amid chaos.

"I won't forget," I promised him—and myself.

The rest of our conversation flowed like ink on parchment—plans for countering Damien's Ascension Protocol using ley lines; strategizing with allies; ensuring every move was deliberate and purposeful.

As we spoke, something inside me shifted—a subtle realignment towards who I wanted to be: an artist whose ink didn't just adorn skin but protected souls; an individual whose heritage didn't define them but empowered them; a person whose choices weren't dictated by fear but guided by hope.

With each word exchanged with Orion, each plan laid out with Tara and Raven waiting nearby, I felt more certain than ever before: My tattoos would be shields against darkness, symbols of unity rather than division—and through them, perhaps we could bring light back into our city overshadowed by Damien's reach.

* * *

The morning light spilled into Orion's bookshop, bathing the dusty tomes and leather-bound volumes in a warm, golden glow. I stood there, surrounded by the essence of ancient wisdom, my fingers tracing the spine of a book that Orion had pushed towards me. The Mark on my arm seemed to hum in recognition of the power nestled within these pages.

"Remember, Alex," Orion's voice broke through my reverie, "you are not just a conduit for these forces; you're their steward. Your intentions, your will... they shape the outcomes."

I lifted my gaze from the book and met his eyes. They held a kind of solemnity that you'd expect from someone who'd seen centuries come and go. I nodded, feeling the weight of his words settle in my chest.

Tara watched from across the room, her brow furrowed with concern. I could tell she was worried about me, about us—about everything that was barreling down on us like a runaway train. But she also had that glint in her eye, the one that told me she was ready to stand beside me through whatever hellfire awaited.

Raven had left earlier after offering those vials filled with magical essences. Allies had sent them; people who believed in what we were trying to achieve—freedom from Damien's tyranny. I picked up one of the vials and rolled it between my fingers, watching the liquid catch the light.

"You'll need to be careful with those," Tara said as she approached me. "We don't know what all of them do yet."

"I know," I replied softly. "But we'll figure it out. We always do."

Orion moved closer, his hands clasped behind his back. "You've grown so much since you first walked into my shop, Alex. Not just in skill, but in spirit too."

I gave him a small smile but remained silent; compliments never sat well with me.

"The city is alive," he continued, "and it speaks through its ley lines like veins coursing with lifeblood. You've felt it—how it ebbs and flows around you. Damien wants to control that flow, to bend it to his will."

I looked down at the Mark again, considering how much had changed since it etched its way onto my skin. It was more than just ink; it was a promise—a promise of balance and guardianship.

"You must be the counterbalance," Orion said firmly. "For every push Damien makes towards darkness, you must offer a pull towards light."

It was a dance as old as time itself—the struggle between shadow and luminescence—and here I was in the middle of it all.

"How can I be sure I'm ready?" The question slipped out before I could stop it.

Orion's response was immediate and confident. "Because you have something Damien will never understand: empathy and connection to others."

Tara nodded in agreement as she stepped closer and placed a hand on my shoulder—a gesture meant to steady both her nerves and mine.

"We're not alone in this," she said firmly.

I closed my eyes for a moment and let their belief in me wash over like a cleansing wave. When I opened them again, something had shifted within me—a renewed sense of purpose crystallized into sharp focus.

I picked up another vial—one filled with an iridescent substance that shimmered with potential—and turned it over in my hand.

"We use these," I began, voice steady now with conviction, "not as weapons but as shields—to protect us and those who can't fight for themselves."

Tara squeezed my shoulder gently. "And when Damien realizes what we've done?"

A fire ignited behind my eyes at the thought of facing him again—the man who believed he could own me and control my gift.

"Then we show him exactly what happens when you try to chain something that was meant to be free." My words didn't waver; they cut through the air like a blade sharpened on stone.

Orion stepped back then, giving us space as if he knew this moment belonged to Tara and me—to those who would stand on the front lines.

"We'll need more than just magic," Tara cautioned after a moment's silence.

"And we'll have it." My voice was firm despite the storm brewing on our horizon.

I set down the vial and pulled out one last item from my bag—the scrying sphere that old man had given me at his cryptic bookstore yesterday. It seemed ordinary enough: clear crystal shot through with fractures that caught the light at odd angles.

"This," I said as I held it up between us, "is how we find where we need to be—where our power will have the greatest impact against Damien."

The sphere pulsed gently in response to my touch—another ally in our cause against darkness.

"Let's get started then." Tara moved towards one of Orion's many tables littered with maps and books about ley lines and arcane history.

As we poured over maps under Orion's watchful gaze—plotting courses along invisible pathways—I felt it: an unshakeable determination anchoring me firmly in place.

This was more than just rebellion or defiance; this was about fighting for something bigger than myself or any one person—it was about fighting for us all—for every soul that sought refuge within this city's embrace.

I stood up straighter as if physically shaking off any lingering doubts or fears because now wasn't the time for hesitation—it was time for action.

And as we laid out our strategy—a delicate operation requiring precision and unity—I knew deep down that whatever lay ahead for us wouldn't be easy or without cost... but whatever price needed paying, I'd meet it head-on because retreat simply wasn't an option anymore—not when so much depended on our success.

Chapter 19

Eclipse of Conflict

I stood in the back room of Orion's bookshop, the walls lined with ancient tomes and artifacts that whispered of a world beyond the one most knew. The musty scent of old paper and the faint trace of incense filled the air. The bookshop, a sanctuary of knowledge and magic, felt like the calm before the storm. My fingers traced over the leather-bound spines, seeking out specific titles I'd come to rely on in recent days. They were guides, companions in my journey to understand the power I now wielded – the Mark of Power.

Tara was there with me, her face set in a determined frown as she checked over our inventory. Vials of enchanted ink lay organized on the table, their contents shimmering with potential. "How are you holding up?" she asked without looking up, her voice steady but laced with concern.

I took a deep breath, feeling the Mark pulse on my arm like a second heartbeat. "I've been better," I admitted. "But I've never been more ready." It was only half-true. The weight of what was coming bore down on me like a physical force, yet there was a fire within me that hadn't been there before – a fire stoked by necessity and resolve.

Orion emerged from the shadows, his eyes finding mine with an intensity that suggested he knew more than he let on. "Remember, Alex," he said in his low, measured tone, "your power is not just in the ink and skin. It's in your spirit – your will to protect and change things for the better."

Raven joined us, slipping into the room like a shadow at dusk. He carried with him a satchel filled with more vials – gifts from those who stood with us against Damien's tyranny. He placed it on the table with care. "These are from allies across the city," he explained. "Use them wisely."

We began strategizing then, our voices low as we leaned over maps of ley lines that snaked through the city like veins. We pinpointed intersections where Damien's influence was strongest and where we could sever it. I felt Tara's hand briefly squeeze my shoulder – a silent message of solidarity.

Victor stepped forward next, his allegiance once questionable but now solidified by shared goals and mutual respect born from past tensions. He unfolded another map atop ours, this one marked with locations critical to Damien's Ascension Protocol. "We hit these spots simultaneously," he said gruffly. "Disrupt his network from within."

The room hummed with focused energy as we assigned tasks and discussed signals for coordination. Cipher would be leading one team to target ley line intersections while Lynx spearheaded efforts to sow confusion among Damien's followers.

As they spoke, I found myself half-listening while my gaze wandered to a corner where an old scrying sphere sat atop a stack of books. Its surface was cloudy, but I knew when the time came it would clear to guide us where we needed to be.

"We should get some rest while we can," Tara suggested eventually, breaking into my thoughts.

Rest seemed like an alien concept now; adrenaline already coursed through me at just the thought of what lay ahead. But she was right; our bodies needed it even if our minds refused.

We dispersed then, each to our own corners of Orion's haven – except for me. I lingered at the table where our plans lay spread out like a patchwork quilt made of hope and desperation.

I reached for one vial of ink – not just any ink but one infused with essences meant to amplify courage and resilience. Uncapping it carefully, I let just one drop fall onto my palette before recapping it and returning it to its place among its brethren.

With practiced movements born from countless hours at Crimson Ink, I dipped my tattoo needle into the drop and began to etch onto my forearm – not far from where the Mark thrummed with life. The design took shape: an unbroken circle wrapped around an eye – an ancient symbol of protection and vigilance.

The needle stung against my skin; each puncture was deliberate as I channeled every ounce of intention into this personal sigil. By dawn, it stood completed upon my flesh – raw but radiant in its simplicity.

Standing alone amidst maps and plans, surrounded by echoes of magic both light and dark, I let myself feel everything: fear for what might come; sorrow for those already lost; anger at Damien for forcing this path upon us all; but most importantly hope – hope that we could turn back this tide before it swept us all away.

Tara found me there hours later as light began to creep into the shop through dusty windows. She didn't say anything at first; instead, she joined me at my vigil over our assembled arsenal against darkness.

"It'll be soon," she said softly as if reading my thoughts.

"Yes," I replied equally quiet. "But we're ready."

She looked at my new tattoo then back at me with something akin to awe in her eyes before nodding once sharply.

We were ready indeed – ready to fight for freedom; ready to stand against oppression; ready to bear whatever cost came with wielding power responsibly for those who couldn't wield it themselves.

In those moments before dawn fully broke over Orion's bookshop and spilled its light across maps strewn with strategies against an enemy who sought only domination through darkness, there existed between us all a unity forged from shared purpose: We would face Damien together; we would protect our city together; we would prevail or fall together because nothing less would suffice when so much was at stake.

* * *

The dim hum of the city above faded as we stood in the underground chamber, our makeshift sanctuary against the world Damien had tainted. My allies flanked me, their faces set in grim determination. Tara, ever the steadfast rock, her eyes scanning our group for any sign of faltering courage. Lynx, with his calculating gaze, mentally charted our course through the battlefield that awaited us. And Victor, a towering figure whose allegiance to Damien had crumbled under the weight of his own conscience.

The air crackled with tension as we prepared to face the vampire gang. The chamber echoed with the sound of leather and metal as my allies readied their weapons. I felt the Mark of Power on my arm pulsing like a second heartbeat, a constant reminder of the responsibility I shouldered.

Raven's magical essences clinked softly in their vials on my belt. Their presence was a comfort—a reminder that even those not physically with us today stood in solidarity against Damien's darkness.

A message from Evelyn had brought us here: a challenge, an invitation to parley—or perhaps it was a trap. Regardless, we had no choice but to meet them head-on.

We moved through shadowed corridors until we arrived at the designated meeting point, an abandoned subway platform that seemed frozen in time. The air felt thick with old magic and dust; it coated my throat and filled my lungs with the musty scent of disuse.

The vampire gang stood waiting for us, their presence menacing in its stillness. Damien was at their center, flanked by Evelyn and Victor's former comrades-in-arms. They were statuesque and otherworldly—beings out of legend—and I fought down the rising tide of dread.

Damien's eyes met mine across the empty space between us. They were abysses that promised endless night, but within them flickered something akin to respect—or was it merely anticipation for the game he believed he was winning?

"Alex," Damien called out, his voice reverberating against the cracked tiles and peeling advertisements that lined the walls. "So kind of you to accept my invitation."

I stepped forward, aware that every pair of eyes was locked onto me—friends and foes alike.

"We're here to end this," I said, allowing my voice to carry with all the authority I could muster.

Damien's lips curved into a sardonic smile. "End this? My dear Alex, you speak as if you have any power here."

I felt Tara stiffen beside me, her hand twitching toward her weapon. But I raised a hand slightly—a silent command for patience.

"Power?" I echoed, tilting my head as if considering his words. "Isn't that what you're after? The Mark of Power?" I tapped my forearm where the Mark lay hidden beneath my sleeve—a feint because its true power rested within me now.

Damien's gaze narrowed slightly at that gesture, but he remained silent, urging me to continue.

"You think you've won," I continued slowly, "because you believe you've bent me to your will. But power isn't about control or dominion." I glanced at Victor then back at Damien. "It's about choice—and consequence."

Evelyn shifted her weight slightly—a predatory readiness that spoke volumes about her stance in this confrontation.

"Choice," Damien mused aloud as if savoring the word on his tongue. "And what choice have you made today?"

"The choice to stand against you," I declared firmly.

A murmur ran through his ranks at my words—a ripple of surprise or perhaps disbelief that anyone would dare oppose them so openly.

"You've made your bed with humans and traitors," Evelyn sneered from Damien's side.

"Better than lying in a coffin with tyrants," Tara shot back before I could silence her with a look.

Damien held up a hand to stay any further comment from his lieutenant and stepped forward—only one step—but it felt like an invasion into our fragile sanctuary of resistance.

"Alex," he began again, his voice lower now but no less dangerous for its softness. "You have something that belongs to me."

My pulse quickened at his implication—the Mark—and how it connected us in ways I wished it didn't.

"You mean this?" Without thinking, I rolled up my sleeve to reveal inked skin—ink that wasn't the Mark but a diversionary glyph instead—a tattoo artist's sleight of hand.

His eyes flashed with recognition then darkened with fury as he realized he'd been deceived—not just now but days before when he thought he'd claimed power over me with his own design on my skin.

Tara edged closer to me as if she could shield me from what was coming next—but it wasn't just about me anymore; we were all part of this tangled web now.

Lynx shifted from foot to foot—a coiled spring ready to release at any moment—and behind him Cipher nodded once sharply as if reaffirming some unspoken pledge they had made among themselves when they chose this path.

I held Damien's gaze knowing this was merely the calm before a storm we might not all weather—but there was no turning back now; we had come too far and sacrificed too much to yield without giving everything we had left to give.

* * *

The damp air of the subway platform clung to my skin like a second layer, thick with the electric charge of magic and anticipation. The familiar weight of the Mark on my arm felt both like a shackle and a scepter of power, a constant reminder of the path I'd chosen. Across from me stood Damien and his entourage, their eyes reflecting the dim lights like predators in the night.

"You think you can stand against me?" Damien's voice echoed, smooth as silk yet edged with malice. "You're nothing but a tool, Alex. A means to an end."

I squared my shoulders, readying myself. "I am not your tool, Damien. I am the keeper of my own destiny."

The gang sneered, their disbelief palpable in the stale air between us. They didn't know about the nights I'd spent honing my craft, the secrets whispered by ancient books and Orion's guiding words. They were unaware of how I'd grown, how the very ink in my veins thrummed with potent magic.

A slight nod from Tara gave me the cue. It was time to reveal just how far I'd come.

With a swift motion, I rolled up my sleeve to reveal an intricate network of tattoos snaking up my arm, each a symbol of protection and defiance. The gang's eyes widened as I channeled energy through these marks, letting it build until it buzzed beneath my skin like a living thing.

"Watch closely," I murmured, focusing on a particularly elaborate design etched near my elbow—a binding sigil interwoven with runes for clarity and truth.

I activated the tattoo with a whispered incantation, and it flared to life with an ethereal glow. The air around us shimmered as if reality itself wavered under its influence. Damien faltered, his usually unshakeable composure cracking as he sensed something amiss.

"You've been marked by your own ambition," I said evenly as I advanced one step closer. "This sigil will make you see things as they truly are—beyond lies and manipulation."

Damien recoiled as if struck, his eyes betraying his inner turmoil. Evelyn glanced at him uncertainly but stood her ground. It was clear that she too sensed the shift in power.

With each step forward, I let more tattoos come alive along my arm—a dance of light and shadow playing across my skin. One depicted an ouroboros, its tail in its mouth—a symbol of cycles and renewal that I had subtly altered. Another was a phoenix rising from ashes—strength through adversity.

Damien's followers shuffled uneasily behind him; even Victor seemed uncertain now. They could feel it—the undeniable force that pulsed from me.

"This is what growth looks like," I continued. "This is what happens when you try to chain someone who's meant to soar."

Raven's essences added potency to my words; every syllable carried weight that hung heavy in the air.

A new tattoo emerged into view—one that no one but Tara knew about. A labyrinthine design encircled by protective wards—a tactical play we had devised together for moments just like this.

"Do you understand now?" I asked Damien as he tried to regain his composure.

"I understand that you're more than we bargained for," he admitted through gritted teeth.

But before he could recover further or launch any counterattack, Lynx burst into action beside me, releasing a volley of energy towards Damien's gang using their own tattoos—another technique we'd refined together over countless practice sessions.

Chaos erupted as members of Damien's gang struggled against the onslaught; some were trying to fight back while others were desperately seeking cover from our unexpected strength.

Victor stepped forward then, his face an unreadable mask. "Damien," he began with caution in his voice, "perhaps it's time we reconsider our stance."

Damien shot Victor a glare sharp enough to cut glass but said nothing. The former enforcer had spoken out of turn—one did not simply challenge Damien without consequence—but this momentary fracture within their ranks gave us an edge.

Tara moved closer to me; her presence was both reassuring and galvanizing as we stood shoulder to shoulder against our foes.

I turned back to Damien then; this was our moment—our uprising against tyranny—and we would not falter now when victory was within reach.

As I held his gaze steadily, there was no mistaking it: he knew that we were no longer mere thorns in his side—we were a force capable of tearing down his empire brick by brick.

The confrontation reached its peak as Damien lunged forward with feral grace only for Lynx to intercept him with precision borne out of necessity and desperation.

In that split second when our collective focus was on subduing Damien's assault, Evelyn seized her chance—her strategy always was survival first—and she vanished into shadows that seemed all too eager to embrace her retreat.

And then it was just us and them—resistance versus tyranny—the final stand on this long-forgotten platform where destinies would be forged or broken under flickering lights and watchful eyes.

* * *

I stood among my allies, our breaths mingling with the stagnant air of the subway, our collective resolve forming an unspoken pact against Damien's looming threat. My skin prickled with the energy of my tattoos, each line and curve a testament to the power I harbored within—a power I had once feared but now wielded as a shield for those I stood beside.

Damien, his silhouette framed by the flickering lights of the underground, held his ground with a chilling calmness that seemed out of place amid the chaos. He wore a smirk that spoke volumes of his confidence—a confidence that bordered on arrogance, but not without reason.

"You think you have power?" Damien's voice echoed through the station, each word dripping with disdain. "You're nothing but children playing with matches while standing in a pool of gasoline."

I clenched my fists, feeling the Mark on my arm pulsate as if responding to Damien's challenge. Tara shifted beside me, her eyes darting between me and Damien, while Lynx readied themselves, muscles taut like a coiled spring.

Victor, once a steadfast enforcer for Damien's will, now looked uncertain—a flicker of doubt crossing his usually impassive features. It was a crack in Damien's armor, and we all felt it.

But then it happened.

Damien raised his hand slowly, deliberately. The air around us grew thick, heavy with anticipation and dread. A dark energy began to swirl around him like a vortex of shadows coalescing into form and substance. It wasn't just raw magical strength—it was something more sinister, something that chilled me to the bone.

The shadows writhed and twisted into tendrils that snaked out toward us. My tattoos flared in response, their glow a beacon against the encroaching darkness. I heard Tara chant under her breath, words of protection weaving through the air like threads of silver light.

"We can't let him do this," I whispered to my companions.

Lynx nodded sharply, their expression set in grim determination. "We knew it wouldn't be easy."

I focused on my Mark, drawing upon its power to erect barriers against Damien's assault. The symbols etched into my flesh came alive, each one burning with an intensity that matched my resolve.

But Damien was relentless. The shadows morphed into specters—figures of nightmare that bore down upon us with eyes hollow and mouths agape in silent screams. I could feel their cold fingers brush against my barriers, testing for weakness.

And then Damien did something I hadn't anticipated; he didn't just wield magic—he became magic incarnate. His body seemed to dissolve into the darkness itself, his essence merging with the shadows as if he were no longer human but an entity born from the abyss.

"Stay strong," I called out to Tara and Lynx. "We can't let him break us."

Tara nodded tersely as she summoned shields of her own—spheres of energy that repelled the specters with bursts of radiant light.

But for every shadow we dispelled, two more took its place—a hydra of darkness that fed on our fears and doubts.

Damien's laughter reverberated through the subway station—a sound devoid of joy but full of malice. "You can't win," he taunted from everywhere and nowhere at once. "I am power."

Victor stepped forward then, his voice steady despite the uncertainty that had plagued him moments before. "Damien," he said firmly, "this ends now."

But before Victor could act on his words, Damien's shadows enveloped him—wrapping around his form like chains meant to bind both flesh and spirit.

"Victor!" I cried out, horror gripping me as I watched our newfound ally struggle against the darkness that sought to claim him.

I turned to Raven then—their vials containing magical essences clutched tightly in their hands. "We need those now!"

Raven didn't hesitate; they threw the vials onto the ground where they shattered—releasing their contents in a brilliant display of color and light that pierced through Damien's shadows like rays of dawn slicing through night.

The specters recoiled as if burned by the magic-infused essences—a momentary reprieve that gave us all a breath we desperately needed.

"Keep fighting," Lynx urged as they launched themselves at a group of specters—each movement precise and lethal.

I turned my attention back to Victor, extending my hand toward him as I channeled energy through my tattoos—a lifeline thrown across an ocean of shadows.

"Take my hand!" I shouted over the din of battle.

Victor reached out—his fingers brushing against mine before grasping hold firmly. Together we pulled against Damien's influence—my Mark flaring brightly against his dark magic.

For a moment that stretched into eternity, we teetered on the edge—a delicate balance between victory and defeat. Then suddenly Victor was free—pulled from the abyss back into our realm where shadows had no dominion over light.

As Victor staggered back to stand among us once again—his expression one of gratitude mixed with defiance—I knew this confrontation was far from over. We had shown cracks in Damien's facade but had yet to shatter it completely.

"Prepare yourselves," I warned my friends—the weight of leadership settling upon me like an old but familiar cloak. "He won't give up easily."

And neither would we.

With every ounce of strength we possessed—with every spell cast and barrier erected—we stood united against Damien's true power: an overwhelming force that threatened to consume us all if we faltered even for an instant.

But amidst it all—one truth remained steadfast within me: this confrontation was not just about survival—it was about reclaiming our freedom from someone who sought to dominate it for their own twisted ends.

And so we fought—not just for ourselves—but for every soul who had ever been touched by Damien's shadowy hand...

* * *

I stood there, the weight of destiny pressing on my shoulders like a physical burden. The subway station, a battleground of shadows and light, seemed to shrink as Damien's power swelled, threatening to swallow us whole. My allies, braced for the worst, exchanged tense glances that spoke volumes of our dire situation.

Damien's laugh, cold and devoid of any humanity, echoed off the walls. "You really thought you could stand against me?" he sneered, his voice a viper's hiss that sent shivers down my spine. "You're nothing but a canvas for my will."

I felt the sting of his words, but I didn't let them penetrate the armor I'd crafted from every lesson learned and every hardship endured. My mind raced, flicking through every possible countermove like pages in one of Orion's ancient tomes.

In the chaos, Tara's voice cut through like a beacon. "Alex, now!"

The Mark on my arm pulsed with an urgent beat. I locked eyes with Damien as I extended my hand, my fingers splayed wide. The ink beneath my skin shimmered with an otherworldly light as I called upon every ounce of strength from the ley lines that crisscrossed beneath us.

"Your mistake," I said with a calm I didn't feel, "was thinking that power only comes from domination."

The shadows recoiled as if burned by the truth in my words. Damien faltered for a moment—a crack in his otherwise impenetrable facade—and I seized it.

I channeled my energy into the protective runes hidden within his tattoo. The glyphs activated, their magic woven by intention and cunning rather than brute force. A surge of resistance pushed against Damien's dark tide, like dawn breaking over a night-blackened sky.

Victor rallied to our side then, his resolve solidifying into action as he drew upon his own newfound defiance to aid us. Lynx and Cipher flanked him, their expressions fierce with determination.

Damien snarled, a beast cornered by its prey turned hunters. "You'll pay for this treachery!"

But something had shifted—the balance of power no longer lay solely in his hands. We moved as one entity: Tara chanting incantations; Raven unleashing vials that erupted into barriers of protection; Victor disrupting Damien's focus with expertly thrown punches; Lynx and Cipher weaving through the melee with grace and lethal precision.

I continued to feed strength into our collective might, tapping into the Mark's reservoir. The tattoos across my body blazed with living light—a tapestry of courage inscribed in ink.

The clash of magic and muscle crescendoed around us as we fought for control over the ley lines that Damien sought to corrupt. In this critical moment where defeat seemed certain just minutes ago, we stood united by shared purpose and empowered by our collective will.

As I pushed forward alongside my friends, each step became a declaration: We would not be broken. We would not yield.

Then it happened—a sudden release like the breaking of a dam. Damien's control slipped as our combined efforts overwhelmed his shadowy constructs.

Evelyn appeared then from her hiding place within the gloom—her eyes alight with an inner fire that spoke volumes of her own struggle against Damien's dominion. In her hand she held an object that gleamed even in the dim light—a dagger that seemed to hum with potential.

Damien noticed too late; Evelyn was already upon him, her movements swift and sure as she plunged the blade into a crevice within his defenses.

A howl erupted from Damien's throat—a sound not just of pain but of profound betrayal—as he staggered back from Evelyn's strike.

I turned to Tara and nodded—the time had come to end this.

With every step toward Damien, I drew upon the teachings Orion had instilled in me—about balance and responsibility—and poured them into each line and curve of ink upon my flesh. As I neared him, I reached out with hands etched in sigils of containment and pressed them against his chest where Evelyn had wounded him.

Damien's eyes met mine; they were pools of darkness waning under the relentless advance of dawn. His lips parted to speak or curse—I couldn't tell which—but no sound came forth as he crumbled beneath our combined might.

The shadows dissipated like mist at sunrise, leaving behind only the tangible weight of our victory—and its cost.

Tara came up beside me then, her hand on my shoulder offering both solace and strength as we surveyed what remained after battle—the fallen not forgotten among triumphs tallying higher than we'd dared hope.

Lynx approached next with Cipher trailing behind them—both bearing scars new and old—but alive and defiant still. Victor leaned heavily against a wall nearby; despite everything he'd been through under Damien's thumb—he stood victorious among friends now rather than alone amongst foes before.

Evelyn stood apart from us all—her gaze distant yet burning still with whatever fire she'd kindled within herself when she decided to turn against her former master.

And there we all were—a group once disparate now united by necessity against a common enemy who had sought to use us all for his own ends but found himself undone by our unwillingness to bend or break beneath his will.

We had won this round—but we knew well enough that more would come; more battles where defeat might loom close before being turned aside by wit or skill or lessons hard-learned along paths none had expected to walk when first they set out on them alone or together alike.

But for now—for this moment—we allowed ourselves to breathe easy again—to revel in victory however brief it might prove—because today we had triumphed over darkness with nothing but our own light leading us onward toward whatever future awaited beyond these bloodstained subway tracks.

* * *

The city lay quiet, a stark contrast to the storm that had raged within the confines of the subway station. Standing amid the remnants of battle, my breaths came in shallow gasps, each exhale a mist in the chill air. My arm throbbed with a heat that matched the pulse of the Mark of Power, its glow dimming as if it too was catching its breath.

Damien stood before me, his figure less imposing now, more human than it had ever seemed. The shadows that once clung to him like devoted hounds had dissipated, leaving him exposed under the harsh fluorescent lights. His followers, those who hadn't fled or been subdued by my allies, looked on with a mix of fear and uncertainty.

I could feel Tara's eyes on me, heavy with concern and unspoken questions. Victor, who'd once enforced Damien's will with an iron fist, stood at my side—his allegiance shifted but his loyalty to our cause clear in his stance. Lynx and Cipher hovered close by, their readiness palpable despite their exhaustion.

"You never understood," Damien spat, blood trickling from the corner of his mouth—a stark reminder of his mortality. "You think you've won? This power you've unleashed... you can't control it forever."

His words hung between us like a dare, challenging me to refute them. I could sense the truth in them—the Mark was a force I'd only begun to comprehend. But standing there, in the aftermath of our victory, I couldn't allow doubt to seep in.

"I don't need to control it forever," I said, my voice steady despite the fatigue that clung to my bones. "Just long enough to stop you."

Evelyn emerged from the shadows then, her gaze lingering on Damien with an unreadable expression before settling on me. "You've done what none of us could," she said quietly. "But be wary—the power you wield now makes you a target."

Her warning was one I'd already considered; wielding the Mark made me both a savior and a beacon for those who craved such power.

A cacophony of sirens approached in the distance—the mundane world encroaching upon our supernatural conflict. It was time for decisions and swift action.

"Go," I urged Tara and the others. "Get out before the authorities arrive."

They hesitated but knew better than to argue during such critical moments. As they vanished into the labyrinthine tunnels that crisscrossed beneath the city's skin, I turned back to Damien.

"Your reign is over," I declared.

His laughter was hollow as he struggled to his feet. "Reigns end, but legacies... they endure." With those cryptic parting words, he lunged at me one last time—a desperate bid for survival or perhaps a final act of defiance.

Instinct took over; my hand shot out, palm forward and fingers splayed wide. The Mark blazed bright once more—a protective shield sprung from skin to air. Damien's advance halted as if he'd struck an invisible wall; his body went rigid before collapsing onto the cold concrete floor.

Victor caught him before he hit ground zero—an odd gesture for a man who'd spent years enforcing Damien's brutal will. But perhaps that was part of this new world we were stepping into—one where former enemies could find common ground.

"We need to leave," Victor urged as he hoisted Damien's unconscious form over his shoulder.

I nodded silently and followed him into the darkened tunnels that had been our battlefield just moments ago.

The weight of victory settled heavily on my shoulders as we navigated through underground passages that felt like arteries carrying us away from one life and towards another—uncertain but alive with possibility.

We emerged into night's embrace somewhere far from where we started—an empty lot swallowed by shadows save for a few stray beams from streetlights struggling against encroaching darkness.

Victor set Damien down against a graffiti-laden wall; even in defeat and vulnerability, there was an air about him that spoke of dangers not yet passed.

"What will you do with him?" Victor asked after a stretch of silence filled only by distant traffic sounds and whispers of wind through abandoned spaces.

I considered Damien—a man who'd sought control through fear and power—and felt no desire for vengeance or retribution. His empire had crumbled; what purpose would punishment serve?

"He'll stand trial," I said finally. "Let him answer to those he wronged." It was justice—not revenge—that drove me now.

Victor nodded once as if satisfied with my answer before turning away into darkness that seemed less menacing now than it ever had before.

As I watched him go—Damien's fate sealed—I couldn't help but wonder about my own future and what costs this victory would exact from me in time.

I glanced down at my arm where the Mark still glowed faintly—a beacon in night's grasp—and felt its power ebb away like tide receding after storm's fury had passed.

It wasn't just Damien who'd been defeated tonight—it was also fear... doubt... oppression...

But at what price?

I didn't have answers; only time would tell if we'd traded one form of darkness for another or if light we sought would truly dawn on us all...

For now though—despite uncertainties and costs yet unknown—I allowed myself momentary respite beneath star-speckled sky as city breathed around me...

We'd won...for now...

Chapter 20

New Dawn Rising

The air hummed with a tension that felt like the quiet after a storm. As I walked through the streets, I could sense the supernatural community's collective exhale, a cautious release of breath held far too long. Eyes, human and otherwise, darted from shadow to shadow, searching for signs of danger that had become all too familiar. But for the first time in what felt like an eternity, there was a whisper of something else—hope.

I kept my stride even and purposeful as I navigated the city's maze of alleyways and thoroughfares. It was strange, this sensation of victory intermingled with unease. My tattoos tingled beneath my sleeves, as if they were attuned to the city's newfound pulse. Every so often, I'd catch a glimpse of recognition in someone's gaze—a nod to the battle we'd won—but always fleeting, like they were afraid to acknowledge it fully.

At the local market, which served as a neutral zone for all beings regardless of allegiance, the atmosphere was different. The usual cacophony of haggling voices and clinking charms was subdued, replaced by murmurs and furtive glances. A vendor caught my eye, her pupils slit with concern.

"Alex," she hissed through pointed teeth. "You've done it now."

I stopped in front of her booth, laden with amulets and talismans. "For better or worse," I replied.

Her scales shimmered with a nervous iridescence as she leaned closer. "They're saying Damien's gang is scattered—like roaches when the light flicks on."

I considered her words, my hand absentmindedly tracing the lines of ink on my arm—the Mark that had turned the tide. "Scattered doesn't mean gone," I reminded her softly.

She nodded, eyes darting to my arm before meeting mine again. "And what about you? The new power in town?"

I chuckled without humor. "Hardly."

But her question echoed in my mind as I continued through the market. Was that what people saw me as now? A new power to be reckoned with? I shook off the thought like an unwelcome chill.

At a crossroads where magic met mundane, I paused beneath an old lamppost whose light flickered inconsistently—a sure sign of lingering enchantments in the air. Across from me stood The Cauldron, a pub known for its supernatural clientele.

The door swung open and out stepped Tara, her expression somber despite our recent victory. She approached me with a sense of urgency that made my stomach clench.

"They're waiting for us inside," she said without preamble.

"Who is?" I asked as we entered the dimly lit interior.

"The Council," she replied under her breath.

My heart skipped a beat. The Council—older vampires who'd advised Damien—had their own intricate webs of influence throughout the city. With Damien's fall from power, it was anyone's guess where their loyalties lay now.

Inside The Cauldron, hushed conversations stilled as Tara led me to a secluded booth at the back. Seated there were four figures whose age was betrayed by their eyes—deep wells of experience and cunning that made me feel like an amateur playing at their game.

"Alex," one greeted me—a woman whose silver hair fell like moonlight over her shoulders. Her name was Lysandra if memory served—a vampire known for her arcane knowledge.

I nodded to each member before taking a seat across from them. "You wanted to see me?"

"We did," Lysandra confirmed, her voice smooth as silk but with an edge that could slice through bone.

The vampire next to her—a man named Mordecai whose specialty was whispered to be shadow manipulation—leaned forward slightly. "You've disrupted the order of things."

"Not intentionally," I said truthfully.

"But effectively," another added—a man named Orion who shared my name but none of my hesitation when it came to power plays within our world.

Lysandra's gaze fixed on me with unnerving intensity. "What do you plan to do now?"

The question hung between us like a spell waiting to be cast—one wrong word could set off an explosion or seal a pact.

"I plan to continue my work at Crimson Ink," I answered carefully. "I'm no leader or conqueror."

"But you are powerful," Mordecai interjected smoothly.

I met his gaze squarely, feeling my Mark thrumming against my skin—a reminder of both strength and burden. "Power isn't always about leading or ruling."

There was a momentary flicker of surprise on their faces before they masked it once again with practiced neutrality.

Orion shifted in his seat, breaking our silent standoff with pragmatic clarity in his tone. "Damien's absence leaves a void."

"And nature abhors a vacuum," Lysandra finished for him.

I nodded slowly; they weren't telling me anything new—nature wasn't the only one who abhorred vacuums; vampires and other supernaturals were equally opportunistic.

"We need stability," Orion said pointedly.

"You need someone to hold back chaos," I corrected him.

Their eyes gleamed like predators considering prey—or perhaps allies assessing each other's mettle.

"Will you help us maintain balance?" Lysandra asked.

I hesitated before answering—a thousand different outcomes flashing through my mind in an instant.

"If balance means protecting those who can't protect themselves—then yes." My voice held steady despite the rapid drumming of my heart.

They exchanged glances before nodding once in unison.

"We have much to discuss then," Mordecai said.

Tara placed a hand on my shoulder—a silent show of support—and I drew strength from it.

As we delved into conversation about ley lines and wards, alliances and protections, I knew one thing for certain: victory had brought change—but change was not always peace; it was simply new ground upon which we would stand or fall together.

* * *

The city's supernatural underworld thrived in the shadows, a twisted mirror of the skyscrapers that clawed at the heavens. But since Damien's downfall, those shadows have shifted, changing shape like clouds on a windy day. There's a new sense of electricity in the air, a charge that tingles across my skin as I walk the streets. It's as if the very essence of the city has awakened from a long slumber, eager to stretch its limbs and explore its newfound freedom.

The night after Damien was carted away by authorities – both mundane and mystical – I could feel the balance of power teetering on the edge of a knife. There were whispers in every dark corner, murmurs in every enchanted parlor. Everyone sensed the void Damien left behind, and it wasn't long before they started to fill it.

In the days that followed, I saw faces I'd only heard about in hushed tones. They emerged from their sanctuaries, eyes alight with ambition or fear. I saw them in my shop, Crimson Ink, asking for tattoos that would mark their new status or protect them from those who might seek to claim it.

One such visitor was an old witch with hair like silver thread and eyes that held storms within their depths. She requested a tattoo of an ancient tree whose roots delved deep into mystical waters and whose branches reached towards realms unseen.

"I need stability," she told me as my needle danced across her weathered skin. "There are those who would see this change as an opportunity for chaos."

I understood her concerns. Damien's gang had been a pillar of darkness that cast its shadow over all others. Now that it was gone, there was room for light – but also for a deeper darkness if we weren't careful.

Another figure who sought my services was a young warlock with fire at his fingertips and ambition smoldering in his gaze. He wanted an ouroboros, but not just any ouroboros – one that would symbolize not just rebirth, but also dominion.

"There will be those who wish to fill Damien's shoes," he said with a smirk that didn't quite reach his eyes. "But they'll find they're stepping into fire."

I could sense his desire to rise above the others, to become something more than what he was. It was the same desire that had poisoned Damien, and I knew I had to be careful with this one.

I made sure to weave protective runes into his tattoo – not just for him but for all those he might come up against. If he were to rise, it would not be through tyranny or oppression.

The power dynamics within our world were shifting like tectonic plates, causing quakes that could be felt in every spell and on every street corner where magic was known to linger.

Evelyn stopped by often during these times of change. She was different now – quieter, more introspective – but there was steel there too, a determination forged in the fires we had faced together.

"We're at a crossroads," she said one evening as she watched me prepare ink for another client seeking strength in these uncertain times. "There will be those who wish to seize control through fear and violence."

She paused, her eyes flickering to the Mark on my arm – a reminder of the power I wielded and the choices I'd made.

"But there are also those who will look for guidance," she continued softly. "You have become a beacon for many, Alex."

Her words weighed heavy on me because I knew she spoke true. With Damien gone, some looked at me with expectation – not just as a tattoo artist but as someone who could lead or at least help guide them through this tumultuous time.

But leadership was not something I'd ever sought out. My art was my voice; my parlor was my domain. Yet now I found myself pulled into politics I'd never had any interest in playing.

It wasn't long before Victor approached me too. His allegiance had always been mercurial at best, but now he came offering information – maps of ley lines that might serve us well if other gangs decided to make their move against what remained of Damien's empire.

"We need to fortify our defenses," he said gruffly as we poured over maps spread across my workbench.

"And we need to think about alliances," Tara chimed in from where she stood beside us, her arms crossed over her chest. She looked fierce and unyielding – a warrior ready for whatever came next.

Tara had always been more comfortable with conflict than I ever was; her strength had been invaluable through everything we'd faced together.

Victor nodded in agreement before glancing back at me. "There are others out there like us – others who don't want to see this city fall into chaos."

He proposed a council of sorts – representatives from each faction within our world coming together to discuss how we might maintain balance without resorting to Damien's brand of control.

It sounded idealistic – perhaps even naive – but as I listened to him speak passionately about his vision for our future, I couldn't help but feel hopeful too.

As new leaders emerged and old rivalries resurfaced around us, there was indeed a sense of opportunity for positive change – one that might allow us all to thrive rather than simply survive under someone else's thumb.

The nights were still filled with whispers and rumors; eyes still followed me wherever I went; but now there was also camaraderie and collaboration where once there had been only fear and subservience.

And so we began our dance anew upon the stage set by Damien's fall – careful steps taken by each player under the watchful gaze of friends and foes alike. It would be easy to trip and fall; easy to succumb to power or pride or pain; but there was hope here too amidst the shadows of our supernatural cityscape.

Hope that together we might find a way forward into a future where light could shine even in the darkest corners; where magic could be wielded not as a weapon but as an instrument for peace; where tattoos inked upon skin could bind us together rather than tear us apart.

* * *

I leaned against the counter of Crimson Ink, the familiar hum of the tattoo machines in the background like a comforting lullaby. My fingers traced the contours of the Mark of Power on my arm, a reminder of what we had accomplished. The walls of my shop, once merely a canvas for artistic expression, had become the bulwark against a tide of darkness that threatened to engulf our city. I could still feel the weight of Damien's glare, a ghostly presence that lingered even after his defeat.

Since that fateful night, whispers about me had spread through the supernatural community like wildfire. I was no longer just Alex, the tattoo artist with an unusual heritage; I was now Alex, the one who had stood up to Damien and his vampire gang. The one who had tipped the scales.

The bell above the door jingled, pulling me from my reverie. A figure cloaked in emerald green entered, their presence commanding yet enigmatic. The air seemed to shift around them, charged with an unseen energy.

"I've heard much about you," they began, their voice a melodic cadence that resonated within the shop's walls. "I am Calliope, a muse from the old world. Your deeds have inspired many."

I dipped my head in acknowledgment. "Thank you," I replied, unsure how else to respond to such a being.

Calliope approached my workstation and glanced at my sketches scattered across it. "Your artistry has woven new legends into our tapestry," they continued. "And with such power comes interest from all corners of our realm."

Interest was an understatement. Since Damien's fall, every creature with fangs or a hint of magic seemed to have an opinion about me. Some saw me as a hero; others saw a threat.

As Calliope left, their words echoed in my mind. Not long after, another visitor arrived—a grizzled werewolf named Garret with scars crisscrossing his face like battle maps.

"You're makin' waves, kid," Garret grumbled as he settled into one of my chairs. "The packs are talkin'. Some want you as an ally; others fear what you might do next."

"I don't want power over anyone," I assured him, trying to infuse confidence into my voice.

Garret nodded slowly. "Just be careful. Not everyone's as grateful as we are."

The door chimed again shortly after Garret's departure—a never-ending parade it seemed today—revealing a pair of nervous-looking nymphs who requested protective sigils etched onto their skin.

As I worked on their tattoos, imbuing each line with care and intentionality, they spoke in hushed tones about how safe they felt knowing someone like me was around—someone who could stand up to vampires and win.

But it wasn't just grateful creatures that sought me out; those wary of my influence were never far behind.

One evening as dusk embraced the city in its violet hues, a stern-faced woman entered Crimson Ink. She introduced herself as Seraphina, an envoy from the Supernatural Council—a group I knew only by reputation.

"Alex," she said curtly, her gaze appraising me like one might examine a curious artifact. "Your actions have not gone unnoticed by the Council."

I straightened up from where I'd been cleaning my equipment. "Is that so?"

"Yes." Seraphina crossed her arms over her chest. "You've disrupted the balance—whether for better or worse is yet to be seen."

I didn't miss the undercurrent of threat in her words. This wasn't just a social call; this was a warning shot across the bow.

"I did what I thought was right," I stated firmly.

Seraphina nodded once but said nothing more before leaving as abruptly as she'd arrived.

Days passed and more visitors came—each leaving their mark on me just as I did on them through ink and magic.

One late afternoon when shadows stretched long across Crimson Ink's floorboards and golden light bathed everything in warmth, Victor dropped by unannounced. His visit surprised me less than it should have; he'd become something of an ally since turning his back on Damien.

"They're scared of you," he said without preamble as he leaned against a wall plastered with designs.

"Who is?" I asked while prepping for another appointment.

"Everyone who's anyone in our world." He pushed off from the wall and sauntered closer. "You took down Damien when no one else could—or would."

His eyes held something akin to respect... or maybe it was fear masquerading as such; it was hard to tell with Victor.

"I'm not looking to replace him if that's what they're thinking," I countered with a slight frown.

Victor chuckled dryly. "Doesn't matter what you want; it's about perception now."

He left me with that thought—a burden heavier than any tattoo gun I'd ever held.

That night as I locked up Crimson Ink alone, Tara's words from earlier rang clear: "You've become more than just our friend—you're a symbol now."

A symbol... The word clung to me like dew clings to morning leaves—refreshing yet laden with unseen depths.

My dreams were fitful that night: flashes of ink transforming into chains or wings depending on whose hands wielded them—a stark reminder that even after victory against darkness like Damien's, there would always be more battles ahead.

Morning light filtered through half-closed blinds when Tara walked into Crimson Ink bearing coffee and news that would set our next steps in motion.

* * *

The door to Crimson Ink closed behind the last client of the night, the click of the lock echoing through the empty shop like a period at the end of another long sentence. I leaned back against the counter, letting out a slow breath I didn't realize I'd been holding. The ink-stained skin of my hands felt tight, a physical reminder of the day's labor and magic.

The quiet was a stark contrast to the cacophony that filled my life now—whispers of creatures in the night, murmurs of alliances forming and breaking, and the ever-present hum of my own power. As I stood there, in the silence of my shop, it struck me just how much I had changed since this all began.

I remembered when tattooing was simply about art and expression, about connecting with clients over designs that meant something profound to them. Now, each drop of ink I laid into skin carried with it the weight of destiny. My work had become a tapestry interwoven with threads of power, rebellion, and protection.

I never asked for this—never wanted to be anything more than Alex from Crimson Ink. But as I reflected on my journey, from a reluctant participant in Damien's machinations to a key player in the supernatural world, I couldn't deny that something inside me had shifted.

In the beginning, fear had been my constant companion. Fear of Damien's wrath, fear for my friends' safety, fear of losing myself to the unknown depths of my own abilities. That fear hadn't disappeared—it had just been joined by other, stronger forces: resolve, defiance, and an understanding that some things were worth fighting for.

The Mark on my arm was a symbol of that transformation. At first, it was nothing more than a tool for Damien's ambition. Now it thrummed with power under my skin—a power I had reclaimed and made my own. It was a constant reminder that choices defined us; I had chosen not to let fear dictate my actions.

I walked over to my sketchbook on one of the workstations and flipped through pages filled with designs—some completed on skin that now walked through the city like beacons in the dark, others waiting for their time. Each one was a piece of me left out in the world—a silent ally in our unspoken war.

Victor's warning earlier still rang in my ears. The Supernatural Council was watching me now. They saw potential where I felt only trepidation. They saw someone who could bring balance or become another tyrant like Damien.

The idea unsettled me—the thought that others might look at me and see a reflection of him—but Victor was right to warn me. With Damien gone and power up for grabs, eyes were inevitably turning my way.

Tara had been by my side through it all. She'd seen me at my lowest when doubt crept in like an unwelcome shadow across my mind. But she also saw something else—something even I struggled to see sometimes—a resilience that refused to break no matter how heavy the burden became.

And then there were others like Raven and Lynx who came into my life offering help without asking for anything in return but trust—a currency that was hard-earned in our world but freely given by them.

I closed the sketchbook and glanced at the clock on the wall; its ticking seemed louder than usual in the stillness. The time passed was marked by each hand's sweep—each tick another moment changed, another step away from who I once was.

As midnight approached, Seraphina from the Supernatural Council would arrive for our meeting—a meeting where we'd discuss what came next now that Damien's influence waned. Part of me dreaded these council meetings; they always left me feeling like an imposter in a room full of ancient beings who wielded centuries of experience like weapons.

But tonight felt different somehow. Tonight, there was a sense within me that while I might not have their years or their wisdom, what I did have was just as valuable—my humanity and empathy which gave me insight they lacked.

So as midnight neared and Seraphina's arrival with it, I took one last look around Crimson Ink—the shop that had become so much more than just a place of business. It was here that everything began; it would be here that we planned our future—one where tattoos weren't just marks on skin but symbols of hope and defiance against those who would seek to control us.

There was no going back to who I used to be; even if I wanted to retreat into obscurity again—the kind before vampires and Marks—I couldn't unsee what had been revealed or unknow what had been learned.

With every passing second towards midnight, I felt it—a culmination not just of today but all the days since this journey began—an acknowledgment that transformation wasn't just about change; it was about growth too.

I stood up straighter as steps echoed outside—the arrival of Seraphina heralding another discussion about balance and order—and with each step closer she took towards Crimson Ink's door, I realized this: whatever lay ahead for us all, for this city entwined with magic both dark and light—I would face it not as Alex from Crimson Ink but as Alex whose ink ran crimson with power earned through struggle and triumph alike.

***

I stood outside Crimson Ink, the early morning light casting long shadows on the sidewalk. The city seemed to hold its breath, as if recovering from a long night of revelry—or in our case, the aftermath of Damien's fall. His tyranny had left deep scars on our community, scars that wouldn't fade with the mere passing of time. I pulled my jacket tighter around me, the chill in the air less biting than the responsibility now resting on my shoulders.

My shop had always been a haven, a place where ink and magic intertwined to create something powerful. Now, it was also a symbol of resistance—a beacon for those seeking not just tattoos but guidance in this new era we were all navigating. With Damien gone, a vacuum had formed, and nature abhors a vacuum. It was up to us, the ones who had fought back, to fill that space with something better.

As I unlocked the door and stepped into Crimson Ink, I couldn't help but feel the weight of expectation heavy on my chest. I flipped the sign to 'Open', signaling not just the start of a business day but also the beginning of a new chapter for us all.

The bell above the door chimed throughout the day as beings of all kinds walked through my door—each one touched by Damien's dark reign in their own way. A dryad with wilted leaves for hair came in first, her voice barely above a whisper as she asked for a tattoo to rejuvenate her connection to her grove, which had been tainted by fear and corruption.

I set to work on her design, intertwining symbols of growth and renewal with her own natural patterns. As my needle danced across her bark-like skin, I felt her strength returning—magic flowing from my hands into her very roots. When I finished, she looked at herself in the mirror and smiled—a small but significant victory against despair.

The day wore on with similar stories. A young selkie sought a mark that would help him reclaim his stolen skin; an old wizard asked for symbols that would strengthen his wards against darkness; and even Seraphina from the Supernatural Council stopped by, not for ink but for discourse.

She perched elegantly on one of my tattoo chairs, her gaze scrutinizing as she spoke of balance and order. "You've become quite influential," she said, "but influence can be... intoxicating."

I met her eyes steadily. "I'm not looking to rule or control," I replied firmly. "Damien's way wasn't just wrong; it was destructive. We need a community where power isn't hoarded but shared."

Seraphina regarded me silently before nodding once. "Just be wary," she cautioned before leaving as quietly as she'd arrived.

In between clients, Victor stopped by—now more ally than adversary—and we talked strategy over cups of coffee that grew cold as we planned. We needed defenses; we needed alliances; we needed hope—ingredients that were hard to come by in times like these.

"You're doing good work here," Victor said with an approving nod towards where Tara was soothing a nervous gnome who'd come seeking protection from predators who once worked under Damien's command.

"We're doing good work," I corrected him with a smile that didn't quite reach my eyes. There was so much yet to do.

Evening came too soon; closing time was upon us when Tara approached me, her expression somber. "There's talk in the alleys," she murmured, "rumors about those who want to step into Damien's shoes."

I sighed heavily at that news—it wasn't unexpected but it was unwelcome all the same. "Then we'll have to be louder than rumors," I declared. "We'll have to show them there's another way."

Tara nodded resolutely and together we locked up Crimson Ink under a sky painted with hues of fading sunlight and rising stars—a sky that watched over us all indiscriminately.

That night we held a meeting—not in some grand hall or shadowy basement—but right there at Crimson Ink among ink pots and sketches strewn across workstations. Lynx and Cipher joined us alongside other faces from our ragtag Resistance—all eyes on me as I spoke about what we could become.

"Our community has been divided for too long," I began, feeling every gaze upon me sharpen with attention. "Damien ruled through fear but what if we led through... through trust?"

Murmurs spread through the group—some skeptical, others hopeful—as I laid out my vision: A network where information flowed freely among us; where power wasn't used to subjugate but to empower; where our differences weren't grounds for exploitation but for collaboration.

Tara stood beside me then, lending me her strength as she added her voice to mine: "We can build something here—a sanctuary not just from physical harm but from injustice too."

Lynx chimed in next: "It won't be easy—we'll have those who'll fight us at every turn—but it's worth fighting for."

As plans were discussed and roles assigned, there was an energy in Crimson Ink that felt like... well, like magic—the kind you couldn't bottle up or sell.

Hours passed as strategies were debated and refined until finally we parted ways with renewed purpose. The road ahead would be fraught with challenges no doubt; darkness has deep roots after all.

But there in my shop—my home—I saw flickers of light beginning to kindle amongst friends old and new alike.

And it struck me then: Maybe this is what hope feels like—not some distant dream or untouchable ideal but something tangible taking shape one tattoo at a time right here in Crimson Ink—the heart of our reborn community.

* * *

The hum of the city buzzed below as I leaned against the cool metal railing of Crimson Ink's rooftop. The night air, a blend of crispness and exhaust, reminded me that even at this height, I couldn't escape the reach of the urban jungle. It was here, among the skyscrapers clawing at the stars, that I felt the weight of Damien's defeat settle into my bones.

His fall had left a void, one that teemed with both uncertainty and opportunity. As a tattoo artist with supernatural lineage, my shop had become more than a parlor—it was now a sanctuary for those who existed in the shadowed corners of our world.

I flipped through my sketchbook, each page a testament to the stories etched in ink on skin. These designs were more than art; they were symbols of power, rebellion, and protection. They represented the trust and hope placed in me by creatures and beings who had long lived under Damien's iron rule.

I paused at an unfinished design—a phoenix rising from ashes. It was emblematic of rebirth, of new beginnings, and I knew it would serve as my personal emblem moving forward. My finger traced the lines as I contemplated my next steps.

A gust of wind tugged at the pages, urging me to look up. Across the rooftop garden Tara had insisted we plant, Victor stood watching me with his thoughtful gaze. "You've got that look again," he said, stepping closer.

"What look?" I asked, closing the sketchbook with a soft thud.

"The one where you're about to change the world—or at least try."

I chuckled dryly. "Is it that obvious?"

He nodded solemnly. "What's on your mind?"

I gestured for him to join me by the railing. "It's this power," I began, rolling up my sleeve to reveal the Mark of Power glimmering faintly on my arm. "It's a tool—a dangerous one—and I need to use it responsibly."

Victor nodded again. "You've always been mindful of your gifts."

"But it's more than that now," I continued. "It's about setting goals for myself and for our community."

"And what goals are those?" he asked.

"Firstly," I said, holding up a finger, "I want to ensure that every supernatural being who comes through those doors leaves with more than just a tattoo—they leave with hope." My thoughts drifted to Evelyn and her shadowy departure during our confrontation with Damien. She'd let me pass when she could have easily turned me over to him. Even she understood that our fight was bigger than any one individual.

"Secondly," I continued, holding up another finger, "I want to use my influence to foster a council—one where voices from all corners can be heard and respected." The memory of Seraphina's warning echoed in my head: 'Influence is intoxicating.' But unlike Damien, I didn't crave control; I sought balance.

"And lastly," I said with conviction as I raised a third finger, "I will protect those within our world from threats both internal and external." My mind flashed back to the young warlock seeking dominance and the old witch asking for stability. They were two sides of the same coin—power could be wielded for good or ill.

Victor studied me for a moment before nodding slowly. "Noble goals," he said finally. "But you can't do it alone."

"I don't plan to." I smiled faintly. "That's where you all come in."

As if on cue, Tara emerged onto the rooftop with her tablet in hand—her face alight with purpose as always. "We've got potential allies reaching out from across the city," she announced without preamble. "Word has spread about Damien's defeat."

"That's good news," Victor remarked.

"It is," Tara agreed before turning her gaze on me. "But we need to be cautious—we don't want another Damien rising from his ashes."

"We won't let that happen," I assured her firmly.

She gave me a small smile but her eyes remained serious—a reflection of her ever-present concern for our safety and future.

The wind picked up again and this time it carried whispers from below—snippets of conversation from passing pedestrians blissfully unaware of the supernatural world existing alongside their own.

"This is just the beginning," Tara said softly.

I nodded as resolve settled deep within me like an anchor grounding my swirling thoughts and emotions. With each tattoo given life under my needle, I'd write our new chapter—one filled with strength rather than subjugation; unity rather than division; freedom rather than fear.

"Let's get started then," Victor said with determination in his voice.

Tara closed her tablet with an audible click—a punctuation mark on our conversation—and joined us at the railing.

Together we looked out over the cityscape—the canvas upon which we'd paint our new vision for our kindred spirits lurking in its shadows.

As we descended back into Crimson Ink—the name now bearing more significance than ever—I felt prepared for what lay ahead: a path lined with uncertainty but paved by hope; daunting yet illuminated by shared purpose.

Inside, Jade waited for us with reports from Lynx about encrypted communications buzzing like swarms of bees eager to spread news of change; Cipher poring over maps highlighting ley line intersections vital for strategic planning; Raven meticulously organizing vials filled with potent magical essences ready for use when needed most; Orion offering guidance through cryptic prophecies we were learning to interpret together—all pieces fitting into place within this puzzle we were determined to solve as one united front against any force daring enough to challenge us again.

The chapter ahead was ours to write—with each stroke deliberate and meaningful—as we aimed not only toward survival but toward flourishing within this ever-changing tapestry woven by destiny itself.

Chapter 21

Ink of a New Era

I perched atop the ancient stone bridge that arched gracefully over the murky waters of the Lachlan River, my city's hidden gem. The bridge was old, a relic from a time when magic thrummed more openly through the veins of the world. Here, amidst the soft whisper of water against stone and the distant hum of urban life, I found a rare peace—a stillness that was elusive in my line of work.

The cool night air brushed against my skin, carrying the scent of wet earth and blooming nightflowers from the banks below. I gazed up at the patchwork of stars scattered across the sky, their light flickering like candles fighting a draft. My city was never truly dark; neon signs and streetlamps vied for dominion over the night, yet here, under this celestial tapestry, I felt a connection to something eternal.

I had come far from the young tattoo artist who merely wished to weave magic into ink and skin. Now, I bore the Mark of Power on my arm—a pulsing symbol that was both a gift and a burden. My fingers traced its outline absently as I considered how it had changed me. The Mark's power was a tempest held at bay by sheer will, but in this tranquil spot, it felt like a silent companion rather than an overwhelming force.

Damien's defeat had left ripples through our supernatural community. Where there had once been fear and submission, now there was cautious optimism—a sense that we could shape our destiny rather than be shaped by it. But with power comes attention, and not all eyes that watched me were friendly or patient.

I drew my knees up to my chest, wrapping my arms around them as I leaned back against the cool stone railing. My friends—Tara, Victor, Raven—each brought their own strengths to our cause. We were an unlikely coalition united by necessity and now bound by purpose. We had all made sacrifices, but we were still here, still fighting for what we believed in.

The wind shifted, stirring the river into a chorus of soft ripples that reflected the city lights like dancing fireflies. This bridge had been here long before me and would remain long after I was gone. It reminded me that we are all just part of a larger story—a story that continues with or without us.

But for now, I was here—I was present—and I would do everything within my power to protect this city and its hidden magic.

The soft sound of footsteps approaching pulled me from my reverie. I didn't need to look up to know who it was; there was only one person who would seek me out here.

"Mind if I join you?" Tara's voice cut through the quiet night with a warmth that made me smile.

I patted the spot beside me on the bridge's wide ledge. "Always room for you."

She climbed up beside me with her characteristic grace and settled in, tucking her legs beneath her. Tara didn't say anything at first; she just sat there with me in silence, watching the stars and sharing in this pocket of calm amidst our stormy lives.

After a moment, she spoke again. "It's hard to believe how much has changed."

"Yeah," I agreed softly. "Feels like lifetimes ago since we were just worrying about normal shop stuff—appointments and ink orders."

Tara chuckled softly. "Normal shop stuff never involved ink orders quite like ours."

"That's true." My laughter mingled with hers before fading into silence again.

"We did good work today," Tara said after a while, breaking our quiet reflection.

"We did," I replied thoughtfully. "But there's still so much to do."

"Always is," she acknowledged. "But don't forget to take moments like this for yourself too."

I nodded slowly. "Balance in all things."

"Exactly." She bumped her shoulder against mine gently.

We fell silent again as we returned our gazes to the heavens above us—a tapestry woven with light against darkness much like our own lives intertwined with shadows and sparks of hope.

Our tranquility was not meant to last; it never did in our line of work. The buzz of my phone against my thigh broke through our peaceful interlude—a reminder that while moments like these were precious, they were also fleeting.

With reluctance woven through every fiber of my being, I pulled out my phone and checked the message lighting up the screen—a simple text from Victor: "Meeting tonight at Jade's place."

I sighed softly and tucked away my phone before turning back to Tara with an apologetic look. "Duty calls."

She nodded understandingly as we both rose from our perch on the bridge. As we made our way down toward solid ground again, I glanced back once more at our little sanctuary by the river—a place where for just a moment everything seemed possible and where peace could be more than just an interlude between chaos.

Together Tara and I walked back toward Crimson Ink—the tattoo parlor that stood as both my heart and battleground—and toward whatever awaited us next in this city where ancient magic flowed silently beneath streets alive with modern noise.

* * *

Perched on my usual stool at Crimson Ink, I swipe a cloth across the counter, clearing away the remnants of the day's work. The scent of antiseptic lingers in the air, mingling with the subtle notes of sage and iron I've grown to associate with my craft. The door chimes echo through the room as it opens, signaling the arrival of my first visitor of the evening.

In strides a man in a neatly tailored suit, his gait confident yet unassuming. His eyes scan the parlor, taking in the framed sketches that line the walls—each a testament to a story inked into skin.

"Alex," he greets with a nod. "Word on the street is you're someone who can make things happen."

I gesture to the leather chair by my station. "Have a seat. Let's talk about what you need."

He does, rolling up his sleeve to reveal an old tattoo, faded and frayed at the edges like a well-thumbed page. "I need an update. Something to reflect who I've become, not who I was."

The design he requests is intricate—a phoenix rising from ashes, symbolizing rebirth and resilience. As my needle hums across his skin, infusing color and life into the design, he tells me of his journey from addiction to advocacy.

"I owe you more than just payment for this," he says as I finish up. "You've become a beacon for many of us out here trying to do better."

His words stir something deep within me—pride mingled with humility. I give him aftercare instructions and watch him leave with newfound purpose etched onto his arm and in his step.

The evening wanes when another figure enters, her appearance cloaked in mystery. Her hood obscures her face, but her aura carries whispers of ancient forests and untamed magic.

"You're Alex," she states more than asks, her voice a melody of hidden depths.

I nod and wait for her to continue.

"I represent the fae community." She lowers her hood, revealing pointed ears and eyes that glimmer with flecks of gold. "We've taken notice of your deeds. You've shifted balances long held static."

"And what can I do for you?" I inquire.

"A symbol," she replies, "one that marks our gratitude and alliance."

Her request is unusual—a vine interwoven with runes that speak of old pacts and new beginnings. My hand steadies as I work on her skin; each line resonates with energy that buzzes through my fingertips like electricity.

As she departs, she leaves behind a single acorn placed upon my counter—a token from her realm and a sign of honor among her kind.

The night grows heavier still when Victor saunters in—his presence always commands attention. He nods at me before taking a seat opposite my station.

"We've got to talk strategy," he says without preamble.

Our conversations often revolve around maintaining peace in our tumultuous world, but tonight he speaks less of conflict and more of camaraderie.

"People respect you, Alex," Victor says earnestly. "Not just because you're strong but because you care. It's rare."

His words leave me grappling with their weight—a responsibility not only to wield power but also to wield it wisely.

Before we part ways, Victor hands me an envelope. Inside is an invitation embossed with symbols representing various supernatural factions—a call for unity under one banner.

"Think about it," he urges as he heads out into the darkness that cloaks our city's secrets.

As midnight approaches, Tara walks in from the back room where she helps manage our stock of magical supplies. She leans against the counter next to me, her expression thoughtful.

"You've done good here," she remarks softly. "The community sees it—the humans who come for renewal and the supernaturals who seek refuge."

Her affirmation warms me more than any spell could.

"I couldn't have done it without you all," I respond truthfully.

Tara chuckles. "You're too modest."

Our conversation is cut short by another arrival—a young girl no older than sixteen, her gaze fixed on me with an intensity that belies her years.

"Alex?" Her voice quivers slightly as she approaches.

"That's me." I offer her a reassuring smile. "What can I do for you?"

She hesitates before pulling out a folded piece of paper from her jacket pocket—an article clipped from a local paper featuring Crimson Ink's efforts in aiding those touched by supernatural forces.

"You helped my brother," she says finally. "He came here lost...and left found."

She hands me a drawing—a heart encased in flames—and asks if I can tattoo it over where her heart beats strongest. It's a simple request but laden with meaning; an emblem of love's enduring strength amidst adversity.

I accept her request with care and begin my work under Tara's watchful eyes—another tale unfolding beneath my hands as ink meets skin once again.

With each customer leaving Crimson Ink marked by their experiences and mine intertwining within this city's supernatural landscape, respect and gratitude become threads woven into my life's tapestry—one filled with vibrant hues and endless possibilities as dawn beckons anew.

* * *

Perched on the worn leather chair in the back room of Crimson Ink, I let the silence envelop me. It was a rare moment of quiet in a life that had become a tempest of ink and magic. The parlor, once just walls and floors, had grown into something far greater—a symbol, a refuge, a battleground. Now, it was time to decide its future.

I picked up a sketchbook, the pages filled with designs of both the mundane and the arcane. The weight of responsibility pressed against my chest as I considered the path forward. My friends, Tara and Victor, had offered their thoughts, but in the end, it was my choice to make. Could I really strip away the magic that flowed through these walls like a pulsing vein? Would I turn my back on those who sought protection within this sanctuary? Or was it time to embrace what Crimson Ink had become—a center for learning about the responsible use of magical tattoos?

My fingers traced over a sketch of an oak tree—the symbol of strength and endurance. It seemed fitting for the parlor's new beginning. "A place of growth," I murmured to myself. The idea blossomed in my mind: Crimson Ink could be a beacon of knowledge where individuals learned not only about magical tattoos but also about controlling their power without being consumed by it.

I stood up and walked over to the window that looked out onto the bustling street below. People from all walks of life passed by, oblivious to the world that existed just beyond their sight. Among them could be future allies or those in need of guidance.

"Turning this place into a school... It's ambitious," Victor's voice broke through my thoughts as he stepped into the room.

I turned to face him, leaning back against the windowsill. "Ambitious, yes. But necessary."

Victor crossed his arms, his gaze steady on mine. "And what about those who need sanctuary? The ones running from things they don't understand?"

His words struck a chord. A vision flashed through my mind—a young girl with wide eyes full of fear, clutching her mother's hand as they sought refuge from supernatural pursuers.

"The parlor will still be a haven," I assured him. "But we can do more than just hide people away. We can give them tools to protect themselves."

Victor nodded slowly, understanding dawning in his eyes. "A dual purpose then—a school and a safe house."

"That's what I'm thinking." I smiled faintly, comforted by his quick acceptance.

The door creaked open and Tara stepped inside, her expression curious as she looked between us. "Making plans without me?"

"Never," I said with a grin. "We're discussing the future of Crimson Ink."

She walked over and perched on the edge of my desk, her presence bringing warmth to the room. "And have we reached a verdict?"

"We have," I replied before outlining my vision for Crimson Ink—a place where knowledge flowed as freely as ink and where those in need found shelter.

Tara listened intently before nodding in agreement. "It feels right."

"I'll need help," I said after a moment's pause.

"You've got us," Victor chimed in with conviction.

"And others too," Tara added confidently. "There are many who owe you their safety—and more who believe in what you stand for."

We spent hours discussing logistics—how we'd set up classes, who would teach them, how we'd maintain secrecy while providing refuge.

The next morning found me behind my tattoo chair once again as Marlon entered—no longer an adversary but now an ally intrigued by our plans.

"I heard rumors," he said as he settled into the chair.

I prepared my needles with practiced ease. "Rumors have a way of traveling fast."

He chuckled dryly. "Especially when they're about turning Crimson Ink into some kind of magical academy."

"It's more than that," I explained as I started his tattoo—a simple band around his arm that symbolized unity within our diverse community.

Marlon winced slightly at the needle's sting but then relaxed into the rhythm of my work. "And what role do you see for people like me?"

"You've got knowledge that can help others understand what they're up against," I said without pausing my work.

He contemplated that quietly for a while before speaking again. "There will be resistance—to change, to learning."

"Change is always met with resistance," I replied evenly.

As Marlon's tattoo took shape under my hands, Raven slipped into the shop quietly—another one drawn by curiosity or perhaps destiny.

"We're moving forward with our plans," I told him without needing to look up from my work.

Raven leaned against the counter, watching intently as ink infused with magic etched into Marlon's skin—a symbol not only for him but for all those who would come seeking knowledge and safety at Crimson Ink.

The day passed in a blur—clients came and went—each leaving with more than just ink on their skin: hope, strength, or protection woven into each design.

As evening fell and shadows stretched across the shop floor, I finally put down my needles and cleaned my station meticulously.

Tara returned from spreading word about our initiative while Victor finalized security measures for those seeking refuge within our walls.

"We're ready," Tara declared as she joined us in closing up for the night.

Ready indeed—for tomorrow we would open our doors not just as a tattoo parlor but as something far greater: A bastion for learning and sanctuary amidst an ever-changing supernatural landscape.

And as we locked up together—the weight of our decision heavy yet hopeful—I knew we were stepping onto untrodden ground paved with challenges and triumphs alike; an endeavor worthy of every drop of ink and magic at our disposal.

* * *

The night had settled like a soft blanket over the city, its sounds a distant hum against the closed door of Crimson Ink. I locked up behind me, a day's worth of ink and magic still pulsing beneath my skin, a tangible reminder of the lives I'd touched. But as I stepped into the cool air, a sense of solitude wrapped around me. In the whirlwind of supernatural struggles and the fight against Damien, my own life had been shoved aside, left to gather dust in the corners of my busy mind.

I wandered through the streets, not yet ready to retreat to my apartment. The streetlights cast elongated shadows that danced around my feet, and for once, I wasn't racing towards a crisis or a strategy meeting. I was simply Alex, with time on my hands and a quiet ache in my heart for things neglected.

A laughter-filled pub caught my attention. The warm glow spilling from its windows was inviting. Once upon a time, I would have been inside, sharing stories and jokes with friends who knew nothing of magical tattoos or vampire politics. They just knew me as Alex: artist, confidant, occasional karaoke enthusiast.

Without quite realizing it, I found myself pushing open the door and stepping inside. The noise washed over me—a symphony of clinking glasses and spirited conversation. It was startling how foreign yet familiar this all felt. Scanning the room for a vacant stool at the bar, I caught sight of an old friend from what felt like another lifetime.

"Hey, isn't that Alex?" Matt called out, his eyes lighting up with genuine surprise.

A few heads turned as recognition spread across their faces. Smiles and waves followed as they beckoned me over.

"I'll be damned," Matt said as he clapped me on the back. "Thought you'd vanished into thin air."

"Yeah," Lisa chimed in from beside him. "You used to be our trivia night ringer!"

Their easy banter enveloped me like a long-lost melody—one I hadn't realized how much I missed dancing to.

"I've been...around," I managed with a half-smile, sidestepping details they wouldn't understand or believe.

As we fell into conversation, old memories resurfaced—trips we'd taken, inside jokes we'd crafted—and for a moment, Damien and his dark schemes seemed worlds away.

Hours slipped by unnoticed until Lisa mentioned trivia night was starting soon. They asked if I wanted to join them, and something inside me clicked. This was normalcy—a chance to reconnect not just with friends but with myself.

"We'd love to have you back on our team," Matt said earnestly.

"I think I'd like that," I replied with more conviction than I'd felt in months.

We laughed and groaned through rounds of questions about pop culture and history—my contributions rusty but gradually improving as the night went on. There was something freeing about focusing on mundane facts rather than magical threats.

After our modest third-place finish—the prize being free appetizers next week—we parted ways with promises not to let so much time pass again. The cool night air greeted me as I stepped outside; it felt less lonely now.

Walking home felt lighter somehow—as if those few hours had untangled knots within me that I hadn't known were there. And there was another part of life that had been waiting patiently in the wings: romance.

Jade's image flickered across my mind unbidden—the intensity of her gaze when she spoke about her art; how she always seemed to challenge and understand me simultaneously. We had come a long way from rivals to allies...perhaps there could be more?

The next day at Crimson Ink brought familiar faces seeking tattoos that held more than just ink—they held stories and trust. Victor strategized quietly in the corner while Tara greeted clients with her warm smile. And amidst it all, Jade walked in—a breeze of possibility amid the everyday routine.

She carried herself with an air of purpose but also hesitation—a mirror reflecting my own internal conflict about broaching what lingered unsaid between us.

"Hey," Jade said softly as she approached my station where sketches lay scattered like pieces of a puzzle waiting to be solved.

"Hey yourself," I replied casually while stealing glances at her between strokes of pencil on paper.

"I've been thinking..." she began before trailing off—a rare occurrence for someone usually so decisive.

"Yeah?" Encouragement edged my tone while curiosity hooked me closer.

"About us—about what's happening here." She gestured vaguely between us before settling her gaze firmly on mine. "And what could happen."

The weight of her words hung in the air between us—a question wrapped delicately within an admission. It took me a moment to realize she was waiting for an answer—an indication whether this path was one we might walk together or one we would observe from afar as possibilities unexplored.

Taking a deep breath, one that felt like it filled every corner of my being with resolve, I set down my pencil and met her eyes fully for what felt like the first time in forever.

"Me too," was all I managed before she closed the gap between us with steps measured but sure—her hand finding mine amidst sketches and ink pots—a touch grounding yet electric all at once.

As our fingers intertwined—a silent pact formed—I realized this wasn't just about reclaiming parts of life put on hold; it was about building new ones entirely—with friendships renewed under softer lights and possibilities explored beneath braver skies.

* * *

The night's veil hung heavy over the city, the stars winking like distant lighthouses as I locked up Crimson Ink. It had been a haven of sorts, a beacon for those who sought to reclaim their power, their agency. My tattoos had become symbols of hope, each drop of ink infused with ancient magics that I was only beginning to understand. I tucked my

hands into the pockets of my leather jacket and took a deep breath, ready to step out into the crisp air.

That's when I felt it—a subtle shift in the energy around me, like the gentle pull of a tide before it rolls back to reveal hidden treasures. The hair on the back of my neck stood up as I turned towards the sensation. In the shadow of the alley across the street stood a figure, cloaked in an aura of mystery as tangible as the ink beneath my skin.

"Alex," a voice called out, neither male nor female, but rich with layers of knowing and experience. The figure stepped into a sliver of moonlight, revealing nothing but the gleam of their eyes.

I hesitated for only a moment. "Who's asking?"

"We are seekers of truths," they said, their voice like a melody played on old strings. "Keepers of the unspoken lore."

I chuckled dryly. "You make it sound like you're from some secret society or fantasy novel."

"In many ways, we are," they replied with an ease that suggested they were comfortable with disbelief. "We've watched you grow into your power, Alex. You've handled it with grace and strength. But there's so much more beyond what you see."

My pulse quickened at those words. So much more? My mind spun with images of worlds upon worlds, layers upon layers—all woven together by magic and will.

"And what exactly is this 'so much more'?" I asked.

They took a step closer, and even though we were still yards apart, I felt as if they were whispering directly into my ear. "A vast network, realms interlocked by magic older than time itself—forces that are waking up as you claim your heritage."

The weight of their words settled on me like a mantle—heady and daunting all at once.

"Why come to me?" I asked.

"You have a gift," they continued. "A talent for creating and shaping magic in ways few can even dream of. You bind destinies with your ink; you alter fates with every line drawn."

I swallowed hard at that notion; it was one thing to tattoo someone with protection or strength—it was another to consider the broader impact I could have on the very fabric of existence.

"And you want me... what? To join you?" The thought was both exhilarating and terrifying.

They nodded slowly. "We propose an alliance—a collaboration that could benefit us both."

"Benefit how?" My curiosity battled with my caution.

"There are places where your tattoos can do more than protect or empower," they explained. "Places where they can unlock secrets, heal ancient rifts, perhaps even save lives."

I couldn't deny that this mysterious group had struck at something deep within me—a longing for connection to something greater than myself. But caution tempered my eagerness; after all I'd been through with Damien and his crew, trust didn't come easy.

"What's in it for you?" I pressed.

"The balance must be maintained," they said cryptically. "And while your actions here have helped stabilize things... there are other areas not so fortunate."

I pondered their words as they hung between us like a riddle waiting to be unraveled.

"Consider this an invitation," they added after a pause that stretched long enough for me to feel the weight of my decision. "We will not press for an immediate answer."

"And if I say no?"

Their gaze held mine—a swirl of starlight and shadow within those eyes—and I felt as if they were looking right through me.

"Then we respect your choice," they assured me. "But know this: The path ahead will unfurl regardless; whether you walk it is up to you."

With those final words lingering in the air like smoke from extinguished candles, they receded back into darkness—leaving me alone once more with only streetlights for company.

As I walked home through streets lined with whispering trees and sleeping houses, my mind raced. This wasn't just about Crimson Ink or tattooing anymore—it was about tapping into streams of magic that crisscrossed realities themselves.

By morning light, after restless dreams filled with glyphs and gateways, Tara found me hunched over my sketchbook in Crimson Ink's back room—my haven turned war room once again.

"What's got you so preoccupied?" she asked, concern etched across her features as she sipped her coffee.

I looked up from my drawings—cryptic designs that seemed almost to hum with potential—and sighed.

"I was approached last night by someone... or something," I began cautiously. "They hinted at a world much bigger than what we've dealt with so far."

Tara leaned against the counter and folded her arms, her expression serious but intrigued.

"They want me to join them," I continued, "to use my tattoos for something... grander."

Her eyebrows raised in silent question; she knew better than anyone what we'd faced together—the dangers we'd overcome.

"They're offering knowledge—access to secrets about magic and power." The temptation danced before me like flames promising warmth in winter coldness.

Tara nodded slowly before setting down her cup with a clink that seemed louder than it should have been in the quiet parlor.

"You're considering it then?" Her tone wasn't accusatory; rather it held a note of understanding—as if she knew all too well how seductive such an offer could be.

"I don't know yet," I admitted truthfully. "There's so much at stake—not just for us but possibly for others out there too."

* * *

The needle hummed in my hand, a familiar buzz that was almost meditative. I finished the last line of a phoenix tattoo on a young man's back. His shoulders relaxed under my touch as I wiped the excess ink away, revealing the bird reborn from its ashes. It was more than just ink; it was a symbol of his survival, his resilience. I knew all too well what that felt like.

I glanced around Crimson Ink, my sanctuary and battleground, now quiet in the late hours. The walls were adorned with sketches and designs, each one a story, a memory of struggles and triumphs. This place was more than a tattoo parlor—it was the heart of a community, one that had been through hell and back with me.

Leaning back in my chair, I let out a long breath. The journey had been arduous. Damien's fall had left ripples through the supernatural underworld, with many looking to me as some sort of beacon. A leader, even though I never asked for it. But perhaps it was always meant to be this way—my heritage made me different, destined for something more than just ink on skin.

The battles we fought were fierce and full of sacrifice. Not just by me, but by friends who stood by my side—Tara with her unwavering spirit, Victor who found redemption in rebellion, and Raven whose wisdom guided us through darkness. Each confrontation left its mark on us, scars that were reminders of what we had endured.

Yet with every scar came strength—a newfound power within me. The Mark of Power on my arm pulsed gently as if affirming my thoughts. It had changed everything; it made me realize that my abilities could shape destinies. And with such power came responsibility.

The losses we faced were heavy—the kind that settles deep in your bones and never truly leaves you. Allies who became memories, their laughter echoing in silent moments like these. But their sacrifices weren't in vain. We had won peace, a chance to rebuild and make something better out of the chaos.

A smile tugged at the corner of my mouth as I recalled how we turned Crimson Ink into more than just a haven for those seeking magical tattoos but also a school for responsible magic use. Teaching others to harness their gifts without succumbing to darkness—that was our mission now.

I stood up, stretching muscles tired from hours of work, and walked over to the large window that looked out over the city. The skyline was a jagged silhouette against the night sky—a mix of old architecture and modern skyscrapers. Lights twinkled like stars brought down to earth; life pulsed through its streets.

This city... it was a part of me as much as I was a part of it—the ley lines beneath its surface connecting us in an intricate web of energy and power. My reflection stared back at me from the glass—tattoos trailing up my arms like vines reaching for sunlight, eyes filled with stories yet untold.

I thought about the mysterious proposition laid before me by the cloaked figure who had appeared earlier that day—a secret group seeking ancient knowledge and desiring to use my tattoos for purposes beyond what I'd ever imagined.

Their offer dangled in front of me like an uncharted path promising adventure and discovery. It intrigued me—the idea of delving deeper into ancient secrets and expanding my knowledge of magical tattoos—but it also warned of risks untold.

Could this be another battle? Or perhaps an opportunity to learn more about my heritage? There was no way to know for sure without stepping forward into the unknown.

I took a deep breath as determination settled within me like armor fitting into place. Whatever challenges lay ahead, I felt ready—curiosity burning bright within me like an undying flame.

My friends—Tara with her tactical mind; Victor with his newfound purpose; Raven with his cryptic wisdom—they would stand by me no matter what path I chose next. And there were others too—Jade with her unwavering support; Lynx with their network within the Resistance; Cipher who never failed to crack the most enigmatic codes—all part of this intricate tapestry we wove together.

Turning away from the window, I picked up my sketchbook from where it lay on a nearby table—its pages filled with designs yet to come alive on skin—and flipped through it slowly. Each page was a promise—a promise to keep pushing boundaries and exploring what it truly meant to wield this ancient craft passed down through generations.

And so here I stood at this crossroads—between endings and beginnings—with gratitude for every step that led me here and excitement for every step yet to come.

The door behind me creaked open, Tara's voice calling out softly as she entered the shop: "Everything okay?"

I nodded without turning around, still facing the cityscape that sprawled before us both.

"Yeah," I replied quietly. "Just thinking about tomorrow... and all the tomorrows after that."

We shared a knowing look—one full of silent understanding—and then turned our gazes back toward the horizon where dawn would soon break—a symbol itself for all our hopes and dreams wrapped up in shades of gold and crimson light.

Tomorrow held no guarantees, but one thing was certain: With every sunrise came new possibilities—and I was ready for whatever came next.

Printed in the USA
CPSIA information can be obtained
at www.ICGtesting.com
LVHW041149180424
777643LV00001B/230